HOMEWORLD

What Reviewers Say About Gun Brooke's Work

Ice Queen

"I'm a sucker for a story about a single mother and in this case, it really adds depth to Susanna's character. The conflict that threatens Susanna and Aislin's future isn't a convoluted series of events. It's the insecurities they each bring into the relationship that they're forced to acknowledge and deal with. To me this felt authentic. The book is a quick read with plenty of spice…"—*Lesbian Review*

Treason

"The adventure was edge-of-your-seat levels of gripping and exciting. …I really enjoyed this final addition to the Exodus series and particularly liked the ending. As always it was a very well written book."—Melina Bickard, Librarian, Waterloo Library (UK)

Insult to Injury

"This novel tugged at my heart all the way, much the same way as *Coffee Sonata*. It's a story of new beginnings, of rediscovering oneself, of trusting again (both others and oneself)."—*Jude in the Stars*

"If you love a good, slow-burn romantic novel, then grab this book."
—*Rainbow Reflections*

"[A] light romance that left me with just the right amount of 'aw shucks' at the end."—*C-Spot Reviews*

"I was glad to see a disabled lead for a change, and I enjoyed the author's style—the book was written in the first person alternating between the main characters and I felt that gave me more insight into each character and their motivations."—Melina Bickard, Librarian, Waterloo Library (UK)

Wayworn Lovers

"*Wayworn Lovers* is a super dramatic, angsty read, very much in line with Brooke's other contemporary romances. ...I'm definitely in the 'love them' camp."—*Lesbian Review*

Thorns of the Past

"What I really liked from the offset is that Brooke steered clear of the typical butch PI with femme damsel in distress trope. Both main characters are what I would call ordinary women—they both wear suits for work, they both dress down in sweatpants and sweatshirts in the evening. As a result, I instantly found it a lot easier to relate, and connect with both. Each of their pasts hold dreadful memories and pain, and the passages where they opened up to each other about those events were very moving."—*Rainbow Reviews*

"I loved the romance between Darcy and Sabrina and the story really carried it well, with each of them learning that they have a safe haven with the other."—*Lesbian Review*

Escape: Exodus Book Three

"I've been a keen follower of the Exodus series for a while now and I was looking forward to the latest installment. It didn't disappoint. The action was edge-of-your-seat thrilling, especially towards the end, with several threats facing the Exodus mission. Some very intriguing subplots were introduced, and I look forward to reading more about these in the next book."—Melina Bickard, Librarian, Waterloo Library, London (UK)

Pathfinder

"I love Gun Brooke. She has successfully merged two of my reading loves: lesfic and sci-fi."—*Inked Rainbow Reads*

"I found the characters very likable and the plot compelling. I loved watching their relationship grow. From their first meeting, they're impressed and intrigued by each other. This matures into an easy friendship, and from there into dancing, kisses, and more. ...I'm looking forward to seeing the rest of the series!"—*All Our Worlds: Diverse Fantastic Fiction*

Soul Unique

"This is the first book that Gun Brooke has written in a first person perspective, and that was 100% the correct choice. She avoids the pitfalls of trying to tell a story about living with an autism spectrum disorder that she's never experienced, instead making it the story of someone who falls in love with a person living with Asperger's. ...*Soul Unique* is her best. It was an ambitious project that turned out beautifully. I highly recommend it."—*Lesbian Review*

"Yet another success from Gun Brooke. The premise is interesting, the leads are likeable and the supporting characters are well-developed. The first person narrative works well, and I really enjoyed reading about a character with Asperger's."—Melina Bickard, Librarian, Waterloo Library (London)

Advance: Exodus Book One

"*Advance* is an exciting space adventure, hopeful even through times of darkness. The romance and action are balanced perfectly, interesting the audience as much in the fleet's mission as in Dael and Spinner's romance. I'm looking forward to the next book in the series!"—*All Our Worlds: Diverse Fantastic Fiction*

The Blush Factor

"Gun Brooke captures very well the two different 'worlds' the two main characters live in and folds this setting neatly into the story.

So, if you are looking for a well-edited, multi-layered romance with engaging characters this is a great read and maybe a re-read for those days when comfort food is a must."—*Lesbians on the Loose*

"That was fantastic. It's so sweet and romantic. Both women had their own 'demons' and they didn't let anyone be close to them. But from the moment they met each other everything felt so natural between them. Their love became so strong in a short time. Addie's thoughts threatened her relationship with Ellie but with her sister's help she managed to avoid a real catastrophe…"—*Nana's Book Reviews*

The Supreme Constellations Series

"[*Protector of the Realm*] is first and foremost a romance, and whilst it has action and adventure, it is the romance that drives it. The book moves along at a cracking pace, and there is much happening throughout to make it a good page-turner. The action sequences are very well done, and make for an adrenaline rush."—*Lesbian Review*

"Brooke is an amazing author. Never have I read a book where I started at the top of the page and don't know what will happen two paragraphs later. She keeps the excitement going, and the pages turning."—*Family and Friends Magazine*

Fierce Overture

"Gun Brooke creates memorable characters, and Noelle and Helena are no exception. Each woman is 'more than meets the eye' as each exhibits depth, fears, and longings. And the sexual tension between them is real, hot, and raw."—*Just About Write*

September Canvas

"In this character-driven story, trust is earned and secrets are uncovered. Deanna and Faythe are fully fleshed out and prove to the reader each has much depth, talent, wit and problem-solving abilities.

September Canvas is a good read with a thoroughly satisfying conclusion."—*Just About Write*

Sheridan's Fate—*Lambda Literary Award Finalist*

"Sheridan's fire and Lark's warm embers are enough to make this book sizzle. Brooke, however, has gone beyond the wonderful emotional explorations of these characters to tell the story of those who, for various reasons, become differently-abled. Whether it is a bullet, an illness, or a problem at birth, many women and men find themselves in Sheridan's situation. Her courage and Lark's gentleness and determination send this romance into a 'must read.'"—*Just About Write*

Coffee Sonata

"In *Coffee Sonata*, the lives of these four women become intertwined. In forming friendships and love, closets and disabilities are discussed, along with differences in age and backgrounds. Love and friendship are areas filled with complexity and nuances. Brooke takes her time to savor the complexities while her main characters savor their excellent cups of coffee. If you enjoy a good love story, a great setting, and wonderful characters, look for Coffee Sonata at your favorite gay and lesbian bookstore."—*Family & Friends Magazine*

"If you enjoy a good love story, a great setting, and wonderful characters, look for *Coffee Sonata* at your favorite gay and lesbian bookstore."—*MegaScene*

"Each of these characters is intriguing, attractive and likeable, but they are heartbreaking, too, as the reader soon learns when their pasts and their deeply buried secrets are slowly and methodically revealed. Brooke does not give the reader predictable plot points, but builds a fascinating set of subplots and surprises around the romances."
—*L-word.com Literature*

Course of Action

"Brooke's words capture the intensity of their growing relationship. Her prose throughout the book is breathtaking and heart-stopping. Where have you been hiding, Gun Brooke? I, for one, would like to see more romances from this author."—*Independent Gay Writer*

"Brooke gets to the core of her characters' emotions and vulnerabilities and points out their strengths and weaknesses in very human terms."
—*Just About Write*

By the Author

Romances:

Course of Action

Coffee Sonata

Sheridan's Fate

September Canvas

Fierce Overture

Speed Demons

The Blush Factor

Soul Unique

A Reluctant Enterprise

Piece of Cake

Thorns of the Past

Wayworn Lovers

Insult to Injury

Ice Queen

Science Fiction

Supreme Constellations series:

Protector of the Realm

Rebel's Quest

Warrior's Valor

Pirate's Fortune

Exodus series:

Advance

Pathfinder

Escape

Arrival

Treason

The Dennamore Scrolls

Yearning

Velocity

Homeworld

Lunar Eclipse

Renegade's War

Novella Anthology:

Change Horizons

HOMEWORLD

by
Gun Brooke

2022

ISBN 13: 978-1-63679-177-7

This Trade Paperback Original Is Published By
Bold Strokes Books, Inc.
P.O. Box 249
Valley Falls, NY 12185

First Edition: July 2022

CREDITS
Editor: Shelley Thrasher
Production Design: Susan Ramundo
Cover Design By Gun Brooke
Cover Photo: Pexels.com

Acknowledgments

First of all, this is a great place to express my gratitude to every single one of my readers. You who buy or borrow my books, read them, and sometimes find the time to comment or write me personally. It makes me so very happy—and it is humbling in the best of ways. And inspiring!

This, the last installment of the Dennamore trilogy, was hard to write, and I want to thank my editor, Dr. Shelley Thrasher. I love working with you and I always look forward to future projects. My first reader, Annika, in Germany—I want you to know that you were invaluable in your patience and ability to point out the flaws, logical gaps, and so on. The fact that you still seemed to also be able to enjoy the story was amazing to me.

As always, Bold Strokes Books staff, with Sandy Lowe at the forefront, provide such a wonderful family to belong to. I treasure you all!!! Len Barot, aka Radclyffe, thank you once again for creating this publishing company. I'm so proud to belong to it.

Writing a trilogy like this was a new adventure for me, in more ways than one. I do feel that there are more stories to be told about the Homeworld, and I have tentative plans to return to it eventually, thanks to my readers and first reader, who encourage me greatly.

Thank you to Malin, my daughter, for her obvious love, encouragement. and support, especially after I broke my wrist. Thank you to Henrik, my son, for all your help, for taking care of me here at the house and cheering me on when I struggled to complete the editing one-handed. Then there is the rest of the family who are always there. I don't think I could thrive as I do and keep writing if I didn't have you in my life.

To my friends, especially Birgitta, Kamilla and Soli, you are true pearls. Also, shoutout to my painting girls! When it comes to my online friends, you are always close to my heart, right here in my computer, which is yet another thing I'm so thankful for.

And I can't help myself…for my sanity, comfort, and unconditional love, I owe a lot to my two dogs, Hoshi and Esti. There. I said it. :-) Woof!

Dedication

For Elon
For my family

PROLOGUE

1777

Bech'taia leaves the long structure they have constructed from the logs of the trees that are indigenous to this part of this planet. Gai'usto, the man she is joined with, is still back there, arguing what seems to be a lost cause. The majority of the crew wants to one day return to Dwynna Major. The captain of their ship, along with the elders among them, refuses. Eventually the arguing has become so loud, Bech'taia has developed an overwhelming headache, and now she hopes that the amazingly clean air of this world, this remarkable, inhabited world, will help. Of course, she can use one of the now-forbidden technological devices, but she finds the purity of this planet's environment an efficient healer.

The elders want them to scuttle the ship, as in crash it into the ocean a few klicks away from their area. This world is still not advanced enough to track their vessel on any sort of sensors, which means it will be easy to do. It will also ensure the crew knows they have no choice but to live their remaining days in this wild paradise.

Bech'taia rubs her forehead as she remembers how she raised her voice to her betters. "But what about the people on Dwynna Major? The ones left behind, hoping to find anything—knowledge, technology, or supplies—to save our world from going under?"

The elders, along with the captain, sneered at her, making sure everyone realized that she didn't know what she was talking about. More concerned with their own personal survival, they ignored the wishes of most of the crew. The Velocity will be destroyed, and the speeders with her. From now on, they will live like the natives, and clearly, they're expected to forget all about their origin.

Having expected this result, Bech'taia knows that she and Gai'usto must assemble their clandestine group and keep working on their alternative solutions. One day they, or their descendants, may want to return to Dwynna Major. Her plan to hide the ship in plain sight may fail, but this way, all may not be lost.

She makes her way to the small log house she shares with Gai'usto. She intends to outline her plan in more detail in the journal she's kept ever since they landed on this world. She sighs at the idea that, instead of making themselves known to the people running this world and learning from them, they will attempt to blend in, and their newly founded town of Dwynna Major will have to become Dennamore.

For now.

PART ONE
THE LAUNCH

CHAPTER ONE

Captain Holly Crowe stood at the center of the bridge, located deep in the belly of the spaceship *Velocity* on deck three. She watched the screens intently. The largest one sat in the middle of the vast bulkhead before her, surrounded by a multitude of smaller screens showing every aspect of what took place with the ship and its crew.

Right now, the main screen showed Earth from high orbit, and Holly knew she wasn't the only one filled with mixed emotions. The yearning to set the course for Dwynna Major, the homeworld of their ancestors, overshadowed the concern of leaving loved ones behind, but not by much. For her, it was an easier choice, as she had lost her parents and her wife years ago, and the people she cared about were on the ship. Others were saying good-bye to family members and friends.

"Samantha to bridge," Samantha Pike, chief helmsman, said over the general communication system. It was still unfathomable that this woman had worked as a librarian until a few months ago.

"Crowe here." Holly tapped her personal speaker, pinned to her uniform.

"We're about to do the last roundup of new crewmembers and their families to the *Velocity*. The people from NASA, and a few from the different law-enforcement agencies, are ready to board *Speeder One* when you give permission."

Holly moaned inwardly. Though dealing with the US authorities was inevitable, it would still be a pain. "How many, exactly?"

"Darian here, Captain," another female voice said, this one sounding sterner. Darian Tennen, a former LAPD detective, was now chief of security aboard their ship. "Six men and two women from NASA, twelve men and eight women from different agencies."

Too many. Returning to the captain's chair, Holly engaged one of the smaller screens. "On screen, Darian." Soon the image of a throng of people below *Speeder One*'s hatch appeared. Most of them wore the obvious go-to black suits and white shirts, some of their jackets bulging at the side, revealing the presence of their sidearms.

"Two from each entity and no weapons." Holly watched the agents' reactions unfold on the screen. Flanked by two of her brand-new subordinates Darian dealt with the situation well. She refused to let anything or anyone on board the *Velocity* ignore her captain's orders. Observing the agents removing their sidearms, she knew she had made the right call. Not that these agents wouldn't be outgunned, but protocol dictated that they outlaw unknown weaponry on board.

With a raised hand, Darian stopped one man, pointing to his feet. Holly wasn't surprised to see him grudgingly remove a clutch piece from his ankle strap.

"All right, Captain. We're taking off with the last crewmembers and their next of kin. The visitors are all seated at the far back of the shuttle and being monitored." Darian spoke rapidly.

"I'll meet you in the shuttle bay." Holly rose as she spoke. "Commander, you have the bridge." She directed the last sentence to the man standing over by an ensign at ops. Formerly a retired chief of police in Dennamore, Geoff Walker was now Holly's next in command. He glanced at her.

"Time to form a welcome committee of one?" He spoke lightly, but the seriousness in his dark-gray eyes showed he knew very well that the visitors en route represented the US authorities. Only the fact that the *Velocity* stayed in a high orbit around Earth had kept the vast array of the US arsenal of weapons from being directed at them.

"It is," Holly now told Walker. "I don't know how long this will take, but I hope for the *Velocity* to break orbit at 0200 hours."

"We'll be ready for it from our end." Walker nodded toward the young man he had just left. "Ensign D'Angelo has almost finished his inventory lists."

"Good. I'll page you later." Holly nodded to Walker and then left the bridge. The elevator in the corridor outside took her down to deck ten so fast, she seemed to be freefalling. Stepping out, she ended up in organized mayhem where wide-eyed new crewmembers emptied *Speeder Two* of their luggage and supplies from Dennamore. Contrary to the federal authorities, every Dennamore inhabitant that had descended from the aliens who landed in the Adirondacks in the late 1700s was eager to help the mission take place. They seemed determined to either be part of the crew or do their damndest to facilitate a safe, comfortable journey to their ancestors' homeworld.

"Captain!" A young woman rushed up to Holly. "Chief Tennen paged that they should dock shortly."

"I know, Ensign Ritter," Holly said after glancing at the uniformed woman's nametag. "We'll need three more security officers."

"On it, Captain." Ritter nodded briskly and turned around while tapping her speaker. "Three security officers to shuttle bay, now."

It still felt surreal to watch more and more people show up in their ancestors' uniforms and see how their Neural Interface Expertise Connectors—NIECs—induced the knowledge they needed to perform their duties from where they sat attached to the back of the neck. The uniforms, unlike the space suits that were form-fitted like a second skin, consisted of black pants over short boots. A sleeveless light-gray, collarless shirt under a mustard-yellow jacket, along with the rank insignias, separated the officers from the crewmen, who wore turquoise jackets. A single golden lapel showed whether the crewman in question wore a NIEC.

A humming sound grew in intensity, alerting everyone that *Speeder One* was approaching. The shuttle-bay door opened, and, unfathomably, only a sensor barrier kept everyone on deck ten from being sucked into space. The sensor barrier crackled and sparkled as the shuttle penetrated it. The doors closed as it set down on its struts next to its sister ship.

Holly stepped closer, stopping six feet from the end of where the ramp would reach once it opened fully. Ensign Ritter and a colleague flanked her to the right, and two other security officers did the same on her left.

"Keep your cool," Holly said quietly. "Nobody is armed, and I fully expect them to make demands and perhaps even threaten repercussions. Be prepared to escort anyone out of line back onto the shuttle if Chief Tennen gives the order—or if I do."

"Aye, Captain," Ritter said smartly.

The hatch snapped open and lowered onto the deck without much sound. In the area above it, Chief Darian Tennen stood flanked by security, much as Holly did. She waved the new crewmembers and the ones among their kin that were able to join them on the space journey to disembark.

Holly shook their hands, even those of the eight children. The crew complement now held about eighteen minors.

"Are you really the captain?" a small, young person asked, jarring Holly from her train of thought. Blinking, she looked down at a small boy, perhaps six years old. He was holding what looked like a large stuffed squirrel and a tablet. Next to him, a young man smiled nervously.

"I am," Holly said, crouching in front of the child. "What's your name?"

"Simon. This is my dad. His name is Mark." Simon beamed up at his father.

"Welcome aboard, both of you. If you follow the welcome committee over there, they'll show you to your quarters and the location of the first information meeting."

Mark and Simon thanked her, and she couldn't blame them for being taken aback by the impressive alien technology around them. The walls were made from a metal alloy that didn't exist on Earth, in a pattern reminding Holly of an intricate katana sword's swirls created by expert forging.

Darian appeared behind the last of the crewmembers and their accompanying family members. With her dark-brown hair in an austere ponytail, she radiated the authority of being the chief of security. Walking down the ramp, she guided the agents and civilians from the different agencies, who were also guarded by Darian's staff.

"Captain." Darian greeted Holly. "Our guests. I'll let them introduce themselves." She spoke noncommittally, but the way she eyed a couple of the guests was an unmistakable sign that she wasn't impressed.

"Thank you, Chief." Holly took a few steps forward and gazed at the unfamiliar faces. Two women and six men stared at her, and among the latter, three of them regarded her through slitted eyes, looking ready to act rashly. "Welcome aboard the *Velocity*, ladies and gentlemen. I won't reiterate the explanations we have already transmitted to your respective agencies, verbally as well as through extensive documentation, but instead—"

"Stand down, Ms. Crowe. We're here to seize this vessel by order of the joint directors of the CIA, NSA, and FBI," one of the hostile-looking men said. He took a step forward. "No matter what hubris this detection has created among you people, you cannot be permitted to—"

"Stop right there," Holly said firmly. "I am Captain Holly Crowe, and this is my ship and my crew."

"You're a schoolteacher, and you've filled the find of a millennium with a bunch of mountain hicks!" the other man, who possessed the same sneer as the first, said. "You have no idea what you're playing with here, and the sooner you realize how many laws, state and federal, you're breaking, the better."

Holly glanced at Darian and sighed. "These were the ones you thought we could talk to?"

"Believe me, there are degrees of hostility and stupidity," Darian said, not taking her eyes off the men.

Holly shook her head and turned back to the group. The two women wore NASA patches on their sleeves. The four men who hadn't yet spoken appeared less riled up, but Holly knew it was a mistake to assume too much too soon. "Your words show you haven't read the English translation of how this ship operates, along with the alien technology. We provided all information to your respective agencies and, of course, to the government and the UN. Nobody but descendants of the original crew of this ship can operate it, and that's a fact. This reality makes it our ship, and though the crewmembers may be new, the Neural Interface Expertise Connectors turn them into an accomplished crew and provide them with their individual ranks instantly. I really don't care if you believe me. That's how it works."

"That's fucking science fiction." One of the men even snarled.

"And yet here we are," Darian said and smiled broadly. "In a huge interstellar spaceship. Sort of takes the fiction out of the science, doesn't it?"

"Captain?" One of the women, a compact, freckled redhead of Asian American descent, raised her hand. "I'm Mireille Wu, a senior astronomer at NASA. I have no military agenda, and I'm grateful and excited to be on board."

Holly didn't allow herself to relax but recognized the mesmerized look in Mireille's eyes as she stared around the shuttle bay. "Welcome, Ms. Wu."

"Doctor. This is my assistant, Emma Andersen." Mireille motioned to the tall blonde by her side. "Can we sit down somewhere and share more information before you embark on your journey?"

Ah. Someone had actually read some of the documentation they had provided during the last few hours. "Certainly. Everyone is welcome to join me in the conference room if they can maintain common courtesy."

"It's not a matter of being courteous," hostile man #2 said. "This is about national, even *international*, security. Who knows what you can uncover if you're allowed to take off with technology you can't possibly know anything about?"

"Are you willing to join us in a civilized manner, or do you prefer to be delivered back to Dennamore without any information for your respective bosses?" Darian stepped in between Holly and man #2. "We can easily arrange either scenario."

The two men looked like they were grinding their teeth, but then man #1 nodded curtly. "By all means. As long as you'll listen to the point of view of the directors."

"Of course. I'm always ready to listen. This way." Holly stepped over to where the elevators were located. "Chief, you're riding up with me. Your officers will take the cargo elevator. Deck three, section two."

Six security officers, some of whom had worked as a store manager, office clerk, and a personal-fitness expert, among other things, less than twenty-four hours earlier, accompanied the visitors into the larger elevator.

"Glad we frisked them twice," Darian said as they stepped into the other elevator. "Those vocal guys, and trust me, they weren't as trigger-happy as their other colleagues, had clutch pieces on both legs, knives, and a double harness holding a sidearm *and* a taser—each."

Holly blinked. "What the hell did they think they'd do with that weaponry even if they managed to shoot some of us? They'd be stuck in orbit on a ship they couldn't operate." She ran her hand along her forehead. "We really hit a nerve, obviously."

"We didn't expect anything less, did we? Consider how our own leader in Dennamore reacted." Darian shrugged.

Holly thought of Desmond Miller, chairperson of the Elder Council in their small mountain town. He had gone from belligerent and vindictive to fearful...and resentful. Never once had he showed signs of feeling the special, inherited yearning to join the crew on the *Velocity*. "You have a point."

They reached the conference room a few moments earlier than their guests. Capable of hosting twenty people around a diamond-shaped table, where Holly's seat was located at the top and center, its bulkhead was lined with something that reduced the hum of the propulsion system to a minimum. Holly admitted that she still had to get used to feeling the reverberation in the gravitation-deck material. It would probably take even longer to become accustomed to the feeling of her feet being magnetized to the deck plating. However, it certainly beat existing in a weightless environment.

The first two security officers stopped just inside the door. "Your guests, Captain," the young woman to the left said.

"Show them in. I want the two of you to remain by the door." Holly shot the woman and the equally young man a sharp glance, but they met her gaze calmly.

"Aye, Captain."

Their guests entered the conference room, and Holly could detect the moment the two women from NASA saw the image of Earth on the large viewscreens adorning two of the walls. It was a poignant, impressive sight.

"Oh." Mireille stopped and gripped the backrest of one of the chairs.

Even the men from the different agencies appeared taken aback for a moment. "That's quite something," a blond man in his early fifties said.

"Please." Holly motioned for everyone to sit as she took her own seat. "Before we continue, I'd like to hear suggestions and demands concisely. I doubt I can meet every demand, but within reason, my crew and I are willing to listen."

As if on cue, the door opened, and her first officer entered. Walker took the seat next to Holly. Soon the senior staff, consisting of the people who had discovered the alien artifacts and the ships, occupied the chairs. Samantha Pike, formerly the head librarian and now the chief pilot and navigator, sat down next to Darian. Claire Gordon, chief engineer, came in with an older woman, the ship's counselor, Camilla Tennen. Previously, Claire had worked at her father's garage as a gifted mechanic, and Camilla had just returned to Dennamore a few months earlier after an extensive career as a scriptwriter in Hollywood. Raoul Viera, a family doctor turned chief medical officer, sat down next to Camilla and murmured something in her ear that made her nod.

"I think that's everyone," Holly said lightly, after introducing the senior staff. "Now, let's see if we can put your mind at ease, at least to a degree." She let her gaze wander from face to face around the table, including her own crewmembers.

"I want to know why you were trying to bring weapons aboard the ship." Walker laced his fingers together and rested his elbows against the table.

"Common sense," one of the impatient men said. "We still have no idea if hostiles are on board, pulling the strings. If you think about it, that scenario is highly likely. How could any of you people even begin to maneuver a ship like this? For all we know, you're a front for an alien attack, or even a domestic one."

Darian snorted and shook her head. "Are you stupid for real? We have provided information and identification of everyone who has felt the yearning—the calling, if you will—to serve on board this ship. They're all regular people ready to take on a challenge and do what they obviously now feel they were meant to. We even have some civilians who aren't of alien descent who are taking on this assignment."

The man stared at Darian as if she had snakes weaving through her hair. "You as a former LAPD detective should know better." He hissed. "We demand to be allowed to examine whatever psychotropic drug those NIECs infuse into unsuspecting US citizens."

Samantha slammed her palm onto the conference table. "Oh, be quiet. We don't use drugs on anyone, let alone anyone who yearns to embark on the *Velocity*. You have to realize that they do so long before they learn of the alien artifacts." She looked over at Holly. "I fail to see why we need to keep repeating ourselves when the CIA agents have preconceived ideas that border on conspiracy theories."

"I hear you, Chief Pike. I do." Holly took a moment. "I want to make something clear. You're here as a courtesy. This vessel is going on its mission to locate the homeworld of our ancestors. You are here only because the senior crew and I believe in transparency. We will return, and when we do so, who knows what information we'll be able to bring back with us. If we find life on Dwynna Major, we might have a chance to establish diplomacy between Earth and another planet for the very first time."

"Or you'll bring back someone ready to attack Earth." One of the CIA agents huffed. "You don't know what will happen!"

"They may become great allies and share technology with us that can help us with climate change, illnesses, etcetera." Holly could tell from the way the man rolled his eyes at his colleague how naive he found her statement. "Guess it depends on how you look at it. I can reassure you that we don't intend to lead any hostiles back to Earth."

The discussion billowed back and forth, and after another hour of circling the same concepts, Holly raised her hand, having had enough. "We will be breaking orbit in five hours. I have a scheduled conversation with the secretary-general of the United Nations in half an hour. While my next in command, Commander Walker, and I do that, I will leave you in the capable hands of my chief of security and her team."

"You're just walking away from this meeting?" one of the FBI agents asked, sounding more perplexed than angry.

"For now, yes. In the meantime, I want you to consider what I'm about to offer you. If anyone is interested, we can include as many as four of you on our mission, to observe and report back to Earth. My chief engineer has arranged to deliver a communication device to the United Nations as we speak, and, at least for part of the journey, we will be able to send digital messages globally and to the crew's family members and friends."

The two women from NASA exchanged a wide-eyed look as Holly rose.

"Commander, with me." Holly nodded to the ones still sitting around the table, noting how taken aback the visitors seemed. As she left the room with Walker by her side, she made some private bets as to who might want to accept the offer.

"That was a curveball they didn't see coming," Walker murmured as the door hissed closed behind them. "I know we briefly talked about it, but I wasn't sure you thought it was a good idea. If one of those CIA guys opts to stay, he's going to second-guess us at every turn and interfere with every minute decision."

"True. But they won't have any authority whatsoever, though they may sow seeds of doubt with the crew, especially the non-NIEC wearers. Stir up trouble unless the chain of command works flawlessly." Holly sighed as they stepped into her office. "We can always hope they're not ready to show real courage."

"Yes, there is that." Walker pushed a stool over to sit next to her as she pulled her computer toward her. Claire had worked on the alien technology and made the communication features compatible with the contemporary computers on Earth. Now she slid her fingertips along the colorfully coded lines and dots where normally a keyboard would have sat. A short hum later, a middle-aged woman of Indian descent appeared on the screen.

"Your Excellency," Holly said, forcing her voice to sound calm even if her heart raced. "I'm Captain Holly Crowe, and this is my next in command, Commander Geoff Walker."

Secretary-general Lilavati Banerjee studied them for a few long moments before responding. "Captain, Commander," Banerjee said without giving away her thoughts. "I understand that you and your team have made the discovery of the millennia."

"Yes, Your Excellency. It can be regarded in that way."

"And also, that you're launching it back into space without placing it under the control of the correct authority." Banerjee clearly was not asking a question.

"I respectfully disagree. There is no correct authority to place it under. As you may have discerned from the documentation we provided the United Nations, only descendants of the alien species who once landed these ships on Earth can operate any of this technology." Holly waited for Banerjee to respond, but the secretary-general only motioned for Holly to continue. Either she genuinely wanted to hear what Holly and Walker had to say, or she was simply giving them enough rope to hang themselves with. The woman was a brilliant diplomat, after all. "A shuttle is on its way to the UN as we speak, containing modified technology that will make it possible for you, Your Excellency, or any member of your staff that you deem fit, to stay connected with us. We aren't certain how long before we'll be out of range, but my chief engineer estimates for at least two-thirds of the distance to Dwynna Major."

This statement finally prompted a reaction from Banerjee. Her perfect, black eyebrows rose, if only for a fraction of a moment. This was obviously not what she had expected to hear. "A military vessel?" she asked slowly.

"No, Your Excellency. A cloaked shuttle, called a speeder, which will hover above the UN building and deliver the communication device."

Holly looked over at Walker, who rattled off the flight information and estimated time of arrival for *Speeder Two.*

"Thirty minutes from orbit to New York?" Banerjee frowned.

"It could go faster," Walker said, "but as it will be in cloak mode, we have to be careful. Our chief pilot and her staff have just launched and are en route to New York. Now, once the technology is in your hands, Your Excellency, it's obviously out of ours." He glanced at his watch. "We're breaking orbit in four and a half hours. We have extended the courtesy to the agents and NASA personnel currently visiting the ship to select four people among them to undertake this journey with us."

Banerjee tapped her desktop with a long, perfect nail. "I see. Do you think any of them will take you up on it, considering they have only hours to decide? After all, it is not only a life-altering but also a potentially one-way trip."

"Yes, I do," Holly said. "Perhaps not as many as four, but this prospect has to at least tempt a NASA astronomer and engineer."

Banerjee raised her gaze to whoever was behind her screen. "Go arrange for security to accompany you on the roof while you wait for the shuttle. Bring the package directly to my office. Then give me the room," Shuffling chairs and feet were audible for a few seconds, and then Banerjee seemed to relax somewhat. "May I call you Holly?"

Holly nodded. "Certainly, Your Ex—"

"Please. I'm Lilivati. I stand on ceremony for the sake of the office I hold, but in this case—well, I suppose the word unprecedented is putting it mildly—I think we're beyond that formality. Whenever we can communicate like this, alone, I'd rather we be on a first-name basis. Will this be amenable to you as well, Geoff?" Lilivati locked her gaze on Walker.

"Absolutely. I usually go by Walker. Either is fine."

"All right, Walker. Holly. Let me be perfectly clear. Once the news breaks, and it will, quite soon, mayhem will erupt. Most likely, neither of you has given enough thought to the ramifications of your discovery and decision for the people of Earth. From a religious point of view, or a political one, the discovery of extraterrestrial life could create chaos. Now, that said, I realize you cannot put the genie back into the bottle, and that's why you must rely on me, and the UN, to do the work at our end. All you can do is stay the course of your mission and keep everyone safe—and bring them back."

Holly agreed that no one among her team, except Philber, had given enough thought to what they were leaving behind on a global scale. "You're right. Yet here we are, and we have to prepare the last details before we go."

Banerjee looked at her cell phone. "Will we have enough time to make sure this communication device you're sending us works before you break orbit?"

"Yes." Holly paused, choosing her words carefully. "I'm not denying that we have a personal, perhaps selfish reason for our journey. The ones among us who carry the alien genetic code, well, many of us feel we have no choice but to seek out the homeworld of our ancestors. That said, I doubt any of us would go if we didn't think we could return home with knowledge and experiences that will ultimately benefit the people of Earth."

"I see." Lilivati didn't comment on Holly's words, but she seemed sincere when she stated, "We'll let you know once we have the communication device up and running."

Holly could have reassured Lilivati that her engineers would know as soon as the hybrid computer was plugged in, but she merely bowed her head. "Until then."

Once she had closed the screen, she allowed herself to slump against the backrest of her desk chair. "That was like being summoned to the principal's office."

"And then some." Walker shoved his fingers through his silver-gray hair. "We better go back to the conference room to make sure Darian hasn't punched some agent in the face."

"God. No joke." Holly rose and straightened her uniform jacket. "I'll be curious to see if anyone accepts our offer."

"I have my doubts, but who knows?" Walker snorted. "After you, Captain."

CHAPTER TWO

Chief Pilot Samantha Pike walked down the ramp of *Speeder Two*, which hovered less than a foot above the UN building's roof, two security officers by her side. Having overdosed the last two days on the surreal feelings of seeing familiar faces from her own town take on their new assignments, no, new *lives*, in their respective roles, she didn't waste time dwelling on how the two men responsible for her safety had been a history teacher and a carpenter only eighteen hours ago.

At the bottom of the ramp, UN security in turn flanked a man and a woman dressed in pant suits. Samantha was carrying the hybrid computer and its backup, something Claire, the *Velocity*'s chief engineer, had insisted on, and stopped a few yards in front of the UN personnel.

"Good evening," Samantha said calmly, secure in the knowledge that *Speeder Two*'s high-projectile force field let people through but not fast objects, like bullets. Any assassination attempt or attack by hostiles would not work. She still hoped that Holly and Walker had reached the heart and common sense of the secretary-general of the UN. The woman had a reputation for being a no-nonsense diplomat, but unknown variables were always at play. Samantha would be naive to think otherwise.

"We're here to retrieve the package and take it to Secretary-General Banerjee," the woman said and took a step toward Samantha.

"Good." Samantha glanced around them and knew her escort had already swept the area with their security-issue trackpads. "We have two packages. One spare, just in case."

"Understood." The man joined his colleague. "We'll be responsible for the items getting to the boss."

"Before I hand them over, I need to make sure you're who you say you are." Samantha nodded to the security officer to her left. "Are we hooked up?"

"Yes, Chief." He showed her a small screen. The face of Banerjee appeared, looking serious. "Your Excellency, Chief Samantha Pike here," she said. "I will have to ask you to confirm that these individuals are the same ones you tasked with obtaining the package."

Samantha's security guard directed the screen to the people before Samantha.

"You have my confirmation," Banerjee said. "You can safely hand over the technology. My IT expert is standing by in my office."

"Good. We'll take off as soon as they are at a safe distance from the speeder." Samantha handed over the two computers to the woman. "I don't need to emphasize that you need to handle these with care."

"Precisely," the woman said and took a few steps back, eyes wide and hands faintly trembling. "Thank you. If I may be so bold, ma'am...Godspeed."

Samantha paused, surprised at the sudden warmth in the woman's voice. "Thank you. And to you. Our journey will no doubt be precarious at times, but so will the situation on Earth." Yet this was the point of no return.

Samantha had begun walking back up the ramp when she heard a noise that didn't come from the speeder's propulsion system. She turned her head and scanned the dark New York sky with her own trackpad. "Helicopters," she said urgently. "Small ones. Not military. News crews, no doubt." She ran up the ramp, not looking back until it began closing behind them. The UN staff members were already at the door leading back into the building, which was all she needed to know. "How the hell did they get permission to fly across Manhattan so fast? If they're risking doing so without a flight plan, the airspace might be full of military jets and helicopters very shortly. Let's get out of here."

Throwing herself into the pilot seat, she saw that Rhian, her copilot, had already started the launch sequence. "We have to cloak, fast." Samantha ran her fingers along the controls and sighed in relief when the computer showed they were no longer visible to anyone but the *Velocity*'s short-range scanners.

"*Velocity—Speeder Two. Velocity—Speeder Two.* Cloaked and taking off. ETA eighteen minutes." Samantha set the trajectory to high orbit, far away from the helicopters and known air corridors.

"*Speeder Two—Velocity.* We hear you," a familiar voice said. Carl Hoskins, now an ops officer on the bridge after having recently lived his life as a high school senior, rattled off information that Samantha's copilot confirmed via her screen.

"The package was delivered according to orders. Identification confirmed with Banerjee." Samantha watched New York shrink below them as they pierced the dark sky, leaving the different layers of spheres until they reached high orbit in the upper part of the exosphere. The signal from the *Velocity* showed they would be able to enter its shuttle bay in less than twelve minutes.

"Good job, Chief," Carl said. "Captain Crowe asks you to remain in the shuttle bay so you can take one last trip to the surface."

"Understood. I gather she wants me to return the agents." Samantha rubbed the back of her head. She had gotten far too little sleep during the last forty-eight hours.

"Affirmative," Carl said. "Bridge out."

Setting the computer coordinates to fully automatic, Samantha closed her eyes briefly. After one last trip back to Dennamore, they would be ready to break orbit, not knowing when—or even if—they'd be back.

"May I ask you something, Chief?" Rhian cleared her throat.

"Of course." Swiveling her chair toward Rhian, Samantha regarded the young, slightly pale face before her. A young mother of small twins, she had often visited the library with her children.

"Are you afraid?" Rhian smoothed down her long, red ponytail.

Samantha waited a few beats before responding, knowing that honesty was key but that Rhian also needed reassuring.

"I have known of our alien ancestry and this technology longer than you, but it's still only a matter of mere months. I can't even begin to understand how overwhelming you must find all this induced knowledge from the NIEC." It was true. Samantha had become used to the oval metal plate with tendrils that attached to the scalp over time. She did remember how it felt like going from zero to a hundred when it came to new knowledge and skills, but in her case, and in the original group's, they weren't thrown directly into the fray like Rhian and the others had been.

"So, to answer your questions—no, I'm not afraid, but I'd be lying if I didn't feel a heavy weight of responsibility for the crew and the civilians." As the chief pilot and navigator, she had her work cut out for her when they began their journey, as it didn't entail simply pushing a "reverse-course" button. Their ancestors had crisscrossed through space before they reached Earth, and they hadn't left much information about how long they'd been traveling when they found what became their final destination. Samantha was relieved that she had managed to plot the correct initial course. She would have to figure out the adjustments when necessary. Unlike their ancestors, this crew knew where they were going.

"I'm still not sure how I was certain, even before I received my NIEC, that I should bring Pierre and the twins with me. And I can't wrap my brain around how fast he agreed, even if he's not from Dennamore." Rhian rolled her shoulder as if shaking off an invisible weight of her own.

"You're not the first of the newcomers among the crew to say this." Samantha nodded at Rhian's screen. "And you're a natural."

"Thank you. It does feel natural, Chief. So does the command structure." She smiled wanly and returned her focus to the controls. "We'll be reducing to docking speed in a minute."

"Excellent. As you heard, we have one more drop-off, and then you're off duty for ten hours." Samantha checked the computer screen and saw the outline of the *Velocity* appear.

"Thanks, Chief." Rhian brightened, as Samantha had guessed she would. Nothing like being with the ones you love to recharge your batteries, she thought.

Darian stood to the side of Holly and Walker. She briefly thought about how she would always use their given names in private, even if they all had to be strict when it came to rank in front of the crew and civilians. According to Philber, their civilian social anthropologist, this procedure was crucial. For Darian, it was not only a familiar way to work, having been in law enforcement for four years, but also a method to unmuddy the water for everyone. Keeping people guessing about the command structure when they had to rely on each other unconditionally as they were hurled into deep space was a sure way to botch the mission—and potentially lose their lives.

Locking her gaze on the agents that were returning to the surface, not trusting a couple of them for a second, Darian was surprised at which ones had decided to stay. Well, perhaps not the two women from NASA. They had been a given. The one guy from the CIA and another guy from the NSA, who hadn't made much noise in the conference room, were unlikely candidates, and Darian wasn't quite sure why Holly had decided to keep them on board.

Speeder Two slid into its bay, and two brand-new mechanics rushed over and began using their special trackpads as if it were second nature. The hatch opened, and Samantha showed up in the opening, scanning the busy area around the speeder. Darian met her gaze, and even if she wanted nothing more than to rush up the ramp and make sure the fatigue in her eyes was not a sign that Samantha was dangerously exhausted, she remained where she was. She loved Samantha, but in this situation, they had their respective jobs to do. As chief of security, Darian was responsible for escorting the agents who were leaving back onto the speeder. Samantha would be piloting, so Darian would have a few moments to check on her on the way back.

"Thank you for visiting us. My regards to the president and his cabinet." Holly nodded rigidly. "It's unfortunate that the US government feels so strongly that our ship is their property, but perhaps they'll have adopted a more forthcoming and reasonable tone once we return."

"And you call yourself a US citizen." The CSI agent who was leaving snarled at Holly. "If you get back, which I doubt, you'll be put on trial for endangering gullible civilians and stealing artifacts belonging to the United States."

"I think it's time for you to go. We have a lot to prepare before we leave. Good-bye." Holly pivoted and left with Walker and one security guard by her side. Darian remained, holding the alien version of a rifle. Small and agile, with a fat body and a barrel about a foot long, it enabled her to control anyone who might act up during the flight down to Dennamore. Unlike the rifles on Earth, which used projectiles, this weapon fired energy bursts. If she needed to render someone unconscious in a safe way, she set the small ridge to 25 percent, and it would knock any subject off their feet and into a deep sleep for a few hours. It was safe to use on any size person or animal, as it located the synapses and simply turned off the light. Darian was relieved she didn't have to estimate anyone's weight or body mass.

The agents entered the speeder and took their seats, buckling up. Darian and one of her subordinates sat down in front of them on a swivel seat as well as behind them. Samantha had retaken her seat at the helm and now slid her fingers along the computer, as did her copilot.

"This is an abomination," the second NSA agent said quietly. "Leaving our homeworld, looking for life on worlds that might not know God."

"Let's hope they have the same open mind we're supposed to have. Freedom of speech, religion, etc." Darian raised her eyebrows at the solemn man. "I suppose coming with us was out of the question for you."

"You're right. They're going to need all the help they can get down there," he said, pointing at the deck of the speeder. "You're revealing truths that we're not prepared for."

"Not going to discuss it with you again. My captain has already—"

"Captain," the CSI agent said, huffing. "A teacher."

"A famous scholar who is our best chance to return with new knowledge and ideas to make life better on Earth." Darian was annoyed that she let the man goad her. "I suggest you enjoy the ride to Earth in silence. You'll find barf bags in the small compartment in the backrest in front of you. Not everyone's cut out for space travel."

When one of the men later threw up several times, Darian knew it was petty of her to grin, but she couldn't help it. He had it coming.

❖

Dennamore lay quiet and embedded in a few inches of new snow. The lights were on in some houses, but many were completely dark, as if waiting for their owners to return. About fifty people stood along the perimeter around the square in front of Town Hall. Police cars had their flickering blue lights on. Some of Darian's former peers had their guns out, although directed toward the ground.

Opening the hatch while Samantha hovered two feet above ground, Darian guided the agents toward the ramp.

"We're still in midair," one of the men said, stopping short of the hatch.

"It's two feet. You can jump. It's that or be harnessed down, which I personally would find embarrassing—in front of your fellow law-enforcement people on the streets." Darian grinned. She was enjoying this situation a bit too much. Samantha was going to notice her pleasure, for sure.

"I suggest you hurry up. We're leaving in four minutes." Samantha joined Darian as her copilot held the ship in place.

"Why don't you set it down?" The NSA agent glared at Samantha.

"Because we don't want to tempt anyone to approach us and risk getting hurt."

The CIA agent acted fast, but Darian was quicker. As he threw himself toward her, she slammed her hip against Samantha, pushing her out of the way, and then fired at the man. He went down as if he'd died on the spot. The fact that he looked quite peaceful where he slumped on the floor reassured Darian that her weapon had worked as intended. To her other side, her subordinate trained his weapon on the shocked men.

"You killed him?" The NSA agent and the others who were returning crouched over the man.

"He's out cold but unharmed," Darian said, not daring to check on Samantha. When she felt Samantha return to her side, Darian willed her shoulders to relax. "I suggest two of you jump off, retrieve him from the ramp, and then the rest of you join them. Now. We're running out of time. If anyone's still on the ramp in two minutes, you're coming with us."

This threat seemed to get through to the agents. Two jumped off, and then the rest unceremoniously rolled the CIA agent off the ramp before they too landed in the snow.

"Close the ramp. Taking off in twenty seconds." Samantha jumped back into her seat. "Damn it. We have incoming. They were expecting us, of course."

Incoming? Darian took her seat to the right of Samantha and pulled up the tactical screen. "I see five of them. Four fast ones and one slower. Military aircraft and a helicopter of unknown origin."

"We're climbing. Not ideal with the hatch not locked into place, but we have to go. How long before we can floor it, Rhian?" Samantha's hands flew across the controls.

"Hatch will secure in twelve seconds." Rhian sounded remarkably calm.

"If they're foolish enough to fire on us, fly out over the meadows," Darian called out. "We can't risk any civilians getting caught in the crossfire."

Samantha pushed the controls, and *Speeder Two* obediently banked as they raced across the houses and out over the large meadows that stretched north of Dennamore. "They're right there behind us."

"Hatch is locked in place!" Rhian tightened her belt, thus reminding Darian to do the same.

"Hold on." Samantha clenched her jaw enough for a vein to become visible on her temple. Darian clung to her armrests as Samantha pushed her entire palm to a red circular light on the console.

Speeder Two seemed to hold its breath before it pushed upward at a ninety-degree angle to the ground. The immense force behind the ship made it howl against the atmosphere, reminding Darian of what fingers on an old-fashioned chalkboard would sound like.

After they reached the exosphere in less than two minutes, Samantha adjusted the controls, and Darian watched her allow the computer to take over.

"Needless to say, we lost them immediately. I can't believe you flew like that on manual. Shit, Samantha." Darian ran an adrenaline-trembling hand across her forehead.

"I can't take the entire credit, Dar." Samantha grinned at Rhian. "If my copilot hadn't performed all the routine procedures at record speed, I would have overshot high orbit by hundreds of miles. A clear team effort."

"Great job, Rhian. Thank you." Darian nodded to Rhian, who seemed as if she might cry and cheer at the same time. Looking over her shoulder, Darian saw her subordinate unbuckle his belt and join them. "And good job on having my back when that guy lost it."

"All in a day's work," he said, patting his rifle. "I'll keep training with this one, Chief, but even so, I'm thankful there's very little risk that I accidentally kill anyone."

"Got it." Darian sighed and leaned back. "I know we're due to break orbit in a couple of hours, but I'd give anything for a pizza."

Samantha chuckled. "Now I know you're okay." She shook her head. "Not sure we can scare up pizza, but I heard in passing that our cooks are really starting to get the hang of the food-prep stations."

"Any chance we might get something other than alien porridge?" Darian straightened. "Nutritious as all hell, and not too bad, taste-wise, but it's been all we've had for days."

"Talk to Brandon when we get back. After all, he's in charge." Samantha refocused on her computer console. "ETA shuttle bay in less than ten minutes."

Darian was relieved. She wasn't sure what to think about the remaining agents and the NASA employees, but she trusted Holly's genius, especially when paired with Walker's common sense. Hopefully they'd become the perfect radar pair that they had the potential to be.

Turning in her chair as well, Darian watched Samantha discreetly. Yes, the woman she loved was tired, but she still performed amazingly amid chaos. Darian thought back to how they'd met in the last moments of summer last year. Literally colliding in the corridor outside the library in Dennamore's Town Hall, Darian had been struck, also literally, by Samantha's poise and beauty. When she also turned out to be brilliant, intelligent, and sexy as hell, falling for her was almost too easy—and not something Darian had wanted, as she'd planned to return to Los Angeles, to her life as a LAPD detective. And then they found all the alien artifacts and proof that they were descended from aliens that landed on Earth, in the Adirondacks, during the late 1700s. Nothing had been the same after that. They risked everything, including their hearts, to discover the truth, and even if they now knew how they felt about each other, they were still risking everything—their lives—their hearts.

Yet Darian wouldn't have it any other way. The point of no return had come and gone a long time ago, both regarding their ancestry and the space journey—and the truth about her love for Samantha.

Chapter Three

Chief Engineer Claire Gordon stood at the center console of her new domain. She had briefly made a ridiculous comparison between this space of advanced technology and her father's garage, where she'd worked as a car mechanic since high school. After being able to say good-bye to her father only over a communication link, she now refused to dwell on the familiarity of her home and how she would miss everything she held dear. She had to file away images of her tall, strong father, the garage, and the natural world around Dennamore that she loved so much. Instead, she had to focus solely on keeping everything tech working on a spaceship that hadn't been used in more than two centuries. It had sat hidden under the famous lake in Dennamore all this time, and nobody had known that it had caused the lake to light up so beautifully every summer at the exact same time. It could have something to do with an automated maintenance cycle, but Claire had yet to confirm that theory.

She glimpsed herself in a glass-covered computer panel as she passed. To respect the uniform and her new position among the senior crew, she had pulled her curly hair back into a low, tight bun. Her eyes were narrow slits, and she probably wore that frown constantly, as she was trying to keep up with the information her NIEC was providing, as well as lead her brand-new group of engineers. She had twelve at her disposal, which meant four were on duty during each of the three shifts.

"Chief?" Trainer, a man in his forties, approached her rapidly. "The converters that will send the signals when we go to ISD all need new fuses."

Claire flinched inwardly. This was very last-minute information. They were breaking orbit in one hour, and once they were on the correct trajectory through this solar system, Holly planned to order the ship to Inter Stellar Drive mode. "How many?"

"Eighty, Chief." Trainer looked pained. "I found backups, but we have only fifty."

Claire lengthened her stride as she tapped her speaker. "Gordon to bridge."

"Walker here."

"All the fuses to the ISD converters need replacing. We may not have enough, Commander," Claire said as she knelt and peered under the console where Trainer had been working. "My staff says we have two-thirds of what we need."

"This is not good news, Chief," Walker said. "Any chance we'll find more in the storage units on deck eleven?"

"I'll let Trainer finish removing the burned ones and go look."

"Report when you have a solution. Bridge out."

Not if, but when. Claire turned to Trainer, who was already pulling out the four-inch-sized, narrow pipes containing the fuses. "I'll page you once I find something we can use. You have engineering until I return."

"Aye, Chief," Trainer said from the floor, as he was elbow deep into the opening.

"Hand me one of the toasted ones for comparison, please." Claire held out her hand, and Trainer gave her the fuse he had just pried free.

Hurrying out the door, barking at two junior crewmen to ask Trainer if he needed help, Claire bypassed the elevator and instead grabbed the pole next to the ladder that they could slide down. Using the crease of her arm that was covered by her uniform sleeve so she wouldn't burn her skin against the metal, Claire reached the belly of the *Velocity* in seconds. A computer panel sat next to the ladder, and she entered the information via her trackpad.

Browsing through the once-so-enigmatic alien lettering, she scanned for spare parts. They needed only thirty fuses to start their journey, but she'd prefer to find a decent stash so they wouldn't run out halfway to Dwynna Major—or back. She had quickly browsed what the ship had in storage several times, in awe at how much the two cargo-bay compartments could hold. Now when she needed something specific, she tried to get her NIEC to find the correct term for it so she could search the database more efficiently. All the many subcategories would keep a person busy for months.

"I heard," an alto voice said from behind, and Claire snapped her head up. "Captain." Claire sighed at the sight of her commanding officer. "I'm sorry for not noticing this shortage earlier. I incorrectly assumed that just because we reached high orbit so easily, no important system on the ship had deteriorated over time."

"Don't beat yourself up. We all made that assumption, I think. How can I help?" Holly moved closer and regarded the long lists of components and their location. "Oh, my."

"Exactly. I've narrowed it down to propulsion system and interstellar drive. This entry lists everything down to the smallest nut and bolt. Not that they used nuts or bolts, though."

"I've noticed that as well. Everything is attached by some heavy-duty rivets, and I have yet to figure out what they used to weld metal together. Or fuse it, rather." Bending, Holly ran her finger down the list. "Here, maybe?" She slid her finger over the controls, opening a new menu. "ISD, propulsion, electronic…what do you think?"

"Great!" Claire leaned in as well. "Yes. This section narrows down the area where they store the fuses we need. Now we just have to pray they stocked up properly. I have it from here, Captain." Pulling out her trackpad again, Claire backed up.

"I'd rather see it through and help you look." Holly smiled. "I need to work off some of my pent-up annoyance with those agents before I return to the bridge."

Claire snorted. "I heard they were charming and that we got to keep some of them."

"Don't get me started." Holly glanced at Claire's trackpad over her shoulder. "Looks like we need to start aft." They weaved in and out among people placing things into storage or browsing for items just like they were.

As they reached the far-aft section, they found themselves alone. Claire called out to the computer to increase the light. Looking up, she gasped at the sheer volume of crates of all sizes. "Damn," she murmured.

"There's no way we can even reach the top shelves. This part has to be thirty feet straight up." Holly sighed and rubbed the back of her neck.

"Wait." Claire closed her eyes as information flooded her mind. She was just about to let Holly know what her NIEC had shared when she became dizzy and staggered into the nearest shelf.

"Claire?" Holly gripped her arm, steadying her. "Are you all right?"

No, she wasn't. A fizzing sound vibrated inside her, and an instant headache made her fumble for support. She felt Holly lower her until she sat on the floor with her back against the shelf behind her.

Holly placed a cool hand on her forehead. "What's happening?"

"I—I don't…" Before she could say she didn't know, the buzzing sensation stopped, and the dizzy spell ended as fast as it had begun. "Whoa. I'm okay, Captain. Seems I just got dizzy for a moment. My NIEC showed me how to do this."

"Huh. Not to hover, but have you eaten today? Or taken a break at all?" Holly rose from where she'd crouched next to Claire and extended her hand, pulling her up.

"The alien porridge. Sure. Twice. I've heard that Brandon and his team will expand the menu later, which I look forward to." Smiling broadly to reassure Holly that she was fine, Claire walked over to a small computer console. "Let's pray this works, or one of us will have to climb, and that'd take ages." She had only to touch the console to make it come to life. Sliding her fingers along turquoise lines and yellow dots, she maneuvered the text on the screen until she found the category Holly had located on the larger computer by the ladder. "We have four possibilities, but I hope we can use this method to determine which fuses we should retrieve. According to this computer, we have two hundred and fifty of each."

"Sounds reassuring," Holly said. "Let's hope it's correct."

Claire tapped the lines of text and then the yellow dots. Above them, a distinct whirring sound echoed down the shelves. Stepping back, Claire gazed up as an arm that resembled gigantic tweezers gripped boxes and seemed to play a game of Jenga with itself as it pulled, pushed, shoved, and slid. Within half a minute, it placed four small crates on a shelf that began to descend toward them.

"I'll be damned. My NIEC clearly doesn't think I need to know this," Holly said. "Perhaps the former captain was less hands-on than I intend to be."

"I think our NIECs will pick up on what we insist on doing that might not be commonplace and teach us regardless." Claire watched the crates that came toward them. As they stopped three feet off the deck, she pushed the lids of the first one open without hesitation. "No. Not these. Too short." She pulled the burned one from her pocket, along with a measuring tape. "It's the same diameter, but it needs to be exactly...eight and a quarter inches long."

Holly blinked. "Really? You brought a metal tape measure from home?"

Claire grinned. "Until the NIEC has showed me every nut and bolt of this bucket, I plan to add tools I'm used to when I need to work fast." She stopped herself, realizing how irreverent she must sound, something that had gotten her into trouble in the past.

"You're calling this marvel of a vessel a bucket?" Holly opened another of the crates. "As long as you're on top of how this bucket performs, I don't mind. May I borrow the tape measure?" She extended her hand, palm up.

Claire gaped for a good two seconds before closing her mouth and handing it over. "Sure."

"Let's see. Ah, damn. Close, but no cigar." Holly handed the tool back. "Let's measure this one." She scanned the fuse. "It's more like the metric system as far as I can see. I think it'll take some getting used to, but we'll get there."

"The way the NIEC crams knowledge into our brains, it'll probably be sooner than we think." Claire opened another crate and pulled out a fuse. When it measured exactly the right length and diameter, she examined it for markings and found microscopic ones that were readable only with the trackpad. No wonder they hadn't located them before. "Fuse-canister. Initiation Propulsion ISD."

"What's wrong?" Holly stepped closer. "Claire?"

The twitching pain dissipated, and Claire waved her hand dismissively. "Nothing. Just a burst of info." Her NIEC kicked in again without warning, and she jerked. "Ow." She raised her hand to her temple. New information existed where it hadn't a second ago.

"We have to switch all of them at the same time. We can't just change the burned-out ones." She stepped over to the computer console and used her trackpad to look up the specific spare part. "Good news. We actually have 1,500 of these in storage, now that I know what to look for and how." She used the console and ordered down the number of fuses they needed and sent the other crates back.

"Let me get one of the carts." Holly reached for a smaller cart, meant to haul items in the cargo bay and the corridors. Magnetic cushions underneath made it hover, and they had yet to stack one full of enough gear to make it touch the deck. They loaded the crates as they arrived on the transport system.

"Good." Claire sighed in relief. "We should be able to leave on time, Captain."

"I never doubted it," Holly said and began walking next to Claire. "I'll be on the bridge."

Claire began pushing the hovering cart toward one of the elevators. "As soon as we're ready, you'll know, Captain. It should take us an hour."

They rode the elevator to deck nine, where Claire stepped off with the cart. "Captain," she said, nodding politely as several of the new arrivals waited outside in the corridor, some looking as if they were lost.

"Chief." Holly returned the courtesy.

Lengthening her stride, Claire hurried back to the main entrance to engineering. Her subordinates dove on the crates holding the fuses like starving vultures, and Claire had to smile. They should be ready well within an hour.

Holly meant to let the elevator door shut and return to the bridge on deck three, but several of the new crewmen crowded the door, preventing it from closing.

"Ma'am," a woman in her fifties said. "I'm not sure where I'm supposed to go. They told me I was to take an elevator to deck seven, but so many stepped off here, and…I can't find the quarters I've been assigned." She was short and had curly, dark-brown hair, and seemed familiar. Holly didn't have Samantha's eye for who people were, but of course it was easier for the former head librarian than for her, who had worked from home ever since she returned to Dennamore nine years ago.

"First of all, just call me captain," Holly said, cringing at being called ma'am in this setting. "What's your name…ma'am?" How ironic that she herself had to use the term she loathed.

"Marjory Hopkins." A young crewman with a large bag nudged the woman from behind. She stumbled forward, and Holly steadied her. Realizing that this group of individuals had fallen through the cracks when it came to guiding them to their quarters or duty stations, she took command.

"Attention!" Holly didn't raise her voice more than necessary, but it was as if she'd cracked a whip. Everyone froze in place, and Marjory gaped. "Who among you are looking for your quarters?"

Six hands went up.

"And who among you are trying to find your duty station?" Holly scanned the group. Another six hands went up. That left four people doing neither.

"All right, the four of you, what exactly are you up to?" Holly lowered her voice half an octave, a method useful in a classroom on a Monday morning when everyone was tired and not very motivated to pay attention. It apparently worked aboard the *Velocity* as well. The four without obvious reason to be in the corridor outside engineering looked sheepishly at Holly.

"We were curious about the, um, engine?" a young girl in her late teens or early twenties said.

"You mean the propulsion system." Holly stepped to the side. "The ones among you who are on their way to their quarters, step inside. The ones among you who know you're due in engineering, the door is down the corridor to the right. The rest of you, enter your name and rank into a console and get new directions. If you're not fitted with a NIEC, turn to the closest person who is and ask them to help you. That's what they signed up to do when they accepted the device." Holly stood quietly while people sorted themselves into the elevator or began walking toward engineering. Turning to the four curious ones, she raised a deliberate eyebrow. "I suggest you familiarize yourself with more pressing matters than sightseeing in engineering. Go to your quarters or the mess hall. Soon enough we will be breaking orbit, and when we do, you want to be close to your designated area. Understood?"

The girl nodded frantically. "Yes, ma'…Captain. Absolutely." She tugged at the young man next to her, and the glare she gave him suggested to Holly that their excursion perhaps was his idea. "We'll take the next elevator, Captain."

"Good." Pressing the elevator console's blue dot, Holly turned to the six inside the elevator, who all looked like they were civilians. "Blue stands for deck six. Orange for deck seven. The identity tags you were issued…wear them at all times, or carry them in your pocket. They will show you where you're allowed to go. They will also open the door to your quarters automatically when you press the sensor next to it. If you have any questions or struggle with adjusting, Chief Counselor Camilla Tennen will fit you into her schedule." She paused, looking at Marjory. "I'm guessing that you're related to Carl Hopkins, my ensign at ops."

"Yes, Captain. I'm his aunt." Marjory looked proud despite her nervousness. "I'm very proud of him."

"So, you should be." Holly gazed at the other men and women. "As should you. I'll be seeing much more of you and the other civilians aboard the ship once we're safely on the right trajectory to Dwynna Major."

The elevator door opened, and everyone but Marjory stepped out at deck six. When the door closed again, she turned to Holly, her round face serious. "I was not certain I should come on this journey," she said in a low, intense tone. "I thought his parents, or even an older sibling, should be the ones taking an interest, finally, in the boy. I should've known better. When my sister and brother proved they had nothing but disdain for his knowledge, but instead berated him for keeping secrets from them, I knew. I'm sure he hasn't told you, Captain, how his brilliance and sweet nature set him apart from the rest of his family members. So…when they couldn't see themselves supporting the boy, I was sure this was my destiny. Please put me to work eventually, Captain. I'm a great cook, an avid organizer, and a good singer."

Holly regarded Marjory for a few beats, seeing nothing but pure determination and love for Carl, the youngest among the group of people who had worked relentlessly to uncover the mystery of Dennamore's past. "Marjory, Carl is lucky to have you in his life and on board the *Velocity*. And don't worry. You will be asked to work. We regard the next of kin as a great asset, not just emotionally for the crew, which is obvious, but as a resource to tap into."

"Excellent. Oh, this is me, then." Marjory hoisted her two bags. "Deck seven. Thank you for taking the time to guide us, Captain. And for listening." She smiled quickly and then hurried down the corridor as the elevator door closed behind her. As it made its way to deck three, Holly realized that though Camilla was the chief counselor, at times the crew and civilians would have to hear from their captain. A new role for her, but something she recognized as vital to the mission. Yes, keeping on top of the alien technology was important, but it was equally important to keep the people on board stimulated, cared for, and reassured that the one ultimately in charge did her best for them.

Clearly, being the captain entailed so much more than she knew when she first put on the captain's NIEC. Much larger than the regular NIECs, it enveloped her head like a crown. As she stepped off the elevator, she was reminded of a quote from Shakespeare's play *King Henry IV, Part Two*: "Uneasy lies the head that wears a crown." The line didn't express megalomania. She knew herself well enough to recognize how grounded she always was. Yet she was venturing into unknown territories, in outer space, where she was ultimately responsible for the many souls aboard the ship.

"Captain on the bridge," Carl said as Holly stepped onto the bridge and took the captain's chair.

Uneasy, indeed.

Chapter Four

Darian took her seat on the bridge, to the left behind the captain's chair, but considering her heightened adrenaline rush, she'd rather be standing up. She wanted to rock back and forth on her soles and be ready to act at a moment's notice. No doubt the cop in her still drowned out her new duties as chief of security and tactical.

"We've heard from engineering, Captain," Carl said from his station. "We're clear to break orbit when you give the order."

"Thank you, Ensign." Holly's calm voice did little to settle Darian's nervous energy. Her skittishness didn't come from fear, but her body was definitely in fight mode. "Connect me to the ship-wide speaker system."

Carl gave her a thumbs-up. "You're connected, Captain."

Holly was quiet for a few moments, but then she spoke in her clear alto voice. "All hands, all civilians, this is your captain. I have received the go-ahead for us to leave Earth's orbit and commence our journey to the homeworld of our ancestors, Dwynna Major. Earlier, I spoke with both the secretary-general of the United Nations and the president of the United States, as we're all US citizens. Secretary-general Lilavati Banerjee wished us the best of luck on our journey and a safe return back to Earth." Holly sent a bemused look toward Walker on her right, and then back at Darian, but didn't expand on how the US president had still tried to get Holly to surrender the *Velocity* to "more apt individuals."

"As for the crew, secure your duty stations and yourselves. You civilians should secure yourself and your family members in your quarters or in whatever common area you happen to be. Nobody, and I want to make that clear, *nobody* can be unrestrained when we go through this solar system and jump to interstellar drive. Once the bridge gives you the all-clear to move about, I urge those of you who might display side effects of the jump to visit the infirmary."

Holly met the eyes of her bridge crew, and for the first time since Darian took her seat at her station, she felt herself settle down. "You will hear the countdown to our breaking orbit over the speakers in approximately five minutes. Crowe out."

Darian adjusted her harness and focused on the information shown on the nine screens of her computer console. From her point of view, they were set to go. Below the captain, on a lower level and facing the largest viewscreen, Samantha oversaw the helm, with one subordinate on either side. Her fingers danced over the controls, and it was hard to believe how much she had doubted her own ability to pilot the speeders, let alone the mothership.

"Two minutes to go, Captain," Carl said. "All departments are signing in that their crew and passengers are secure."

"Good." Holly tapped the side of her massive NIEC. The thing had to weigh a ton, but Darian had never heard her complain. "Begin the prelaunch sequence, Samantha."

"Aye, Captain." Samantha was clearly prepared, as she only pushed one orange, glowing dot on her console. The hum around them seemed to change in tonality. A muted vibration traveled along the ship's struts and the hull, and into the deck under their feet. "Systems working."

Carl gripped the edge of his console. "One minute."

"Tactical?" Holly glanced back at Darian. "No space debris or any shuttles launched at the last minute from Earth to get in our way?"

"Nothing on sensors that poses a risk to us...or anyone else, Captain." Darian nodded as she browsed through the different screen settings. "We are so far up in the exosphere, no working satellites can reach this far. I see minor dust, but all my indicators remain blue, which is a good thing." Orange or green ones could have alerted them to a problem.

"Thirty seconds." Carl's voice was tighter now, but his face showed pure concentration.

"When we're at fifteen seconds, start the countdown," Holly said.

Glancing around the room before she refocused on her console, Darian saw the same tense concentration on the faces of the rest of the bridge crew. Fourteen people could work there at one time, but only at critical moments like this did they need a full bridge crew.

Behind Walker, Camilla—Darian's grandmother—whom she lovingly referred to as Gran, sat with her hands calmly laced on her lap. She didn't even blink as the countdown began. It was unfathomable that her formerly frail Gran now looked so strong, so healthy, after receiving alien medication and having undergone alien surgery, performed by their ship's doctor. Now working as their chief counselor and responsible for the crew's mental wellbeing, she looked entirely in her element.

"Five—four—three—two—one." The computerized voice droned on. It wasn't speaking English, but it felt like English to Darian, which was another odd sensation as their NIECs provided the translation. Even the passengers and crewmembers who weren't outfitted with a NIEC understood, as they'd all received small translators, even the very young children.

"Breaking orbit," Samantha said. She used both hands, running her fingers up and down small indentations. The pressure as well as the speed mattered when you piloted the ships. Now Darian watched on the external sensors how Samantha eased the large spaceship from the high orbit they'd inhabited the last few days. The course had been pre-plotted, checked, and double-checked, and once Samantha steered the ship away from orbit, she would set the propulsion and navigational system on the aliens' version of autopilot.

The ship moaned as it broke free from the last remnants of Earth's gravity. The way it changed from humming and stomping to almost silent mode made Darian's heart jump. Was something wrong? Had the propulsion stopped working? Were they drifting? She reeled herself in, forcing herself to pay attention to the information on her screens.

After another couple of minutes, someone in the far back of the bridge gasped and then whispered, "Oh, look."

Darian stared up at the main screen that was surrounded by eight smaller ones. On one of them, she saw Earth...and it was visibly shrinking. They were nowhere near interstellar-drive speed, but they were moving very fast, compared to ships containing Earth technology. The moon was already visible and also shrinking exponentially on the same screen.

"Speed is now 2 percent of ISD." Samantha spoke tightly.

"And if that's this fast…" Holly murmured and shook her head. "Breaking orbit was a little bumpy, but that is why we need everyone strapped down. We just don't know how it's going to feel."

Or what jumping to ISD would do to them. After all, they were all mostly human, some of them *all* human. Darian was searching for anything that might pose a tactical problem when her security alarm went off. "Darian here. Report!" she barked into her speaker, noticing how Holly, Walker, and Gran whipped their heads her way.

"Chief, it's one of the agents, the one from the CIA, Neville Brewer. He unhooked his harness in the common area on deck two and is on his way to the bridge." The woman speaking sounded out of breath. "I'm in pursuit."

"Use caution, Ensign. I'm leaving the bridge and heading toward you." Darian unbuckled her own harness as she spoke. "Tennen out." Darian pushed at her console and stood.

"What are you doing?" Walker asked, frowning.

"We have a loose cannon. CIA Agent Brewer is on his way here."

"You need to be strapped in, Chief," Walker said.

"I need to keep that fool off the bridge." She turned to the woman behind her station. "You have my tactical station." Speaking through clenched teeth, Darian then hurried across the bridge and out into the corridor, which was still empty. She engaged her speaker again. "Tennen here. I need Brewer's location."

"He ran toward the elevators." Her subordinate had answered immediately. "Or the ladder, rather, as the elevators are not operational before a jump."

"True." Darian stopped at the bulkhead that separated the corridor outside the bridge with its surrounding offices and workstations from the senior crews' living quarters. A large screen showed the layout of the ship, and she ran her trackpad along the side of it to identify herself. In seconds, she saw a complete, layered blueprint of the eleven decks. She couldn't be certain that Brewer was actually heading to the bridge, but he could do potential harm in plenty of other areas.

Sliding her left index finger along a blue line ending in a yellow dot, Darian could now detect all the speakers, trackpads, and TAGs. As everyone should be strapped into harnesses at this point, she should be able to see only three moving targets: herself, the ensign in pursuit—and Brewer. She scanned the deck above that held the common areas and saw a moving dot halt about ten yards to her left, near an elevator and a ladder. She heard, before she saw, the swooshing sound when someone slid down the pole.

A woman she recognized as Ensign Sarah Lawson came into view as she touched down with a thud. "Ensign."

Sarah pivoted, her hand on her sidearm. Seeing Darian, she nodded briskly. "Chief. Did he come through here?"

"Not that I saw." Darian turned back to the screen. "There. He's right next to the ladder...on deck nine." She cursed under her breath. "Shit. Engineering. The main weapon lockers." She began to run toward the ladder. Lockers were located on all decks of the ship, but on deck nine an entire corridor was lined with them. "Tennen to bridge. Brewer is on deck nine. Alert the crew. Ensign Lawson and I are in pursuit."

"Understood," Holly said. "What harm can he cause? He had no access to any vital systems."

"I hope that's enough. I'll report when I know more." Darian wrapped her arm around the pole and barely squeezed it, which meant she more or less fell the six decks before she managed to stop herself from fracturing her ankles. She barely got out of the way before Sarah landed next to her. "Use your trackpad and look for anything moving that shouldn't be. I'll go aft toward the weapon lockers. You make sure he hasn't gained entry to engineering."

The ship-wide speakers came to life with a high-pitched tone. "This is the captain. We should hit 20-percent ISD speed in five seconds." The computerized countdown started again.

"Hold on." Darian nudged Sarah toward the wall, equipped with a railing. They both clung to it as the deck shook under their feet. After a few moments, it stopped, and Darian took off toward the aft section of deck nine. The corridor wound its way between bulkheads, and her

NIEC informed her that there were no long, straight corridors aboard *Velocity*. This way, no crewmembers could fall the entire length of the ship—perhaps to their death—if the inertia controllers malfunctioned. Unfortunately, someone like Brewer could easily hide.

She knew she was on the right path when she heard a muted clunking noise farther down. Darian pulled her sidearm and eased forward. The corridors had two more bends before she reached the massive weapon lockers. She had gone through them all, and her NIEC had provided what information she might have missed.

Tall, matte-black, and deep, the lockers held everything from sidearms to rifles and some harpoon-like weapons meant for an array of arrows. They also contained more of the glass-encased grenades they'd found in the archives beneath Town Hall. Brewer couldn't get his hands on any of these items.

Darian stopped at the last bend in the corridor. Peering around the corner, she saw him kicking the ladder next to one of the lockers over and over. She murmured into her speaker. "I have him in my sights, Ensign. Join me by the lockers."

A mere click came through her speaker, which meant Sarah had understood.

Not sure of Brewer's reasoning, Darian stepped into the corridor, not having spotted any weapons in either of his hands. "Stop right there, Brewer." She spoke firmly but didn't raise her voice.

Brewer swiveled and glowered at her. "How the hell did you find me this fast? You put a tracker on me?"

"We're all tracked, one way or another. I'm sure you understand that's for everyone's safety." Darian held her weapon trained down and with her finger away from the trigger. "What are you doing?"

"You stripped me of my gun, and I haven't been able to get through to any of your security people, which is hardly surprising, as they're all amateurs." Brewer had stopped kicking.

"Do you think going against the rules and regulations is a clever way to win us over?" Was the man suffering from some strange sort of space sickness? For the love of—that was a quick reaction if he was.

"Rules and regulations? Stipulated by whom?" Brewer sneered, clearly unimpressed.

"I can answer that question in several ways, but for now, let's just say that I expect you to abide by the same chain of command you've done all the years you've been an agent. I'm a former detective, and we served under the same code of conduct."

If Darian had thought referencing their similar backgrounds would help, she'd been wrong. Brewer gave the locker another futile kick. "I came along to get you to see that you're all like children playing with a new toy you know nothing about. It's just that this particular toy has dangerous weapons—potentially of mass destruction."

"We're explorers," Darian said, even if she didn't think this response would have any impact on Brewer's reasoning. She was correct.

"So you say. You pluck the greatest find in human history from the ground and decide that it's your own personal joyride. It's insane!" Starting to kick again, Brewer growled in frustration when the door to the locker didn't so much as dent.

"Perhaps you have heard the quote, often attributed to Einstein, 'The definition of "insanity" is doing the same thing over and over again and expecting different results.' That would suggest that you're the one not of sound mind, as you've tried kicking down a door made of extremely durable alien metal alloy for several minutes now. Stand down. It's not going to budge. You might actually sprain something."

Rapid footfalls came closer behind Darian. Sarah rounded the corner with her weapon drawn, breathing faster, but not out of breath. "Chief?"

"No harm done, except perhaps to Agent Brewer's leg—or pride. Restrain him. We're taking him down to the brig on deck ten until the captain can advise how to proceed. We'll all strap in there, as I have a feeling our next jump might kick us on our asses."

While Sarah put wrist and ankle restraints on Brewer, who seemed to have opted for sullen silence, Darian paged the bridge and gave her report.

"Good job, Chief," Holly said. "Now be safe. Ten minutes to the 100-percent ISD jump."

"We'll be in our harnesses by then. See you once we're stable, Captain."

"Affirmative."

Darian didn't gain any satisfaction out of perp-walking the recently so belligerent Brewer as she and Sarah escorted him one deck down, which was no small feat as he had to climb the ladder still wearing his restraints. In LA, she had often felt a sense of accomplishment when she was able to march a suspect to interrogation or a cell. That was her old self. But no matter his motives, Brewer wasn't a criminal. He was misguided, certainly, and he had managed to alienate them and break tons of rules, but they couldn't very well turn back and drop him off, which meant Holly and the rest of the senior crew, including herself, would have to come up with something they all could get behind—including Brewer.

CHAPTER FIVE

Holly entered her quarters and barely dared to look at the bed. If she did, she might fall onto it and not wake up for days. She hadn't slept more than an hour here and there during the last four days, and now that they'd jumped to full ISD and the ship was slicing through space like a hot-edged razor, she had handed the bridge over to Walker. He had gotten some decent rest and seemed surprisingly refreshed, considering he was pushing seventy.

Holly engaged her speaker. "Crowe to engineering. I need a final report before I'm off duty." Ha. She was the captain and never off duty.

"Like I told Commander Walker just now, all systems are working fine, Captain. I'm going to follow your example and leave engineering to my subordinate." The faint slur in Claire's consonants spoke of how equally tired she was.

"I'm having something to eat before I get some sleep. Want to share some food in my quarters, Chief?" Holly surprised herself by asking. She was probably just afraid she might face-plant into her meal if she didn't have anyone to talk to. "I believe your quarters are directly across from mine." All the senior-staff quarters were located on deck four.

"Sounds great. Let me clean up my act. I'm stepping onto the elevator as we speak. I heard from Samantha that Brandon and his team broke the code for the food dispensers."

"He did. And, I dare say, they spruced it up quite a bit from the alien porridge we've had so far." Holly pulled off her clothes and entered the ensuite bathroom. She had used it only very briefly before and was dying for a hot shower. "Just pop over when you're ready. I'll ask one of the crewmen in the galley to bring us something." She fully intended to eat in the mess hall once they got used to their routines, but for tonight, she wanted to get ready for sleep as soon as possible.

The shower looked more like a narrow metal tube than anything else. After stepping inside, she flinched when it closed around her, leaving about two inches on either side of her and no room to maneuver. "What the hell?" Glancing back and forth, trying to find a way to slide the door open, she jumped as a circular spray began to travel from her head down. It moved slowly, and the scent was pleasant, thankfully not overly perfumed. Her skin tingled as the tiny sprays wet her. When they reached her shoulders, they changed pattern, creating the number eight as they managed to reach every crevice of her body.

"Like a damn carwash," Holly muttered. She was in the shower for approximately five minutes, which had to be the quickest shower she'd ever taken, before the ring of spray nozzles did a final once-over and then stopped. Still the door wasn't opening. Perhaps it was a good thing that Claire was popping in if this thing malfunctioned, or Holly would have a damn uncomfortable sleep.

A faint tremor created a soft tone, and something sucked every drop of water from her skin and hair. The process took less than ten seconds, and she gasped at the unfamiliar sensation of getting goose bumps as each minute hair follicle was engaged. When the door opened, she hurried out, still not trusting the strange shower stall… tube…thing.

Apparently, their ancestors still wanted to examine their reflection when getting ready, as a full-length mirror sat next to the bathroom door. Pulling on familiar clothes made her feel more normal—light-blue sweats and some white tube socks, over cotton underwear. The ship provided all the uniforms and gear they required, and even some generic clothing, but that was it.

A quick knock on the door, followed by a chime, announced Claire's presence. Damn, the food! Holly cursed her foggy mind and pressed the sensor next to the door. To her surprise, Claire was holding two boxes as she stepped inside.

"I come bearing gifts…or food. Ran into Camilla and Brandon, and they had food boxes to spare." Claire smiled. "And boy, was that shower thing brilliant. Clean and ready to go in minutes. Good thing we have the gym room where we can swim, or I'd miss not getting a good soak every now and then." She set down the boxes on the dining table to the left and tossed her long, tight braid over her shoulder. Her dark-brown eyes narrowed. "Captain? You all right?"

Holly closed the door behind Claire and forced herself to focus. "Good. About the food, I mean. And please, when it's just us and we're not in an official setting, keep calling me Holly." She motioned for Claire to sit. "I see you've taken the opportunity to wear something more familiar as well." Claire was dressed in a red turtleneck, black jeans, and sneakers.

"It helps with the strange feeling I've battled for the last few hours." Claire smiled quickly. "Don't misunderstand me. I don't regret one thing, but I did have a quick audio conversation with my father on the hybrid communicator I placed in one of the smaller common rooms for the crew to use while we're still in range. He's proud of me, but he's worried, and since he and I have never bullshitted each other, I couldn't do like some of the others, you know, downplay everything." Claire opened the lid of her box, and the enticing scent promised that they wouldn't be having porridge again. Holly did the same.

"You're an only child?"

"Yeah. I am. I know he and Mom hoped for more, especially since they wanted someone to take over the garage, but that didn't happen." A shadow ghosted across Claire's face. "I had many reasons to stay in Dennamore, and that was one of them."

"I see." Finding a forklike utensil in the box, Holly picked it up and began to eat. No matter what the dish had originally been, Brandon's talents had increased the taste a lot, Holly guessed.

"What about you?" Claire tilted her head as she pushed something resembling a meatball into her mouth and chewed. "Mm. Not bad."

"What do you mean? Oh, relatives?" Holly shook her head. "As you may remember, I was adopted. It still boggles my mind that I had accepted not being of Dennamore alien descent only a few days ago. Going from that to being the captain, and realizing that somehow one or both of my parents were from Dennamore, or at least related to one that was…well, you can imagine." Holly was momentarily stunned at how easy it was to confide in Claire. Here, in her quarters, dressed normally, it was as if she'd been transported back to the weeks leading up to finding the *Velocity*. This behavior might not be very captain-like. On this mission, she would have to act larger than life and be somewhat unattainable. Forming an inappropriately close bond with a subordinate wouldn't help her achieve that demeanor. And yet… Claire regarded her with understanding.

It didn't escape Holly how beautiful Claire was. Back on Earth, at moments—fleeting, but clear moments—she had briefly acknowledged that she found Claire attractive. Having stayed away from much personal socializing after she lost Frances, her wife, and then her mom a year after Holly returned to Dennamore, she rarely even noticed someone. Nine years alone was a long time, but in all good faith, it hadn't seemed like a decade had passed.

"Holly?" Claire put down her fork.

"What?" Blinking, she wondered how much time had passed. "Oh. Well, fate must have stepped in somehow." She finished her meal quickly. "Thank you for keeping me company. I was afraid I might fall asleep while eating.'"

"Same." Claire rested her elbow on the table and propped her chin in her hand. "Isn't it odd that now that we're going full steam ahead, so to speak, it doesn't feel like we're moving at all? I mean, aside from the faint hum of the propulsion system and sensors, we could be sitting ducks and not know it."

Grateful to Claire for steering the conversation onto less personal subjects, Holly nodded. "Yes, I know. The ship's in remarkable condition after having been stationary for centuries. Tomorrow I'm going to put together a team that will inspect her from stern to aft, starboard to port, and locate every single function and piece of technology we haven't discovered yet. We have to be sure we have every advantage. I have a feeling we'll need it." Holly covered her mouth with a hand and tried to stifle a yawn.

"And…that's my cue." Claire grinned and stood, taking her box, mug, and utensils to the counter by the door. "Checked this out yet? One of my favorite features for sure." She pushed the box into a slot in the bulkhead, then the utensils and mug. "And there it goes."

Holly stood, surprised when the items disappeared with a soft hiss. "Where did they go?"

"Brandon told Darian, who told me, that everything showed up in the galley, clean and ready to be used again. Any leftovers are composted, according to Patsy."

"Who's Patsy?" Holly wracked her brain, but no face appeared in her fatigued mind.

"Our florist-turned-botanist. She's slept about as little as the senior crew has, more or less taking up residence in the far end of the second cargo bay, where she found traces of an aquaponic bay."

"That's definitely on the list of what we're going to look at tomorrow." Holly walked Claire to the door. "Get a good sleep now."

"You too. Something tells me we need to be rested." Claire ducked out and gave Holly a little wave with her fingertips before she entered her own quarters.

Returning to the table, Holly repeated Claire's maneuver with the food box, and it obediently disappeared into the wall and swooshed away. With barely enough energy to brush her teeth, Holly forced herself to do it and then removed the captain's NIEC, since she couldn't possibly sleep wearing that damn crown-helmet hybrid. Periodically something of an insomniac, she had no idea the next morning if she had managed to hit the mattress before she was out cold.

CHAPTER SIX

Darian let her gaze take in the circle of people that had met in the conference room. Divided into three teams of four people each, they'd been chosen to explore the ship in more detail. It would take a lot longer than one day to cover the expanse of the large vessel, but it was important that they start ASAP. Next to her stood Gran, Holly, and Carl. Philber—the social-anthropological scientist who had been part of unlocking the mysteries of Dennamore's past—headed one of the teams and stood next to Nate, a former cop like herself and now one of her senior security guards. From the first moment, he had insisted on joining the crew. One of the women from NASA, Mireille Wu, had also been selected to join them for this assignment.

"All right," Holly said, placing her hands on her hips. "A senior officer will lead each team." She waved over Mireille Wu and two young women from Dennamore. "You're with me. Darian, you'll head a team with Camilla, Lieutenant Sommer, and Crewman Rhodes over there."

Darian recognized Lieutenant Sommer as Nate, a former cop from Dennamore who had been among the very first to heed the yearning to join the crew. Crewman Rhodes was an unfamiliar middle-aged man who apparently had worked as an accountant until now. Darian had to hide a smile at the man's eager steps as he crossed the circle of people and stood to her right.

"Carl, you'll be responsible for Ensign Brett and for Crewmen Johnson and Santorini." Three young people, though all of them older than the nineteen-year-old Carl, joined him, looking as excited as Rhodes did.

"You have grids to cover, and you'll find them in your respective trackpads. You will scan and document everything you discover that is not already available in our database. Our ancestors of course knew of every feature of the *Velocity*," Holly said, "but our NIECs can clearly infuse only a limited amount of information and knowledge during this short time span. We have to find out ourselves, like this." Walking inside the circle, meeting everyone's gaze firmly, Holly lowered her voice. "I don't have to tell you that everything you find is confidential unless I, or any of the senior staff, tell you differently."

The team members nodded, the seriousness of the situation obviously not lost on them. Darian wondered how the new crewmembers could function. They had to be overwhelmed.

"Let's go, people. We report back to this room at 1200 hours." Holly waved the three women she would work with to join her and left the room.

Darian turned to her grandmother, who already had her trackpad out. "Where do we start, Gr—Counselor?"

Gran tapped the trackpad with the perfect-oval nail of her index finger. "Deck five. Infirmary and science labs, beginning aft, which is the labs."

Darian nodded and turned to the other two. "I know you had a brief orientation when you were outfitted with the NIECs, which makes this search easier, since you have prior knowledge. Let's grab an elevator and head down." She began walking to the closest elevator. Holly and her team were already stepping into it, and as it could easily hold ten people, Darian motioned for hers to do the same. Next to their elevator, Carl's team slid down one of the ladders, one by one.

"We're on our way to deck eight," Holly said, turning to Darian and Gran. "The hydroponics bay is a bit of a mystery to me, which means I hope to learn a lot. We have new crewmembers already working hard there."

"We're on our way to the science labs." Gran held up her trackpad. "I imagine we'll run into a lot of new crewmembers down there too, and I fully expect to do double duty." As the ship's counselor, Gran was in charge and responsible for the crew's mental health and general coping ability.

"Understood. I've told you before, Camilla, that if you need more people on your staff, I will make that happen." Darian understood the serious note in Holly's voice. She too worried for the psychological impact the journey and circumstances would have on the crew, especially the ones whose yearning to be part of this mission had struck them immediately, with little time to reflect.

"And I'll keep you posted, Captain," Gran said firmly. It was hard to fathom that the grandmother Darian stood next to on the elevator only recently had been suffering from severe rheumatoid arthritis and a heart condition. After Raoul had treated her using alien technology and remedies, she walked unhindered and moved like someone much younger than seventy-four. Once she was outfitted with a NIEC, a harrowing experience for Darian, as she was terrified of losing the woman who raised her after her parents died, Camilla had appeared stronger than ever. Always confident and an accomplished screenwriter, she had appeared larger than life to Darian, but now, she seemed even more so.

"This is us," Darian said as the elevator halted on deck five. "Look forward to our respective briefings later, Captain." She smiled at the others in Holly's team before exiting. Turning to her own team members, she motioned for them to follow her. "First, we'll make sure the respective labs are where they're indicated on our trackpads. I know our ancestors appear to have been meticulous, but we should never assume anything. I don't want anyone to end up in the wrong place during a potential emergency. Rhodes, you're with me." She glanced over at the other two. "Sommer, you're with Counselor Tennen." Obviously, Nate Sommer knew who Gran was to Darian, because he squared his shoulders as if to say he would guard her with his life. Gran's faint smirk showed that she had noticed.

Rhodes, a tall, lanky young man in his early twenties, was studying his trackpad closely. "At the far aft, we should find the chemistry and biology lab, Chief," he said. "Right now, we have three people assigned there per shift."

"All right. Then this is where we'll start." Darian lengthened her stride to keep up with him. Knowing that it was also part of her duty to get to know the crew, she took the opportunity to get personal. "Speaking of people, who do you have with you on board, Rhodes?"

He snapped his gaze up, looking surprised. "Um. My mom and my sister. My dad's back in Dennamore with my nanna. She's old."

He looked uncomfortable. "He wasn't happy." Rolling his shoulders, he returned his focus to the trackpad. "Looks like the other Chief Tennen and the lieutenant will take the starboard labs. That means we'll be looking in on the physics lab and the…" He frowned and tilted his head, as if that would help him decipher the information on his device.

Darian glanced down at her trackpad. "Creative lab." She smiled at Rhodes. "If it's any consolation, I have only a vague idea what it might entail, so clearly it has little to do with security."

Rhodes's shoulders returned to a more relaxed position. "I'm normally assigned to the cargo bay, so I have no clue at all."

"All the more fun to explore. And besides, the people working in there will be able to fill us in." Passing several doors, they reached the one at the end of the winding corridor and entered.

The large space was brightly lit, and Darian immediately noticed the floor-to-ceiling cabinet with what looked like glass doors. The deck was clad in a stark-white material that resembled high-gloss resin. A woman in a white uniform stepped into a circle outlined with black on the deck, which turned out to be a round plate that promptly elevated her halfway to the eighteen-foot-high ceiling.

"Cool." Rhodes breathed the word, then caught himself. "Sorry, Chief."

"You took the word out of my mouth. It is cool." Darian walked up to a man sitting at a desk at the far wall. "Lieutenant Boyd?"

The man glanced up and immediately stood at attention. "Chief Tennen. Didn't notice you come in. I heard there'd be an inspection today. It's really not fair, as we have only scratched the surface—"

"Let me stop you right there, Boyd." Darian held up her free hand. "This isn't that type of inspection. We're not here to put you on the spot, nor do we expect you to know everything after only a few days aboard. We want to get an overview and find out if we've missed something vital this early in our journey. The captain may have said that she wants us to go over the ship with a fine-tooth comb, but realistically, we will keep learning about the *Velocity* as we go."

Boyd didn't look as if he entirely believed her but motioned toward the multitude of cabinets. "In here, we have enough extraterrestrial samples to keep us busy for years, perhaps even decades. As I browsed the catalogue, I realized only a few moments ago that it must have taken our ancestors even longer to collect them."

"You mean the ones who settled in Dennamore had been traveling for years—decades?" Shocked, Darian forced herself to sound composed. This was not good news.

"No, not necessarily. Nothing says they started from nothing with the samples. They, however, found it necessary to bring all these, and we're hoping to find out why." Boyd turned to a woman who was using a piece of technology that looked like a long metal tube that ended in a square glass box. It was not glass, she guessed, but a durable, transparent material. "Vanya? Can you brief us about what you found last night?"

"I posted a report on the server," Vanya said, sounding absent-minded and not even raising her head.

"I think the lieutenant means you need to brief me." Darian didn't raise her voice, but any of her former colleagues in LA knew what her stern tone meant.

Vanya glanced up and nearly fell backward as she moved too fast on her narrow stool. "Sir! Chief. I didn't..."

"Hear us come in." Darian grinned. "At least you're all very dedicated and diligent about your work. And 'chief' is fine." If the crew was flailing about the command structure and their new positions, so was Darian. Sure, she had her police training to fall back on, but that was more useful during an emergency or at a crime scene.

Vanya grabbed her computer and hurried over to Boyd's desk, where she set it up and angled the screen toward them. "This is what I found."

Darian and Rhodes studied the screen, even bending closer to analyze its content. "Are these DNA strands?"

Vanya moved to Darian's left, pointing to parts of the images with their alien captions. "Yes, and look how they're labeled. From what my NIEC tells me, these are ten different DNA strands, collected from several different planets."

Darian straightened. "Does it say anything about these planets?"

"No, but I suggest a search for cross-references in the database." Vanya paused, looking hesitant. "I'm actually a high school biology and chemistry teacher and noticed something definitely familiar about the DNA."

"You're clearly in the right place, then." Darian returned her focus to the screen and wished she knew more about what she was looking at. She could read the captions, but they were littered with abbreviations and words she had no reference to even in English. Then she noticed a sentence at the bottom of the screen, and only her training kept her from flinching. "Have you seen that?" She pointed to the screen while looking over at Vanya and Boyd. "It's a warning to not examine any specimens or samples outside of a containment unit. Are you aware of it? Have you opened any of these damn pots and jars?" She indicated the ample collection surrounding them.

Vanya shook her head. "Nothing's been opened, Chief." She flushed a deep red. "Although I hadn't noticed that part yet."

"Nothing's been opened—Trent! Stop!" Boyd had looked up at the woman on the raised platform and turned pale. "Put that back. Immediately." Walking over to where Trent stood, now balancing on one leg, probably because his booming voice had startled her, Boyd steadied her. "Put it back. That's it."

"Lieutenant?" Trent, a brown-haired woman in her forties, replaced the two small crates she had plucked from a cabinet.

"Just come down, and we'll talk about proper procedure immediately. It's all right." Boyd waited until Trent had returned to the floor. "Thanks to Chief Tennen, we've realized we can't be cavalier about what we do and assume the NIECs have already given us everything we need to know." He looked apologetically at Darian. "We all could easily get carried away, Chief. We know of so much now that we didn't a few days ago, and it's easy to become overzealous."

Darian glanced over at Rhodes, but he was already taking notes. "This experience has been eye-opening. If nothing else, then for that insight. That goes for all the departments—senior crew included. Everyone should move forward with caution." Darian thought of how reckless she and Samantha, and their friends, had been when they first started researching the remarkable finds in Dennamore. Yes, they carried the alien DNA, but ten generations, at least, separated them and the space travelers from Dwynna Major.

"All right," Darian said, "we'll soon be out of your hair, but before we leave, we need you to show us around the main equipment."

"Absolutely," Boyd said, sounding relieved. He hurried around the desk and motioned toward the piece of technology Vanya had just vacated. "This is a microscope that can rival anything we have on Earth, according to Vanya."

"And what were you examining earlier?" Darian asked, stopping a few feet from it.

"Don't worry, Chief," Vanya said quickly. "I was exploring the microscope, not alien samples. I used a few strands of my own hair. It's remarkable the information it draws from that."

"Such as?" Darian relaxed and walked closer.

"Look here, Chief." Vanya motioned to the metal cylinder.

Darian knew she wouldn't understand what she was looking at and, vaguely remembering feeling out of her depth in high school during these types of classes, she peered into the cylinder. At first, she couldn't make out what she was seeing, as it was magnified to a degree that made the strands look like firewood. A vast amount of information was listed underneath the image.

"What you see underneath is my complete genetic makeup, with tons of information about my health status, down to my nutritional intake the last few years."

"Years?" Darian snapped her head up.

"Someone with short hair, like the lieutenant here, wouldn't find data about more than a few months, but as my hair has been growing out for over two years, it holds a lot of information. What's also important—it shows how you're related to our ancestors. Apparently, I'm related on both sides of my family, to such a degree I'm starting to feel inbred." Vanya crinkled her nose, tension around her eyes.

Darian nodded slowly as a sudden thought made her want to talk to Raoul. What if Vanya had a point? What if the amount of alien DNA played a part in how individuals responded to the NIECs and, in Gran's case, to alien medical treatment?

"I may want you to crossmatch your findings with the medical department, Vanya," Darian said matter-of-factly. Something told her that their learning curve was steeper than anyone could have foreseen, as in a ninety-degree climb straight up.

CHAPTER SEVEN

Holly regarded the long benches that ran the entire length of the ship, broken up by bulkheads every ten yards. Surprised to see more people filling the benches with something resembling fine gravel than were assigned to each shift on this deck, she approached a diminutive man whose bald head clearly showed his NIEC.

"Ensign...Potts." Holly glanced at his nametag and held up her hands as the man jumped and pivoted so fast, he nearly toppled over.

"Captain!" Potts changed from skittish to beaming in a single beat. "So great for you to visit us. Look at this! We'll have fresh produce in a few days."

"Excuse me? Days?" Holly blinked.

"Yes, ma'am." Potts looked like he was about to salute her, but instead he motioned for Holly and her team to walk with him to the deep shelves along the inner bulkhead. "This substance is damn near magic for an old gardener like me. It resembles vermiculite, but it's infused with an amazing compound that I can't translate the term for, as we don't have it on Earth. If we did, famine would be a thing of the past, I tell you."

"You have quite a few people here. Civilians?" Holly noticed how Mireille was taking notes and kept her focus on Potts. The man looked like he was about to combust from eagerness.

"I'm sure you know we have a thriving gardening society in Dennamore, which I'm chairman of, and even if we never were able to rival that Lake Light Festival, our garden tours are nothing to sneeze at." His face fell. "I didn't think of that. Now that we've left with the ship, the lake lights won't happen, will they?"

Holly hadn't even contemplated that effect of their departure. "I suppose not." She motioned toward the people hauling canisters from the shelves to the raised beds. "So, these workers belong to your garden society?"

"Some. Others are friends or family members who are excited and, I wager, quite adamant about producing fresh vegetables and fruit."

"But what about seeds, etcetera?" Mireille asked.

"As soon as I felt the yearning, I pulled out my collection of seeds and even had my staff bring the truck around with a lot of what I had already sown in my greenhouses. Don't worry. I left enough for the people back home. Call me crazy, but I don't want my business to go under." Potts chuckled.

Holly took the time to send the two young women in her team to observe what was going on in the hydroponic bay in more detail. Turning back to Potts, she asked, "And your NIEC is working well for you?"

"It's brilliant. All I had to do was enter this deck, and I immediately knew what to do. It was startling at first," Potts said, "but it all happened organically—no pun intended."

Even Holly had to smile. "How long can you use the beds now, before the soil, for lack of a better word, is depleted?"

"It won't be depleted for a long time. Years, in fact, as we'll be fertilizing with the powder the ship collects from the lavatory system."

Mireille's eyebrows rose as she stopped taking notes for a moment. "Dust?"

"Exactly." Potts waved them to the center of the vast area and pointed aft. "Down there is a massive storage system for our waste. It turns the dust into small marbles, and when we mix them into the 'soil' and add water, the result will keep everything fertilized. Something in the material we're pouring in right now elevates and expedites the process when it comes to the plants. I'll enjoy showing you the first results." He rubbed his hands together.

"I look forward to it." Holly walked after Potts, watching how his exuberance spread to those working with him to initiate their food production. They filled the benches with the odorless material and then opened nozzles on pipes that followed the entire ceiling.

This part Holly already knew, how they produced enough water to sustain everyone for a long time in space. All urine was recycled. The bulkheads were filled with fresh water, most likely from the lake in Dennamore, and Claire had explained to Holly how the system converted energy from space dust to keep the bulkhead topped up. Two days ago, the chief medical officer, Raoul Viera, had reported on the vast stock of rehydration capsules kept in the cargo bay, which would keep everyone alive should they be subjected to a catastrophic event. And Samantha had her NIEC's knowledge of how she could scan for water sources on planets that contained ice or regular water.

"Won't the water evaporate?" Mireille asked, leaning in over the hydroponic bed next to her.

"Yes, but very slowly. The rate it needs to be refilled will barely register on our water gauges," Potts said, now sounding serious. "And the benefits for us from eating homegrown vegetables and fruits far outweigh any concerns about the water." He brightened again. "And then there are all the alien seeds. It'll be amazing to try them out in a few of the beds."

"Alien seeds? As in turning into something edible?" Holly looked around. "Are they in here?"

"In a cordoned-off area behind locked doors," Potts said, again looking serious. "We can't risk cross-contamination when we sow our first batch of Earth plants. Once we've worked with the chemistry department and researched the long-term effects and so on, we can create a mixed environment behind other locked doors. Don't let my excitement fool you, Captain. I know what I'm doing."

"I have every faith in you, Ensign—*what* was that?" Holly snapped her head back to the aft section. A strange, almost howling outcry echoed through the hydroponic bays again. Turning to Mireille, Holly frowned. "Did that sound like a rooster to you?"

"It did." Mireille's hazel eyes were round from shock.

"It is." Clearing his voice, Potts looked nervous. "I didn't know about it until this morning, but apparently Crewman Schneider couldn't part with his birds." Scratching his now-deep-red neck above the collar of his uniform, Potts smiled carefully.

"Birds. Plural." Not waiting for an explanation, Holly marched toward the agitated-sounding rooster. The closer she and Mireille got to the aft section, the more clearly Holly could make out the sound of clucking hens. When they finally turned the last corner of the winding corridor, they entered another cordoned-off area. Behind a fortified fence, a rooster stood between them and, Holly counted, eighteen hens. These weren't regular fowl either. Even she, who had no interest in farming whatsoever, recognized Brahma chickens. Huge, with feathers adorning their legs like lace-trimmed bloomers, they moved quite majestically. "Crewman Schneider?" Holly approached a young man who stood just inside the fence, tossing whatever the chickens ate among the birds.

Turning around, Schneider paled, then blushed. "Captain. Ah. You're here. Right now. I mean, you know."

"I do now." Holly approached the fence only to stop instantly as the impressive rooster appeared to be hissing at her before he crowed again. "Tell me this first, Schneider. Will these birds survive on board the *Velocity*?" She hoped so.

"I absolutely think so, Captain," Schneider said quickly. "I'll set up daylight lamps for them and build something so they can go inside and perch. We'll have eggs, and I hope they'll continue to breed as well. Also, they're brilliant as pets once they get used to their environment. They're a little startled right now."

"Did you say pets?" Mireille gaped.

"Sure." Schneider smiled, more relaxed now, probably because Holly hadn't chopped him off at the ankles. "The kids on board might miss their pets. I bet they will. They can come here once the girls have settled in and cuddle them."

"Mental-health benefits, right there," Mireille said, returning his smile. "What do you think, Captain?"

Holly looked at the hens and noticed how some of them had begun to eat. That had to be a good sign. "So far it sounds doable." That was as far as Holly was prepared to go. "Schneider, you'll obviously be in charge and responsible for these birds, but you also need to find at least three other adults who are ready to assist you on a rotating schedule."

"That won't be hard, Captain. A lot of the gardeners are super excited about them."

Holly nodded and motioned for Mireille that it was time to continue their tour. "I have to say I didn't expect to see chickens on the ship," she murmured.

"Me either, but if it works out, they'll be a major source of nutrition and, as he said, something for the kids to care for." Mireille jotted down notes as they walked back toward Potts.

"Well, unless they have a stowaway cow somewhere, let's continue to learn more about what we actually came here for." Holly braced for impact as Potts rushed toward them with his arms outstretched.

"You did ask about fertilizing," he said. "Let me show you under a very fancy microscope how the process happens."

Holly bit back a moan. From chickens to glorified manure. Fantastic. She was starting to realize this journey would provide her with just as many challenges inside the ship as understanding how to maneuver interstellar space would.

Nodding to Potts, who looked like he was about to show them the Hope Diamond, she said, "Lead the way" and followed him to the laboratory part of the hydroponic bays. Her captain's NIEC immediately infused her brain with general knowledge, which also explained more of what Potts had talked about earlier regarding the "soil." Relieved, as that meant Potts didn't have to drone on in detail for her to grasp what he was talking about, Holly dutifully used the microscope and had to admit she was increasingly impressed.

She was about to ask a follow-up question, when her speaker buzzed.

"Engineering to Crowe." Claire's voice came through as clearly as if she'd been standing next to Holly. This clarity made the urgency in her voice obvious, and Holly stepped away, out of earshot of anyone else.

"Crowe here."

"We need you in engineering right away." Claire was out of breath. "And preferably with a few strong people."

"On my way." Not bothering to explain, Holly called out to Mireille to finish in the hydroponic bay. She hurried toward the closest ladder, at the same time summoning security, including Darian, to engineering. Hooking one arm around the pole, she slid down to deck nine. She paged Claire back after smacking her boots onto the deck and starting to run. Were any of the agents trying for the weapons' storage again? "Almost there. Security on their way."

"It's not a security matter, per se. We need brute force, as in muscles!" Claire groaned the last words out.

Holly ran faster. What the hell was going on?

Chapter Eight

Claire pushed past the metal grid she had just shoved to the side. Yellow light blinked in the narrow space under the propulsion drive, its correct alien name best translating to *Sub Transit Helix*. STH, for short. It had spun almost inaudibly until five minutes ago, but now the engineering alarm system roared above her as she pushed herself farther in. Her NIEC might as well have lit a path for her, for she knew exactly where she was going, but it was a crowded space, and dragging a tool kit behind her didn't help.

"I wish you'd let me go instead," one of her young male subordinates shouted behind her. "Chief, it's hot as hell in there!"

It was. Something that had gone wrong with the STH was causing it to heat up, and if she didn't fix it ASAP, it could potentially destroy the ship. She had paged Holly before she shoved her head and shoulders into the opening, and now the heat was singeing her face.

"Shut off the damn alarm!" She couldn't move enough to look back at the man behind her. "And call out the data to me over my speaker."

"Yes, Chief!" It took a few moments, but then the klaxons stopped blaring so quickly, they seemed to leave an echo.

"Temperature is rising, not as fast as before, but too fast," the ensign behind her called out. She suddenly couldn't remember his name. "If we don't cool it—"

"I know! I know…" Claire coughed again and then felt a firm hand around her ankle. "Ensign!" She kicked to free herself.

"It's me," Holly said behind her. "Ensign Larsen is at the console by the STH, your other officers are running diagnostics—and I'm here."

"We may have to start evacuating onto the speeders," Claire said huskily. "It'll be standing room only, but we should be able to eventually make it back."

"Giving up so soon?" Holly asked, sounding so calm Claire feared she might not have understood the potential danger. "Work the problem, Claire." The use of her first name jolted her into action, and she realized that a moment's lapse in her NIEC had allowed her to panic.

Pulling out her engineer-issue trackpad, she scanned the painfully bright light ahead. "Wait. Getting more readings. It's…It's the cooling system. Something in the inner bulkheads could have created a blockage or dented one or more of the conduits." Wiping the sweat stinging her eyes away with her sleeve, she squinted at the trackpad. "If it wasn't so hot in here, I would've flushed the system, but if we cool it too much, we might rupture the joints. The metal alloys used to construct the *Velocity* are damn near indestructible, but that means there's less give as well. If one compartment blows, the force behind it can cause irreparable damage." Claire felt Holly's hand farther up her leg and realized that she had pushed herself into the space as well. "What are you doing, Captain? It's tight enough with one person in here!" Coughing again, Claire wheezed as she tried to breathe the hot air.

The trackpad beeped, and new data ran across the screen, making it hard to keep up, as the smoke was now twice as thick as before. Something else pushed at Claire's hip, and she was about to hiss at Holly for pushing even farther in, when she felt a mask of sorts in her hand. Turning onto her side, she pushed it over her face, where it slid into place and followed the contours of her face perfectly. Clean air and added oxygen filled her lungs as she greedily inhaled. The life-giving gas seemed to kickstart her brain and make it reconnect to her NIEC.

"We need to calibrate the STH to new numbers. Tell Ensign Larsen that I'm transferring them to his trackpad." Claire pushed deeper in after sending the data. She could see the glowing conduits farther in. "I need four conduit repair kits, instantly." Claire heard Holly relay the orders behind her.

"Here, Claire." Holly pushed four small crates into Claire's hand, one by one. "How can you fix them when the drive's running?"

"It's a liquid porcelain substance. All I have to do is pour it onto the conduits, and it will seal them and keep them going until we need to replace them permanently." Claire eased forward and opened the first crate. A soft, gooey substance, the same viscosity as thick honey, easily allowed itself to be administered to the first conduit. Obediently, it filled every little gap that was invisible to the naked eye and sealed the leaks. She repeated the procedure three more times, and by then the ventilation system had finally kicked in and drawn out the mist, making the air cooler. Oddly enough, Claire now became aware of how much her face, neck, and hands hurt.

"I'm done," she said, hating how her words ended in a moan.

"Then back out. I've got you." Holly tugged gently at Claire's light-gray uniform pants.

"Ow. Careful." Starting to hyperventilate against the pain, Claire groaned. "I must've singed myself."

Holly's face appeared above Claire when she ended up sitting on the engineering deck once she was out of the crawl space. Claire tipped her head back to look up at the captain and raised her hand to remove the mask.

"Oh, God. Don't." Holly stopped Claire's hand. "You've more than singed yourself." She glanced behind her. "We need a gurney!"

"I'll be okay." Sure, her skin stung a little, but not too much. Claire found Larsen among the pale faces around her. "What's the new data saying?"

"We're…eh…we're back to normal, Chief. The STH is working smoothly again. If you hadn't thrown yourself in there like you did, we could have sustained severe damages to the entire conduit system." He looked away.

"Monitor it meticulously until we know we can trust the patch job I did. I—" Feeling her face grow cold on the inside, even if she could still sense the heat in her cheeks, Claire flinched. "Damn. Now that does hurt."

"I'll say." Holly shifted to the side as a gurney was lowered onto the deck. "Your chief has to go to the infirmary instantly. I need two people to assist." She stood next to the gurney as two of Claire's crew lifted her onto it and raised it until it hovered between them.

"Ensign Larsen, you're in charge of engineering until Chief Gordon has healed. You will file reports every forty-five minutes until further notice, to Chief Gordon, Commander Walker, and to me."

"Understood, Captain." Larsen looked down at Claire, who was now focusing on breathing through the pain. "I'll keep her running, Chief."

"Come on," Holly said and motioned for the two crewmembers to push the gurney while she strode toward the exit. Outside, she slammed her palm against the controls and barked, "Captain's code. Emergency."

The elevator door opened within seconds, but the pain made each passing moment feel like an hour. Claire was whimpering now and raised her hand, shocked to see blisters forming on the back of it.

"Crowe to infirmary. We're coming in with a burn victim." Holly held her hand on Claire's shoulder. "It's Chief Gordon."

"Affirmative." Raoul sounded calm yet urgent. "We'll be ready."

The elevator sped them four decks up, and the elevator doors opened to show Raoul and two of his staff waiting. "We've got her, Captain. We'll keep you posted." He glanced at Claire and then pushed the gurney through the door to the infirmary. As it shut behind them, Claire couldn't feel Holly's reassuring touch against her shoulder anymore. Closing her eyes and cursing at the tears that stung her face behind the mask, she wanted desperately for the pain to stop. Holly had so many duties, and so many crewmembers to consider, but she missed the reassuring touch more than she could say.

"Claire," Raoul said. "I'm going to administer pain relief before we remove your mask and your uniform. When you wake up, you'll feel a lot better."

Something icy cold hissed at her neck. As the world shrank to a faded gray around the edges, Claire could sense the pain lift like mist on a moor. She allowed herself to sink into the darkness, and just as she became unconscious, she heard herself say, her voice husky and trembling, "Holly...don't go..."

❖

Holly experienced a strange, reversed déjà vu from when she had been the one on the remedial bed, the premier, best-equipped examination gurney in the infirmary, and Claire had hovered over her. It hadn't been that long ago—on the night they had found the ship under the lake and the captain's NIEC had attached itself to her.

Raoul worked quickly, assisted by one of his medics, using a wand, similar to the one he'd administered to Camilla's swollen joints, across Claire's scorched skin. The angry reddish welts and seeping blisters, which on Earth would have marred Claire's beautiful, deep-toned skin, appeared to dry up and begin to flake in minutes.

"She'll be all right, Captain," Raoul said, after glancing up at Holly. "This heals the wound from within, as well as cleans it. We'll hang some fluids to deal with the risk of dehydration."

"It's amazing." Holly didn't move. She told herself she was there because she was responsible for every single soul on the ship but had to admit that wasn't the whole truth. This was Claire, whom she'd gotten to know very quickly when the two of them joined Samantha, Darian, and the others in their quest to solve Dennamore's mind-blowing mystery. Claire, who loved to camp and hike in the forest around their hometown, who was obsessed with anything remotely to do with science fiction, and who had selflessly stayed near home to help her father by working as a car mechanic in his garage.

What had possessed Claire to go into the crawl space without protective gear? Holly gripped the edge of the bed, knowing the answer. She hadn't had time. Or, at least, Claire had made the judgment call that she had to act immediately.

"Captain? You better let me look at your hands." Raoul had finished the procedure with Claire and now sidled up next to Holly. "Have a seat."

"I'm fine—oh, all right." Raoul would pull some CMO rank on her if she insisted, but he should focus on Claire and leave her be. She sighed and sat down on one of the other beds. Holding out her hands, she flinched and made a face. As if seeing her own blisters brought the pain forward, she moaned and closed her eyes briefly. "Damn."

"Exactly." Shooting Holly a knowing glance, Raoul needed only a minute to heal her second-degree burns. "I realize your hands look fine now, but I still want you to put on lotion."

Holly blinked. "Lotion?" The alien showers furnished a built-in cleansing solution, but body cream? That would be too much to ask. She had packed some essentials at the very last minute but had focused on technological practicalities rather than personal hygiene. Right now, she could remember bringing only her toothbrush and toothpaste.

"Ah, yes. Just a moment." Raoul walked over to a large workstation, where he ran his finger along the controls. He nodded toward one of the medics over by the far wall, who opened a frosted-glass door, pulling out a cylinder the size of a decent cigar, which he gave to Holly.

"Here you go, Captain. This is the ointment you need. We'll be putting the same on Chief Gordon and will send some with her when she's released."

Claire moved as if to get up. "I'm ready to go now," she said.

"Oh, no, you don't. Raoul says you need fluids and ointment. If I listened to him, you will too." Holly placed a gentle hand on Claire's shoulder. "And then, when you're back on your feet, we're going to work on safety regulations and protocols. Apparently, our ancestors didn't think to infuse enough of that type of information into the NIECs. Perhaps they, rightfully so, thought it required simple common sense."

Claire frowned. "Hey, I didn't have time—"

"I know. That's why we need to review it. We have to minimize the risk of this happening to anyone else if we can avoid it."

Claire sighed. "Yeah. You're right, Captain. Safety regulations and protocols. Got it."

"Good. And don't feel singled out. This step goes for every soul on the ship, down to the smallest child."

"You mean even baby Alicia?" Claire's expression shifted from slight exasperation to mirth. "She's eighteen months old."

"Excuse me?" Not having gone through the crew and passenger manifest in that great a detail, as that was Walker's and Camilla's task, and they hadn't had time for it yet, Holly couldn't believe her ears.

"We have twelve children between eighteen months and fifteen years old," Raoul said. "I received the detailed manifest only an hour ago. I'm going to see them all very shortly and work my way through the crowd from there."

"I see." She really didn't. Holly had known children would be on this trip, but she had surmised they'd be at least twelve or fourteen. The responsibility of having a toddler on a potentially, most likely, dangerous journey weighed on her even more. Not about to let her reaction show, she decided it was time to leave. "I'll return to hydroponics. Thanks for the lotion." She tucked the cylinder into her breast pocket as she headed for the door. Just as it began to hiss shut behind her, she heard Claire mutter, "Oh, she took that piece of information really well."

Chapter Nine

It was late in the senior staff's conference room next to Holly's office, and only the fact that Claire's team in engineering had managed to calibrate the system that mimicked daylight at the appropriate hours compared to Earth made Samantha's body believe it. She sat to the left of Holly, with Darian on her other side. Walker had been showing Holly something on his computer and just now snapped it closed and took his seat beside the captain. Camilla looked remarkably unaffected by the late hour, while Claire slumped in her chair, her deep skin tone displaying a grayish undertone. Her ordeal earlier in the day had startled them all, but Raoul, who sat next to Darian, reassured them she just needed some decent rest.

Philber was busy jotting down notes using pen and paper, and whatever he was working on had him looking like the proverbial mad scientist, with his hair in complete disarray. Somehow, he'd managed to pull a torn cardigan over his pale-beige uniform, which added to the imagery. Carl, like Camilla, appeared as if he had just had a solid eight-hour sleep and was ready to throw himself into his new job as ops officer, when he had in fact worked a double shift helping his counterparts find their stride. They had all pulled double duty like that at some point during the day, as it was essential to establish the three shifts required to maneuver the ship. Walker was setting up a roster that would allow them to work in different constellations, both to get to know each other and also to comfortably perform together and not become an A, B, and C crew.

Samantha was pleased with the two ensigns who would take the helm when she wasn't on duty. One man and one woman, both in their late thirties, the woman actually a newly minted helicopter pilot, had been able to absorb everything their NIECs offered and put the new knowledge to practical use. Samantha would, together with her new copilots, train others to maneuver the speeders and, later, at least know the basics of handling the helm.

"I have a question," Carl said, thus starting the meeting even if they were missing Brandon and Raoul.

"By all means," Holly said as everyone else quieted. "Ask away."

"Is it true that we have chickens in the hydroponics bay?" Carl's eyes glittered.

"It is indeed." Holly smiled, which reduced the tension around her almond-shaped eyes. "According to Crewman Schneider, we'll have eggs—and pets."

"Pets." Walker raised his bushy eyebrows. "Please tell me they won't be assigned to us in our quarters."

Holly chuckled, which made her hair dance around her cheeks. "I'm tempted to suggest it. But as a favor to the chickens, not to mention the impressive rooster, they're getting a proper chicken coop where they currently reside." She laced her fingers and placed her hands on the table. "I learned a lot today, not just about the chickens, even if that situation was rather surreal. I now realize we have *very* young children on board, which means we have to be diligent when it comes to their protection, as well as their schooling and general development—physically, mentally, emotionally. I happened upon a lovely woman in the elevator yesterday, Marjory Hopkins—"

"My aunt!" Carl lit up.

"Exactly. She seems to be something of a renaissance woman, possessing many talents, and judging by how she spoke of you, she might be perfect as a liaison between civilians and crew, and the children especially. However, I leave the final decision in your capable hands, Walker, Camilla."

"You read my mind, Captain," Camilla said. "I ended up at Marjory's table in the mess hall today. She's immensely proud of you, Carl."

Reddening now, Carl seemed to think they'd talked enough about his relative. Samantha took the opportunity to address them. "On that note, not just the kids need an education. We all have so much to learn about the ship, and I've noticed that our respective NIECs don't always, well, bother to show us even the basics. It took me the better half of an hour to figure out the shower. And everyone should understand how the entire process of recycling and waste management works, even if specific personnel will handle the maintenance."

"Noted—and I agree, of course." Holly nodded. "Suggestions, Commander?" She glanced at Walker.

"We've already discussed rotating schedules when it comes to our respective specialties, which will help us get to know our peers. That's not enough, not right away, since we have to get more used to being on board, but we should plan to do rotations in other departments. You had similar thoughts, Camilla." The look he gave Camilla warmed Samantha's heart. Walker had nourished a crush on Camilla when he was only fourteen and she a stunningly beautiful senior in high school. When Camilla heeded the well-known yearning to return to her hometown after fifty years in LA, they'd found each other, and the love between them was tangible.

"I do," Camilla said and patted his hand, a habit that no difference in rank would break, Samantha knew. "Mental health and emotional stability mean we cannot allow ourselves to become complacent. We're in a honeymoon phase of sorts. Everything's shiny and new right now—the ship, being in space, this fantastic adventure—but that won't last. We have to do rotations among ourselves as people as well." She looked around the table.

"How do you mean?" Darian asked.

"We risk forming cliques. Lower desk versus bridge crew. Civilians versus crew. Young people versus the older generations. Those who are alone aboard the ship," Camilla said—glancing at Philber, who didn't appear to notice as he still was deep in thought at his notes—"and those who brought several family members or friends. We have to keep the doors open between these subgroups. All jobs matter to keep the *Velocity* running smoothly, and all of us as individuals count—equally."

Claire straightened in her chair, then spoke. "We have a diverse group of people aboard," she said slowly. "The biases and prejudice that exist back home haven't magically been erased just because we're all in the same situation while on this mission. Having different ethnicities well represented within the senior crew sets the tone, but I agree with Camilla. We can't afford to become complacent, or naive, as much as we might hope we'll all remain in this lovely sense of 'us-against-the-universe kumbaya.'" She shrugged and pulled up one corner of her mouth in a half smile. "In my experience, eventually, no matter what their best intentions are, people are people."

Samantha nodded. "Well said. And yes, as important as it is to be vigilant about our work, our assignments, to keep us all alive, the ones among us born privileged must recognize the truth in your words, Claire. As the senior crew, we can't allow complacency, biases, or prejudice."

"Agreed. Who has an NIEC and how the individual using one is chosen is another potentially combustible issue down the line," Walker said. "Some may be relieved not to have to wear one, but others might eventually question why they don't."

Carl cleared his throat. "We have a golden opportunity with the youngest of our passengers, and crew too, to bring them along to help set a tone of tolerance."

"You're right," said Brandon, who, with Raoul, had joined them in the middle of the discussion. As they took their seats, Raoul patted Carl on the back.

Brandon continued. "We should put what you all just said in writing. Make it part of our, well, not rules and regs, perhaps, but statement of principle. And let's not kid ourselves. This trip is going to be a constant work in progress."

"Lead by example on all fronts," Samantha said as Darian took her hand under the table.

Holly rapped her fingernails against the table. "Camilla, Claire, Brandon, and Carl. Form a group and start working on the document."

Samantha listened to them say "Yes, Captain," but she focused primarily on how Darian caressed the back of her hand with her thumb. This journey would be challenging, but right now, with Darian by her side, she was optimistic. She was where she wanted to be, and if the others yearned for Dwynna Major as strongly as she did, so were they.

PART TWO

SPACE

CHAPTER TEN

The alarm klaxons jolted Holly out of bed, nearly making her fall and break her neck, since her legs were still tangled in the blanket. It was the third time this week and was quickly getting old. After more than eight months in space, most of it at ISD speed, which she now knew all there was to know about, thanks to her captain's NIEC—and to Claire—they were six light-years away from Earth. The technology that made it possible for the *Velocity* to move at such speeds—while at the same time calculate trajectories, avoid asteroids, meteors, and so on—was becoming, if not commonplace, then at least an everyday thing.

"Crowe to bridge. Report!" Tapping her speaker, Holly pulled on her uniform with practiced ease and attached her NIEC.

"We're down to 75-percent ISD, again." Samantha spoke curtly. "Can you feel the tremors, Captain?"

Holly was heading out into the corridor, but now she stopped. She was so accustomed to the *Velocity*'s usual faint hum, it wasn't hard to distinguish the pulsating vibrations that pressed against the soles of her boots. "I do. I'm on my way. And cut the noise." Damn it, this was more than the glitches they'd fixed earlier in the week. A simple reboot of the system had appeared to be enough, but perhaps they'd only managed to make the underlying problem worse. "Crowe to engineering." Holly entered the elevator, which whisked her to the deck above her in a few seconds. The corridor between it and the bridge was filled with people hurrying to their duty stations.

"We're all here, Captain," Claire said over Holly's speaker. "We're running diagnostics, but I recommend reducing speed further until we've figured this problem out."

Holly knew Claire was right, but it still irked her. "How much?" She took her chair and tapped the sensor that lit up all her screens and identified her as the captain. They flickered with so much information, she feared she might have a seizure if she didn't slow them down.

"We need to limp along at 10 percent for a while." Claire sounded about as disgusted with the idea as Holly felt. "As soon as we've located the issue, we'll be back at 100 percent."

"All right. I'll work the problem from the bridge, but if you locate it from your end, page me. I want to see it firsthand."

"Aye, Captain." Claire's clipped tone conveyed how focused she was on her task.

Holly turned her attention to the ops station, where Carl had just taken over the main computer. His hair stood on end, and he yawned behind his hand. "Carl. What do you have?"

"From my point of view, nothing's wrong with our systems that raises any flags. Apart from the reduction in speed and the alarm going off because of it, all systems are a go." Carl lifted his hands, palms up.

"Commander?" Holly shifted her gaze to Walker, who was reading his screens.

"None of the departments are reporting any malfunctions." Walker scratched his temple. "Starting to think we have gremlins in the machinery."

"Hm." Holly turned forward and found Samantha waiting to give her report. "Go ahead."

"I'm glad I was at the helm when it happened this time. The other two times, junior officers have manned the controls, and even if they reported back to me in minute detail, it's not the same as a personal experience. At 0231 hours, I felt a faint tremor. Mere seconds after that, I could have sworn the ship rose under my feet. Or perhaps heaved is a better word. Then, after what felt like a short, sharp stomp, the reverberations began. That's when the alarm went off."

"Sounds like a mechanical problem," Holly murmured and read from her screens.

"Not entirely. We may have a tactical situation," Darian said from behind.

Standing up and rounding her chair, Holly walked over to the tactical station where Darian and Nate stood, their fingers flying across the sensors. "Go on."

"I just got here, as Nate manned tactical, but he caught these coordinates instantly." Darian swiveled one of the smaller screens. "This view shows that something other than space dust, asteroids, or meteors is out there."

"And you're sure about this?"

"We are, for a simple reason." Darian exchanged a glance with Nate. "They're on a parallel trajectory to ours, at the exact same speed."

Holly blinked. "Excuse me?"

"That was my reaction," Darian said.

"What distance?" Holly asked, her mind racing.

"Too close for comfort, I'd say," Nate answered. "I've run the calculations on the star chart, and whatever's out there is holding at eight kilometers."

"Damn, that's close," Walker said as he showed up next to Holly. It was. In space that counted as bumper to bumper.

"I am scanning around the ship, and I widened the area we're looking at to a radius of thirty kilometers." Darian pulled several fingertips along the screen and then made a pinching motion. "Captain." Her eyes narrowing, she stepped aside for Holly to read.

"You have four contacts." Holly's stomach felt as if she'd just downed ice water. "Two at thirty kilometers, on either side of us, and two at the same distance above and underneath us."

"Should we increase speed and see if whatever it is does too?" Nate asked.

Holly was tempted but then shook her head. "No. At this point, we don't know if the contacts have anything to do with living beings. They could be buoys or sensors. Or surveillance. We can surmise it's not something organic to space." Holly stepped to the side. "Keep monitoring these contacts. I'll go down to engineering. If whatever's out there is managing to disturb our ISD, I want to be of assistance there. Commander, you have the bridge back."

"Aye, Captain." Walker retook his chair. "Before you go, Captain, Camilla paged me that she's setting up what she calls emotional triage in the mess hall for those who might find these alarms frightening, especially the children."

"Excellent." Holly hurried back to the elevator and rode it down to deck nine. Camilla was a godsend when it came to keeping the crew and passengers as mentally sound as possible. People of all ages simply adored her. When Holly asked her a while back who Camilla turned to when she needed a shoulder, or to vent, she simply smiled and said, "Who do you think, Captain?" then winked at Holly. Of course, Camilla turned to Walker. They lived together, and their love was obvious. It was good to know that Camilla helped keep frayed nerves at bay.

If deck three had been busy, engineering was controlled mayhem. Claire had her subordinates running diagnostics while she and two others were pulling on protective gear.

"Report," Holly said as she stopped next to Claire.

"Ah, you're here, Captain. Great. That means you can take over the main work console and another one of my ensigns can join us in the crawl spaces." Claire walked over to the console as she motioned for the woman to gear up. "What can you tell me?"

Holly briefed Claire regarding what the bridge crew had found. "You have to be on the lookout for something that might seem manually turned off or manipulated, in case that's what these contacts are able to do."

Claire turned to her subordinates. "Did everyone understand what the captain just asked of us? You're going to be responsible for one crawl space each, and you need to be thorough."

"Yes, Chief," Bergstrom, the young woman that had just vacated the main console, said. "We're on it."

"Good. If you find something, send the information to the captain, who'll be monitoring. Do not touch anything until we've had a chance to evaluate and diagnose it properly. You don't want to repeat my mistake from that first week after we broke orbit."

Several people from the group in protective gear said, "No, Chief," and one of them visibly shuddered, probably remembering Claire's burns all too vividly.

"Let's go then." Claire nodded at Holly and began to walk toward the starboard-to-stern corner of engineering. Halfway there, she stopped, pulled off her helmet, and placed it on a work bench.

Holly had logged in as captain on the computer before her but kept a curious eye on Claire, who now pulled off her NIEC and reattached it. Frowning, Holly wondered what that was about and made a mental note to ask Claire later.

Soon, all four were deep into their respective crawl spaces, their suits registering heat and potential radiation. Holly found she could follow their individual progress by means of internal sensors, which made it marginally less worrisome to have the *Velocity* swallow them up into a dangerous area.

Ten minutes went by, and so far, none of the engineers had found anything out of the ordinary. Holly pulled a stool closer and sat down. She kept in contact with the bridge and learned that the mysterious contacts hadn't shifted from their previous positions, maintaining the same course and speed as before.

"Darian." Holly tapped her speaker, as she had just thought of something and dreaded the answer. "How often, and how wide, do you perform your scans?" She had a vague idea, but she had decided from day one not to micromanage her departments.

"We scan routinely whenever we go on each shift. Twenty-kilometer radius at regular setting. Five-kilometer radius on high resolution. If they're both negative, we wait eight hours until the next one. I scanned with the high-resolution sensors on the other times we had issues with the propulsion earlier this week and found nothing. Either these things weren't there, or they held at a longer distance." Darian's prompt answer was not reassuring. For all they knew, someone, or something, could have been out there stalking them for light-years.

Holly relayed the information to the four engineers in the crawl spaces. As they were letting her know they heard her, one of them gasped.

"Captain! Wait." It was Ensign Bergstrom, now deep into the starboard-aft crawl space. "Something's glowing in here that shouldn't be. Or, at least, not according to my NIEC."

Holly opened her mouth to reply when another ensign called out, "Here too, Captain!" from the port-aft crawl space. "Four square metal crates, approximately eleven times eleven inches, and two inches thick. On my end, they're pulsating."

"Nothing here, so far," Claire called out.

"Here either, Chief," the third ensign parallel to Claire's position said.

"I want you two to back out of there and wait until we finish searching the other two crawl spaces," Holly said. Then they would explore the pulsating crates in an orderly fashion.

"But, Captain, I'm already here. Why can't I just go on?" Bergstrom asked.

"Back out of there. That's an order." Holly infused her, by now reputable, stern tone into her command.

"Yes, Captain," Bergstrom answered, sighing.

Claire and her counterpart pushed on, and Holly could see them advance through the crawl-space system until, after half an hour, they were at the end.

"We found nothing that alerted our NIECs," Claire said. "Ensign Kozak, we're going to exit the space straight up, into one of the supply areas on this deck, but it beats backing up all that way."

"Good plan, Chief," the ensign said. "See you outside." He sounded quite relieved and would probably never have volunteered extra time in the crowded space.

Holly watched Claire hurry through the door, pushing her protective gear down to her waist and tying the sleeves. "Prepare crawlers. They're not the most advanced, but their instruments will do for now."

The engineering crew was already bringing out the small, rectangular boxes that were outfitted with something looking like skateboard wheels. They were remotely operated, and their scanners were second to none aboard the ship.

"Why didn't we send these in right away, instead of risking our people?" Holly murmured to Claire when she joined her by the closest opening to a crawl space.

"Believe it or not, these machines are more fragile than they look. We had to make sure there was no radiation, or we would have fried them. In our suits, we were protected, and let's not underestimate our ability to make useful deductions and the advantage of human intuition." Claire reached in front of Holly to push a lever next to the console. Her arm brushed along Holly's front, and she yanked it back. "Sorry, Captain."

Holly merely took a step back, providing Claire more room. Claire didn't look at her but kept pushing and pulling the four levers. "I'm venting the crawl space before we send in the first crawler. That'll give it more time, in case the heat increases."

"And if what they found emanates radiation?" Holly looked at Claire's quick hands as they shifted between the now-so-familiar, colorful controls and the low-tech levers.

"If there's radiation, they'll fry—at least the sensors and possibly the coating on the wheels. One of my ensigns decided to try one on the hull a few weeks after we broke orbit, when we were afraid some of the plating had corroded because the ship sat under the lake for so long." Claire huffed. "Needless to say, we lost that crawler because space dust and radiation perforated it."

Holly was about to answer when Claire flinched and gripped the railing in front of the computer console. She drew in a breath between her teeth and once again pulled off her NIEC, glowering at it.

"What's wrong?" Holly asked, lowering her voice.

"Not sure, but this thing has a habit of zapping me every now and then." Clare pushed the oval-shaped unit back against the nape of her neck, and Holly watched the metal-tipped filaments find their way into Claire's tight French braid.

"But you're okay?"

Claire turned her head back over her shoulder and smiled. "I'm fine."

Holly wasn't so sure, but as Claire kept working the controls without a glitch, she had to take her word for it.

Claire's thoughts whirled, and it was as if the two halves of her brain each worked on a separate issue. One half was fully occupied watching the crawler disappear into the crawl space and make its way to the glowing rectangular boxes. She handled the remote with care, mindful of what could happen if the crawler touched anything that could short-circuit it because it lacked a protective layer. The crawlers reminded her of nerve endings laid bare in order to feel every single thing they came in contact with. Right now, this one was steadily moving toward her ensign's find.

The other half of Claire's brain was panicking over her NIEC's increasingly weird behavior. She had to reboot it several times a day, which was driving her insane. Usually, that helped, and it required only a second or two for the device to reestablish contact with Claire's central nervous system. Not so today. It had taken several seconds longer, which were like dog years for this type of technology. And it had happened right in front of Holly. Wanting to moan out loud, Claire forced herself, and her NIEC, to focus on her task at hand.

Of course, she had fucked up and grazed against Holly's chest and stomach with her arm, just because she'd been distracted. Not only was she trying to deal with a moody NIEC, but she now had also run the length of her arm along Holly's breasts. So embarrassing. Perhaps, if Claire hadn't on occasion stealthily studied Holly, how she moved, how she looked, and, oh God, how she sounded, she could have chalked it up to a meaningless mishap.

"We're closing in," Claire said, breaking out of the unwanted reverie. "The space is half a degree Celsius higher than the area by the hatch."

"Nothing that alerted the suits," Holly said. "You were well protected at all times, according to internal sensors."

"I thought as much. Here we are." Claire moved into position by the console, vaguely aware that the engineers not needed on other workstations stood in a semicircle around her and Holly. Images began streaming to the smaller screens around the larger one in the center of the workstation. Claire squinted through her glasses, watching data and images fight for attention.

"They're mostly made from a carbon-lead alloy," Ensign Bergstrom said. "Eleven point six inches times seven point four inches. Thickness…one point seven two inches."

"The casing is perforated in six directions, in the dead center of each side." Claire slid her finger along the center screen.

Bergstrom ran her fingers along her trackpad. "Each hole is one sixty-fourth of an inch. Or almost point four millimeters."

Claire studied the way the boxes were placed. There was still enough space to crawl through them, as they sat in the same formation as the perforations: one on the bottom of the space, one on the ceiling, and one on each side. Pulling up an exact outline and magnifying it, she heard Holly, next to her, draw in a breath.

"I'll be damned," Holly murmured and slapped her speaker. "Crowe to bridge. Send your latest information of the distances and schematics of the contacts—as detailed as you can make it." Her voice was higher than her usual alto, making Claire study the data that the crawler had provided again.

"What are you seeing?" She spoke both to Holly and to herself.

"Surely someone isn't trying to sabotage us, Chief?" Bergstrom asked. "As far as I could tell, they're well fitted into the system."

"No. They've been there the whole time," Holly said slowly, and Claire realized her mind was racing.

"Captain?" Bergstrom frowned.

"You've done an excellent job, Ensign," Holly said, visibly snapping out of her train of thought. "Chief. I need you on the bridge."

"Yes, Captain." As Holly left engineering, Claire put her key people to work, informing them that new orders might soon come in fast. Pulling off her protective gear, Claire hurried toward the door. Something told her Holly was starting to piece all the scattered information together and that this was truly an all-hands-on-deck situation.

Chapter Eleven

Holly regarded the members of the senior crew, all gathered in the conference room, some bringing a subordinate. The people she'd come to care for and consider family over the last months looked expectantly at her. At times leading them all had felt daunting, yet that was nothing to what she felt right now.

"I've reviewed the data, and Carl has run several diagnostics. We have more information to gather, but this is what we have right now. Carl?"

Carl rose and pushed his trackpad against the large screen on the wall. "Here are the specs of the glowing rectangular crates in the crawl spaces. Let me magnify one of them." He slid his finger along the bottom of the screen. "With the help of the database, I have managed to extrapolate an approximate image of what it looks like on the inside, but it was not easy. We have no complete blueprints of this apparatus, and that's why I'm forced to make an educated guess." He swayed back and forth on the soles of his boots. "We've found perforations, tiny ones, on either side of each crate, and the measurements not only coincide with how they're placed together, but also with how the contacts are located around the *Velocity*."

"What?" Raoul said, looking back and forth between Carl and Holly. "Are you saying that the finds you made in the crawl spaces and what's stalking us are connected?"

Holly shook her head. "In a way, yes, but I'm not sure we're being stalked. To be sure, we need to examine exactly what is out there."

"And how will we do that?" Darian asked. "Our scanners are amazing, but their resolution and what they can relay are limited."

"I know. That's why I want us to bring the *Velocity* to a full stop and launch *Speeder One*." Holly let her gaze travel around the table, taking in everyone's immediate reactions.

"I see," Samantha, Holly's third in command, said slowly. "What if the contacts out there don't stop? What if they continue on and we're left stranded?" Her tone was somber.

"Whatever they are, they've been matching our course and speed meticulously," Darian said. "What if we stop the ship and monitor their actions, and if they seem to continue without us, we can start up again?"

"That's one way," Samantha said slowly. "I wouldn't recommend coming to a full stop, though, Captain. We have a feature called maintenance speed, something you can also use while in orbit if you don't feel comfortable shutting down completely. That way, you're ready to accelerate normally, should you need to. It's no more than what a race car on Earth has."

"You're suggesting we reduce to maintenance speed, and if the contacts follow suit, we can safely launch the speeder and still be able to keep up and reach the contacts at the same time?" Holly wasn't opposed to the idea.

"I am. I know how to do a cold start in space in theory, but I'd rather try it under controlled circumstances and not when the lives of a hundred-and-eighty souls hang in the balance." Samantha studied the specs on the screen. "What other explanation for this similarity can there be?"

Claire stood and joined Carl by the screen. "I haven't seen all the diagnostics, but I have pinpointed two potential explanations for how it happened, with varying degrees of probability. The crawl-space crates and the contacts could be two sides of the same coin, subject to some law of attraction in space that we know little or nothing about. Or the crates on the ship could set off alarms when they run into the contacts, which could be part of a minefield or simply sensors, placed by an unknown entity."

"I find it odd that we don't have enough information via our NIECs," Philber said, looking up from his ever-present writing pad.

"If either of these things belongs to the ship, or was built by some of our ancestors, we should have *something*."

"I agree," Claire said, her frown deepening. "It's strange that we've found such scattered information. If this were any other piece of technology, I'd say being stuck under a lake for two hundred and thirty years might cause a glitch." Her wry grin made everyone chuckle. "But that's flawed reasoning. Everything else is damn near pristine, and we've been great at maintaining the upkeep of the parts that do wear down. The NIECs make that routine easy, and I've received no reports from any of my subordinates to the contrary."

A shadow ghosted over Claire's face, and Holly wondered if anyone else noticed the tension around Claire's eyes. Probably not, unless they had furtively studied Claire the way she had. Guilt and unease at the fact that she allowed her attraction to the brilliant woman across from her to appear front and center in her mind when a crisis was at hand made Holly reel herself in.

"Anyone else?" Holly asked the other department chiefs, referring to potential NIEC malfunctions, but they shook their heads no.

A raised voice outside the door sent Darian to her feet. "Not again. I swear that man is going to be the death of me."

Unsurprisingly, it was Agent Neville Brewer, demanding entrance.

"Why wasn't I summoned?" he asked, as soon as Darian opened the door.

"You're not part of the senior crew," Darian said with more exasperation than anger. "And I feel like a broken record for having to repeat that fact on a near-weekly basis."

"You wouldn't have to if you got it in your head that I represent US law enforcement." Brewer spat the words out. "What's going on?"

Holly motioned for a vacant stool by the wall where some of the invited lieutenants and ensigns sat. "By all means." She refused to dignify his constant referral to his position back on Earth. It had no bearing on the *Velocity*. "In short, Mr. Brewer, we're planning to reduce speed further and launch one of the speeders to investigate an anomaly."

"Wait…what?" Brewer had just sat down but now stood again. The man was really too intense for Holly's liking. "What anomaly?"

"You'll be informed of the details along with the rest of the crew and passengers, but our sensors have detected four alien contacts. We believe they may have something to do with the *Velocity* being yanked out of interstellar drive. If we intend to reach Dwynna Major before we become a generational ship, we need to check out the situation."

"I have to join the team." Brewer lowered his voice, and for once, he didn't sound agitated.

"And why is that?" Darian asked, sounding less than forthcoming.

"The same reason as always, but also because I know how to handle myself in a tactical situation. Your crew is good, Chief, but they're still wet behind the ears from a law-enforcement point of view, except Nate."

"So, I'll go myself or send Nate." Darian wouldn't budge, Holly could tell. She and Brewer had butted heads since day one, and Darian would probably never see anything positive in the volatile man. They hadn't entirely succeeded in their attempts to integrate crew and passengers. Walker had done his best when working with the crew and the passengers, as had Camilla. The statement of how everyone was expected to work and conduct themselves toward each other had proved useful, but she was well aware of the cliques that had formed, or perhaps the term subgroups was more apt.

"Sit down, please, Neville," Holly said, thinking it was long overdue to call the man by his given name here in the conference room. "I haven't decided yet who will go on this mission. It will have to be a mix of senior and junior crew." If something went wrong, and they lost people, she couldn't lose all her senior staff just because she thought they'd be better at the mission at hand.

"Yes, Captain," Darian said and sat down.

Neville did the same and appeared to listen with great interest.

"We need two pilots, two security officers, one engineer, one science officer, and one medic." Holly gazed around the table. "Darian, Claire, and Samantha, you're on the team. Darian and Samantha, take one backup each. Raoul, you pick your best medic. Philber, do the same in the science department." Holly glanced at the screen. "Be ready to launch in half an hour."

After acknowledging Holly's orders, everyone but Claire left the conference room.

"Yes?" Holly turned off the screen and started walking toward the door to take her chair on the bridge.

"I—I just have a feeling you're sending us to confirm your suspicions about what's really going on." Her voice low, Claire stepped closer.

"I beg your pardon?" Holly stopped in front of Claire.

"Am I wrong?" Resting her hip against the conference table, Claire tilted her head. "I can't figure out why you're not being more forthcoming with your theory."

"I'm not prepared to discuss my reasons for my orders, Claire. Do you not want to take part in the mission?" She was surprised. Claire was usually almost too brave, sometimes taking foolhardy risks.

"Not at all. You couldn't beat me off with a hockey stick. No, as the engineer on this mission, I feel I should know what, if anything, you think these contacts may be."

Holly stood in silence for a few beats, her mind whirling. "I'm not evading your question, but I also wonder why you haven't brought up more theories yourself."

Coloring, Claire tucked her hands into her pockets, making Holly wish she hadn't used such a harsh tone. "I'm not sure they're valid, as I haven't had time to run them through the computer system. After we found the crates, we spent what little time we've had in engineering dealing with the crawlers' data." Claire raised her chin and moved her hands to her hips.

"I'm not criticizing you," Holly said calmly. "I depend on you, and if something is keeping you from voicing your opinion, I'd like to know."

"I voiced it right now, and you *are* evading the question."

"No. I do have theories, several, as to what might be going on, but as they are speculations—and farfetched, to say the least—I don't see the value in sharing them. I don't want the team unduly influenced but to examine the contacts with an open mind."

Claire looked like she was about to call Holly's statement a cop-out, but instead she sat down on the table. "All right," she muttered, rubbing the back of her neck. "Damn it." She removed the NIEC and examined the small metal feet at the ends of the filaments.

Holly knew now that something was truly amiss. "What's wrong?" She stepped closer and peered down at the limp NIEC.

Claire sighed and shifted her grip on it. "Just a headache. One of the filaments isn't connecting well. I'll look into it later."

"Are you able to function?" Holly placed a hand on Claire's arm when she moved to hop off the table. Feeling Claire's velvety skin against her palm sent such a strong jolt up Holly's arm, she was certain Claire must've felt it.

Claire briefly covered the spot on her arm where Holly had grabbed her. "I am." She blinked slowly, her gaze probing Holly's for a few moments. "Honestly."

"May I see your NIEC?" Holly held out her hand.

Claire looked like she wanted to go around Holly and dismiss herself from the conference room, but eventually she relented and placed the device in Holly's hand. "By all means," she muttered and rubbed the back of her head.

Turning the NIEC over, Holly tried to inspect it for breakage or see if it was simply off-line. "It looks all right from the outside, but you need to scan it—"

"I have!" Claire flung her hands into the air. "Several times. Nothing's wrong with it—not that I can find." Obvious frustration made her voice raspy.

"Has Raoul examined the back of your head?" Holly still kept the NIEC.

"Excuse me?" Claire rushed from frustration to consternation in one beat.

"For a skin issue, or another connectivity problem that keeps the NIEC from functioning correctly."

"There's not. Nothing's wrong with my skin!" Claire glowered at her but then relented. "Take a look and you'll see."

Holly refused to let her reaction to her proximity to Claire stop her from helping her. "I'll just check beneath your braid, all right?"

"Sure. Fine."

Holly handed the NIEC to Claire and then lifted the thick braid from where it rested between Claire's shoulder blades. Using gentle fingertips, she felt over the flawless skin and through the hair where the NIEC-filament feet rested and contacted the scalp, but she couldn't detect anything alarming. "You're right, of course." Holly let go of Claire's hair but plucked the NIEC from her hand before Claire could react. "Allow me, please." She lifted the braid again with one hand and placed the metal alloy oval against the nape of Claire's neck. It obediently snapped into place, and the tiny feet extended and disappeared into the curly black hair. Holly found it nearly impossible to pull her hands away from Claire and ended up overcompensating, taking a quick step back and bumping into a chair.

Claire turned around, her eyes wide. "Captain?"

"Looks like it attached all right." Holly cleared her throat.

"Well, then. All's fine." Claire stood as if nailed to the floor. "Thank you." Claire sounded hesitant and polite.

Holly checked the time. Claire's gaze made her feel weak. She gathered her computer and trackpad, nodding at Claire as she passed her. "Very well. Carry on." Hurrying out the door, Holly felt her heart race as she took her chair on the bridge.

"Reduce to maintenance speed," she ordered, her tone much harsher than she intended. The ensign at the helm scrambled to follow orders.

Holly tried to force her mind away from what had happened in the conference room. Not only had Claire questioned her approach to the mission, which was all right, as she expected questions and counsel from her senior staff, but the way Claire made her feel when they'd stood so close together worried her. The command structure they operated under made every single person on the *Velocity* unapproachable. It was enough that Claire's knowledge of the ship stood between them and complete disaster. If Holly were to give in for so much as a second to the undeniable attraction she felt for her, all kinds of vital boundaries would be forever blurred.

"Maintenance speed, Captain," the helmsman called out.

"The contacts?" Holly turned her head over her shoulder to Carl.

"Matching our course and lack of speed," Carl said. "Hang on, Captain." He frowned and began tapping in commands. His screens lit up his face, creating multicolored patterns as he read the latest information. "Eh, they're right where they were before, but... something strange is going on."

"Explain." Holly stood and crossed the bridge to stand next to him.

"Look here." Carl pointed. "They're spinning."

Holly took over and increased the resolution. Zooming in as far as the sensors allowed for, she observed that each object was indeed spinning around on its own axis. Was this because they had reduced to maintenance speed as well? Or, if these were space mines, could an attack be pending? She engaged her speaker. "Mission team. Launch mission immediately." No way was she going to waste time. The mission needed to get underway as soon as possible. "All hands, ready your stations and secure your area. Passengers, move to your designated safety areas. Tactical teams, in position." Returning to her chair, she looked at Walker, who was scanning the crew's progress. He gave her a quick glance.

"Captain?"

"Not taking any chances. We've had smooth sailing, a proper honeymoon phase, until now. We have no idea what those things truly are, or if they have ill intent."

"Agreed." Walker motioned at his screen. "Departments are confirming that everyone's secure."

Retaking her seat, Holly made sure everyone on bridge duty was in place. "This is our first trial by fire, my friends. This is when we have to rely on our NIECs and be prepared for anything." Too focused to feel an onset of nerves, Holly kept her hands steady as she strapped herself into her seat. "All hands. We're about to launch a mission using *Speeder One*. Remain secure until the bridge crew tells you otherwise."

"Samantha to bridge." Samantha's voice followed just after Holly's ship-wide message. "We're set to launch."

"At your discretion, Chief," Holly said. "Good luck."

"We'll bring answers home for you," Samantha said. "Departing in fifteen seconds."

"External port and starboard sensors on screen." Holly gripped the armrests as Carl sent the imagery to the main screen. "There they go."

Holly studied the perfect trajectory of the speeder as Samantha piloted it toward the starboard contact. Hopefully it wouldn't be long before they had some information and thus a plan on how to deal with their propulsion malfunction.

"There." The ensign at ops pointed to the main screen. "*Speeder One.*"

Creating a white line away from the ship, the speeder made a beeline toward the contacts. "*Velocity—Speeder One.* We have you on screen and are following your progress."

"*Speeder One—Velocity.*" Samantha spoke curtly. "We're approaching with caution. ETA four minutes."

Four minutes for a mere eight kilometers meant the speeder was literally crawling. A quick glance at one of the screens showing the object proved Holly had a right to worry. It appeared to spin exponentially faster. She hailed *Speeder One*, knowing things had just gotten a lot worse. They could still see the ship make its way toward one of the contacts but received no reply.

Chapter Twelve

Samantha let her most seasoned copilot, Molly, deal with the computer readings while she focused on the approach. She could see the spinning object grow on her main screen as they neared it.

"We have lost voice contact with the *Velocity*," Darian said, her tone stark. "I get what I suppose is static, but something's interfering."

"Dollinger." Samantha called out to the science officer in the back. "Anything harmful causing our lack of communication?" This was her main fear about the four objects surrounding the *Velocity*.

"No, Chief. Just your regular space dust and radiation. Nothing our bulkhead or suits can't handle."

"All right. Keep trying, Darian." Samantha gripped the manual controls, preparing to take over from the computer if necessary.

Carl sighed. "They have to be freaked out back on the ship. I mean, not being able to get through."

Samantha agreed but didn't voice her opinion. She was in charge of this mission and could ill afford to speculate. "Brett. Just to be safe, scan our NIECs to make sure they haven't picked up anything."

Brett, a bulky man in his forties, looking more like a pro wrestler than a nurse, moved lithely through the aisle in the back of the speeder while pulling out his medical trackpad. Methodically he ran it over their NIECs and studied his results. "We're all sticking to our baseline, Chief."

"Excellent. Let's keep it that way."

"One kilometer to go," Molly said starkly.

"Going to manual." Samantha wasn't sure they could rely on the automatic technology to circle the object before them, as it had had a strange effect on the *Velocity*'s propulsion system. After months at the helm of the mothership, she found it challenging to maneuver the speeder but, she admitted, also a thrill. "Darian, what do you see?"

"It's a smooth, metallic, charcoal-gray rectangular box." Darian adjusted her instruments. "Dollinger. Any readings on the alloy?"

"The instruments won't penetrate whatever's shielding this thing." Sounding disgusted at not being able to answer promptly, Dollinger shoved his fingers through his barely existent tufts of hair.

"Life signs?" Samantha asked.

"Can't say." Dollinger groaned. "Sorry, Chief. A lot of use I am."

"I'll get us closer. When I'm at a hundred yards, try scanning again. Focus on anything that might kill us." Samantha was only half joking. She pushed the levers, finding them a lot easier to use when flying manually than the colorful consoles that weren't as intuitive when she needed to act fast.

"Careful," Darian murmured.

"Trust me. I'm ready to hightail it out of here in a tenth of a second," Samantha said. She eased the speeder closer, keeping between the *Velocity* and the object. "Up close, this thing is huge."

"Two hundred, one-seventy-five, one-fifty…one hundred," Molly said.

"Halting." Samantha made sure she kept her distance. "Talk to me, people."

"One of the short sides has a round, black circle," Darian said, leaning closer to her screen. "And it looks indented. I mean, concave."

"An entrance?" Claire appeared from the storage area at the back of the speeder, followed by another engineer, Trainer, who was carrying two crates and a computer. "Or an exhaust of sorts?"

"Good speculations, both of them." Samantha held the levers firmly. "Anything else?"

"Goddamn it, it's slowing down." Claire took a seat at the console next to Darian. Trainer began hooking the crates to the computer on some empty counter space to her left. "The rotation was a hundred and twenty per minute earlier, and it's declining."

Darian whistled softly. "Huh. Are the other three doing the same? Can we even determine that from here?"

"No. The closer we get to the object, the less reliable our instruments become." Trainer sighed. "Which means we have to rely more on our eyes and ears, and what samples we might gather, than on the computer. Good thing you're flying manually, Samantha. Otherwise, *Speeder One* could have slammed right into it."

"Charming," Samantha muttered. "I'm taking us in closer. Any arguments against that?"

"Not from me. We have to determine what this thing is, and if radiation and space dust are all we have to worry about, we're good."

"Agreed." Claire plugged one of the crates into her computer and placed it next to her console. "I'm going to try to boost our range and clear up any disturbance."

"That'd be great." Samantha glanced at Molly. "I'll need your hands on the controls as well. If we have to get out of here, we can't risk them being sluggish."

"Yes, Chief." Molly gripped her controls with deceptively slender hands. "Ready."

"Give me a new number for the rotations," Samantha ordered as she pushed the controls in a soft semicircle.

"Ninety-eight and slowing," Claire said. "There. How are your readings, Darian?"

Samantha glimpsed Darian sliding her fingers along her console.

"Hey. Whatever you've concocted there seems to work. It's not crystal clear, but it's better."

"Eighty yards. Seventy. Sixty, fifty." Molly's clear voice guided Samantha as she caressed more than gripped the controls.

"Ow, fuck!" Claire called out, startling Samantha, who instinctively relaxed her hold on the levers to avoid creating a disaster.

"What's wrong? Claire...Claire!" Darian caught a slumped-over Claire. "Brett!"

Brett was already behind them. Samantha grasped the controls again and hated that she couldn't see what had just happened. "Report." She barked the order as Molly kept reading their distance from the object.

"Blood pressure 170/100, respiration 20 and shallow, saturation 98%." Brett lifted Claire into his arms. "Unfold the LSC-bed."

In the back, Dollinger was already shifting the seats and creating space for the emergency Life-Support-Care bed.

"I'm putting you down, Chief," Brett said, his voice gentle. "Just stay still."

"My NIEC. It showed me." Claire's hoarse voice was barely audible. "When the…rotations cease…we have to d-dock."

"Twenty yards," Molly said, and Samantha halted the ship.

"Rotations now?" Samantha asked, turning to Darian, whose knitted eyebrows showed her concern for Claire.

"None. It's stopped." Darian ran a hand over her face. "Shit, she scared me. She just went down."

"Molly, take over." Samantha unfastened her harness and got out of her chair in a practiced movement. Hurrying back to the bed, she bent over Claire so she could meet her eyes while Brett was scanning her. "Hey. How are you feeling?"

"Better." Claire's voice was a mere whisper. "Sensory overload, I think."

"How do you mean?" Samantha took Claire's cold, clammy hand.

"I can answer that," Brett said darkly. "The chief's NIEC downloaded a crapload of information in a single instant. Our brains aren't equipped to deal with that amount. I've seen enough crewmembers with migraines from just ordinary usage."

Samantha had heard of people having headaches. "And now?"

"Her vitals are almost back to normal. Chief, I bet you have a hangover of sorts for a few hours." Brett frowned. "Something must be wrong with your NIEC. It's definitely not supposed to do this."

"At least I know we can dock at the black circle," Claire said and waved their hands away as she slowly sat up. "Oh, damn."

Claire gripped the side of the bed in a way that told Samantha she wasn't well. "Easy. Holly will have my head if I put a dent in her chief engineer."

Claire glared at Samantha, but apparently this movement hurt too, as she flinched and squeezed her eyes shut. "I don't have time for this."

"You can still help. If it won't make you worse, can you access the information your NIEC flooded you with?" Samantha could tell her question didn't please Brett, but Claire brightened.

"Yes. Absolutely. But perhaps I need to lean back a bit."

Brett adjusted the bed and pulled a blue blanket over Claire's trembling body. He ran a wand over her forehead, and her features relaxed for the first time since she passed out.

"Ah, better." Claire kept her eyes closed. "Normal docking procedures. When you're ten yards from the hatch, eject the bulkhead tunnel system."

"The what?" Samantha was about to ask for clarification when her NIEC provided her with brand-new information. "Ah, yes. Understood."

"At least you weren't completely flooded and subjected to an overload," Brett muttered and took a seat on a stool by the LSC-bed.

"*Velocity—Speeder One.* Come in. I repeat, *Velocity—Speeder One.* Do you copy?" The voice belonged to Walker, and Samantha took her seat again as Darian replied.

"*Speeder One—Velocity.* We read you loud and clear now."

"Holly here, Darian." The concern in their captain's voice was barely masked. "Report."

"As we neared the object, our external sensors stopped functioning properly, which included coms. We're currently halted twenty yards from it and are about to start the boarding procedure."

After a moment of silence, Holly came back. "Boarding? Explain how that'll be possible."

"Claire added supplemental technology to her console and suffered an episode, well, a fainting spell—"

"Is she all right?" The starkness in Holly's tone made Samantha look over at Darian, whose lips described a perfect "O."

"She has a headache, but her vitals are normal, Captain," Brett said from behind them. "Her NIEC may not function in a safe way."

Another beat and then Holly merely said, "I see."

"So how are you planning to dock with that thing?" Walker came back over the speaker system.

"Claire says she can guide us through it, and I've already gained more knowledge via my NIEC." Samantha gave the bridge crew on the *Velocity* a schematic explanation. "I have a question. Are the other three objects still spinning, or have they stopped as well?"

"We can read the others enough to see that they're spinning, but even if we can communicate with *Speeder One*, we can't scan your object."

"It's aligned with the *Velocity* again, as far as we can judge from our sensors," Samantha said. "We're starting the procedure now, which involves an extendable bulkhead tunnel that I had no idea even existed until a few minutes ago. Darian is documenting everything for your review later, as we can't transmit properly." Samantha nodded at Darian, who held up her trackpad, showing she was prepared.

"Trainer, take my station until we're docked. Then I need you to be my eyes and ears. All right?" Claire asked.

"Of course, Chief." Trainer sat down next to Darian.

"Careful with that computer you hooked up. Not sure what it'll do to anyone's NIEC, malfunctioning or not," Samantha said as more information appeared from her own device. "We're ready to go. Close your space suits. Once Molly has us safely docked, I want Darian, Trainer, Carl, and Dollinger with me." Brett, Molly, and the other security officer would mind the speeder. "Any questions?"

"Geez. Do I have to be in this soap bubble?" Claire groaned. "Freaking incubator for adults."

Samantha turned to look and had to smile. Since it wasn't optimal for a patient on the LSC-bed to be in a closed space suit, a see-through bubble was extended around it. The access ports on the sides did indeed make it look like a huge incubator. "Safety procedures," she said.

"Ha. I see you agree with me." Claire growled, and Samantha understood her frustration.

"We'll keep an open speaker link with *Speeder One* and will be wearing body vids." Samantha opened the hatch to one of the smaller storage units above the helm and took out what looked like thin headbands. Two pin-size cameras sat evenly spaced on the ribbons. "As you know, you'll be able to monitor all four of us, two cameras each, on the screens." Samantha handed them out to the others, who were already suited up. Darian pulled on the ribbon, and the cameras began transmitting immediately.

"I suggest we stick to the front camera only, unless we have a good reason to watch what's going on behind us, or we'll get motion sickness trying to keep up," Claire said, turning on her side, facing the screens. "That okay, Samantha?"

"Absolutely." Samantha closed the last fastening of her space suit and grabbed her helmet. "Once we latch both hatches, you can remove your helmets and the incubator, but not before." All crewmembers had trained on safety protocols during their eight months in space, but Samantha needed to be sure. Turning to her team, she saw they were ready to go.

"Chief?" Molly called from the helm. "I need you to supervise."

"On my way." Samantha moved in behind Molly, who was using the computer to initiate docking. "You're doing great."

"I'm not doing much. This is fully automated, but I'm ready to take over if something goes wrong." Molly kept her gaze on the screens. "The tube is almost fully extended. Nearly there. Now. Docking."

A faint thud indicated that they had contacted the object. Molly slid her fingers over a short magenta line on the helm. "Clamps are engaged. Seal is deployed. Evening out pressure."

"Very good." Samantha straightened. "You have the conn until I return."

"Aye, Chief." Molly remained at the helm, obviously not about to risk missing any alerts or indications by instruments.

Samantha motioned with one hand toward the hatch. "All right. Time to move out."

CHAPTER THIRTEEN

Darian took the lead, followed by Samantha, Carl, Dollinger, and Trainer, connected to each other by silicon-looking cords. Darian was carrying a flashlight as well as an alien sidearm. She missed her old Glock, but projectiles such as bullets were not a good thing in outer space.

The tunnel looked deceptively frail, as if made of aluminum foil. A sponge-like surface provided them with a stable, artificially gravitational area to walk on, but Darian still trod carefully.

The hatch closed behind them, making Trainer yelp. "I knew that was going to happen, but it still startled me."

"Let's hope it'll let us back in," Carl muttered.

"Yes. Let's." Trainer rolled his shoulders. "Call me crazy, but I find this first mission a bit advanced for a space-travel newbie."

"Hm. He's not wrong," Darian said and continued moving toward the hatch on the other end. When they reached it, she pulled out her trackpad and scanned it. The instrument flickered for a few moments, and then a bright-pink circle appeared on the screen. "What the hell?"

"Let me see." Samantha moved closer. She gripped Darian's shoulder firmly and shuddered.

"Not you too?" Darian's heart began to thud painfully as Samantha clung to her.

"No. I'm okay. Just trying to sort out the information." Samantha shook her head as if to jolt her thoughts into place. "Damn, that was confusing."

"What was?" Carl moved closer, and Darian saw how Carl placed a protective hand against Samantha's back.

"I know we're supposed to press the circle to open the hatch, but I saw other things—other symbols—I didn't understand." Squeezing her eyes closed, Samantha then blinked several times. "Ah. Better. Felt a headache coming on, but I'm okay."

"If it happens again or if it gets worse, we're turning back," Darian said.

"All right." Samantha released Darian's shoulder after patting it gently.

"Let's go." Darian pushed a gloved index finger against the circle, and it took a couple of moments, but then the hatch before them split in two, showing complete darkness. Turning on her flashlight, Darian let the beam sweep from one side to the next, and soon it was joined by the others' lights. An empty space extended directly inside the opening, and Darian gingerly stepped into it. Bright, yellow-tinted lights switched on, showing corridors extending in both directions. As soon as they were all inside, the hatch closed behind them.

"Now this isn't creepy at all," Carl said, pulling out his trackpad. "Running basic scans." He moved the device from ceiling to floor and side to side. "I'm not detecting any other life forms."

Trainer did the same, using his trackpad. "The bulkhead's made from a different alloy than that of the *Velocity*, but I see similarities. As you can tell, we have some gravitation in here. Same as the moon back home, approximately. At least we're not bobbing like Ping-Pong balls."

"I have good news too. The air in here is breathable." Dollinger used a bio-chem scanner that resembled a large fork. "No toxins or biohazards, Chief."

Darian hesitated but then unfastened her helmet and pushed it off. She inhaled carefully, and even if the air was stale, it was breathable. "Helmet or no helmet is optional," she said, not about to force anyone to remove theirs if they didn't want to.

Samantha pulled off hers, and so did the others. "Easier to communicate," she murmured while looking around.

Darian hooked her helmet into the strap on her back meant for this purpose. "I suggest we split up. Carl, you, Trainer, and Dollinger go left. Samantha and I will go right."

The men saluted, and Carl detached himself from Samantha's suit.

"Speakers on an open channel to each other and to *Speeder One*. We rendezvous here in no more than an hour." Darian paused, meeting every team member's eyes. "I don't have to tell you to be careful."

Carl shook his head. "No, you don't, but it's still a good reminder. It's easy to get carried away."

"Document everything you come across for Claire, Dollinger, and Trainer to study." Samantha tucked her flashlight away. "Be safe."

"You too, Chief," Carl said and motioned for the other two men. "Let's go."

Darian saw them begin to walk and then turned to Samantha. "You and I in a strange corridor. Feels like the good old days." She started moving and scanned the surface.

"Old and old. It's been about a year since we found the tunnel under Dennamore." Samantha walked one step behind Darian, doing her own scans. "Have you noticed how quiet it is? No hum from a propulsion system."

Darian realized the truth in Samantha's observation. "Not the slightest tremor. I suppose that changes when it's spinning. I hope it doesn't start that with us in here. I don't do well on carousels." She grimaced at old memories of severe nausea at the amusement parks of her childhood.

"I don't think it will. At least, in theory, it should sense that something has docked with it, and it would be logical that this fact prevents the spinning."

"Then again, can we assume that logic in space is a given?" Darian moved her trackpad along the inner bulkhead, but the device showed only "the basics," as Carl had put it. After a while, they came to a ninety-degree turn but still no pieces of technology or entrances.

Once they had made more progress down the new, longer corridor, she felt the trackpad hum with added information. "Hang on." Darian read from the small screen. "Always something. The corridor runs the entire length of this thing. It's a hundred and ten yards long. Height is twelve feet, and it's eight feet wide."

"Considering the size of this contraption, it would suggest at least one more deck, or something else, above us." Samantha gazed up at the ceiling. "I don't see any pipes or manifolds. Must be in the walls."

As they neared the halfway mark of the corridor, both their trackpads blinked a bright green. Only seconds later, their speakers buzzed.

"Carl here. We've reached a hatch of sorts." Carl's excitement was undeniable.

Darian scanned the inner bulkhead and then smiled. "So, it would seem, have we."

"We're at the fifty-yard mark," Carl said.

"Same here." Samantha ran her fingertips against the barely noticeable outline of the hatch.

Darian couldn't see an obvious way to open it and didn't intend to do so half-cocked. "Darian to *Speeder One* and Carl," she said into her speaker. "Carl. Helmets back on. We're not taking any risks. Claire, we've reached the center of the vessel. There's a hatch. Samantha and I are entering."

"Helmets are on," Carl said after a few moments.

"Noted. We see it on the cams. Looks like Carl and his crew have found its counterpart on their side," Claire said, sounding intrigued.

"Keep your eyes trained on stuff we might otherwise miss, Claire." Darian made sure the seal of Samantha's helmet was engaged, and Samantha returned the favor, then ran her trackpad around the hatch. Another pink circle appeared on its screen again. "Pink circle here, Carl."

"Ours is blue," Carl said.

"Let us go in first. We'll be able to judge if the space behind it is safe, and if it stretches over to you." Darian waited for Carl to acknowledge and then pressed the circle like before. The hatch slid open, disappearing into the bulkhead. The pitch-blackness didn't surprise her. She used her flashlight to make sure a floor actually existed beyond the tall threshold. What looked like a fire-engine-red carpet did surprise Darian, and she stepped inside, the soles of her boots sinking into the surface. Samantha followed her, and, like earlier, the hatch closed.

"I'm trying to not let these prison-like actions of the hatches get to me," Samantha said.

"Yeah. It's a bit creepy." Darian had barely gotten the words out when new lights switched on. "Holy crap." She gaped.

"Chief?" Carl said. "I'm watching you on my trackpad. Is this what I think it is?"

"I want to know too," Claire said, sounding fully alert.

Darian moved in farther, not sure if this was a smart idea, but she and Samantha were the ones actually seeing the unexpected sight. "If by that you mean if it looks like a huge pool filled with water, that's correct."

Samantha joined her, busy scanning. "It's ninety point five yards long and twenty yards wide. Content is H2O and…a mineral oil of some kind."

Darian used her trackpad to scan the total space. "I'd say this pool fills almost the length and width of this…damn, I keep calling it vessel, not knowing if that's the correct term…well, of this vessel." She looked up. "There are what look like walkways every ten yards or so. I'll make my way over and see if I can spot your hatch, Carl."

"I'll join you," Samantha said, but Darian shook her head.

"No. I want you to remain here and continue the scans. Send whatever you find back to Claire."

"Yes, please do," Claire said over the speaker. "I'll force Brett to push a computer into the incubator."

Darian stopped and turned back to Samantha. She was fairly certain she would be able to climb up to the closest walkway and make her way to the other side, but there were no certainties in space. Not caring if the others were seeing them on their respective screens, she pulled Samantha in for a quick, firm hug. Tipping her head back, she wished she weren't wearing a helmet, as she wanted to kiss Samantha, but a hug would have to do.

"Be careful," Samantha said quietly. She ran her gloved hand along the visor on Darian's helmet. "Okay?"

"Okay." Darian let go and walked over to the grid that seemed to be placed there in lieu of a ladder. Tucking away her trackpad, she began to climb, mindful that she had barely any sensation in her hands and feet, thanks to the suit. When she reached the top, she looked back at Samantha, who wasn't scanning a damn thing. Instead, she seemed transfixed by Darian's progress. "So far, so good." Darian sighed and looked at the "walkway." It wouldn't be easy to maneuver on. Most of it was created like a grid, with only parts of it clad with metal sheets. Darian debated whether to crawl or walk over the narrow—only two-feet-wide—space, which lacked a railing. If the vessel began spinning or moved in an unexpected way, she could tumble into the water below, and what that could do to her, and to her suit, was anybody's guess.

Swallowing hard, she pushed herself forward on all fours. "All right—here goes."

Chapter Fourteen

Samantha watched in disbelief how Darian pushed up onto the narrow structure that was hardly a walkway. Walkways had railings, for one thing. Samantha barely dared to blink, as if taking her eyes off Darian for a single moment would cause her to plummet from its side.

A crackling noise from her speaker made her jump. "Samantha here," she said, tapping it.

"This…Crow." A voice spoke through a strange sound distortion.

"Captain? Hello?" Samantha moved back to be able to follow Darian's progress. Darian was still walking determinedly and perfectly balanced. Samantha tapped her speaker again. "Holly? Are you reading this?"

"Yes. Barely. Energy…ave…" Holly said before the speaker went silent.

"Samantha to team. Did anyone else capture what the captain was saying?" Samantha couldn't back off any longer, and Darian was starting to reach the point where she'd be out of sight.

"I heard her, but she couldn't receive," Claire said. The sound quality wobbled, but her words came through loud and clear. "You all need to brace yourselves, no matter where you are in the vessel."

"What?" Samantha blinked. Then she began to run toward the ladder. "What's going on?"

After a few seconds of complete silence, Carl's voice came over the speaker. "The audio is skipping. I heard Claire. An energy wave's approaching."

Samantha gripped the ladder harder as she was climbing. "Carl. Don't wait for Darian. Get inside the door. It has to lead into here somewhere. She's high up on a structure and—" Desperate, Samantha reached the top of the ladder and gripped the narrow, long stretch of metal sheets. "Darian. Hold on. Energy wave!"

They had come across energy waves while aboard the *Velocity,* but the ship was constructed to ride out such storms. Here, they had no idea what such a wave would do to the small vessel.

"I heard," Darian called out. She crouched and appeared to grip the edges of the walkway.

Samantha did the same as the vessel lurched under them, rising as if trying to throw them all out the airlock. Unable to stop herself from crying out, Samantha gripped the metal bars as hard as she could. In front of her, she saw Darian, about ten yards away, clinging to the walkway, her arms and legs wrapped around it.

"Carl, where are you?" Samantha yelled, hoping her speaker hadn't closed the open setting.

"We're through. A bit of a maze of corridors, but—"

Another wave, stronger than the first, jolted the vessel, which now began to roll. The water sloshed beneath the walkway.

Samantha groaned as her aching fingers began to lose their grip. She was slipping inside the gloves and debated whether to get on top of the structure, though afraid to let go long enough to do so.

A shriek from Darian's direction made Samantha forget her own fears and push herself closer. "Dar!" She blinked as the walkway was empty—no sign of Darian. "Darian!" Samantha's cry drowned out what Carl was saying the first time he tried.

"Samantha, we're here!"

"She's fallen off, Carl. Where is she? Where is she?" Close to full panic now, Samantha had to bite the inside of her cheek to not lose it completely and stared down into the water. "What the…?" Barely able to close her eyes, she watched the water slosh up against her, but she didn't get wet. Instead, what had to be a force field kept it in place. It certainly hadn't been there before, when she'd scanned the water.

"Unnnggg…" Samantha heard a staccato groan over her speaker.

"Darian! Where are you?" Samantha slid farther along the walkway. At the other end, Carl's head popped up. "Can you see her, Carl?"

"No. Did she go into the water? Hey, what the hell?" Carl was staring at the water that splashed against the force field. "Did she go in before that thing turned on?" He sounded so shocked, Samantha almost lost her grip.

"I just heard her." Not caring about anything but finding Darian, Samantha hooked a leg around the edge of the walkway and slid over to the other side, praying she wouldn't fall. She bent her neck backward and stared with tear-filled eyes along the bottom of the walkway. At first, she couldn't see anything, but just as she heard another groan, she saw Darian.

The woman who held Samantha's heart was hanging upside down, her head and shoulders against the force field that crackled around her. "Oh, God, no! No, no, no!" Samantha heaved herself up and began crawling along the structure. Soon the hard edges of the bars had made her knees raw, but as long as they didn't penetrate her suit, she didn't care. She just wanted to get to Darian. "Carl, she's there, closer to you than me. Underneath."

Carl repeated Samantha's maneuver and then started crawling at a much faster speed. He waved at one of his team to follow him, and when Samantha reached them, they had put their hands on Darian but weren't moving.

"Pull her up! Why aren't you doing anything?" Samantha reached down and found Darian's ankle. "Darian? Can you hear me?"

"She's unconscious." Carl was pale. "I just briefed Brett. We need to stabilize her neck and spine before we pull her up."

Samantha forced air in and out of her lungs at a stable pace rather than hyperventilate. They were right.

"Her vitals are okay," Trainer said, and only now did Samantha realize he was the one who had joined Carl.

"But she could be wounded." Samantha thought fast. She was carrying one of their med-kits, and Carl had the other. She sat up on the rocking walkway and pushed it off her. Pulling out a neck-spine brace and then a thin wire, she unfolded it and hooked the long, rigid brace to her harness. "We're tying the tether to the walkway, and then you two are going to hold on to my feet."

"Please, Chief, let me—" Trainer stopped when she quickly raised her hand. "No. You're both stronger than I am. You can pull us up. I just have to secure her back and neck first. Here are the wires to the brace. Make sure to balance it as much as possible once I've attached it to her. Have Dollinger report to Claire and Brett."

"All right." Carl climbed past Samantha, tugging on her harness and the wire before she slipped over the edge. Strong hands grabbed her legs just beneath her knees, and other hands held onto her harness.

"Okay. Lower me." Samantha held on tight to the neck-spine brace, which she couldn't drop. Carl also carried one, but if she had waited for his, they would have wasted valuable time.

Studying Darian as the men lowered her, Samantha saw no obvious injuries, but a lot could be wrong internally. If they could get Darian back to the shuttle, Brett would be able to stabilize just about anything before they returned to the *Velocity*.

"Sam..antha..." Darian's slurred voice made Samantha jerk, but she was almost in place.

"I'm here. Don't worry. We'll get you out of here." Samantha called up to the men. "She's conscious. Push me farther to my left." She swayed sideways. Cautiously, she wrapped her arm around Darian's leg, where her foot was stuck on the walkway.

"Ahh!" Darian cried out. "My foot."

"I'm sorry." Samantha steadied herself while trying not to hurt Darian. "I'm going to attach the neck-spine brace to you, all right? It might hurt some, but we have to get you out of here." Samantha didn't like the crackling sound the force field was making against Darian's helmet. It could be compromising her space suit.

"I thought I was going into the water," Darian whispered. "That I had traveled through space only to drown on my first mission."

"You'll be all right." Samantha wrapped her arms around Darian and tugged at the straps. Once she had attached one firmly around Darian's chest, she began to breathe easier. With one strap around the stomach and four around the stuck leg, she had to settle for one around the flailing leg. She wrapped the last two around Darian's head and secured her arms close to her body. "When you pull her up, be gentle.

I need to come up once you have her almost at the edge. Her foot is stuck underneath the structure, and it might be fractured." Samantha was sure it was, as the angle of it made her sick.

"Got it, Chief," Trainer said. "Here. Pain meds." He reached down at a precarious angle and handed Samantha an infuser. "That's got to hurt."

"No painkillers," Darian muttered. "Need to stay sharp."

"You'll be plenty sharp, Dar. I promise you, once we've freed your foot, that you're going to be glad we insisted. Please." Samantha bent and turned her head to look into Darian's eyes. Appalled at Darian's pale-gray complexion, she found the port under the helmet fastener and shoved the infuser against it, making sure she reached the skin. "Dar?"

"All right." Darian groaned and then relaxed instantly once the medication reached her bloodstream. "Okay. You're right—again. Damn it."

"I'll remind you that you said that." Samantha signaled the men to start pulling.

Darian still cried out, despite the potent pain medication. Samantha wanted to tell the guys to stop, but they had to get Darian up and out of danger before the vessel performed some other crazy move. After Darian was suspended parallel to the walkway, Carl and Trainer secured the wires and pulled Samantha up to Darian's level.

"How's the foot?" Carl asked, trying to peer through the grid of the walkway.

"Cut it off," Darian said, slurring her consonants.

"We'll do no such thing." Samantha pulled herself closer. "Actually, if I can unbuckle her space boot, pull it off, and give it to you, Carl, we can attach it once she's up. We need to keep her suit intact until she's back on *Speeder One*."

"Got it." Carl saluted with his right index fingers before grabbing the wires again. "Ready on our end."

Samantha pressed the small metal clasps on Darian's right boot, and her foot slipped right out.

"Fuck!" Darian seemed to arch against the neck-spine brace. "Please, get me out of here."

"You're free now. Hoist her up." Samantha pushed her away, which hurt her as she wanted only to hold Darian close and protect her. "There you go. Carefully."

Carl and Trainer pulled the neck-spine brace up over the edge, and when Samantha saw they had made it, she barked her next order. "Secure her left leg properly, then get me up. We have to carry her over to the speeder right away." She handed the boot to the men.

"I hear ya', Chief," Carl murmured and tugged at Samantha's wire. "Mind that edge. It's sharper than it looks. We don't want you to be the next to fall."

"No kidding." Samantha's arms were trembling when she tried to help heave herself over the edge. Once she was up, lying on her stomach, she looked at Darian. "How is she?"

"She's loopy," Darian replied. "And you can use your usual name for me. Dar. Darling. Either of those." She hummed something inaudible.

"I gave her one more shot," Trainer said apologetically. "Her vitals showed she was about to go into shock."

"Aha. Good." Samantha might have been embarrassed at any other given time, but right now, she just wanted Darian to be safe and taken care of. "We have to get her back, and then I'll return to go through whatever technology—"

"No need, Chief," an unexpected voice said. "Dollinger and I are on it, and we can use Carl too. We're already downloading information." Claire poked her head up at Dollinger's side of the walkway. "And before you get all cranky about my being here, I'm doing tons better—definitely better than Darian. Besides, I brought help. Brett came with me."

Relieved at the last sentence, Samantha knew better than to waste time. "All right. Let's get her off this damn walkway." She crawled after the men who were pushing and pulling the board. Dollinger and Claire steadied it as they lowered it onto the deck, and when Samantha finally did lose her footing on the way down, Trainer caught her.

"Thank you." Samantha shot Claire a brief glance while she hurried over to Darian. "You look pale."

"I have the mother of all headaches, but that's all it is. I'm going to work as fast as I can with these two." Claire motioned at Carl and Dollinger. "Trainer and Brett will carry Darian."

"Just give me my stupid boot. I must have lost it." Darian's eyes rolled as she seemed to try to focus on them. "I can walk."

"Not likely." Samantha gently placed a hand on the swollen foot. "Brett, can you do anything about this? I want her to wear the boot, if possible, when we go through the tunnel to the speeder."

"Sure." Brett pulled out a short, fat wand, made from a red metallic alloy, and pushed it against the top of Darian's foot, which made her tremble.

"Now that's downright mean." Darian glared at no one in particular.

"Just hang tight." Brett kept it going for half a minute and then switched to do the same to the sole of Darian's foot, and finally the back of her heel. "How's it now?"

"Hey. You're not so bad after all." Darian smiled. "I think I really can walk—"

"Eh, no. You get a free ride. I believe Chief Pike's coming with you." Brett put his instruments back, and then he and Trainer lifted the neck-spine brace after he put Darian's boot back on.

"I would think so. I always want her right by my side. You know. Close." Darian sighed and closed her eyes. "Like a cradle," she said and waved her fingertips like a discreet music conductor. When she remained quiet for a minute, Samantha realized Darian was fast asleep. She was still pale but at least not gray. Carrying both their gear, she was starting to feel her own aches and pains but kept pace with the men. Once she saw the docking port, she breathed easier. Darian was obviously too open when she was high on medication, but she wasn't wrong.

Samantha belonged at Darian's side and vice versa.

CHAPTER FIFTEEN

The conference room one was filled with not only the senior crew, but their immediate subordinates. Holly sat at the end of the table, drumming her fingers impatiently against her leg out of sight. They were still waiting for Claire, Carl, Dollinger, and Trainer to join them. The team had been back for four hours, and nobody on the team had stopped to eat or rest.

Brett had taken Darian to the infirmary and worked on her fractured ankle with Raoul. Samantha hadn't left Darian's side until five minutes ago, but instead worked on her computer by the LSC-bed.

Molly, Samantha's copilot, had proved herself worthy of the trust placed in her and was now overseeing the post-mission maintenance of *Speeder One*. Holly made a mental note to enter into her official record how pleased she was with the young woman.

Rapid steps announced the missing crewmembers before they pushed through the door.

"Good. We're all here, except Darian. Now, we're all eager to be briefed." Holly nodded at Claire. She had already learned the basics of Claire's findings, but she had a lot of questions that she hoped the four new arrivals could shed some light on.

"Same goes here, Captain." Claire skipped the usual protocol, which suggested she should stand when giving a briefing. Claire was evidently still tired after her ordeal with the NIEC issues on *Speeder One*.

"First of all, it took us an extra hour because we struggled with the language of the computers on the vessel. And we can stop calling it, or its counterparts, vessels. They're not. The best term we've come up with in English is 'rig.'"

"Rig?" Walker leaned back farther in his chair. "In what capacity?"

"Think sailing." Claire pulled out her trackpad, and the large screen across the table from Holly came to life. "Here's a quick sketch." Claire used a marker on the screen and remained in her chair. "This is the *Velocity*." A bright-green dot pointed to a familiar 3D outline of the ship. "These are the four rigs." Blue dots indicated the four contacts on either side of them. "This is the location of the internal casings we found in the crawl space of engineering." Yellow dots appeared close together in the aft part of deck nine. "This was all we knew when we set out to explore one of the rigs. It turned out to be more perilous than we counted on, as the damn energy wave jolted it, sending our chief of security flying off a walkway. Once she was taken care of, Carl, Dollinger, Trainer, and I continued to work on the two computer consoles in the area where the water was kept. I think you've all seen pictures of the water, both when the force field was engaged and not? Good." Claire cleared her throat. "The water isn't entirely pure. It contains an unknown mineral oil, which suggests we have to expand the periodic table. Whether it's to prevent corrosion or lubricate the mechanics behind the pool, I'm not sure yet, but either choice seems logical.

"As I mentioned earlier, we had problems with the language of the computers. If it had been entirely alien, that wouldn't have been a surprise, but the language wasn't unfamiliar. However…it was different, and our NIECs, not just mine, had a problem understanding it completely. It was as if we had pieces of the puzzle missing." Claire changed the image on the screen, showing a full page of alien letters or signs. "Check this out. We found every third or fourth letter completely different from the language of our ancestors."

Holly read through the rows, from right to left, bottom to top, frowning. Claire hadn't exaggerated. "Have you managed to decipher any of the unknown letters?" She looked at the team of four.

"It took us a while, but eventually, we got lucky." Claire motioned to Carl, who rose and opened the door, waving at someone outside. A young girl stepped inside, looking nervous. She wasn't in uniform and was no more than fifteen, if that. "This is Belle. Her mother works in engineering, and Belle was visiting her after school. Once I put the text up on our main screen, it became obvious to Belle's mom that her daughter could read most of it, as long as she was wearing her TAG. As soon as she removed that, she just saw strange, unfamiliar signs, like the rest of us. I tried her TAG, and so did several others, including her mother, but it did nothing for us. In combination with Belle, it did a lot. Without them, we'd still be struggling."

Whatever Holly had expected, this wasn't it. She studied Belle, who stood next to Claire, and realized only belatedly that she was making the child even more uncomfortable. "Take a seat, Belle," she said, hoping she didn't sound too harsh. She still had to calm down from having worried about Claire and forcing herself to keep working and not let her concern show. Even if Claire seemed fine now, Holly didn't trust the clearly malfunctioning NIEC to not do irreparable damage the next time it acted up. "Please, continue."

"Carl. Your turn." Claire sat back after patting Belle's arm.

"As Claire said, we had the text up, and no matter how we tried using our translator software, we couldn't get it to make sense. That's when Belle and her mom came up to us and offered to help. Belle began reading the document like the rest of us read our ancestors' language when we first began. A bit hesitant, but once she settled on what the signs meant, she kept going faster and faster. Trainer was already recording everything, and that way Belle didn't have to repeat herself. Saved time." Carl pushed his black mop of hair back. "As it turned out, what we found by finally understanding the data didn't make it easier to grasp its meaning at first."

Holly had to force herself to remain seated. Filled with nervous energy, she wished she could have had more than a few minutes over the speaker with Claire earlier. What the hell was wrong with her? But she couldn't allow herself to become attached to a crewmember on a personal level. She would be too tempted to refuse to send Claire into a dangerous situation, to keep her safe and thus endanger someone else instead.

"Let's begin with the water pools, or tanks. Force fields keep the water inside the pools when the rigs spin. Or, like today, if energy waves jolt them. They function like gyroscopes. Granted, we haven't scanned or visited the other three rigs, but they're most likely exactly the same." Carl nodded at Trainer.

"Exactly. We ran diagnostics of the casings in the crawl spaces in engineering and could tell they are exact miniatures of the ones in space. They too spun when their larger counterparts did."

Claire took over again. "Most remarkable is how Belle came upon the words 'solar sails' over and over in the documents. She read through at least 50 percent of the data we collected, and the term came up many times."

"This sounds familiar somehow," Walker said. "I've read about this in theory, back on Earth."

"So have I," Claire said. "As a sci-fi nerd, I always loved popular science, and this is where it gets even more interesting. The term 'magnetic sail' also kept appearing in the data."

"Please share what these sails are and how they differ from solar sails too," Holly asked. The short brief she'd received earlier hadn't been this detailed.

"Scientists on Earth have theorized about solar sails, but apparently, our ship has functioning ones. Or will have, once we're able to deploy them. Using the radiation pressure of sunlight, these sails provide propulsion. As if that's not spectacular enough, they are apparently doing double duty as a magnetic sail, which uses a static magnetic field to deflect charged particles radiated by stars as a plasma wind. Between the two systems, combined with the *Velocity*'s propulsion system, the ship's speed will increase more than tenfold."

Philber looked up from his notepad and tapped the back of his pencil against the table. "Why hasn't this technology appeared until now? Why haven't the NIECs belonging to you engineers and scientists indicated their existence in the first place? What does this have to do with you being unable to decipher alien letters?" He looked angry, which was his standard expression when he was deeply concerned.

"Glad you asked," Claire said and sighed. "The ship has to find itself in a less dense part of space for this system to work. The ship can handle the asteroid belts and meteors we encounter when on regular ISD. These sails are thin, and even if they can filter space dust without a problem, a meteor, or an asteroid, would irreparably damage them, and the ship…and us."

"As for the unknown signs and the NIECs," Trainer said, "we think the answers to those concerns are linked. Remember, Belle's not wearing a NIEC, yet somehow, she could decipher the signs. Carl has an interesting theory."

Holly motioned for Carl to continue.

"I talked this over with Claire because she's the only one who's even more into sci-fi and fantasy than I am."

A few of the people around the table snickered, and Carl's cheeks turned red.

"Hey. I don't see any of you kids doing the kind of job Carl does." Philber growled, and those among the subordinate crew who had found Carl's words funny quieted instantly. Having a grumpy old guy in the senior crew had its advantages, Holly thought, not for the first time. Kept some of the young hawks in check.

"Anyway, I'm not saying we can find explanations in science fiction, but reading it does influence your way of thinking. I couldn't comprehend why we suddenly didn't understand or know about certain technology or couldn't read the alien language of our ancestors, which is second nature to most of us by now." He grinned at one of the science officers who had laughed. "Even you, Noah." It was the other man's turn to color.

"What did you come up with?" Walker asked.

"That's just it. I didn't. I thought of one elaborate idea after another, but nothing made sense, until I gave up and went to the mess hall and grabbed my daily coffee. Perhaps it was the caffeine. I took a note from Philber's book and pulled out a pencil and drew on a napkin. Mostly I just stated what I didn't know." Carl stood and slid his fingers along the console to the main screen. "Like this. We don't understand these signs. Our NIECs don't recognize them either. We didn't know about the technology in the crawl space or the rigs surrounding the ship. Our NIECs hadn't taught us to even search for any of them." Carl placed his bullet points to the left on the screen and then pulled out his trackpad. "First point, not understanding the signs. They're not our ancestors' language, though sometimes they resemble what we've learned from our NIECs. The fact that our NIECs don't fully recognize them supports my theory. Also, we had no clue about the technology. If another alien race, or species, installed it on the ship, that would account for the language mystery as well."

"But what about Belle?" Camilla smiled at the young girl and then returned her gaze to Carl.

"That will take even more wild speculations, but what if her DNA shows markers from yet another alien race?" Carl hesitated. "Or a mix."

"You're saying that two alien races landed on Earth at the same time? On the same ship? That sounds farfetched," Trainer said, not unkindly. "We haven't found any such evidence in the old journal or any database."

"I know. These are educated guesses at best, but nothing I or any of the other scientists or engineers have come up with can explain what we're looking at."

Holly raised her hand. "All right. Do we know enough about the sails to use them? To shave off a tenth of our journey from now on would mean a lot to everyone. Not to mention those who have family and friends waiting for their return home." She let her gaze linger on Claire.

Claire raised her trackpad to another screen. "Once we broke the code on most of the signs, thanks to Belle, we found blueprints that we actually *can* read. As soon as we saw these, our NIECs were back on board." She grimaced, and Holly guessed that Claire still wasn't pleased with her own NIEC's performance. Making a mental note to talk about this problem with Claire in private later, she walked up to the screen. Holly's own NIEC absorbed the lines and signs easily, and it took her only a few minutes to learn the basics of the solar-magnetic sails.

"This is unfathomable." Holly motioned to the screen. "How could our sensors not notice when the rigs detached from the ship and moved to their position?"

Claire stood and joined her. She placed a hand on the wall, making Holly realize that she hadn't entirely recuperated, no matter what she said. "Because this is a fully automated function, I think. Also, each rig has shielding around it to protect other pieces of technology from its electromagnetic fields, so the sensors ignored them and/or were blind to them."

"And the casings in the crawl spaces?" Walker asked.

"Same goes for those. They're shielded, apart from the pin-prick holes on either side, where they communicate with the rigs." Claire pulled up specs for the casings. "I'm sending all of you this material." Returning to her seat, she sat down with a thud, proving she truly wasn't feeling well.

"All right," Holly said. "I need all hands on this. Commander Walker will put you on a duty roster to find out as much as you possibly can. I want to know if this system will harm humans, if we can deploy it safely, and if not, how do we redeploy the rigs and continue as we were before we had problems with the propulsion system? Samantha, you, Claire, and Carl will head this study up, including me. Any questions?"

Camilla raised her hand. "What do we tell the rest of the crew?"

"I see no reason not to be transparent," Holly said. "We're all on this adventure together, and everyone has a right to know what we're working on when it involves something that can be either an incredibly good thing or something of a greater challenge. I place that assignment in your capable hands, Camilla. Everyone here will set aside any time required to answer your questions."

"Thank you, Captain."

Holly was about to dismiss the crew when Raoul raised a hand. "I have a question. I have everyone's DNA samples and bloodwork stored in the infirmary. Do I have permission to examine them for potential unknown alien markers?"

Holly tapped her lower lip. "Good question. I almost gave you permission without another thought—but privacy is important. I suggest such examinations be voluntary. I doubt many of the crew will object, but some of the passengers might. Why not send out a form to everyone's computer and study only the ones returning a favorable response within a certain timeline."

"Understood," Raoul said.

They always tried to balance the greater good against the right of the individual. Holly had discussed the subject with Camilla and Raoul on several occasions, and they agreed to respect an individual's freedom of choice unless the situation involved survival, like a virus or contamination.

"Nothing else for now? Well, I'll expect reports every hour on the hour from now on. Dismissed." Holly stood and gestured discreetly for Claire to remain back.

After the others had left the conference room, Claire approached her slowly. Tucking her computer into her over-the-shoulder bag, she leaned against the table. "I know, I know. I'm going to let Raoul scan me again. Still got that damn headache."

"That's a good idea, but it's not enough." Holly pulled up a chair and motioned for Claire to sit down. Once Claire slid onto it, again obviously too tired to do so in a coordinated way, Holly took a seat in her own chair and rolled it closer, making them sit directly in front of each other. "Your NIEC is malfunctioning, and I think it's hurting you. I haven't gone over your head and spoken to Raoul, but I will if you don't mention this situation to him. Who knows? The NIEC could harm your brain indefinitely. What if it causes a stroke, or seizures?" Holly nearly added how devastated she would be if something happened to Claire but stopped herself. This was not about her but about Claire's health—her *life*.

"You're being serious." Claire gripped the armrests hard. "You'd go to Raoul and tell him I can't perform my duties anymore?" Whether she was furious or hurt, Claire's dark eyes filled with tears.

Taken aback, Holly shook her head and placed a hand on Claire's knee. "That's not what I said, or meant, at all."

"But you—"

"Listen." Holly squeezed Claire's knee. "My concern for your performance doesn't factor in. Yes, you're invaluable as my chief engineer, but that's not why I'm desperate to have you level with Raoul. Your health matters more than anything. We don't gain anything by playing ostrich and pretending that things aren't bad."

"But I can't work without my NIEC. If he takes it away from me, I'm useless." Claire raised her voice. "I've tried to retain as much as I possibly can, but it's a damn big ship, and then, of course, it has its fucking secrets...like solar sails and text that isn't even our kind of alien!" Tears overflowed, and Claire pressed a hand to her forehead. "Ow."

"Claire. Please." Holly recalled when they were only regular inhabitants of Dennamore and getting to know each other while trying to solve an irresistible mystery. She had been drawn to Claire from the moment they met, and now, seeing her in pain and panic, she felt the captaincy melt away. "Hey." Sliding off her chair, Holly knelt between Claire's knees and took her trembling hands. "You've done a remarkable job after you got back from the rig. Now it's time to just look after yourself for a few moments and let Raoul make sure you're okay. And just so you know, you can never be useless to me. Ever."

Claire squeezed Holly's hands and raised her gaze to meet hers. "What if the NIEC can't be mended?"

"Is that your worst fear?"

"Yes." Claire spoke without hesitation.

"Then let me tell you my worst fear. I can't imagine not having you here. You're part of this crew, the senior staff, but most of all, you're one of the few people I can call a close friend." The half-truth in that statement made Holly's stomach tighten. As captain, she could never allow herself to tell Claire she felt more than friendship. You didn't want to take a woman to your quarters and get to know all her intimate secrets if friendship was all you were after. Backpedaling her thoughts so fast she nearly grew dizzy, Holly allowed herself to cup Claire's tear-stained cheek. "I'll help you find a solution for your NIEC no matter what the problem is, no matter how long it takes. That's a promise."

"R-really?" Claire drew a deep breath and then one more.

"Really." Wiping at new tears that dislodged from Claire's eyelashes, Holly smiled. "You know I'm a stickler for rules and regulations. That goes for promises made as well." Holly let go and pushed back up into her chair.

"I know that." Claire straightened her back. "All right. Might as well get it over with. Raoul and I will brief you on the outcome later. That's a promise too." She stood, looking less wobbly. "Thanks, Holly."

"Very good. We'll figure things out." Also getting to her feet, Holly found she could exhale for the first time in several minutes. As she watched Claire make her way around the table and out the door, she ached inside. Claire's fears were valid. What would happen if they lost their chief engineer? And what would losing her usefulness, her skills, do to Claire?

No matter what, that couldn't happen.

Chapter Sixteen

D arling, how are you?"
Darian looked up from where she sat in one of the infirmary beds used for patients that no longer needed life-saving care. "Gran!" She put her computer down. "I was just thinking about you."

"Same here." Gran walked over and pulled up a stool. As graceful as ever, she slid onto it and bent to kiss Darian's forehead. "I'm sure I give you terrible dèjá vu by nagging you like you're a teenager, but should you be working? You had a severe concussion."

"I know. Raoul isn't happy, but right now, we need all hands on deck." Darian closed her computer to appease her grandmother. "I was allowed to listen in on the meeting earlier but not weigh in. Just take notes. I did. Copious. Just sent them to the entire senior crew."

"Yes. I heard a ping on my trackpad." Gran lifted the blanket at the level of Darian's feet. "And your ankle?"

"Fused. I'll be on light duty for a week or so, and if Raoul's scans are clear then, I'll return to my normal routine."

"You've hurt yourself several times the last year. Falling down that hole that led us to the ship and dislocating your shoulder..." Gran shook her head. "If I wasn't already completely gray, it would have happened then. Or the time you took a bullet in LA. Neither of your jobs has been very safe."

"I know. But given the circumstances, this job is the safer one, from an injury point of view." Darian took Gran's hand, as always amazed at how slender it was. Raoul's technique with the alien medicines and instruments kept Gran's rheumatoid arthritis and heart condition at bay. When it came to sitting at a loved one's hospital bed, Darian had done that many times the last ten years, with Gran. "How are you doing? You have a lot on your plate, being on the team that keeps crew and passengers informed."

"We've drawn up a plan. The previous crew on this ship had a lot going for them, but they weren't that big on planning for potential mental-health issues. Or if they did, they didn't leave that information for us to find."

"I wish we knew more about them, on a personal level. It might help solve the mystery of the discrepancies regarding the solar-magnetic sails and the signs we can't read—hey, wait." Sitting straight up in bed, Darian winced as the headache she was trying to get rid of pierced her skull. "Ow. Crap."

"Careful!" Gran stood and cupped Darian's cheeks. "I'm getting Raoul."

"No, no. Not necessary. I want you to ask Carl to find the box he and I discovered in the library archive back home. It's not very big and is full of small scrolls. We opened one of them and realized it contained biographies of crewmembers, but they had completely slipped my mind. I meant to give them to you, to look into…" Darian groaned and rubbed her temple.

"But it's been one thing after another. I understand. I'll ask Carl to get them to me and see if I can uncover something useful. You're going to convalesce until you can move without wincing."

"But I'm needed." Darian knew Gran was right. She could never stay still very long and was rapidly starting to sound like her teenage self. "But I will get better. As long as you guys keep me informed, I will."

"We will. And remember that you trained your staff well—and you have Nate, and Geoff too, in a pinch, to head tactical if need be."

"All right. I'm convinced. I'll try for a nap after I complete the extended DNA-scan permission thingy. Have you signed it yet?" Darian pulled up the document on her computer.

"I have." Gran looked away, her eyebrows pulled together in an unusual frown.

"It's not mandatory." Darian dislodged her trackpad from the computer and clicked the document with her identification.

"Of course not, and I'm fine with it. Truly." Gran's blinding smile showed that she was overcompensating, which was not like her either. "I'll let you sleep a bit, darling. I'll stop by later and bring Geoff with me."

Darian nodded and pushed the computer over to a side table. She was relieved that Gran and Geoff Walker had found each other, especially if anything happened to her. Walker would never abandon Gran, no matter what. He had told Darian that he was living the dream with Gran and being aboard the ship with family, friends, and neighbors. Curling up against the pillow, Darian allowed sleep to overcome her, hoping it would last only half an hour, at most.

❖

Claire knew when she was beaten. Having been on her feet for eighteen hours, she handed engineering over to a subordinate, instructing him to wake her if the *Velocity* did something out of the ordinary that they couldn't handle. Tomorrow afternoon, they planned to attempt to deploy the sails, and in the meantime, all teams were busy reading the translated material. Young Belle was quickly becoming famous on the ship for her ability to read and translate the signs.

"Claire?" Holly approached from behind as Claire headed toward her quarters, directly opposite Holly's, and they stopped between their respective doors.

"Long day," Claire said. "And before you say it, I know I pushed myself the last few hours, but I figured I'd get better quality sleep if I made certain I didn't miss something when briefing my subordinate. Trainer and I are both off duty, and it wasn't fair to send Sike into the fray without making sure. He was in the conference room, but we didn't cover every minute detail of engineering specific details there."

"Good thinking. And, that said, I can see you're propping up the bulkhead, which makes my idea redundant." Holly sent a pointed glance at the hand Claire used to support herself.

"What idea?" Claire thought about straightening up, but she was exhausted and jittery.

"Chamomile tea. Sweetened. No caffeine, as much as it pains me. I was going to offer you a mug, but you look like you could fall asleep against the bulkhead."

"Yeah, perhaps." Claire studied the tense skin around Holly's almond-shaped eyes, their beautiful shape and dark-green irises, probably a mix from the Asian part of her heritage. "You know what. I think some of the treatment is creating some lingering jitters. If you don't mind having the tea in my quarters, I'd love some."

Holly's shoulders lowered an inch. "I'll go change and then bring the tea over."

"Great. I'll do the same. Later." Claire's speaker unlocked her door automatically, and she pressed the sensor to open. Slipping inside, she pushed off her uniform and tossed it into the recycling chute. Not having to do laundry was one of the many, many perks of being a space-faring adventurer, at least on this ship. The reproducer scanned every garment, even their private clothes. Claire giggled when she remembered how they had used one of Walker's beloved flannel shirts as a test subject, much to his dismay, and sent it through the reproducer. She entered the narrow cleansing tube that engulfed her like an embrace and began spraying her down. Walker's shirt had emerged in the maintenance section, not only looking brand-new, but also with his name stamped inside the collar. Each crewmember had three uniforms, all marked. Their space suits and boots adjusted to any length and body size, and there were plenty to go around. Claire had heard the younger children called the space suits "smurf-wear," which she found hilarious.

Stepping out of the tube, clean and dry, she pulled her hair into a looser type of braid, which made sleeping more comfortable, and opted for her favorite sweats, light gray. Claire, as an engineer, had broken the code on how to keep them soft despite the reproducer's attempt to renew them. She reset the cycle from scratch every time they went into the reproducer, which meant that each "wash" left them a little more worn, as the technology interpreted the clothes as new garments, which it didn't have a template for,

The door chime sounded, and Claire pressed the sensor. Holly stood there, looking so beautiful, Claire forgot to step aside for several moments. Dressed in a crisp, white leisure suit, she returned Claire's gaze and then slowly raised her perfect, dark-brown eyebrows. "Don't you want to be more comfortable when you have your tea?"

"Hm? Oh. Oh! I'm an idiot. Come in." Claire took the mugs from Holly and walked over to the small sofa under the screen that showed what the external sensors were picking up. It wasn't the same as a window, but it was better than a blank bulkhead. Holly's quarters were located against the outer bulkhead and had large viewports and an actual view of the surrounding space on her side of the ship.

Holly sat down on the sofa and sipped her tea. Claire had meant to use the chair that sat perpendicular to it, but the harder seat didn't appeal to her when she ached all over. She sat down next to Holly, only then realizing that they had ended up with less than five inches between them. Claire turned to face Holly and leaned against the armrest so she wouldn't crowd her late-night guest.

"Some day, huh?" Claire said, groaning inwardly as the clichéd phrase sounded only marginally better than "how 'bout them Yankees" or some other trite icebreaker.

"I can speak from only my own point of view. It was certainly not easy to be so far away from you…all of you…and listen to a less-than-stellar audio transmission of how things were eroding from challenging to disastrous." Holly studied the steam rising from her mug before looking back at Claire. "I had a quick report from Raoul that he's prioritizing the DNA study and your NIEC." She tilted her head in a clear question.

"And I'm prioritizing the sails and my NIEC. In that order." Claire hoped Holly would understand. "I know you were adamant about it, and I understand, but I have to balance the NIEC against my duties as an engineer."

"Very well. I get that. As long as you maintain a reasonable balance." Holly motioned toward Claire's mug. "Drink it while it's hot."

Normally, Claire would have said "Yes, *Mom*" to anyone else pointing out something like that to her, but no way could she refer to Holly in mom terms, even as a joke. Dressed in her uniform, Holly had a formidable presence as their captain that made the crew and passengers revere her more than Holly would ever understand, and certainly not acknowledge. This Holly, however, wearing soft, becoming, private clothes, with her golden-brown hair not in her usual razor-sharp do, but instead in soft beach waves, was stunningly beautiful and sexy. Her skin held a faint olive tint, and the stars on the viewscreen ignited sparkles in the dark forest-green of her eyes.

"There you go again," Holly murmured. "Not doing as I say and slipping away. Makes me curious where you go when you grow still like that."

To counter Holly's much-too-observant statement, Claire took a big gulp of her tea, burning the back of her tongue as she swallowed. Coughing, she placed the mug on a shelf behind the couch.

"I didn't mean for you to drown." Holly set her mug down next to Claire's. "Are you all right?"

"Fine." Claire wheezed. "Just swallowed wrong."

Holly smiled, something she didn't do often, which sent Claire into another coughing fit. "I see. Need help?"

"Help?" Claire nearly forgot to breathe. "With what?"

"Breathing. I'm well trained in CPR."

The air in Claire's lungs rushed out as fast as it went in. At least she could restrain her coughing, but she needed to occupy herself with something and grabbed the mug again.

"Stop." Holly took the mug. "This is mine." She sipped from it, her eyes glittering even more.

Her cheeks warming, Claire took her own mug and drank with great care. This time, she could actually taste a hint of cinnamon, sugar, and a spice she couldn't identify…nutmeg? No matter what, it relaxed her even after only a few sips.

"Good?" Holly put her mug back on the shelf.

"Yes, thank you. Once I stopped trying to inhale it, it started doing the trick." As if to show just how well, an irresistible yawn made Claire cover her mouth. "I'm sorry."

"Don't be. This *was* the intended effect." Holly stood. "I take that as my cue to leave. I'm about to start yawning any moment myself." She held up a hand as Claire moved to get up as well. "I can see myself out."

Claire stood anyway. "I can't stay on the couch. That'd be some lousy sleep. Trust me. It's happened a few times too many." She took the mugs and put them in the reproducer. "Thanks again."

Holly stopped by the door. "You're welcome. I hope you sleep well." She looked like she wanted or meant to say something more, but instead she laced her fingers in front of her.

"You too." Claire wiped her suddenly damp palms against her pants. "Um. I'm glad we cleared the air and sort of reached an understanding." Why did she have to suddenly sound so formal? Claire swayed back and forth on her soles. When she looked up again, she saw Holly staring at her feet and stopped moving.

"Purple nail polish." Holly smiled again while studying Claire's toes. This time her comment had the same effect as the chamomile tea. Feeling entirely comfortable around Holly for the first time since the day she became captain of the *Velocity*, Claire acted without thinking. She rose on her toes and placed a gentle kiss on Holly's right cheek. "Sleep well, Holly. See you tomorrow."

Holly didn't freeze exactly, but her eyes widened, and the smile turned into a perfect "O." She pressed the sensor and quickly stepped out into the corridor. "'Night." As she disappeared into her quarters and Claire's door hissed closed, Claire was surprised that she didn't regret her spontaneous action, even though she obviously caught Holly off guard. No matter how fast Holly had moved, for a fraction of a second Claire had heard her trembling intake of breath, and Holly had leaned toward her ever so slightly.

Yawning again, Claire cleaned her teeth and used the bathroom. The next morning, she couldn't remember even seeing the bed, let alone crawling into it. She did, however, remember kissing Holly's cheek.

Chapter Seventeen

Holly took her seat on the bridge, strapping herself in. She had just given the command for all hands and passengers to secure themselves no matter where they were. Her senior bridge crew was present on the bridge, including Darian, who did look pale but insisted that she was fine.

"Ops." Holly looked over at Carl.

"Ready." He made a thumbs-up.

"Tactical."

"Ready," Darian said.

"Engineering."

"Every system checked and double-checked, Captain," Claire said over the speaker. She sounded confident.

"Good. Helm?"

"Standing by." Samantha didn't turn around but raised her hand in a quick wave.

Moving on to Walker, Holly probed his expression closely. "All sensors engaged, Commander? We need to know immediately if something goes wrong."

"All internal and external sensors are functioning." Walker slid his fingers along his console. "We're ready, Captain."

"All right." Holly let a few moments pass, steadying herself. "Helm, increase to 20-percent interstellar drive."

"Aye, Captain." Samantha and her two copilots worked in trained unison at the helm, their hands rapidly creating patterns on their consoles. "*Velocity*'s obeying commands within normal parameters."

"On my mark, deploy the sails." Holly gripped her armrests hard but immediately let go. It wouldn't do to show how nervous she was. This was a hundred times worse than when they broke orbit and left Earth and all their loved ones behind. She swallowed hard. "Mark."

"Deploying sails." Samantha ran her fingers across the helm, and a whooshing sound engulfed them, like air flowing from the vents.

Holly kept her eyes on the main screen. The sensor was attached to the tallest antenna at the top of the ship and showed a three-hundred-and-sixty-degree view of the *Velocity* from above. At first, she saw no change, but then something shot from both sides of the ship, a shiny material that reflected the light from the surrounding stars as it unfolded in different directions.

"Change the main screen to the stern sensor." Walker drummed his fingertips against an armrest.

The main screen shifted to display the amazing sight of something resembling metal butterfly wings extending from the ship. They weren't completely out yet, and the outer rims weren't in the sensor's view.

"Captain, I'm getting telemetry from the rigs." Carl sounded baffled.

"Go on." Holly wanted to unstrap her harness and pace.

"We're in clear contact with them. And they're showing how something is approaching from us to them, simultaneously."

"Claire?" Holly engaged her speaker. "Are you seeing this?"

"If by 'this' you mean the projectiles heading toward the rigs, then yes. And that's not all, Captain. They're leaving the ship through the casings in the crawl spaces. We can feel a distinct whirring sound in the deck here in engineering."

"Tactical, ops. Can we magnify?"

"I can boost the signal," Darian said.

"And I can do one better," Carl said brightly. "The sensors on the rigs are transmitting too. We can see what's going on from their end as well."

"On the main screen, Carl. Regular sensors on the side screens, Darian." Holly had already forgotten about the harness and tried to lean forward. Cursing under her breath, she didn't take her eyes off the screens for a minute. "Helm. How're we doing?"

"Keeping steady at 20 percent. I recommend going to forty. My computer suggests it," Samantha said

"All right. Go to 40-percent ISD." Holly squinted at the main screen. "Is that the strongest magnification?"

"For now, Captain, yes," Darian said. "Wait…is that? What's that?"

Holly saw it too. A small, narrow object, like a spear, grew in size with each passing moment. "How big is that thing?"

Carl used both his computer and trackpad, and sweat had broken out at his hairline. "Eighteen yards long and two feet in diameter."

"It's going to hit the rig," Darian said, her voice half an octave higher.

"Same goes for the others," Carl said. "They're traveling at the exact same speed, and they're pulling a wire—of sorts."

"So, they're attached to the wings. Is that what you mean, Carl?" Holly's NIEC stirred, and new information flooded her mind. "Ohh."

"Captain?" Walker said, reaching for her.

"I'm fine. Just a NIEC surge." Blinking, she refocused on the screens. "How are the rigs lined up? The docking port the team used is on one of the short sides."

"No such luck, Captain." Carl had gone from eager to subdued in less than half a minute. "The rigs have one of their long sides toward the arrow, or whatever we end up calling it."

"Actually…" Claire said over the speaker system. "My NIEC tells me they're called, um, the best translation seems to be 'javelins.'"

"All right. The javelins are on a collision course with the long sides of the four rigs." Holly was perspiring too, small droplets sliding down her temples.

"So it seems." Claire sounded almost apologetic. "Monitoring continuously from engineering. We can pull the plug at any time from here, Captain. If all else fails, we'll cut power. Just say the word."

"Good to know, but not yet."

"Captain!" Darian called out. "The rigs are spinning!"

Holly turned her focus back onto a smaller screen that showed a view of their port rig. The rectangular, flat structure was gaining momentum where it spun around its lengthwise axis at an increasing speed. "It's turning. Samantha, can you judge the angle compared to the *Velocity*?"

"It's spinning at an insane speed. I'm sure glad not to be inside there now. As for the angle degree, it's closing in on forty-five degrees, the short end without the docking hatch closest to us." Samantha worked her consoles, and her back looked rigid.

"That makes no sense," Holly murmured, and she could tell Walker heard her. He nodded solemnly.

"Ninety degrees and holding." Carl called out the numbers, and Samantha shot him a quick smile.

"Time to javelin impact?" Holly barked.

"Two minutes and four seconds," Darian said.

"Give me a countdown when twenty seconds are left. Carl, transmit the telemetry to my console." Not sure if she could interpret the data the way Carl did, thanks to his NIEC, she admitted it was too much information to try to read on the larger screens on the bulkhead before them. Her left screen pinged and showed a flow of data on one side and images from internal sensors inside the rig on the other. "Status on the sails."

"Almost fully extended." Samantha sounded as calm as always, but the tension in her body was clearly visible. "They're beautiful."

Holly tore her gaze from the telemetry and looked at the main viewscreen. They were indeed. Like vast fields of gold and silver, they extended from the ship and were connected somehow to the javelin. Holly had been under the impression that the wings would have been able to draw the jigs in and connect directly, or even be remotely guided, but this—she tried to scan her mind to find more information left in the last surge from her NIEC, but either she was too stressed, despite her best efforts to appear calm, or it simply wasn't there.

"Twenty seconds," Samantha said.

"Here we go," Darian murmured behind Holly.

"Seventeen."

Holly glanced back at the telemetry, but her attention was redirected as she saw movement on the rig's inner sensor. Something was shifting.

"Fourteen."

"Check the rig sensors, Carl." Holly had gone beyond stress now. What would happen—would happen.

"I see it, Captain. It's opening a chute of sorts," Carl said.

"Eleven." Samantha quickly turned her head back and looked at Darian, neither of them saying a word.

"Eight seconds."

"Engineering. Claire. Report." Holly's vocal cords felt dry as she uttered the three words.

"All is still going very smoothly from our end, Captain. We're presently just monitoring." Claire sounded excited and confident.

"Four. Three. Two. One."

Holly stared at the large viewscreen and the one adjacent to the left, where Carl had also placed the images of the rig's inner sensors. As if in slow motion, the javelin appeared to pierce the short side of the spinning rig. But instead of destroying it, or causing an explosion, the javelin appeared on the inner sensors, where it slid into the chute. Clasps, or hooks, locked onto it on either side.

"Helm?" Holly kept her gaze on the javelin.

"I have current information on my screen, Captain," Samantha said, sounding mildly dazed. "This I can read without a problem. We have access to EISD. Enhanced Interstellar Drive."

"Are all the javelins secure in their respective rigs?" Holly asked, turning to Carl.

"Yes, Captain. I have confirmation."

"As have I on my end," Claire said over the speaker. "The casings are spinning at exactly the same speed as their rig counterparts. Seven hundred and twenty rotations per minute."

"Look!" Walker gripped his harness and inhaled sharply. "If we thought they were beautiful before..."

Holly stared at the screen. The four sails were now billowed out and fully extended. Completely smooth and slightly concave, their intricate pattern made her think of thin veins.

"How far do they reach?" Holly asked, thinking that the rigs were a mind-blowing eighteen point six miles away.

"Each wing extends five miles from the ship. The area of each wing is approximately three million square yards. So, times four."

"Damn," one of the junior officers whispered loud enough for Holly to hear, but she was thinking the same thing.

"And what's connecting it to the javelin? Claire?" Holly rapped her blunt fingernails on the surface holding her computer.

"If you're asking me what it's made of, I have no clue. According to a set of new specs Trainer pulled from the back of his NIEC, it's practically strong enough to wrap around a planet if we find one we like and want to take it with us."

Holly blinked, and then she couldn't stop a bubbling laugh from erupting. The rest of the bridge crew joined in, as much a welcome release of nervousness as Claire's analogy being funny.

"We get it, Claire," Walker said. "It's strong." He turned to Holly. "Your decision, Captain. Do we use them? Are we skilled enough? Or even prepared?"

Sobering, Holly turned to Samantha, who had swiveled in her pilot's seat, awaiting her orders.

"Well, we can't very well remain here forever. We have a planet to explore and hopefully people to see." Holly nodded to Samantha. "Begin pre-EISD protocols, Chief."

"Aye, Captain." Samantha turned forward again and began the procedure.

"All hands, Captain Crowe here. We're about to start the next part of our journey, and at a much greater speed. Remain in secure seats and especially take care of our youngest passengers. We'll announce when we're taking off again. Crowe out." Holly tapped her speaker. "Claire, what's the status in engineering?"

"All systems are a go, and we're all strapped in."

"Excellent." Holly wanted to ask Claire to take care, but this was not the place for personal remarks.

After a much-too-long wait of eight minutes, as Samantha insisted on double- or triple-checking every step of the EISD protocol, she turned to Holly and nodded. "We're ready."

Holly announced the information over the ship-wide speakers and then gave the order with a completely calm voice. "Engage EISD on my mark. Mark."

Samantha placed her fingers on the four magenta-colored dots on her console at the same time. Afterward, she would remember how the *Velocity* seemed to take a deep breath and then heave forward. The otherwise so sophisticated, smooth technology they had gotten used to seemed to work more by force than by advanced mechanics, as the sound from the propulsion system roared behind and beneath them. The ship stomped for a few frightening seconds, then lurched as if trying to dislodge everyone from their chairs.

"Report!" Holly called out from behind.

Samantha, busy checking her screens, was relieved when Carl answered the captain.

"It's not the ship. It's the rigs. I think they're calibrating against their counterparts in engineering."

"Claire. Check the inner rigs." Holly's voice was like a whip.

"Already half through a diagnostic. The calibration is taking a little too long. Remember, this ship has sat still for a while."

Samantha knew they should be happy that so much worked seamlessly despite the ship's long sleep under the lake in Dennamore. But if the ship was going to show its age, she'd rather it do so while cleaning clothes rather than right now.

"It's catching on, Captain!" Carl hooted and then turned the youthful sound into a feigned cough. "The rigs are aligning."

Samantha felt the tremors slow down, and just as she began to relax marginally, the ship lurched again, but this time, a strong gravitational force pinned Samantha back. She couldn't even turn her head to her side to check on her copilots, let alone move her hands over the console. She barely managed to read the data on her screen. "Speed already twice the maximum ISD and increasing," she gasped as the forces pressed her into her chair.

"Keep reading the data," Holly said, sounding strained.

"Four times ISD. Six." Unlike when she read the seconds until the javelins hit the rigs, Samantha didn't have time to be nervous. She kept her eyes on the instruments and computer screens, praying she wouldn't have to make any corrections, as she was still unable to move. "Nine times ISD. It's increasing faster. Ten."

Everything went quiet so fast, she thought she had gone deaf. Then she noticed the ship's normal humming and heard the other crewmembers gasp for air much like she did. Blinking to clear her mind as much as her tear-filled eyes, Samantha checked her screens.

"Level ten of enhanced interstellar drive. We're plunging through space at ten times our usual speed. All my systems are at peak performance, according to my instruments. I do, however, intend to double-check our course and the computer's ability to make course corrections. At this speed, a thousandth of a degree can be disastrous."

"Good job, Samantha," Holly said, unfastened her harness, and stood. "All hands and passengers, stand down safety protocol for now. Crowe out."

Samantha followed Holly's example and saw Darian do the same. "You have the conn," she said to her copilots and made her way to Darian. "Are you all right? That was some g-force."

"I'll say. We were up and touching g-6. Considering that this ship manipulates inertia like a champ, that's saying something. If we had been in a weightless environment, we'd all be rice pudding on the bulkhead—oh, God." Darian covered her mouth.

"What?" Samantha lost her breath. "You didn't say how you're doing. Are you—you should sit down. Your concussion—"

"No, no. I'm okay. Headachy, but okay. Raoul cleared me for duty. That's not it." Darian stared at Samantha with widened eyes.

"Then what?" Holly came up to them, joined by Walker. "What's wrong?"

"We went all the way up to six g's, Holly." Darian swallowed hard.

"All crew and passengers came through it well," Walker said, placing a hand on Darian's shoulder. "They've all reported in."

"Yes, but has anyone been down to the cargo bays?" Darian shook her head. "Has anyone checked on Crewman Schneider's chickens?"

CHAPTER EIGHTEEN

Darian opened the door to the corridor and found her grandmother standing there, still in uniform.

"Hey, Gran! This is a pleasant surprise. Come in. Can I get you something?"

"No, no. That's not necessary, darling." Gran stepped inside but remained just past the threshold, looking fidgety—and Gran never fidgeted.

"What's wrong?" Darian stepped closer and gently cupped Gran's left elbow. Immediately concerned, she thought back to the two weeks since they began traveling using the EISD. Things had gone smoothly, and the crew and passengers seemed at ease. It was, however, apparent that Gran was not.

"Nothing's wrong. Just…well, I have an appointment with Raoul, and I don't want to worry Geoff, and it's really a family matter…" She sighed and pinched the bridge of her nose. "I would like for you to go with me if you're free."

Darian's stomach felt as if a pound of ice had taken up residence there. Gran used to be so ill, and now that she'd been practically cured by the alien medical treatment, Darian had begun to relax and push back the old, constant worries. Now they rushed back and so did the fear of losing Gran. "What's wrong? I mean, what symptoms?" Her mouth was so dry, she had to clear her throat twice.

"Symptoms? Oh, darling, no. My symptoms are kept at bay. That's not it—at least not this time. Raoul has shown me how my body is responding somewhat reluctantly to some of the alien medications, but so far, I'm doing very well. No, this is about the extended DNA screening."

"You said a family matter." Darian tried to follow what Gran was saying. "Is something wrong on that front? With the DNA of both of us?"

"Not wrong exactly. Or not at all. Just a surprising discovery. I want you there because it concerns you as well. And Holly is joining us."

Darian blinked. "Holly?" What the hell was going on?

"I'd rather let Raoul explain everything, since he'll be able to answer the technical questions. I'll try to fill in the blanks, so to speak." Gran was fidgeting again.

Realizing she was only prolonging Gran's obvious stress by asking so many questions, she bent and kissed Gran's cheek. "Let's go, then. We'll sort things out. I promise."

Camilla relaxed her shoulders and sighed. "Thank you."

As they made their way to the infirmary, Darian didn't say much because her grandmother seemed preoccupied and apprehensive enough to squeeze Darian's arm hard. Just yesterday, Samantha and Darian had had dinner at Gran's and Walker's joint quarters, and all had been normal. They had, again, teased Darian about her concern for the—thankfully alive—chickens after the deployment of the sails. A different Gran now clung to Darian as they took the elevator down to deck five.

Holly was already there when Darian and Gran stepped into Raoul's inner office. He was busy showing her multicolor charts but turned off the screen as soon as he saw them.

"Camilla. Darian. Please take a seat," he said and motioned for the chairs around a small round table. "You too, Holly."

"Please, get to the point quickly," Holly said. "I'm not much for this cloak-and-dagger way of relaying information."

"Nor am I, normally," Raoul said, sounding serious. "Bear with me, please. This is a sensitive matter, and it's important to get it right."

Holly frowned and looked from Raoul to Darian and Gran. "A sensitive issue concerning the three of us?"

Darian thought about Gran's words. Something about their DNA. The sensation of ice in the pit of her stomach had disappeared but now returned, even stronger, especially as Gran unobtrusively took her hand. Gran's fingers were just as cold as the sensation under Darian's breastbone.

"As you know, I've completed the extended DNA scans and was just showing Holly some graphs."

"Very schematically. You have to go through that again with the senior crew." Holly's smile appeared tense.

"I will." Raoul took his computer and turned it so they could all see the screen. "These are the results for the three of you." He pointed out which graph belonged to whom. "When I ran the initial scans so we could use the NIECs, I never went further than that. When I ran the new scans, I needed to see if certain clusters among everyone on board had markers in common, and that's when I found something I didn't expect. I wrestled with it until I spoke to Camilla this morning."

"And this is where you stop stalling," Holly said, now sitting straight up in her chair.

"These graphs show that you three are biologically related," Raoul said and looked at them one at a time.

"What?" Darian whispered. Gran let go of her hand.

"You're joking?" Holly had lost some color now and gripped the edge of the table. "I'm related to my friends. You're sure?" She looked over at Darian with narrowing eyes. "You're really sure?"

"I am. One hundred percent. I ran the tests twice." Raoul leaned back in his chair.

"But how?" Darian said and looked back and forth between Gran and Holly, her head spinning.

A prolonged silence stretched out, only Holly's and Gran's labored breathing audible. Darian felt dazed. How could this be? "How closely are we related? On the mother's side or the father's?"

Raoul looked over at Gran, who pulled a tissue from a dispenser on the wall to wipe the corners of her eyes.

"I can tell you that," Gran said, her voice thick. "Just give me a second." She discreetly blew her nose. "I have lived with a very faint suspicion for some time, but now I know the undeniable truth." She placed a frail hand on Holly's lower arm. "You're my niece, Holly. You're the child of my younger sister Grace."

Darian caught Gran just as she burst into tears. Kneeling next to her chair, Darian held her trembling grandmother and could only stare at the shocked Holly.

"I'll give you all some privacy. Just call me if you have questions I can answer." Raoul patted Gran's shoulder before he left the office and closed the door behind him.

Darian was barely able to get the words out. "How…how's this even possible? All I know of my great-aunt Grace is that she died really young."

"She was my mother?" Holly reached for a tissue with robotic movements. Her eyes kept producing silent tears, and she mopped her cheeks, but her movements were still jerky, as if her coordination was off. Darian was torn between soothing her grandmother's anguish, telling Holly they would figure things out, and finding the last few minutes entirely mind-blowing.

"I may have assumed too much. Raoul did warn me." Gran spoke so quietly that Darian had to lean into her to hear. "We should have ascertained if you really wanted to know, Holly."

Holly's expression went from shocked to annoyed. "Of course, I wanted to know. I've wondered all my life why my birthmother didn't want me!" She pushed her chair backward as she stared at Darian and Gran.

"Still, this was too…too abrupt." Gran was obviously set on taking the blame for everything. She was shaking visibly now, and perhaps that was what made Holly stop glaring at her. Holly pushed her fingers through her hair and inhaled deeply. After expelling the gulp of air, she pressed her hands under her legs, literally sitting on them. Darian could relate to that way of maintaining control. She'd done so herself, many times.

"May I tell you what I know?" Gran used the tissue she was clutching to dab at the corners of her eyes.

"Yes." Holly didn't sound all that convinced, but Gran continued as Darian held her hand again.

"I left Dennamore when I was twenty, dreaming of writing, of making movies. It took me a while to get to Hollywood—two years. Back then, of course, and this was in 1965, when Grace was five years old, I was the odd one out and expected to stay, marry, and take care of my mother, who was a single parent by then. My father died in the last throes of World War Two, before I was born. Mother fell in love a good decade later and had Grace when I was fifteen. Her father never lived with us and lost interest in our family once Mother was pregnant.

"I loved Grace. She was such a little cutie. Very energetic and always up to mischief. My mother, who was raised quite conservatively—which made her having Grace out of wedlock remarkable—tried to raise this little girl like she did me. I was more resilient. Grace rebelled in different ways." Gran squeezed Darian's hands but then rose and moved her chair closer to Holly. "Better." She hesitantly took Holly's hand, and Darian got up, ready to wrap her arms around Gran if Holly rejected her. Instead, Holly just sat there, motionless, and listened.

"In the letters from my mother, she talked about how Grace was acting out, visiting friends in Albany, not wanting to stay with Mother, etc. I was wrapped up in my career, had gotten married, and we were starting a family. That's no excuse. I probably chalked up Grace's behavior—as Mother described it—to teenage rebellion. Perhaps that was why Mother stopped mentioning so much about Grace after a while.

"Mother died when Grace was sixteen, and she went to live with an aunt on my father's side, in Albany. When I learned of this arrangement, I figured it was better for Grace to remain in the area. I had a young son, and with so much going on, I told myself this was best for my little sister—when it was probably only best for me. And I doubt that now." Grace shuddered. "We barely had any contact after that. I did call and write, but she never wrote back, and the calls were brief. A few sentences and that was it. Then, when Grace was seventeen, she got pregnant. I had no idea." Sobs began shaking Gran, and now both Darian and Holly held her hand.

"Camilla—if this is too much," Holly said, stroking the fragile skin on the back of Camilla's hand, "we can continue later."

"No. If it's all right, I'd rather tell you all I know now." Gran freed her hand and cupped Holly's cheek. "It's the right thing to do—and what I owe you and Grace."

Darian wanted to take Gran back to her quarters and tuck her into bed, but her grandmother had never allowed anyone to decide her actions, and this time was no different, no matter how much the situation worried Darian.

"My great-aunt notified me that Grace had passed away. She never mentioned that Grace had died giving birth. When I learned of your existence, Holly, too much time had passed. Six years. My aunt confessed that she had persuaded Grace to sign the adoption papers just before she lost consciousness, not knowing that Grace would die a few hours later. Apparently, the amniotic fluid entered her bloodstream, and…that was that. The baby, you…it was a closed adoption, and I couldn't find out what happened to you. All I knew was that the child was a little girl, and I prayed that you had been placed in a loving family."

"I was." Holly drew a trembling breath. "The best."

"And in Dennamore, at that." Gran shook her head. "When the captain's NIEC worked for you and proved your DNA to be similar to ours, I stopped sleeping as soundly. Remember, as ship's counselor, I have access to everyone's file, and your date of birth made it possible. That, and a faint memory of Mother talking about Grace dating a boy of Asian descent from Albany. Back then, that was considered a stigma." Gran clung to Holly's hand. "I'm sorry, but I don't know the first thing about him. I meant to broach the subject, but I told myself that I was most likely wrong. Too farfetched. Tons of adoptions had to be happening in the area."

"And yet, here we are," Darian said. "I don't mean to oversimplify, but I for one am glad that you two found out the truth, even it if is traumatic. On a very selfish note, I'm happy you're my cousin, though not sure when that'll start to feel commonplace." Darian wrapped an arm around Gran's shoulders. "Please, Holly, I hope you can see this as a gift. Perhaps, when the shock lessens, you will. I sure can't even begin to understand how much this has rocked both your world and Gran's."

Holly looked at Gran and then over to Darian. "So…she didn't abandon me. Not voluntarily, I mean. She was tricked, and then she died." Her raw voice sounded as if every syllable hurt.

"In a nutshell, yes." Gran straightened on her chair, placed a hand in the small of her own back, and grimaced. "Can we call Raoul back? I need some of that alien medicine. Guess I've become increasingly tense during the last few months."

Darian stood, opened the sliding door, and motioned for Raoul to join them. "Gran's not feeling too well."

Raoul didn't waste time but knelt in front of Gran and checked her vitals. "BP is elevated, though not dangerously so. But I see markers for a renewal of the original inflammation in your joints, Camilla. From a medical standpoint, I want you to wrap up this session ASAP." He looked sternly at Holly and Darian. "You two are fine, but our favorite counselor needs her rest. I can administer the medication in your quarters, or you can stay here, Camilla. Either way, I'm paging Commander Walker."

"I'll do that," Darian said. "Gran. Here or at your quarters?"

"Quarters. I'm just a bit tired."

"This took a lot out of her," Holly said, suddenly looking every inch the captain. "Are you certain she's safe to remain there, Raoul?"

"As certain as it's possible to be in my line of duty." Raoul was working at his computer. "The medication is being mixed and packaged in the chemistry department. I'll just wand her joints before she goes."

Darian stood and paged Walker. "Gran is all right, but she needs you in the infirmary. Are you able to hand over the bridge?"

"Samantha, you have the bridge," Walker said without disconnecting his speaker. "I'm on my way. Walker out."

"Darian to Samantha, private." Darian looked helplessly at Holly, who now stood with her hands on Gran's shoulders while Raoul ran the wand he'd used on her before, back on Earth, on her wrists.

"Darian?" Samantha spoke quietly, and her concern was obvious.

"Once Walker is here and Gran's back in her quarters, Holly and I'll join you on the bridge. Gran's a bit shaken, as we had some news, but she's going to be all right. I'll tell you more later, okay?"

"I'll be here. Page me if you need me before you get here. I can summon the next shift early if need be."

"Thanks." Darian wanted to be in Samantha's arms more than anything right now, but Gran's well-being took precedence, and then there was Holly, who did almost too good a job of seeming unfazed.

Walker hurried through the infirmary and entered Raoul's office, filling it with his presence. Darian bent to kiss Gran's cheek. It had taken Darian a few months to accept that Walker was now Gran's closest next of kin in most ways. She needed him now, not her granddaughter or Holly. At least not yet. "Look who's here, Gran," Darian said. "Walker and Raoul will help you back to your quarters, and in the meantime, Holly and I'll be with Samantha on the bridge. If you need me, I'm just one deck away."

"I'm fine, darling." Gran's voice did sound marginally stronger. "Just all this emotional commotion…and the fear of causing so much pain to someone I've come to feel so strongly about." Gran looked at Holly.

"Camilla," Holly said softly. "No matter our newly found history, one thing is clear. You're not responsible for it. Neither is Darian nor I. Please, take care of yourself, and we'll talk more when you're feeling stronger."

"A lot stronger," Walker said firmly, and his gaze when scanning Darian and Holly wasn't soft at all. "Camilla will rest, but I would like to be briefed later."

"Geoff. Stop barking." Gran stood and took his arm.

Walker blinked. "But you're white as a sheet and—"

Gran leaned her head against his shoulder. "Stand down, Commander. I don't need a watchdog. Just the man I love."

Walker's stern glance and rigid form melted before them. "Who am I to argue, then?" His gaze was still firm when he looked back at Darian. "But still. An explanation isn't too much to ask for."

"You're right, Commander," Darian said.

"We'll be on the bridge." Holly appeared as if she couldn't get out of there fast enough.

"Later, Gran." Darian hurried after Holly and caught up to her at the elevator just as the door opened. "I know you hate the question as much as I do, but are you all right?"

Holly was quiet for a few moments as the elevator took off toward deck three. "My gut reaction was to say no, as my world has been turned upside down. But then I thought, has it really? The information I always struggled to fathom, how and why my mother decided to give me up, was answered in a way that will take some time to process…but also in a way where I one day may be able to truly feel I wasn't cast aside. And I have biological, live relatives that I love dearly. That's another thing I need to process." She stopped talking and walked out of the elevator. The corridor was empty, and she turned back to Darian. "And so have you and Camilla. You now know who I am. I think Camilla is glad to know Grace's child, but…" She crossed her arms over her chest and studied her boots for a beat.

"I can only second what you just said. I have a biological, live relative, a cousin, in fact, that I already care so much about." Darian exhaled. "So, cousin, what do you say we go put in some extra time on the bridge, before Samantha implodes in there."

Holly raised her gaze, her dark eyes showing less tension. "Good plan. We have approximately three more months to go before we reach Dwynna Major's star system. That gives us plenty of time to communicate."

Darian couldn't help herself. She flung her arms around Holly's neck and hugged her. The embrace was so brief, she didn't give Holly a chance to either reciprocate or recoil. "Sorry. I just had to."

Snorting softly, Holly merely shook her head and began walking to the bridge. "No problem, cousin."

Chapter Nineteen

Claire knew something was up just from the way Holly took her seat on the bridge. Something had been weird for the last week. Not one to socialize with the crew and passengers much to begin with, Holly had retired to her quarters as soon as her duty shift was over. Claire admitted to being disappointed. She wouldn't have minded spending some more quality time with Holly, like she had that evening when they had tea in Claire's quarters and something inexplicable happened between them. Instead, if Holly had invited anyone into her sphere, it was Camilla or Darian and Samantha. The exclusion not only stung—it hurt—which ticked her off even more. She wasn't prone to jealousy, but apparently when it came to Captain Holly Crowe...nothing was as it used to be with Claire.

Grimacing, she pulled off her virtually useless NIEC and rubbed her temples. The damn thing did little to add to her knowledge of the ship and its functions. She had promised Holly to be transparent if her NIEC caused more health issues, but that wasn't it. It was just slowly going dormant. Granted, Claire had studied specs and documents about the ship until her eyes came close to popping out and thus didn't need the technology as much anymore. She had scanned the metallic oval and its filaments several times a day, and from what she could tell, it was merely shutting down.

Claire's computer pinged at the same time as Carl's. "Captain," she called out. "Course correction."

The first few times the *Velocity* went through course corrections, Holly had issued a ship-wide alert, as they had no idea how violently the ship would respond. They soon learned that it was a much smoother maneuver than a car turning the corner on a busy street.

Holly still didn't take any chances. "All hands and passengers. Brace for course correction."

Claire knew this procedure was prudent, as there was no "same ol', same ol'" in space. Just when they thought they had it all figured out, they would travel through a denser area or a sector with larger solar systems—even twin suns. The ship compensated for the most part, but that didn't mean they could relax.

This course correction was long and level, whereas the previous ones had been more abrupt. Claire kept her attention on the curve displayed on one of the larger screens.

"Fifteen degrees port and still turning." Samantha looked tense where she sat, gazing steadily at the screens.

"I see it," Holly said calmly.

"Eighteen. Twenty. Twenty-one. And that's it. We're on a completely new course." Samantha began to tap and slide her fingers on her computer.

"Time until we reach Dwynna Major's solar system?" This time, Holly's voice showed more emotion.

"Carl, check my calculations." Samantha swiveled her chair and looked over at Carl, who was busy at his console.

"Wait. Hang on. What? Can this…yeah. Yeah." He popped up, eyes huge in his narrow, boyish face. "You're correct, Chief."

Samantha nodded and turned her attention to Holly and the rest of the bridge crew. "According to this new course correction, and unless we run into something unforeseen, we'll arrive at Dwynna Major's solar system in seventy-two days."

Claire had already seen the information confirmed on her computer but still felt goose bumps all over her arms. Seventy-two days. Two and a half months. That was unreal.

"And here you thought we'd have to round the upcoming dense area of planets with asteroid belts." Walker grinned. "Now this is cause for celebration."

"And intensified training—for everyone," Darian said, her tone firm. Claire could tell she wasn't entirely pleased with cutting short their time to prepare, but—again—this was space travel for you. Unpredictable.

"Set up a new roster for tactical training on all levels," Holly said. "Commander Walker will do it with you to make sure we make the most of the remaining time, as he's in charge of the regular duty rosters."

"Yes, Captain." Darian nodded at Walker, who gave her a thumbs-up.

If Darian had her way, they'd train even the smallest child to fight, perhaps even the damn chickens, but Holly had set the age limit at fifteen. That left out only fourteen children and meant one hundred and sixty-two people could do battle if need be. But the risk of that happening was minimal—or so Claire told herself.

The next shift strode onto the bridge, and Claire briefed Trainer on what was in play at her console. He took over easily enough but then stopped her with a "Hey, Chief. You forgot this." He held up her NIEC that hung limply from his fingers, his expression curious and concerned.

"Thanks." Opting not to offer any explanations, Claire took it and headed for the exit.

"Claire?" Holly caught up with her, motioning at the NIEC in Claire's hand. "What's wrong?"

"Nothing. I mean, it's not hurting me. Just sluggish and goes offline a lot." Trying for a casual tone, Claire hooked her arm around the pole next to the elevators and slid down to deck four. Holly did the same and kept an even pace with her as they walked toward their quarters. Claire was fully expecting Holly to do what she normally did, say "Have a good evening" and slip into her quarters, but this afternoon, she stopped closer to Claire's door than her own.

"Yes?" Claire feigned innocence. She knew this was about the NIEC.

"I haven't seen any reports on a deterioration. You promised me." Holly's eyes were opaque, showing very few emotions, but a deepening frown proved otherwise. She was not pleased.

"It hasn't affected me adversely. I mean, health-wise. It's just been, well, dormant."

"I still want to know." Obviously trying to soften her tone, Holly stepped closer and touched Claire's arm.

"You haven't been very accessible after hours," Claire heard herself say. "I didn't think I should bring up the topic of my moody NIEC on the bridge or in the conference room, when it really is a non-issue—for now."

Holly's frown became twice as pronounced. "What are you talking about? Not accessible? I'm on duty around the clock."

"Aha. So, I should have called you in the middle of the night and reported that my NIEC is dying on me? You've clearly had a lot on your plate lately, and as we can't do anything about it, I figured I'd just wait until we can." Claire could hear how she raised her voice. Her stress was talking, but there was a time and place for addressing the issue with her NIEC—and right now, other things were more important. "And I'm not blind. I can tell that something's been going on with you lately. I know," she added holding up her hands, "I know it's none of my business, but I also wanted to be considerate."

Holly's expression turned pensive, but she was still hard to read. "We need to talk, and in a more private setting. This discussion isn't going the way I hoped." She motioned behind her. "Care to have some dinner in my quarters?" Matter-of-fact and nearly casual in her tone, Holly still seemed apprehensive.

Claire waited a few beats, her thoughts whirling. "All right. Thank you."

Holly pressed her sensor to open the door to her private space, stepping aside to show Claire in. "Please."

Claire had thought she would have time to change out of her uniform and perhaps use the cleaning tube, but apparently Holly wanted to deal with this issue right away. Fine. Perhaps clearing the air was the right idea.

Holly's table was cluttered with technology, notepads, and pens. Several fiction books were piled on one of the chairs. Holly didn't apologize for the mess, merely pushed the papers and pieces of technology out of the way before she headed over to the recycling unit to order food from the galley. She paused, looking back over her shoulder at Claire. "Please. Have a seat. Your choice?"

Claire slowly sat down. "Vegetarian casserole, please." This was her favorite, as the hydroponic bays produced amazing vegetables and fruits under the watchful eyes of the gardeners.

"Two vegetarian casseroles, please." Holly spoke into the small speaker unit attached to the compartment adjacent to the reproducer. The reproducer was one of Claire's favorite features aboard the ship. Its many functions sure made life easier. Not having to worry about dishes or laundry would never get old. Right now, though, Claire's attention was completely on Holly, who appeared rigid and twitchy where she stood instead of her normal graceful self, waiting for the boxes to arrive. When they did, she yanked them to her and carried them over to the table.

"Smells great." Claire tried for casual as well but could hear the tension in her voice.

"Yes." Holly fetched forks and then sat down, opening her box. "So, your NIEC?"

Claire had just opened her own box and reached for a fork, but now she stopped and tried to gather her thoughts. So that was Holly's approach—ignore what was going on with herself—which was part of why Claire hadn't brought up her sluggish NIEC.

"As I told you earlier, it isn't causing any pain or injuries. It's just not working well. It goes off-line, yes, but when it *is* functioning, I'm working it hard to stimulate my brain so I can retain as much information as possible."

"I see. Have you cleared this situation with Raoul?" Holly was merely stirring her casserole, not eating anything yet.

"I've communicated its decline, yes. I haven't subjected myself to any more scans as of now, as I don't think they're necessary. Neither does Raoul, or he would have insisted." Anger stirred under Claire's skin. Yes, Holly was the captain and ultimately responsible, but this was Claire's medical issue, and she shouldn't have to report to the captain as soon as she had a hair out of place.

"You have a point. But we had an agreement. You have to realize that I worry when—" Holly pushed the food away and sighed. "What I mean to say is, I trust you to level with me and not come up with excuses."

"What excuses are those, exactly?" Claire pushed her box of food away as well.

"It's not for you to second-guess your captain's state of mind or ability to cope. If we have an agreement, I have to be able to trust you to follow through and not change it on your own accord." Holly's breath visibly caught in her throat, and she coughed twice.

Taken aback, Claire wondered how Holly could be this upset about what she saw as a mere detail, a non-threatening glitch. "What's going on?" She gently took Holly's left hand. "Somehow, I don't think we're only talking about faulty alien technology here."

"Don't—change—the subject." Holly drew a new deep breath.

"I'm not. Not really. I may be way off base here, but it's not farfetched to ponder if your reaction has something to do with what's happening with you." Claire realized how badly she had framed her statement the moment the words came out of her mouth. Before Holly's newly enforced scowl turned into a proper dress-down, Claire gripped her hand tighter. "No, that's not what I meant. That came out wrong. I honestly think we have a case of mutual concern going on, and that makes us both miss the point the other one is trying to make."

"How is that?" Holly spoke curtly but didn't remove her hand from Claire's.

"Okay. I'll go first." Claire braced herself, knowing that the truth might reinforce Holly's impression that she'd been hiding things from her. "I've been worried about potentially letting the crew down. That's why I've studied and crammed as much as I could into my brain about the ship and every piece of technology I've come across. I've been busy, but not so busy that I haven't noticed that you've withdrawn as well. Something else is going on, and it seems to involve Camilla, Walker, and Darian, perhaps Samantha as well. I'm not asking you to confide in me, but that's where my thoughts have been." Suddenly hungry and hell, yes, needing something to hide behind, Claire pulled her casserole closer again and pushed her fork into a piece of squash and a tasty bright-yellow alien vegetable that reminded her of a carrot.

"I see." Not revealing her reaction to Claire's monologue, Holly slowly tugged her food back as well. After a few bites, she put her fork down and rested her elbows on the edge of the table. "I'm the captain."

Claire stopped her fork halfway to her mouth. "Yes. You are." Where was this going?

"I'm proud of that fact. I think I'm good at it," Holly said, sounding as if she was working through her own train of thoughts.

"Agreed." Not sure if Holly even needed a reply, Claire kept hers to one word. Holly was pale, except for two pink spots at the top of her cheekbones. "That means I can't get involved with a crewmember. Privately. No matter what."

Claire's stomach began to tremble, and she knew she couldn't manage another bite of the casserole. What was Holly talking about? Get involved? With her?

"And yet, when it comes to you, the lines...the damn lines..."

When Holly didn't continue, Clare eventually murmured, "Lines?"

"What?" Holly flinched. "Yes, the lines. With you, they get blurred. With Camilla and Darian, they're blurred as well, and I have no idea how to deal with the fallout from that mess." Her eyes grew sharp again. "And that's why I need you to at least follow what we agree on and not keep me guessing!"

This was getting ridiculous. Claire scooted her chair closer to Holly's and now held her hand with both of hers. "If you think that was clear, I have to disappoint you. You have to explain more. I have no idea what you're talking about when you speak about blurry lines and messes. What mess can Camilla and Darian possibly have made that has you this unraveled? And what does it have to do with me?"

"That? Nothing." Perhaps Holly heard how harsh she sounded because she covered Claire's hands with her free one. "And you're not wrong."

"About which part?"

Holly snorted. "About it spilling over into what I do and say."

Claire ignored the risk of sounding presumptuous. "You might need to talk to someone, and since Camilla is our counselor, and she's involved in this mysterious mess...I can keep a secret."

"You sure can," Holly said slowly, tilting her head as if she seemed to genuinely consider Claire's offer. "It's not a secret per se. I mean, it won't be for long, as there's no need. I just need to wrap my head around it, and, I think, Camilla too, especially." Then it was as if Holly suddenly noticed how their hands were interlocked. She dropped her head and drew a trembling breath. "Camilla is my biological aunt, and so Darian is my cousin. Or, rather, my cousin's daughter."

Whatever Claire had envisioned, and she had gone through so many scenarios in her head the last week, this wasn't it. "Wait…your birthmother was Camilla's sister?"

"Yes."

"No wonder you've been on edge. That's a lot to process."

Holly chuckled mirthlessly. "For all of us. I'm starting to intermittently wrap my brain around it."

"And how do you feel about it?" Claire had so many other questions, but it wasn't her place to ask.

"I'm…Actually, I'm starting to get used to the idea. Ha. That's odd." Holly blinked and met Claire's gaze. "I didn't realize that until this minute."

"Perhaps you needed to just say it? I'm not trying to be some amateur Freud here, but my dad always says that if you put words to your woes, then they're not as woeful anymore."

Holly removed one hand from their grip and pushed her hair back from her forehead. "Clever man, your dad. I'd like to meet him when we get home."

Claire's heart skipped more than one beat, she was certain. "He'd like that. So would I. He's pretty cool, and just so you know, his daughter can do no wrong when he's talking to other people." Claire felt her eyes fill with tears at the thought of her father all alone in their house, where she resided on the second floor and he on the first.

"Hey. I didn't mean to upset you." Holly shifted so fast that Claire had no time to react. Shocked, she watched Holly slide off her chair and kneel next to hers. "I apologize for not being able to keep my private issues from spilling into my work."

"You have nothing to apologize for. Nothing." Claire turned on the seat so she could face Holly. "What did you mean when you said that stuff about blurring the lines and not being able to get involved with a crewmember?" she murmured, her hands finding their way to Holly's silky hair. She smoothed it from Holly's face and knew she would remember this moment for a long time.

"Just that. I can't be the captain I must be if I'm emotionally, or romantically, involved with someone." Holly cleared her throat and covered Claire's hands with hers. "With you."

Claire slid off the chair and ended up on the floor next to Holly. The chair slid back as Holly shifted her grip and steadied her. "I haven't been imagining things." Claire took in every expression that crossed Holly's face and was exposed in her eyes. Those stunning eyes that could appear so focused and almost cold now appeared to emanate heat.

"No. And still, this, between us, can't happen," Holly said.

The warmth in Claire's belly helped her tune out the truth in Holly's tone. She didn't want her standpoint to be real. They had a command structure, sure, but they were also just people from Dennamore. How could Holly possibly mean—

Then Holly put her hands on Claire's shoulders and just held her in place, their mouths an inch apart. "Listen, Claire. I'm not going to lie and say that I don't feel anything when I'm around you—because I do. That's why this ends now."

Claire tilted her head and tried to understand. She sank down until she sat on the floor. Holly was not going to change her mind. "Of course, you're right," Claire heard herself say. "You're the captain. Everybody's captain. You can't have anyone think even for a moment that you're playing favorites or that you won't be able to send every member of your crew on equally dangerous missions."

"Exactly." Holly was still holding onto Claire's shoulders, but that wasn't why Claire's heart started beating so painfully. Fat tears ran down Holly's cheeks, just one on each, but that was more than enough. No matter what the captaincy entailed, it pained Holly to reject her.

Pulling back, knowing somehow that Holly wouldn't be able to physically push her away, Claire felt Holly's hands slip from her shoulders. The distance between them was now barely more than a foot, but they might as well have been on opposite sides of the ship.

"Don't cry," Claire whispered. She wanted to wipe the tears from Holly's face, but from now on, she would have to be strong. For Holly. For herself. She stood and rounded Holly, who struggled unsteadily to rise.

"Thanks for dinner." Claire stopped by the door. "And just so you know, what I said still stands. If you want to vent about finding out who your birthmother was and so on, I'm a good listener."

"Thank you." Holly suddenly looked entirely composed, as if their joint emotional vortex hadn't happened. "That's good to know."

And from the way Holly spoke those words, Claire knew they wouldn't have a heart-to-heart about Holly's family. As she left Holly's quarters and walked over to her own, the symbolism didn't escape Claire. She pulled out the NIEC, glared at it, and then threw it against the wall.

PART THREE
PLANETSIDE

CHAPTER TWENTY

Samantha rolled her stiff shoulders as she checked the data on her console. They had reduced speed for the last two weeks, as they were nearing Dwynna Major's solar system. Before the ship began to reduce the EISD, they had experienced another lull for more than two months. As of the last two weeks, the sails had been retracted and the rigs returned to their compartments just inside the hull.

The crew and passengers knew the ship from stern to bow by now, and Darian had them all in the best physical shape possible. Samantha hoped they hadn't missed anything important, as time was running out. Truthfully, none of them knew what they might find waiting for them on the planet.

"Captain?" Samantha mirrored her screen to the large one on the wall. "Here is the latest graph. We're on a perfect course, still."

"Looks good." Holly had been on her feet and pacing for the last half hour. "Any changes in the schedule?"

"We'll be inside the solar system within two hours and entering high orbit around Dwynna Major in an additional six." Samantha heard the bridge crew murmuring behind her and understood that the two-hour-faster approach had ignited a few nerves.

"All right. Before we reach the solar system, I want a meeting with the senior crewmembers. Once we're inside it, you're back at the helm, Samantha."

"Aye, sir."

"No time like the present." Holly raised her voice. "Senior staff, hand over your stations to your next in command and join me in the conference room." The familiar rapid cadence of Holly's boots showed she was already on her way.

After entrusting the helm to her two copilots, Samantha waited for Darian to do the same with Nate at tactical. When they walked through the door to the conference room, they found Holly standing with her back to them, staring at the largest viewscreen, which showed the imagery of the starboard sensor. Ever since they had dropped in speed, it had been possible to see individual streaks of stars in the far distance, and right now, they seemed to have hypnotized Holly.

Camilla and Walker joined them and took their usual seats. Claire sat down in the chair next to Holly's, and the two women exchanged glances before quickly looking away again, Claire at her trackpad and Holly back at the viewscreen. Something had to have happened between them. They were friendly enough toward each other, and nobody could fault the professionalism of either, but during the last two months, something had changed. Darian sat down, and Samantha followed suit. When Darian pinched Samantha's thigh lightly, she realized Darian had noticed the interrupted looks as well. No doubt this topic would come up the next time they had a moment to themselves—whenever that would be.

Holly turned to look at them. "Ah. We're all here. Good." She took her seat, folded her hands in front of her, and began the briefing. "Darian, I've told you before, but it bears repeating, how well you've prepared everyone. I hope we don't have to use any of the skills you've taught us, but knowing we are familiar with the *Velocity*'s external weapons' arrays, rifles, and sidearms, and, to some extent, hand-to-hand combat, is reassuring."

"Everyone's put in countless hours after their duty shifts. The passengers too," Darian said. "It's given me time to figure out who is best suited for any given position."

"Excellent." Holly slid her fingers against her trackpad. "As you know what happened on the bridge, we now have two hours less before we reach orbit. We will still take time to prepare to go planet-side, depending on our readings, and here's where we need to be diligent when briefing our respective subordinates. Camilla, I trust you to bring your civilian contacts up to date."

"Absolutely," Camilla said. "All I have to do is contact Marjory, Carl's aunt, and she'll make sure everyone knows to be prepared earlier than scheduled. She has worked hard on establishing what she called a phone chain."

"Sounds good." Holly paused while using her trackpad. "Claire, what's the status in engineering? Anything you need because of the updated schedule?" Holly swiveled her chair to look at Claire.

"We're still examining the minor components that tend to burn out faster when we do quick maneuvers, such as going into orbit. If any NIEC-wearing staff can help the people down in the cargo bays, as that is labor intensive, that'd be great." Claire raised her chin, and Samantha guessed she was defying anyone to comment on the fact that she wore hers only when she used her computer for short bursts of time, which was obviously not a secret. Claire had showed Samantha her modified TAG, temporary access grant, which helped her use any non-sensitive equipment. It gave her more access than the passengers had, but when she needed to log on to anything in engineering, she had to use her faulty NIEC. Samantha had witnessed her do it, and it seemed like a painful, frustrating experience.

"Commander, see to that?" Holly glanced at Walker but then looked back at Claire. "Anything else?"

"Not at the moment," Claire said softly. "I'll let the *commander* know if I need more boots in engineering."

Samantha thought she saw Holly flinch, but if so, she did it subtly. Was it because Claire had made it clear she was going to run her request by Walker...when Holly had seemed to want to be clued in?

The meeting lasted another half hour, and then Holly stood. "We all have our jobs cut out for us, but we've planned for this occasion for almost a year. I'm going to the mess hall to make my daily appearance among the civilians and grab some coffee. See you back on the bridge in an hour. Dismissed." She nodded to no one in particular, then strode out of the conference room.

Darian wrapped her arm around Samantha's waist. "Coffee, huh? Sounds like a brilliant idea. What do you say? Should we follow the captain's example and grab a mug of the real stuff in the mess hall?"

Samantha tickled the small of Darian's back. "I really should get back to the helm." Noticing Darian's disappointment, she realized that just this morning she had thought how seldom they saw each other, as they often ended up on opposing shifts. "But coffee in your company outweighs doing that by far."

Brightening, Darian kissed Samantha's lips lightly. "Now you're talking. After we reach orbit, I doubt we'll be cozying up over coffee very often, at least not initially."

"I know you, and I have speculated about what Dwynna Major will be like. But what do you think it'll feel like to see it for the first time? And what will being there do to our yearning tendencies?" Samantha began walking, her hand still on the small of Darian's back.

"Well, goose bumps, for sure." Darian grinned. Then she grew serious. "That brings up something we've all mentioned at one point. We have very few images of the planet in the database from a close distance, and no everyday snapshots of the surface. We know something about the typography but no views of buildings, structures, or houses. That gives me pause. Sometimes I feel our NIECs can't give us access to everything, much like the language and signs that Belle so easily read."

"I know Holly, Walker, and Claire have gone through as much of the computer database as they've been able to, but most of the information focuses on the ship and the part of the trajectories that has been logged."

"Well, thank God for that, or we wouldn't have been able to find Dwynna Major in a timely manner." Darian stopped at the elevator.

"Exactly."

The mess hall was about half full as they made their way to the shelf where someone had put up old-fashioned coffee drip filters. Earth coffee was heavily rationed, as it was the most popular hot beverage aboard. After they poured some into espresso-sized mugs, they found a small table for two by the far bulkhead.

Samantha saw Holly standing among a group of civilians, patiently answering questions and sipping her coffee. "She looks more relaxed now, with the passengers," she said quietly.

"You mean Holly? Yes, she does. And just so you know, I nearly got into real trouble with Gran last night when I complained about how distant Holly feels. Gran thought I was trying to test the waters about the captain's mental status. As if! Gran observes strict confidentiality, and I would never suggest she break that. I'm just hoping Holly's rigid approach to her job of late won't get us into trouble if we need to think creatively."

"Camilla is no fool, Dar. She would turn to Walker if she thought anything compromised the captain—or any of us. She's dealt with what few cases of space fatigue we've had like a pro."

"I know. And I told her that I wasn't prying. All's good." Darian sighed but then smiled and seemed ready to change the subject.

"Listen. After we've completed the next stage of our journey, I plan to insist on R and R for the two of us. We can barricade ourselves in our quarters with a pound or two of Earth coffee." Darian grinned and sipped from her mug.

"I like how you think." Samantha reached for Darian's hand across the table, which made Darian blink. Their relationship was no secret, but she was a private person and not comfortable being demonstrative. Darian sometimes hugged, and even kissed her, in public, but never on duty. Right now, knowing that they'd have barely any alone time for the foreseeable future, Samantha was ready to pull Darian across the table and kiss her senseless. "I'm all for being barricaded—and alone—with you. These last few months since you recovered from your injuries, I've felt so blessed. I can't imagine my life without you."

Darian pulled Samantha's hand to her lips, kissing the back of it. "I love you too," she said huskily.

"Oh." Samantha reciprocated the hand kiss, not caring who else was in the mess hall. Everyone was probably too focused on their own family and friends anyway. "I love you, Dar. With all my heart." Images of how she and Darian had literally run into each other almost a year and a half ago, at the Town Hall in Dennamore, flickered through Samantha's mind. She had sat among all her newly printed documents, watched them fall like enormous snowflakes and land around her and the handsome woman before her. Not knowing anything about Darian, Samantha was enthralled, and when Darian had told her she lived in one of the original houses from the late 1700s, it was the perfect combination. In retrospect, she knew that her curiosity about the old log house was by far overshadowed by how mesmerizing Darian was. And, unfathomably, here they were, having crossed an unimaginable expanse of interstellar space and now holding hands among people who were family to them.

"What were you thinking about right now?" Darian asked, tilting her head, making her short ponytail do a little dance.

Samantha smiled, her cheeks warm. "You. Us. On the floor at Town Hall."

"Classic." Darian chuckled. "I think it's a testament to your allure when—despite my very sore tailbone—all I could see was you."

Samantha had opened her mouth to reply, when a cackling sound stole her attention. Snapping her head to the left, she stared as two chickens made their way through the mess-hall patrons, followed by a flustered Schneider.

"I'm so sorry, I'm so sorry. I'm on my way to deck two, to the common area, but Chief Gordon needed the elevator to go back to the bridge. When I set it to deck one, someone must have called on it here, because it stopped, and when the door opened and so many of the lower-deck crewmen stepped on, they spooked my girls, and they literally jumped from my arms." He bent and captured the white chicken. "Please grab Ruth, someone?"

"Ruth?" Darian murmured but then bent and scooped the brown-and-white chicken off the floor. "I've got her."

"Oh, thank you, Chief."

"Why were you transporting them like this?" Samantha emptied her coffee and stood.

"We're going to have the kids pat and cuddle with them. The counselor suggested this for the youngest kids before they have to buckle up as we enter the solar system."

"I see. Well, you better hurry and get to the common area, then." Samantha scanned the mess hall and waved a teenaged boy over. "Dylan? Why don't you help Crewman Schneider with one of these? They're due in the common rooms."

"Hey, that's Ruth, isn't it?" Dylan said and flicked his long bangs from his face with a practiced move. "No problem." He took the chicken from Darian, and the two guys left the mess hall.

"Nobody will ever believe that part, that's for sure," Darian said, snorting.

"True." Samantha checked the time on her trackpad. "I know it's a little early yet, but I'm going to use the latrine and then return to the helm."

"All right." Darian sighed but had clearly slipped into her work persona as well. "I'll join you on the bridge as soon as I've made sure we're all set from a tactical point of view. I'm going to walk the lower decks and am taking Agent Brewer with me." She held up her hands before Samantha had time to comment. "I know. You've told me to watch my back with him for a long time, but he's good to have in a fight. You've seen his martial-arts skills."

"I still don't quite trust him." Samantha began making her way to the door, Darian just behind her.

"Oh, I believe that once we get back, he might try to screw us over, from an agency point of view. But out here, where we all depend on each other for survival, he's being a good boy."

"All right. I trust your judgment." Samantha gripped the pole next to the steps. "See you on the bridge."

"Yes. I'll be there before the big show." Darian kissed Samantha's cheek. Smiling, Samantha let go and allowed herself to slide down toward deck three. This had been a nice break with Darian, and she had needed it more than she knew, but now they would reach the outer perimeter of Dwynna Major's star system in only forty minutes. She would have to reduce speed continuously, or the ship would barrel straight past their homeworld. As she landed with both feet next to the pole on deck three, nervous jitters erupted in her belly.

Looking at the serious faces of the current bridge crew as she entered, she could tell she wasn't the only one feeling the suspense. She squared her shoulders and took a cleansing breath as she made her way to the helm.

This was the moment they'd all been dreaming of, no, yearning for, since they unearthed the ship. This was it.

CHAPTER TWENTY-ONE

"Ten minutes until we reach high orbit!" Carl called out from ops.

Holly gripped the armrests harder. Ever since they had neared the planet, the *Velocity* had stomped and moved restlessly under their feet. Everyone was strapped into their seat, but she was seriously considering the risk of half the crew having whiplash injuries.

"Course is steady and we're on the right trajectory, Captain, no matter how it feels." Samantha had to raise her voice, as something in the very upper layers of the planet's atmosphere was sending a reverberating roar through the ship.

"Maintain course and speed," Holly barked. "Steady as she goes."

"Speed is down to 5-percent ISD, Captain," Carl said, probably seeing that Samantha and her two copilots had their hands full.

"Once we're locked into high orbit, cut down to 2-percent speed, just to keep the ship right side up, so to speak," Samantha said.

"Good. Carl, I want you to start scanning the space around the planet, as well as the surface for signs of life and technology," Holly said. "We need to be prepared for satellites or space debris."

"I'll make sure we run continuous scans for both," Carl said.

His reply bothered Holly. She hadn't found it strange that they hadn't come across other signs of life in space on their way to Dwynna Major, since they had traveled at such an unfathomable speed. If they had indeed passed an inhabited planet, they would have streaked by it so fast, their sensors wouldn't have been able to pick up anything.

As they were literally creeping up on Dwynna Major, they should be able to detect transmissions and see signs of their no-doubt vastly more advanced technology in space. The fact that they didn't made her stomach clench.

"One minute to high orbit," Carl stated. "Isn't it beautiful?"

Holly had deliberately avoided thinking about the planet before them in those terms. She saw oceans, vast ones like on Earth, and landmasses, but light-gray clouds obscured a lot of them. A formation resembling what a hurricane looked like from space hovered over one of the oceans, probably causing havoc.

"Any signals or transmissions?"

"None. Not even static," Carl answered from behind Holly.

"High orbit established. Reducing speed." Samantha slid her palms along her console. "There. The graviton pull of the planet will keep us in place. Speed 2 percent. Correction. One point five."

"All right." Knowing she had to harness her impatience, wanting nothing more than to hurry over to Carl's console and watch as the results of his scans trickled in, Holly tapped her speaker. "All hands, this is the captain. We have now arrived at Dwynna Major and are locked into steady high orbit. You are free to move around the ship, but pay attention to potential alerts." Another tap opened a link to engineering. "Bridge to engineering. Status report."

"Claire here, Captain. All systems are operational. Samantha took us in smoothly, and except for an elevated amount of magnetism at deck level, we had no surprises. Running diagnostics on all equipment."

"Magnetism?" Holly had unbuckled her harness and now stood, pulling out her trackpad. She scanned the bridge deck. "Nothing out of the ordinary on the bridge, Claire. What's going on at your end?"

"Apart from the magnetism, nothing. I'll send out engineers to scan along the corridors on all decks," Claire said.

"Report back ASAP."

"Aye, Captain." '

Holly could hear Claire begin issuing orders before the link disengaged.

"Magnetism?" Walker raised his bushy, gray eyebrows. "Like in the space sails?"

"I have no idea. Claire will have a report for us as soon as she knows more." Walking over to Carl, Holly arrived in time to see him go pale. "Carl?"

"Captain. I…I can't believe this. I have to rerun the scans. This can't be true." Carl's hands weren't entirely stable as he entered new commands. "Damn."

"Talk to me, Carl." But Holly was already seeing the readings from his initial scans. No transmissions came from the planet below them. In fact, there were barely any emissions of any kind.

"Atmosphere breathable. Oxygen levels comparable to Earth, same goes for nitrogen, and traces of carbon dioxide. But pockets of radiation exist."

"Radiation?" Holly bent closer, impatient to read the information, but then let Carl continue.

"Magnetic radiation, but not all over." Carl tapped his speaker. "Bridge to engineering. I need a deeper analysis of the magnetism in the deck."

"Claire here. Sending as we speak, Carl."

New information streamed along Carl's screen. He began putting the data next to the sensor readings from Dwynna Major. "Not exactly the same, but close enough, if you ask me, Captain," he said and rubbed the back of his neck. "Something's been going on down there that causes magnetism to linger on the ground and in the atmosphere."

"I see." Holly engaged her speaker. "Bridge to the infirmary. Raoul, have you seen the latest data?"

"I'm looking at it." Raoul sounded preoccupied, suggesting that he was reading through it while he spoke.

"What can we expect to see in the form of health issues regarding the magnetism in some decks and, later on, the magnetic radiation on the planet?" Holly asked.

"I'll have to scan the database and make comparisons, but as far as the ship's concerned, I don't think we're currently in any danger. We're not carrying any passengers or crewmembers with pacemakers or other medical equipment that potentially could be affected."

"I see. Report back when you know more. Crowe out." Holly turned to Samantha. "Once we hear back from Raoul and Claire, I want the speeders to go into low orbit for a closer sensor sweep and scan of the surface. In the meantime, launch four of the advanced probes to circle the planet on the lowest possible flight path."

"On it, Captain," Samantha said and began instructing her copilots. "Sending out the probes now, set to fly a thousand feet above the surface. They're equipped with high-resolution sensors, which will make it possible to zoom in very closely."

"Excellent. Once that's done and all the data is in, I'll decide about potentially going planetside—and how."

"Aye, Captain." Samantha returned her focus to her console.

"You look worried, Captain," Walker murmured when Holly had retaken her chair.

"I am. And I can feel the eagerness from everyone to just jump into a speeder and fly down there to experience where they stem from. I feel it too, the pull. That means we have to keep a united front, Walker. We can't let them all become cowboys and set safety aside." Holly sighed. "I always knew there was a risk, and a proper one, that I might lose someone on this mission, and I took on the captaincy anyway. I am, however, not prepared to lose anyone because we couldn't contain ourselves and follow procedure."

"I think everyone is still taking your orders at face value," Walker said, looking around furtively.

"For now. And up here among the senior crew who know me well and trust my judgment, yes. But on the lower decks, and among the passengers...when I was in the mess hall earlier, I could feel the anticipation in the air. It was tangible. Some of the younger people, teens and young adults, were nearly vibrating. If things don't happen as fast as they would like them to, the security situation could become a problem."

"I'll take that up with Darian, but I have a feeling she already knows. She's made a point to get acquainted with every single passenger while providing tactical training." Walker smoothed his mustache down. "And you're not wrong, Captain. If I, who pride myself on being a person with decent self-control, can feel this jittery about being in orbit around the place that part of my ancestors came from, the young people could be bouncing off the bulkheads soon."

"Exactly."

"Imagery being uploaded to the database," Samantha called out, putting an end to the exchange of concerns.

"On main screen," Holly said.

The first imagery showed a canyon, or a vast ravine, with bright-orange jagged cliffs and bedrock poking through what looked like off-white, fine sand. As the probe flew west along its trajectory, Holly saw flat areas, covered with the same sand, and whatever bedrock poked through was either orange, silver-gray, or charcoal in color.

"There. A few degrees north!" Samantha called out and adjusted the probe's flight path. "Isn't that a ruin? Taking stills." She sent the stills to the right of the main screen and zoomed in. "Oh, my…"

Holly blinked, but the photos showed the same view. A grid of squares, circles, and rectangles, some with part of the walls still attached, others clearly caved in, proved that structures had been there before. But how long ago?

"Mark the coordinates." Holly spoke curtly.

"Yes, Captain," Carl said, and his hands flew across his console. "The readings are different here. I'm getting new data from the probe, and here, the magnetic radiation is lower."

"And there's more," Samantha said. "More ruins. And…oh, my God!"

Holly knew why the otherwise so calm and collected Samantha sounded so shocked. A river stretched across the photo, from north to south, and amid the ruins she saw the impossible. A fully intact bridge stretched from the west shore to the east. "It looks pristine. New."

"But no signs of life." Carl flung his hands up. "The probes haven't detected anything other than different types of wildlife ranging from the size of elephants to foxes. I'm not saying there's no wildlife smaller than that, only that our sensors don't detect it—yet."

"Wildlife but no people. Ruins, but a bridge that looks new. I can't even begin to guess," Walker said.

"You and me both," Holly muttered. "How big was this place when it was inhabited?"

Carl ran his index fingers along his console. "Fifty-six square kilometers. About the size of Albany, I'd say."

"And judging from the foundations of their buildings, and I admit I'm guessing to some degree," Darian said, "these were high-rises. Look at the sturdy bases for the walls."

"That's an astute guess," Walker said. "I was just thinking the same."

"Now that I know what to look for," Carl said, "I see similar settlements in ruins all over the continent, though not as large as this one. Plains down toward the equator from here show signs of having been cultivated at one point. The sand has been pushed aside into large piles."

Holly looked from one screen to another, all of them showing signs that Dwynna Major had once been populated, but apart from the bridge, she saw no indication that anyone had been around for a very long time.

"Was this why our ancestors left? Some war with magnetic weapons leaving the planet a desert?" Philber's voice from the door made them all turn their heads.

"Good. Glad you're here. Take a station." Holly pointed to a free one behind her, but Philber walked to stand behind Samantha.

"I've only had a chance to look at the photos we have access to very briefly," he said "but I think it's safe to say that something catastrophic happened here. Once we go down to the surface, we'll be able to carbon-date any object we find, as we'll have access to the soil."

"You mean sand." Carl snorted unhappily.

"No, soil. Yes, it appears as sand as it seems all dried up, but I bet this is what used to go for soil around here."

"And the bridge?" Holly asked.

"That is something of an alien variable, no pun intended. Being less fortified than most structures, it should have collapsed before the rest of the buildings did." Philber pulled at the collar of his uniform, which Holly knew he loathed to wear. He did so only because Holly had personally requested it. They needed to show the junior crew and the passengers exactly who they were.

"I'd like to bring the agents from FBI and NASA to the bridge to give their opinions," Walker said, holding up his hands as if to ward off any annoyance from Holly. "Some of this situation ties into their respective expertise."

"Are you sure?" Holly frowned.

"Why else did we bring them and allow them to take up valuable resources if we didn't think they'd be useful?" Smiling now, Walker tilted his head.

"All right. Fine. Just keep an eye on Brewer. He's the loosest cannon among them."

"He is." Walker nodded at Darian, who relayed the order to tactical. The FBI agents were allowed outside their quarters and the common areas only when accompanied by an armed escort. Brewer had been on the bridge a handful of times, but only very briefly.

Shortly, Agent Brewer stepped through the door to the bridge, Nate by his side. Behind them, the other agents followed, their eyes huge.

"Welcome to the bridge," Holly said shortly. "Please take one of the visitors' chairs. My next-in-command is certain that hearing any potential opinions from any of you could be valuable."

"But not you, Captain?" Brewer said as he sat down. He looked over at the photos on the screens and went tense. "That's the planet." It was not a question.

"Ruins. Whole cities in ruins?" Mireille Wu said, looking stricken.

"It appears like it," Holly said. "I know you can't interpret the alien data at the same rate as someone wearing a NIEC, but I would appreciate any thoughts you may have about what we see in these photos."

As Carl put up more photos from the four probes, Holly started to feel dizzy. Reluctant to admit how badly she'd slept the last couple of weeks, and how sudden exhaustion could set in unexpectedly, she gripped the armrests hard and forced herself to focus.

"Roads. Surely those are roads?" Emma Andersen, the other NASA engineer, pointed at one of the smaller screens.

"Move image on four to main screen," Walker said.

Holly leaned forward, as if getting a foot closer would help her see clearer. "You mean the lines?" Squinting, Holly made out lines that truly were too straight to be a natural occurrence. "Magnify."

A collective gasp gushed from everyone at the sight of the photo.

"Damn," Darian said behind Holly. "Yeah, those are roads. New roads."

"What the hell?" Walker turned to Holly. "What do you and your NIEC make of this?"

"No references to this situation are coming through," Holly said, her momentary bout of fatigue gone for now. "But every analysis it makes tells me those are roads. We need to find out where they originate and where they lead. Either someone's bothered to maintain old ones in pristine condition or these are indeed new. We have to figure out which—and why."

"Understood." Walker turned to the rest of the bridge crew and issued the orders. "Samantha, deploy smaller, more agile probes to follow the roads, one in each direction. Carl, analyze what was used to build—or maintain—them. Darian, make sure tactical teams are ready—just in case." He hesitated and then looked over at the bulkhead just inside the door where the visitors sat. "Agent Brewer. I want you and your colleague to make yourselves available to Chief Tennen as she assigns duties to her teams. We need every person available on this assignment if we're going to maintain a safe ship. Doctors Andersen and Wu, please report to the lab units on deck five. They have access to all data and will need help with their analyses."

Holly kept her gaze furtively trained on Brewer, but to her surprise, he looked more relieved than anything. As Darian waved the two FBI agents over to her console, Holly got up, as nervous energy made it impossible to remain seated.

"Engineering to bridge." Claire's voice came over Holly's speaker.

"Crowe here. Go ahead." Holly stepped aside from the conversations going on at the different consoles.

"My initial report is on its way, but I wanted to let you know that the magnetism in our decks is similar but not the same as the radiation on Dwynna Major. As my staff scanned the decks, we triggered new technology in engineering."

"New technology?" Holly rested her hip against a railing.

"I think you need to see this for yourself, Captain. It might help answer a lot of questions as we discover more." Claire paused. "Trainer is unlocking one unit after another."

"I'm on my way." Nodding at Walker as she passed his station, she felt strangely rejuvenated. "I'll be in engineering. You have the bridge, Commander."

CHAPTER TWENTY-TWO

Claire inwardly tapped her foot as she waited for Holly to join her and her crew. Forcing herself to remain calm among the people gathered in a semicircle as they ran scans, she looked over her shoulder as the double door hissed open. Holly strode in, eyes sharp and jaw set as she took in engineering.

"Captain," Claire said and motioned for the crew to back off. "Once we had established a secure orbital trajectory, this wall turned itself inside out, much like the opening leading down to the tunnel below Dennamore. Our NIECs hadn't registered its existence until it appeared."

Holly halted next to Claire and merely stared. "What the hell? This was inside the bulkhead?"

"Yes. Not only that, but my engineers are scanning it, and so far, we can tell that it has not only been hidden, but also cloaked." Claire adjusted her NIEC. "I have enough juice left in my NIEC to receive this information."

Holly stepped close but then backed up. "I think it's smart to keep a certain distance," she said, grimacing. "My NIEC is working fine, but the flood of information is giving me a headache."

"I hear you." Claire studied the wall that had emerged, much like someone flipping a deck of cards. Approximately ten yards long, it filled the space between two of the inner bulkheads. Six feet tall, it held computer consoles, screens, storage areas, and instruments she would have to figure out as soon as possible.

"Chief! Over here." Trainer, who was kneeling by the wall, waved at Claire, who inched close to him, unwilling to relive the pain of her malfunctioning NIEC.

"What do you have?" She crouched a few feet from her next in command as he held a storage door open.

"NIECs." Trainer pulled out a shelf. "Not quite like the ones we're using, but—" He flinched and touched the back of his head. "Damn."

"Trainer?" Holly had joined them and now placed a hand on his shoulder.

"I'm good, Captain." He shook his head. "I know what they are now. Damn, Captain." He pulled out one of the small transparent crates. No scrolls were attached to these NIECs. "Here you go."

Also crouching, Holly accepted the crate and held it out for Claire to see. Slightly larger than the normal NIECs, and faintly triangular, the device was made from a matte charcoal alloy. "Does your NIEC give you the information?" Holly asked.

Claire shook her head. "It will in a bit. It's still accurate when it works, but it's slow."

"Then I can inform you that this NIEC is meant to be used in wartime." Holly pressed her lips into a fine line. "This entire wall of consoles was created for that purpose. Right, Trainer?"

"Aye, Captain." He looked somber.

"Damn." Claire could barely believe it but knew that was true, even if her NIEC hadn't caught up yet.

"That's not all." Holly stood, and the others joined her. "This console doesn't just appear for no reason. Something about Dwynna Major made it deploy, and we have to find out why."

"But why here? Why in engineering?" Trainer asked and scratched his jaw.

"That's yet another surprise that the *Velocity* decided to spring on us. This area of the ship is the emergency wartime bridge." Holly motioned along the wall of instruments. "This wall is a condensed version of the bridge."

Claire blinked. "You mean, in case the main bridge is compromised?"

"Exactly."

Her mind reeling and panicking at all the latest information she would have to learn the hard way now that she'd been thrown yet another curveball, Claire studied the NIEC in Holly's hand. "I need to try that on." She took the case before Holly had a chance to object.

"What?" Holly reached out for it, but Claire kept it out of her reach. "Claire…"

"I have a NIEC that barely functions. Only because we've been in a lull since the sails deployed, and it's been smooth sailing, have I managed to remain as chief engineer and help keep us safe. We're here now, and each of us needs to bring our best game. I can't do that with this thing!" Claire tore the offending NIEC from the back of her neck, holding it out between them. "Look at the filaments. They're fucking orange!"

Holly's eyes narrowed as she studied Claire's equipment. "It looks…deceased."

Claire realized they had quite the audience. "Trainer. Keep scanning every inch of the new panel and report to me. Captain. My office." Realizing she sounded as if she'd ordered Holly to come with her, Claire was still agitated enough to not care. In her small desk area, she pointed to the chair in the corner. "Have a seat." Pushing computer tablets and scrolls from her desk, she placed the transparent case in the center, keeping a hand on it.

"I'm not going to snatch it from you," Holly said dryly as she pulled the chair closer to Claire's desk. "Are you really ready to risk trying this NIEC?"

"I am. That is what Samantha and Darian did back home. They had absolutely no idea what they were doing and what the repercussions would be. We, at least, know that they only attach to people with the right DNA marker and that they have had—so far— no harmful side effects."

Holly nodded slowly. "I know. And if I survived this thing," she said, motioning to the crownlike captain's NIEC she wore every day, "it might be all right. I know you want to slap it on right away, but page Raoul first."

Claire considered the order and nodded. "Good idea." She used her speaker, and Raoul turned out to be two decks below seeing to an injured cargo-bay crewman and would join them within a few minutes.

Claire studied the NIEC. "It looks rather badass," she muttered. "I mean, the design."

Holly looked up, surprise on her face. Then she smiled, a faint upturn of the corners of her mouth. "It does. In other words, it'll fit you, if you can wear it."

Claire knew she was gaping but couldn't do anything about it for the first few seconds. "What? You think I'm a badass?"

"In the best sense of the word," Holly said. "The way you've handled the challenge with your NIEC, and for a lot of other reasons."

"That's not how I've felt at all." Claire pressed against the backrest. Not sure if this was the right time and place to be frank with Holly, she hesitated briefly. "I've been battling with old feelings of déjà vu, actually. Perhaps in part because it's seriously exhausting to cram in all the knowledge the old-fashioned way that the rest of you get from the NIECs, but…it's not the first time I've felt like I didn't belong. That I was judged by a different standard. Dennamore is a wonderful place for the most part, but—" She shrugged.

"I've felt like an outsider many times," Holly said quietly, "for not being originally from there, but also for being biracial. Is that what you mean?"

"Not the first part—my ancestry is pretty mixed, but my dad's sister tracked us back to the early 1700s in the area. Even before the aliens. No, in my case, it was a mix of biases and sometimes racism. I had my gang of friends at school, thank God, and we were a cool group of kids from all walks of life. It was mainly the grownup world that tried to limit my options, my dreams, whether they realized that or not. It made me escape into reading—and into the woods, hiking."

"Where we found you." Holly's expression had grown both dark and soft, which made it impossible for Claire to take her eyes off her.

"Yes. You did." Claire cleared her throat. "Not sure why I'm telling you this now. So random."

"Not at all. I assumed that coping with the faulty NIEC had been easier on you than it was. You made it seem easy by being brilliant at what you do. And that in turn made you think of when people made assumptions about you back home that weren't correct either." Holly's firm gaze didn't waver.

"I felt useless some days, and I spent so much time double-checking everything going on in engineering. If it hadn't been for Trainer, I would have developed an ulcer, I think." Claire tried to smile, but the words were too true. "I felt I had the potential, but something out of my control was preventing me from experiencing it, excelling at it. All too familiar. In this case, it was mechanical, sure, but it still made me feel thwarted."

Holly leaned forward and placed her lower arms on Claire's desk. "If it's safe for you, this NIEC could change that feeling. You're always brilliant, but this can give you a level playing field, and I can finally relax about the other NIEC physically injuring you."

The fact that Holly had worried about her, thought of her, made Claire's heart tremble. Holly had been polite, sometimes friendly in a detached, cool way, after that evening in her quarters. After the "I can't, I'm the captain" speech, they had both kept their distance, yet here they sat, suddenly being so open with each other.

"All right. What's the emergency?" Raoul's voice from the doorway interrupted them.

Holly flinched but pointed to the new NIEC. "This thing. Newly discovered in the panel out there."

"What panel?" Sticking his head out the door, Raoul reappeared after whistling. "You're not kidding. That's new."

"It is. And it held a whole cabinet of these. Claire wants to try one. You need to monitor her." Holly's speech sounded cropped, the way it did when she was concerned. Claire knew her well enough by now to determine that difference.

"Ah. I see. All right." Raoul studied the NIEC. "Bigger. Triangular. Okay, Claire. Jacket off."

Claire removed her leather-like jacket and tugged at the short sleeve of her T-shirt. "That okay?"

"Yes." He attached an Earth-type blood-pressure cuff around Claire's right arm and a pulse oximeter on the index finger on the same arm. "One forty over eighty. Slightly elevated from your baseline, but we're all excited, so that's normal. Ninety-eight percent oxygen level. You're good to go." Raoul rested his hip against the desk.

Claire opened the case and removed the NIEC from the form-fitted indentation. "Damn, look at those filaments. Eight on each side."

"Still okay with this?" Raoul asked.

"Hell, yeah. Here goes." Despite her bravado, Claire felt an onset of nerves that made her glance at Holly.

"We've got you, Chief," Holly said softly and rose to stand next to Claire. "We'll yank that thing off in case you run into trouble."

"Not unless I say so—or if my system is compromised." Claire shot Raoul a stern look.

"Got it," he said calmly.

Claire pushed the triangular piece of technology against the nape of her neck. Assuming that it went on with one of the rounded tips up along the back of her head and the other two on either side of the base of her skull, she pressed it firmly under her braids.

The NIEC behaved as if it had waited too long to get to work. It snapped against her with a click, and the filaments appeared to extend, attaching to her scalp after slithering into place in an intricate pattern. The next moment, Claire's brain flooded with so much information, she had to close her eyes. Fumbling for the armrest of her chair, she instead felt hands grip hers. Holly's slender hands. She'd recognize them anywhere. Strong hands held onto Claire's shoulders. Raoul.

"Claire?" Raoul said. "Talk to us."

"Give me—a moment." Claire gasped. Images, data, knowledge. It all swirled like carnival balloons let go in a tornado. She clung to Holly's hands. "D-don't let go."

"Never."

The impossible words. Did Holly really say never? Claire focused on the word, used it as an anchor in the mental storm that was overrunning her at ISD speed. Perhaps this was a big mistake? What if all this information was too much for a mostly human brain? She might implode, or come out the other side in a vegetative state. She should tell them to remove the NIEC. This was more than a NIEC. It held images and knowledge she didn't want, never asked for. She was an engineer, and all she required was the information about how to deliver the people aboard, people she loved, to their destination, keep them safe. Why did the NIEC force this overload on her? Claire tried to speak, tried to tell Holly and Raoul that this wasn't what she signed up for. She would let them know as soon as she was able to open her mouth and say something.

"Claire? Please. Look at me." Holly sounded so worried that it had to be a dream. Her tone woke Claire right up, and she tried to move her arm to reach the glass of water that she always kept by her bed. Now, this was strange, but her hands seemed locked in place. Was she strapped in? What was going on?"

"Claire? Can you hear me? Open your eyes."

It was definitely Holly's voice. Claire shook her head to clear it.

"Now, Claire. Look at me *now!*"

That was an order. Claire forced her heavy eyelids open. The light pierced her retinas for a few painful moments before her eyes adjusted. Holly's beautiful face filled her entire field of vision, and she looked pissed. No, worried. Or perhaps pissed *and* worried.

"That's better," another voice said. "Blood pressure and O2 saturation normal. I'm going to scan you now, Claire."

"Raoul?" she murmured, still looking straight at Holly.

"That's right. You paged me to monitor you, remember?" Raoul appeared to Claire's left. He held a medical trackpad and began scanning her. "What the hell...?" Raoul tapped the trackpad and scanned again. "Nothing."

"What do you mean?" Holly snapped the words out. Her grip on Claire's hands grew close to painful.

"She seems fine, but my trackpad...it can't scan her brain. I can see her eyes, nose, mouth, her entire face, and even her bone structure, but that's it." Raoul set his trackpad on the desk. Pulling out a wand, he ran it at half an inch distance around Claire's head. "It's as if it's shielded."

Holly let go of Claire's left hand. "Let me try. Mine isn't a medical trackpad, but it's the captain's model." She mimicked Raoul's movements and then blinked in confusion at the result. "Not entirely shielded. I can see that her brain tissue is all there, but I'm not getting enough data to—"

"All right, all right," Claire said and waved her free hand. "Stop talking about me as if I'm not here." She felt better, steadier. "I'm okay. My brain's still there, for God's sake."

"Coherent speech. Thank God." Raoul looked relieved. "Mind standing up to show me your motor functions are in working order, Claire?"

Claire stood and performed some rudimentary neurological tests—pointing to her nose with her eyes closed, balancing on one leg—and then allowed Raoul to test her reflexes. "That's it. I'm not going to do cartwheels. I'm fine." She pulled off the blood-pressure cuff and the pulse oximeter. "Thank you for making sure I didn't melt my brain. I'm truly doing all right. Bit of a headache, but it's getting better as we speak."

"Good to hear." Raoul gathered his equipment. "I'd like to know what makes my trackpad go blank though, when you have the time, Chief."

"Of course." Claire felt her annoyance dissipate, along with the initial headache. "And I didn't mean to snap at either of you." She looked down at Holly's hand, still holding hers. "Thanks for being here, Holly."

Holly let go, which induced an acute sense of loss. "These NIECs are a major discovery, and so is everything else in that new wall of instruments. I would never forgive myself if something happened to you because I wasn't here—or Raoul." She nodded at Raoul. "How's the wounded crewman, by the way?"

"He'll be fine. Just a sprained ankle." Raoul hesitated. "I'd prefer if you'd accompany me back to the infirmary, Claire."

"Headache's nearly gone, and I feel better than I have ever since my old NIEC began acting up. To be honest, I haven't felt this clear-minded—and relieved—for months." Claire patted Raoul's arm. "I promise I'll page you if I experience anything strange. And I'll even ask Holly and my staff to keep an eye on me, okay?"

Raoul studied Claire for a few moments. "I'm going to hold you to that."

Claire nodded. "A promise is a promise." She meant it. It was one thing to be resilient and another to be foolhardy. The latter was not an option after living with a painful, malfunctioning NIEC for so long.

After Raoul left them, Holly ran a hand over her face. "Now that was a bit more dramatic than I normally care for." She sighed. "You bounced back quickly though."

"And now we need to see what this thing is capable of. I can feel its weight, which I never did with the other one. It's made from a different alloy. Makes me wonder how heavy the captain's crown is."

"Crown?" Smiling faintly, Holly shook her head. "All I can say is, you get used to it."

"Ha. Okay." Rolling her shoulders a few times and feeling down her braids, Claire stepped out into engineering, where she found her crew all looking around at the same time. Their concern for her was tangible, but then they refocused on their tasks and kept working.

Trainer came over and stared into Claire's eyes until she began feeling awkward.

"It hasn't turned me into an alien zombie or something, Trainer," she said and pushed against his shoulder. "Cut it out."

"Sorry, Chief." Trainer stepped back.

"No problem. Just don't creep me out." Claire grinned at him. He was a good friend, as well as her next in command.

As she turned to the bulkhead with the new instruments, another surge of information hit. This time, Claire didn't lose consciousness, but she gripped Holly's right arm to steady herself. "Shit."

"What do you mean?" Holly didn't appear to care that they were in plain sight of everyone in engineering. She wrapped a steadying arm around Claire's waist. "Claire?"

"There's another cabinet with another version of these NIECs." Claire blinked. "They're meant to be attached on top of the existing ones. There's a captain's version in that storage cabinet." She pointed to a smaller cabinet to the left of the center console.

"We haven't been able to open that one, Captain," Trainer said.

"Only possible if you wear the crown," Claire said. "This panel was created for the captain only. We've already figured out it is a panel meant to be a second bridge. It was always meant to deploy if and when the *Velocity* returned to Dwynna Major. It turns engineering into a situation room and a war bridge."

Holly let go of Claire and stepped closer to the panel. After placing a hand on the small cabinet, which obediently clicked open, she pulled out an intricately designed NIEC with a multitude of filaments and their corresponding little metal "feet." Glancing at Claire, she gave a wry smile. "My turn."

Chapter Twenty-three

The shuttle bay hadn't been in proper use since they investigated the rig for the solar-magnetic sails. Now Samantha looked around as it bustled with activity. Crewmen from the lower decks, especially the cargo bays, were stocking up *Speeder One* and *Speeder Two* with crates and canisters, and Samantha felt she ought to know in more detail what went into them. But all she could do was trust the people she was about to ship to the surface to know what they had taken with them and how to use it.

"Hey. Glad I caught you." A kiss from soft lips landed on Samantha's cheek, and she inhaled Darian's familiar, sweet scent. "I have to ask. Don't you feel it's rather heavy?"

"Excuse me?" Samantha blinked and turned to face Darian. "What's heavy?"

"The add-on to the NIEC. I heard someone among the crewmen call it the wartime bug." Darian shrugged. "Small crew. Word gets around."

"I've heard that too. Perhaps that's what's giving it an emotional, sort of perceived, weight," Samantha said, refocusing on the crew loading via the aft section of *Speeder One*. "We know why it was constructed. The ship has obviously noticed something that suggests we might need it. Now *that's* heavy."

"And philosophical. Anyway, it took me a few hours not to feel weird about it, and I'm a cop. You seem very calm regarding it. So does Gran."

"Camilla's wearing one?" This news caught Samantha's full attention. "You're joking. She's the ship's counselor."

"Apparently the add-on agrees with her. She's now a wartime counselor." Darian shrugged, but Samantha could tell she wasn't happy about her grandmother's decision.

"Can she be, you know…overcompensating? I mean, in a misguided way to show Holly that she's going to make her niece proud, no matter what?" Samantha murmured the words into Darian's ear. They had spoken about Darian and the fact that Holly was her great-aunt's daughter, but not lately. On the surface, everyone seemed to have just accepted the relationship for what it was, but Samantha guessed that story might have more chapters.

"Who knows? Gran's always been stubborn and had a very well-developed mind of her own. Remember back home when she was frail and not able to do much? She still ruled the house, and God help me if I 'hovered.' Now, I feel she's hovering, as if she has something to prove."

A signal echoed from the ship-wide speaker system. "Department heads, report progress to the bridge. Estimated time for launch to the surface is twenty minutes."

"Twenty?" Samantha jumped. "I thought I had another hour."

"Sorry. I meant to tell you. People are scrambling, and we're getting ready sooner than expected. Don't worry. You have everything you need, according to your loading crew. I asked them earlier."

"And you?" Samantha forced herself to relax her stiff shoulders.

"I'm leading a tactical team of sixteen from your speeder. Nate's doing the same from *Speeder Two*. Both speeders will also carry scientists and medical staff."

Samantha knew all this, but she was glad Darian had repeated the information, as it seemed to ground her.

"Just so you know," Darian continued, "Agent Brewer's on my team. The other agent is on Nate's. Not entirely ideal, perhaps, as they spent the entire first half of the journey being major pains in the ass. They've been doing all right since about the time we deployed the sails. Despite being a bit full of themselves, they're highly trained in law enforcement, with all that it entails. To be honest, we need them."

"I know. Not sure I like it, but we do." Samantha motioned for Darian to walk with her up the ramp. "We might as well get started."

The helm of the speeder felt strangely small since Samantha was so used to the impressive console on the bridge when piloting the *Velocity*. To her right, she had her copilot, and she'd handpicked Molly, who had been at her side the last time she flew. At the helm of *Speeder Two*, Holly would be assisted by Rhian, who had flown the speeder to the UN building back on Earth.

It took the rest of the crew only ten minutes to settle into their seats. They were all dressed in space suits, helmets on their laps.

"*Speeder One* to bridge. We're closing our hatches and will be ready to launch on time." Samantha watched Darian swivel her chair into a locked position.

"Bridge to *Speeder One*. Affirmative," Walker replied. "*Speeder Two* is almost ready."

"Understood." Samantha closed the link to the bridge and instead engaged the local system within the speeder. "All hands, this is Chief Pike. In a few minutes we will launch, and even if I know that your respective department heads have briefed you, I still want to emphasize a few things. Nobody leaves their seat unless Chief Tennen or I say it's all right. Once we set down, you disembark only when we give you permission as well. This regulation is non-negotiable, regardless of your rank. Security officers report to Chief Tennen, and scientists report to me." Samantha motioned for Darian to continue.

Darian raised her voice. "Listen up, everyone. We're setting down in what looks like the ruins of a vast city, which means the ground can be treacherous. We know the air is breathable, but the helmets stay on until you have permission to remove them." Darian paused. "Any questions?"

"I worry about having my sea legs, so to speak," a female scientist said. "We've been living with artificial gravity for more than eight months. We're bound to feel the effects."

"The gravity on Dwynna Major is comparable to that of Earth, so yes, perhaps you'll feel some of it. We did, to a degree, when we visited the rig a few months ago," Darian said over her shoulder. "Let's keep an eye on each other for potential ill effects, all right? That's our best bet, as we can't anticipate every detail about setting foot on an alien world."

"Bridge to *Speeder One*. *Speeder Two* is ready to begin countdown."

"*Speeder One* to bridge. Affirmative. Commencing countdown to launch." Samantha nodded at Molly. "Ready."

"Ready, Chief." Molly nodded, her expression stark and her eyes focused.

"Ten, nine, eight, seven…" As Samantha performed the countdown aloud for the benefit of the crew behind her, she regarded the other speeder that sat next to them via the smaller left screen. *Speeder One* would launch first and *Speeder Two* only seconds after, once Samantha had cleared the port. "…three, two, one, launching." Pushing the sliders on her console, Samantha sent her speeder toward the open port within a few moments. The different sensation in the controls and how the speeder seemed to swell around them told her the moment they were free. The weightlessness of space didn't actually make the ship swell, but it felt like it did.

"We've cleared the hull. Ready for 10-percent speed." Molly had her gaze locked on her screen. "And there's *Speeder Two*, right behind us."

"Initiating course for the old city." The flutter in Samantha's stomach grew as she pulled her speeder into a perfect glide path toward the trajectory that would take them to their destination on a—hopefully—uneventful journey.

"*Velocity—Speeder One. Velocity—Speeder One*," Samantha said over the speaker system.

"Walker here. We see you. All's looking good from our point of view, Samantha." Walker sounded faintly relieved. "Same goes for the other speeder. They're eight seconds behind you."

"Thank you, *Velocity*. We'll report back when we've landed."

"Sounds good. We're monitoring your trajectory. Walker out."

Their descent described a perfect drop-shaped curve toward the surface. As they neared, Samantha saw seas of sparkling turquoise water, billowing, golden fields, and charcoal-colored, jagged mountain ridges. Perfectly straight lines among the mountains and across the fields suggested a vast civilization had once resided here. Samantha had to force herself to focus on flying the speeder rather than speculating about what could have erased an entire species.

The flight down to the planet took twenty-five minutes, as Samantha and Holly had agreed to go slower than they had back on Earth. When they reached their destination, Samantha brought *Speeder One* into a hover at six thousand feet above sea level. Something inside her, perhaps the yearning, made her fingers itch to just set down on any area level enough and go outside, to fully return home. She couldn't let that part of her brain determine her actions though. Clenching her hands, she let the speeder hover as *Speeder Two* appeared at their port side.

"*Speeder Two—Speeder One*. All's well on our end. Are you ready to proceed?" Holly's voice was distinct.

"Affirmative, Captain. Just waited for you."

"Then let's go. Lead the way, Chief. Crowe out."

Samantha pushed the sliders into position as she tapped her speaker with her free hand. "In a few minutes we'll be setting down in the old city. Remain alert, and prepare to put on your helmets."

"Remember, we'll enter the troposphere in one minute. It can get bumpy."

Samantha opted to fly the last stretch of the approach manually. Deploying the two thin metallic levers on either side of her console, she guided the speeder between clouds and looked for any unexpected obstacles.

"There! Ten degrees starboard!" Molly called out. "Some sort of birds and they're huge."

Fairly sure that running the speeder into birds wouldn't damage it, but as it most likely would kill the creatures, Samantha gripped the levers firmly. "Adjusting course point five degrees."

"*Speeder Two* following suit," Molly said. "Smooth maneuver, Chief."

"Those were some weird birds," Darian said. "I snapped a photo for the scientists back in the crew seats. I know they're psyched about studying wildlife."

"One minute to touchdown." Samantha pulled the levers toward her. "Speed .5 percent. Point three."

"We're kicking up a lot of dust, but we're free of debris," Darian said.

"Hovering. Check the sensors on the belly one more time." Darian was right, but this was Samantha's responsibility, and she wasn't going to crush anything under the speeder if she could help it. Even if it was nothing important, inanimate objects might damage the vehicle.

Speeder One seemed to give a sigh, and then all was still for a few moments. "We have touchdown. Put on helmets. Ready your weapons and bring your gear. As Chief Tennen said—just like we trained." Samantha sent a short message to the *Velocity* after she put on her own helmet. After checking her weapon's harness and making sure her sidearms were secure, she pulled her impressive backpack from the starboard-side storage area and hoisted it into place.

"Goodness. You have more stuff than I do, and I carry enough firepower to take on a small country." Darian snorted. She was fully geared up and stood by the hatch, with Agent Brewer on the other side of it. They were going to be the first out the door, followed by two more security officers. Once they gave the all-clear, the rest of them would exit the speeder.

Samantha would be the fifth one out the door, and even if she had just set down her speeder on Dwynna Major's soil, it still felt surreal to have finally reached their goal—the birthplace of their yearning.

Darian winked at Samantha and said, "Here we go, Chief," before opening the hatch. Dust-filled air swirled outside as the pressure evened out. Once the ramp was in place, Darian motioned for Brewer to follow her and then ducked out through the opening, immediately obscured by the dust.

Samantha could have sworn she heard someone say, "Honey, I'm home!"

Chapter Twenty-four

Darian changed the filter for her helmet visor as the dust took its sweet time to clear. Until they could see their surroundings, they couldn't give the go-ahead to the rest of the teams.

"Nate to Darian. I'm outside with my agent. We can't see shit." Nate's voice was so loud and clear, Darian felt as if he stood right beside her.

"Understood. Brewer and I just changed to visor five. It helps a lot."

"Hey. Yeah. It does. The captain's eager to get outside," Nate said. "Are those cobblestones we're standing on?"

Darian looked down again. "Close enough, anyway. They're perfectly octagonal as far as I can see. Makes sense."

"How do you mean?" Nate asked.

"We know from our ancestors back home that they're brilliant when working with bedrock." Darian pulled out her trackpad. "I have deployed my sidearm, and so has Brewer. Am scanning the area now." Holding the trackpad closer to the visor, Darian squinted to make out the readings. A feature that let her see the screen of the trackpad was displayed on the helmet's visor, but Darian didn't want to mess with that when she needed to pay attention to everything around them.

"I'm not seeing anything. No people. No major wildlife. Just structures that nature is taking over in different stages." Darian sighed. "For now, it looks like the people who lived here either left or perished."

"Don't jump to conclusions, Darian," Holly said, entering the conversation. "We know far too little about this world, and who used to live in these structures, to deduce anything."

"I hear you, Captain." Darian stepped around Brewer. "You get anything?" Brewer had been outfitted with a wartime NIEC after demanding to try one. Nobody thought the device would work for the ornery agent, as he had no connection to Dennamore, but it turned out that this type of NIEC didn't discriminate. This device gave them all a last-minute edge, as several others among the passengers didn't carry the alien DNA marker but could be useful in an emergency. Now, Brewer stood swiveling his trackpad in a wide arc several times.

"I'm not sure, Chief," Brewer said absentmindedly. "Most things around us are built of a granite-like bedrock, but not a structure farther up this—what is it—a square? Anyway. That building seems as worn down by time as the rest, but I see something made from metal."

"Good job locating that clue." Darian nodded, looking around. The dust seemed to be settling, and the contours of the structures around them became increasingly visible. Darian stared. Some looked so high it was impossible to guess their height. Her trackpad insisted that one of the buildings was 2,460 feet tall. Cone-shaped, it was mostly made from the type of bedrock Brewer had mentioned.

"Darian to Nate. Let's scan the immediate perimeter, and if we don't find anything, we can allow the rest of the others to join us." Darian cast another glance at the surrounding buildings, some as tall as the cone-shaped one and others only half its size.

Moving in a coordinated pattern, the eight of them soon established a secure perimeter. After she placed one security guard in each corner around the speeders, Darian gave the go-ahead for Samantha and Holly to proceed. Soon they all stood between the ships, as they provided shelter for the crew in case something happened.

"Look at the masonry." Mireille Wu took pictures of the ground after brushing away some of the fine dust that had just settled. "Amazing."

Darian stood in the small group consisting of Holly, Claire, Samantha, Carl, Raoul, and Brandon. The latter wore a wartime NIEC with pride, and considering his checkered past included a stint with the secret service, he was one of those unexpected assets. Darian waved to Brewer to join them before turning to the others.

"Brewer found some odd readings farther down the square. I suggest I head up a team to investigate while the rest of the tactical team safeguards the scientists as they begin gathering samples and exploring. I don't want anyone out of sight of the speeders for now, though. That's non-negotiable."

"I want to go on that team," Brewer stated firmly.

"Finders keepers, you mean?" Samantha shook her head.

"Something like that." Brewer didn't look like he was about to back down.

"Pick your team, Darian, but I'm going," Holly said. "While we were in space, I was reluctant to send too many senior officers on the rig mission, as we couldn't afford to lose all of them. Now that we've reached our goal, no matter what we find, I have to deploy the best people for each situation, regardless of their rank."

"All right, then. Captain, Brewer, Samantha, Claire, and Brandon." Darian turned to Raoul. "I need you to set up an infirmary in *Speeder One*. I hope we won't have to use it, but we have to be prepared."

Holly nodded. "Good plan, Darian. Carl, you will let everyone know that you expect them to report to you every fifteen minutes. That goes for this team as well. If anyone fails to do so, you report to me immediately."

"Aye, Captain." Carl nodded. "I'll go reel in the giddy scientists and let them know." He stopped midstride. "Be careful over there. None of these buildings looks very safe."

Darian agreed with Carl, but she was more excited than nervous right now. "You be safe too, Carl. I could never face your Aunt Marjory back on the *Velocity* if something happened to you."

"I'll be okay." Carl began jogging over to the scientists.

"How's the air, Raoul?" Darian asked before he started walking up the ramp to *Speeder One*.

"Let me run the medical trackpad again." Raoul moved the device in a figure-eight motion before he checked the results. "You can remove your helmets, but keep them with you. I'll send out a message to everyone's trackpad to warn them at what value they need to put them back on again. If we don't kick up more dust than this, we should be safe."

"Should?" Holly frowned.

"A certain percentage of my work on this planet will be guesswork for quite some time." Raoul shrugged. "Can't be helped."

"I understand, but I don't have to like it." Holly unfastened her helmet and was the first one to remove it.

Darian followed suit and drew a careful breath once she'd removed the helmet completely. To her surprise, the air smelled clean, even if the finest of dust still lingered. "Whatever happened here, either the air wasn't affected," she muttered, "or it was so long ago it has cleared up on its own."

"Hopefully we'll find out." Holly waved at the team to fall in. "Let's go."

Holly took the lead, and they rounded *Speeder Two*, where it sat on its struts. Passing one of the security guards watching the perimeter, she nodded at him, as he seemed on edge. "Good job, Ensign."

"Thanks, Captain. Be safe." He gave a wary smile.

"You too." She used her confident tone, one she'd cultivated over many years of lecturing and giving speeches, but most of all during the past months on the *Velocity*.

Claire appeared at Holly's right and Brewer on her left.

"The crumbled material from the buildings," Claire said and ran her engineer trackpad along the wall of the structure they were approaching, "looks more like it happened over time than all at once."

"What do you mean?" Holly changed the grip on her rifle, making sure to point it away from Claire.

"The debris. The way the climate has treated it…some of the pieces of bedrock are severely eroded, and some look like they fell off the building yesterday. And they seem to be cut with the same precision as the ones back home in the basements and the tunnel."

"And you think the ones suffering from erosion were initially just as perfect?" Holly had to admit this theory made sense.

"Yes, exactly."

"A natural disaster? A war?" Brewer asked.

"Could be. Or a plague." Holly hid a smile when Brewer flinched and then grimaced.

"I know the doc inoculated us with something, but that's still a freaky thought," Darian said from behind them. "I like my threats big enough to fire on."

"I hear you." Brewer gave a rare smile, which in Holly's book gave his normally set-in-granite face an eerie expression. Somehow, it was as if his normally rigid facial muscles weren't used to turning the corners of his mouth upward.

The towering buildings, which covered most of the turquoise sky by their sheer height, loomed over them as they made their way along the debris from crumbled walls. As they approached the building that sensors had flagged as unusual, Holly raised her hand.

"I know we haven't seen any signs of life—yet—but still, weapons drawn, everyone. On shock setting only, unless I say otherwise."

"Shock setting," Brewer said, his disdain obvious.

"That's right." Holly held her rifle against her shoulder as she, after allowing Darian to go first, moved faster toward the building. They had trained for this scenario so many times that walking heel-to-toe was second nature to her by now. The rubble on the ground made it impossible to be as quiet as she'd liked to, despite their by-the-book approach.

At one point, a glass door had led into the tall building, judging by the remnants hanging from the hinges. Even such hardware looked to be made from marble-like stone. Darian took the right side of the entrance, Holly the left. Behind them, the rest of the team lined up.

What looked like it might have been a lobby ran the entire length of the building. Columns of glittering bedrock held up what was left of the floors above it. The ceiling had collapsed in places, but furniture, appearing rustic and made from wood, had survived.

"That looks remarkably like oak," Samantha murmured. She ran a gloved hand over the surface of an armrest.

The walls were made of the same glittering material. Claire ran her trackpad along it and then raised her eyebrows. "Marble." She glanced at Holly. "Not *like* marble, but exactly marble. Wow."

A shiver ran through Holly. Another similarity to Earth. God only knew how many they'd end up finding. "That looks like what's left of a counter over there." She pointed to the far wall of the space.

Sending a wary glance up toward the ceiling, she hoped it wouldn't come down on them. As she passed a piece of the fallen piece of furniture, which was also half crushed under a crumbled pillar, she glanced down to make sure she wasn't stepping on glass or anything else sharp. Their space suits could take a lot, but piercing objects were their enemies.

Holly stopped walking abruptly, making Claire stumble into her from behind. She automatically reached out and steadied Claire, still staring at the floor. "What's wrong with this picture?" she said in a faint voice.

"Captain?" Darian came up to them.

"Damn," Claire whispered and gripped Holly's arm with her free hand. "Someone's maintained this floor. Or at least this part of the floor."

Holly nodded slowly. "Everything else is covered with dust. This part, this *path*, has only a thin layer. Hang on." She knelt and turned on the sharp light at the top of her rifle. Directing it parallel along the floor, she drew in a sharp breath. "And unless I'm hallucinating, those are footprints."

Chapter Twenty-five

Darian knelt next to Holly, peering along the floor. Some kind of footwear had disturbed the fine dust. It wasn't pawprints, unless the animals on Dwynna Major wore something with soles.

"Someone's been in this building," Darian said quietly. "And recently."

"Exactly." Holly stood, looking around, her rifle raised again. "See any stairs? No one could use an elevator. The structure's not level enough."

Samantha joined them. "Crumbled stairs over there, in the center," she said. "But that's not where the cleared path leads."

Walking next to the path to not disturb it further, Darian realized Samantha was right. The path looked like it might stretch across the building, but after the counter, it veered ninety degrees to the left. "There," she said, pointing with her rifle. "It continues that way."

Holly gestured at Brandon, Samantha, and Brewer. "Circle around and keep checking the floor. We'll follow the path and see where it ends."

"Aye, Captain," Samantha said and motioned for the men to follow her.

Darian kept walking along the cleared path but found it impossible to avoid stepping on it because of all the rubble on either side. Holly and Claire were right behind her.

A wall partition that didn't go all the way to the ceiling made Darian raise her hand and stop. "Let me check this out." Immediately peering carefully around the corner, she saw no sign of any individuals, but the cleared area widened until it reached what looked like a flat box, approximately four yards wide. From their angle, she couldn't determine how far it stretched into the vast space beyond it. "Looks clear." Darian waved for Holly and Claire to follow her.

"Hey. What's that? A podium?" Claire scanned the structure that did indeed look like a large podium or a stage.

"Your guess is as good as mine," Darian said. She and Holly had their rifles trained on it. "But it's clear of dust."

"Samantha to Holly." Holly's speaker was so loud, Darian pivoted, ready to fire.

"Holly here. Go on." Holly didn't even blink.

"We've found what looks like an elevated square, covered in dust though," Samantha said.

"We found something similar without dust," Holly said. "Unless you see anything that's been cleared of debris and worthy of immediate investigation, scan for our signals and join us."

"Affirmative. Samantha out."

Darian stood ready with her rifle while Claire scanned the "podium." It was nine by thirteen feet. "Anything?" She was growing impatient and had a gnawing feeling that they were overstaying their welcome. She detected no movements, no signals other than from the rest of their team and, at a greater distance, the teams over by the speeders. She tapped her speaker. "Darian to Carl. Report."

"Carl here. All's well. Everyone is present and accounted for. I was just starting to worry about your team. Find anything?"

"Potential signs of life, but it's too early to tell. The scientists?" Darian turned in a slow circle, keeping her eyes trained on the empty octagonal openings that might have once been windows, which now left the entire bottom floor open to the elements.

"You'd think it was Christmas, Hanukkah, and Eid all rolled into one." Carl chuckled. "Any ETA of your return?"

"Not yet. I'll page you again in half an hour." Darian heard a crunching noise and rounded on it, her rifle at her eye. When she spotted Samantha coming across the expanse of debris, relief flushed over her. She didn't wave or call out, but she could see Samantha's smile through the sight of her rifle.

"There it is." Claire sounded tense. "The metallic alloy our scans showed. It's there. Under the elevated area."

Holly looked over Claire's shoulder at the readings. "Damn. You found the origin of the readings. Or one of them."

"Yeah, and I had to really tweak the settings, as this thing," Claire motioned at the elevation, "is damn near impenetrable to scans."

"Is all of it metallic?"

"No. That's just it. Not all of it. Most of it appears to be constructed of the same marble as the structure, but from the data, I'd say it's lined with something. And the metallic parts are in the corners here, I'm certain."

Darian walked closer to the elevation that reached her hip. Examining the surface that looked like high-gloss, lightly veined, white marble, she pushed her rifle onto her back and placed her hands on it.

"Darian?" Samantha's voice, laced with concern, reached her from behind.

"I'm okay—" The sudden tremor under Darian's hands made her jump back, snapping her rifle forward and up to her eyes. "Watch out!"

The elevation began to rise, and Darian retreated farther. Using her left hand, she signaled to her team members to spread out and keep their weapons ready.

"What the hell's that?" Brewer stood two yards to Darian's left. "Did you trigger a weapons array?"

"How should I know?" Darian growled. "It's still rising."

"I detect a cavity inside it now," Claire called out. "No life signs, not that my trackpad can detect, anyway."

"All right." Holly, who stood to Darian's right, raised her hand. "Just hold your positions."

Darian counted another twenty seconds before the elevation stopped moving. "Claire?"

"It's nine and a half feet tall at this point." Claire moved closer as she kept scanning the structure before them. "The metal parts in the corners run the entire height of this thing. Permission to approach closer to get better scans, Captain."

Holly's hesitation was so brief, Darian nearly missed it. One beat, and then Holly nodded. "All right. Be careful."

Claire made her way along the cleared path that led to the middle of the elevation. She ran her trackpad and then seemed to lose her balance.

"Claire?" Holly took a step forward, but Darian was quicker. She covered the distance with quick steps and took hold of Claire's arm. "Hey there."

"Just my new NIEC going crazy for a moment. I'm all right." Claire held up her trackpad. "Suddenly got a lot of added information, and it seemed to go to my head, so to speak."

Darian smiled at the pun but grew instantly serious when a whirring sound emanated from the structure. She pushed Claire behind her and raised her rifle again.

A crack in the middle of the glossy surface on the wall facing them parted and folded back into itself in an only-too-familiar way. Staring into the opening, Darian saw what looked like a small room and blinking dots on what had to be a computer console.

"Captain?" Darian didn't have time to finish the word before Holly was by her side. "An elevator. Not exactly like the ones in Dennamore, but close enough."

"I see it."

Holly engaged her speaker. "All senior crew. All tactical staff. This is Captain Crowe. My team and I have found an elevator that appears to be in working order, and with a live computer inside. I want all scientists back on *Speeder Two*, ready to return to the *Velocity* on my orders or on Ensign Hoskins's. Commander Walker, be prepared to initiate the protocols for emergency extractions if our speeders are compromised."

"Understood, Captain," Walker said.

"Carl to Crowe. Should I send more tactical officers to your coordinates?" Carl could be heard ushering people to board the speeder while he waited for Holly's reply.

"Negative, Carl. Keep everyone safe, and be ready to leave. Proceed through most of the start-up sequence with Molly and Rhian."

"Will do. Carl out."

Holly looked around the team, meeting everyone's eyes. "This is why we came here. To find out who our ancestors were. To see if life still existed here, and if not, what happened to the inhabitants. I'm going to use the elevator, and I'll need Claire to go with me, as well as at least one more."

"I'm going," Darian said quickly.

"And so am I." Samantha stepped up to Darian. "I'll order Molly to remain in *Speeder One*, to fly it out with the rest of the remaining crew if something goes wrong." She placed a hand on Darian's shoulder. "As you said, this is why we came here."

Darian half expected Brewer to insist on going, but whether he had an onset of nerves or realized they'd ask him to keep guard along with Brandon, he remained quiet.

"All right." Holly pushed her rifle onto her back. "Brandon, Brewer, you're the only ones who know exactly where we went down, and I need you to stay on an open link to the *Velocity* and to Carl on *Speeder Two*."

Samantha, who had quietly ordered Molly to return to *Speeder One* with two security officers, said, "Include Molly as well. She'll be ready at the helm on the other speeder in two minutes."

"Brewer, you're in charge of the open speaker to the ships." Claire raised a hand. "If Brandon uses these settings on his speaker, he should be able to hear us on an open link unless that thing takes us too far down. Everything depends on the sediment and bedrock beneath us. Sending it to you now, Brandon."

Darian didn't care what anyone else might think. She went over to Brandon and kissed his cheek. "We'll be all right," she murmured. "Tell Gran that."

Brandon looked sternly at her. "Tell her yourself, Darian."

"I will. We will." Returning to the opening leading into the elevator, Darian scanned all of it with her tactical trackpad before waving to the others to join her. "From my readings, this is simply an elevator. That said, helmets on." She shrugged. It could be something they had never heard of, or experienced, and they wouldn't know until it was too late.

Nothing happened for a good five seconds after the four of them stepped through the opening. Just as Darian thought they might have to risk tinkering with the console, which to a degree resembled the ones they were used to, the wall folded into place again, hiding them from the two men outside.

"At least a light's on," Holly murmured. "Should we try to decipher the—" She gasped and had steadied herself against the wall when a loud clonking sound rang out.

And then she felt as if they were falling.

"Hold on!" Holly yelled. "Damn, this thing is fast." Grateful that some time had passed since she ate, Holly swallowed the rising bile in her throat. After a few more moments, her system seemed to catch up with the elevator's insane speed. Relaxing marginally, she was then flung sideways when it unfathomably changed direction and went sideways. Pressed against one of the walls in a heap of arms, legs, and rifles, Holly pulled at Claire, who was pressed face-first against her, whimpering.

"Claire? Are you hurt?" Holly managed to right them both.

"Trackpad. Caught me across the throat." Claire's wheezing cough sounded painful.

"Can you swallow?" Samantha asked.

Claire swallowed and then grimaced. "Yeah." She glanced at her trackpad. "We've been in here eight minutes and counting. Three of them were straight down. Then sideways."

"Holly to Brandon. Do you read?" Holly kept one hand on Claire's shoulder.

"Brandon here. We hear you, barely." Brandon sounded as if he were speaking through water.

"I'll try to boost the signal further." Claire coughed again. "Ow. Damn."

"Can you feel it?" Darian asked. "Is it just me, or is it slowing down?"

"It is," Holly said, the elevator pressing less against her back. The reduction in speed was gradual—until it wasn't. The last jerk made them stumble, but they all remained standing. "Weapons."

Holly barked the word out, raising her rifle and aiming at the door. The others, except Claire, who was scanning, did the same.

The doors, if that was the right word for the wall folding back into itself, opened smoothly. Holly hadn't even thought of what to anticipate, but it wasn't the sight that met them.

In front of a rock wall, about four yards from the opening, four figures stood facing them. Dressed in gray pants and light-yellow jackets, each of them wore a silver-colored harness and what looked like a sidearm strapped to their right hip. They also wore what looked like a form-fitted helmet that covered everything but their nose, mouth, and jaw. As soon as they saw Holly and her team, they reached for their weapons.

"Not so fast," Holly said, not sure if these people could understand her. Instead, she pressed the sensor on her rifle that triggered the telltale tone that it was ready to fire.

The figures stopped with their hands only a few inches from their weapons.

"We don't want to shoot. We're not here to cause trouble." Holly and her senior crew had debated about how to make themselves understood if they found life on Dwynna Major. The general consensus, because what little else did they have to hope for, was that their NIECs would translate for them. Now, Holly realized that even if that turned out to be the case, the people standing in front of them, looking like sentries, might not understand a word of what she'd just said. "Lower your weapons, but keep them charged," Holly told her team. Holding up a hand, palm forward, she pointed the muzzle of her rifle toward the ground. "Please. We're here as visitors. Explorers."

The figure to the far left raised their hand to their lapel, making Holly wince, not knowing what to expect. They ran a gloved fingertip along the edge of the lapel, which made it glow faintly. Holly saw that they appeared to have a human hand under the glove, judging from the form. Then they pointed to Holly and flicked their fingers. She didn't understand.

"I'm sorry. I don't know what you mean."

The figure rolled its hand in the air, now seeming impatient.

"Try again, Holly," Claire murmured from behind. "From the beginning."

Holly nodded faintly. "We don't mean any harm. We are visitors. Explorers."

The figures exchanged glances.

"Visitors. From where?" the left individual asked, sounding like a woman.

"The hell? That's not English, and I still understand it," Claire whispered and stepped closer to the opening, studying her scanner.

"Careful, Claire. We have NIECs, they have…that, or something else," Holly said quietly before turning to the one on the left. "We are from a planet called Earth."

"Why have you—"

"Number One." The figure on the far right interrupted. "Sound the alarm. We need reinforcement and our elders to gather. Don't forget your place."

Elders? Holly thought fast. Did these people still use the system with elder councils? If so, was that a good way to explain where they came from and why?

"Affirmed." The person on the left twisted something on their wrist, and a loud, booming alarm rang out. Within seconds, the sound of a multitude of boots hammered against the polished rock floor and quickly grew closer.

"We're going to be seriously outgunned. We have to fall back, Holly," Darian called out.

"Agreed. Close the opening if you can, Claire!" Holly took two steps back and raised her weapon. "Come on!"

"I can do it. Just give me a sec!" Claire ran her fingers along her trackpad, and Holly sighed in relief as the walls began to roll back into place.

Just as they had only two feet left to go, a gloved hand shot through the opening and grabbed Claire's wrist.

"Claire! No!" Holly cried out as she let go of her rifle to reach for Claire. Instead, she found herself fumbling in the air as Claire disappeared through the opening. Only the fact that Darian yanked Holly back saved her hands from being mangled when the walls closed.

Thrown against a wall when the elevator accelerated, all Holly could think of as she crumbled to the floor was that she'd lost the one person who really mattered. But then she pushed herself back onto her feet, standing, feet wide apart, in the center of the elevator, gripping her rifle hard.

No matter what it took, or what she had to do, she intended to get Claire back.

Chapter Twenty-six

Claire tumbled through the elevator opening just before it closed, falling onto her knees with her arms protectively around her trackpad. Looking behind her, she saw nothing but a smooth wall and a computer console.

Next to her, the one who had reached in and pulled her through rose and then stood at attention. The other three did the same.

"Sir Neo'Toya, sir!" The four sentries spoke in unison and then performed a gesture that could have been some sort of salute. They placed their left hand on their right shoulder for a few moments and then jerked it back to their side.

"Shut off the alarm," a deep voice that held a booming command ordered. "Who is this individual?"

Claire didn't intend to meet the people she sprang from on her damn knees. Standing up while still holding her trackpad, she turned to face the newcomer. As it turned out, the man wasn't alone. The wall behind the sentries had shifted, and behind the looming, burly man, she saw what looked like a sea of helmets in a wide corridor. The man in charge, Neo'Toya, didn't wear a helmet, but instead a metal band that went under his jaw and up around his head. Long, black hair billowed around his shoulders, but his complexion was pale, almost shimmering white.

"They and three others came down with the transporter. We thought it was our missing team that's two rotations overdue." The one who had grabbed Claire spoke. "As soon as I saw it wasn't them, I decided to act and captured this one."

"What faction wears this type of uniform?" The man in charge stared down at Claire, towering at least two feet over her five-foot-four height.

"How about asking me directly?" Claire wasn't sure where she found the courage to speak, but she was already in a world of trouble. In the back of her mind, she could still hear Holly screaming her name. It could well be the last time they ever saw each other.

"Remove the helmet." The man motioned toward Claire's head.

Having checked the quality of the air in the corridor already when Holly was trying to address the sentries, Claire knew it was safe to do so. Folding her trackpad and placing it in her leg pocket, she unhooked the fastening hooks of her helmet and pulled it off. Her long, thick braid fell down her back.

"Look! Look at them!"

"Their skin. What happened?"

"What are they?"

The words from the closest people washed over Claire. They stared at her, open-mouthed, and only then did she realize that perhaps nobody on this planet had as deep a skin tone as she did.

Neo'Toya was the only one truly keeping it together. If he was as stunned as the others, he didn't let on. "Who are you?" he asked, placing his hand on his sidearm.

Claire looked at the weapon and then at his face, deliberately raising her eyebrows. Not so cool and unyielding after all, perhaps? "I am Chief Engineer Claire Gordon of the space vessel *Velocity*. Neither I, nor any of my crewmembers, mean you and your people any harm." *Well, perhaps with the exception of Brewer, if he got an itchy trigger finger going.* "I understand if your subordinates were curious about me, or even afraid, but I must protest against being handled this way." Trying to not sound like something from a science-fiction show and still get her information, and indignation, across, Claire folded her hands behind her back. Damn if she was going to say "take me to your leaders," or anything equally trite and ridiculous.

Neo'Toya studied her closely, and for a second, Claire thought he might actually reach out and touch her hair, which wouldn't be the first time a stranger did that without asking. She glared at him, and even if he seemed unperturbed, he didn't come near her.

"The *Velocity*," Neo'Toya said. "It's in orbit?"

"I'm not prepared to answer any questions until I've been in contact with my captain."

"She could be one of *them* in disguise," someone said from behind Neo'Toya, who merely grunted and effectively shut the fool up.

Checking a rectangular plaque on his left arm, Neo'Toya tapped it a few times. "Your crewmembers are back to the point you entered the transporter. I would very much like to know how you were able to access the system and, of course, how you can understand our language. Our technology can easily deal with your rudimentary syntax, but neither machine nor man can easily grasp our language."

Claire didn't point out that she was not a man but stood her ground. "I'd be happy to explain some of that, after I've talked to my captain and we've reached a mutual non-violent understanding."

"You are not in any position to demand anything," Neo'Toya said. He motioned to the area behind him, where at least thirty people stood ready to engage.

"I'm one person. I pose no threat. I do, however, have information you need." Claire certainly hoped these people didn't have some freaky truth serum or lobotomizing equipment to extract what she knew from her brain.

Neo'Toya studied her further. "Surrender your weapon."

As Claire didn't plan to shoot anyone, she handed over her gun.

"And the piece of technology." He pointed at her pocket.

"No. I gave you my gun in good faith. You have to show equal respect, or I won't tell you, or your people, a single thing." Claire hoped how much she trembled inwardly didn't show on the outside. More than anything, she wanted to be back by Holly's side, working and exploring. Perhaps she was naive, but she had never even considered going through this whole first-contact thing on her own.

"Very well. For now." Turning to the large group of sentries, he raised his voice to a booming level again. "I'll need four sentries. The rest of you—dismissed." As if he had pushed a button connected to their rears, most of them performed their strange salute and then turned to fall into a jog down the wide corridor. A few at a time, they disappeared into openings that appeared in the walls along it.

The four remaining, not counting the ones guarding the elevator, no, transporter, moved to place Claire in the center. "Follow me."

Neo'Toya strode down the corridor, which of course was made from shiny white rock. Claire didn't want to give the sentries an excuse to push her so lengthened her stride and managed to catch up with him. It strained her legs to keep his pace, but she would be damned if she was going to walk two steps behind anyone, ever.

As they made their way down toward what looked like a well-lit arch in the distance, it dawned on Claire that the air was starting to smell quite sweet and fresh, and not at all stale, raw, or dusty, as she would have imagined it could underground. Was this a bunker? Who stayed here? And, thinking back to what the interrupting sentry had said, who were "them"?

The arch turned out to have two sets of double doors, and once they went through the first set, a mist gushed over them, quickly replaced by a swift, warm breeze. Claire held her breath, afraid of what it might entail, but she hesitated to pull out her trackpad, afraid they'd snatch it from her.

"Decontamination. The dust up top is harmless these days, but we are not taking any chances," Neo'Toya said brusquely. The fact that he bothered to explain anything at all was hopefully a good sign.

"Thanks for letting me know," Claire said as they proceeded to the second double door. Like the others, they folded into themselves, and stepping through next to Neo'Toya, she stopped so suddenly, one of the sentries walked into her. Covering her mouth with her hand, Claire gasped. "Oh, my God." The sight was so unexpected, so overwhelming, she couldn't process it.

"Keep walking," Neo'Toya said impatiently, but it was impossible for Claire to move.

They stood on what could only be described as a wide balcony inside the door, behind a transparent railing. Beneath them, beyond the balcony, stretched a city for as far as she could see. Tall buildings, parks, infrastructures, hanging gardens…Claire didn't know where to look first. "Please. Give me a moment." She gripped the top of the railing, and for a terrifying moment, the fact that it was transparent gave her vertigo. "I've never seen anything like this. I mean, not underground." Tears formed in her eyes, and she wiped them with one hand while holding on hard with the other. When she finally returned her attention to Neo'Toya, she saw what she thought was a hint of surprise, or confusion.

"Ready?" he asked and started walking toward the left end of the balcony. There, another door, this one smaller, folded back. Neo'Toya stepped inside, and Claire walked in behind him, grateful to lean against the wall. She lowered her head and tried to swallow the nausea caused by the vertigo. "You're dismissed," Neo'Toya said, and she snapped her head up.

The four sentries looked like they wanted to object but saluted and let the door fold back between them and their commanding officer and Claire. He pressed his hand against the console, and two wide straps shot through a slot next to them.

"Put it on." He wrapped the harness around his stomach and clicked it back into its slot.

Ah, that made so much sense. This was another transporter. If she ever got to ride the first transporter again, she now knew how to not get knocked around. She buckled up and tugged at the belt to make sure it was attached.

"Hold on." Neo'Toya slid two fingers along the integrated console, and the transporter went into what felt like freefall.

"Shit." Closing her eyes, Claire covered her mouth. She wasn't going to alienate this man by throwing up all over him. She barely had the chance to finish the thought before the transporter stopped. Unprepared, she cursed under her breath again when the back of her head bounced against the wall.

Stepping off the lethal transportation method and onto another, smaller, balcony, Claire realized they hadn't ridden all the way to the ground level. Beneath them, shuttles flew between buildings, as well as above them, their flight paths appearing entirely random. How did they avoid slamming into each other?

"We'll catch a ride now," Neo'Toya said. Was it Claire's wishful thinking, or did he sound less harsh? She wasn't sure.

"Where are we going?" she asked.

"Elders Hall." He didn't elaborate.

"I'm not going on any of those deathtraps. They're all over the place." Claire didn't move.

"You're not going on any of the public shuttles." Neo'Toya shook his head at her, looking exasperated, as if she should have been able to figure that fact out. "We're riding that." He pointed to the side of the railing at what had to be their version of a motorcycle. It hovered in place, yet Claire couldn't hear a live propulsion system. Her wartime NIEC was working overtime, and she suddenly knew the term for it, even if the model was unfamiliar.

"You have your own twin cruiser. Sweet." She was clearly not right in the head because she opted to give him a thumbs-up, followed by a grin.

Neo'Toya blinked and then stepped well within Claire's personal space. "How can you know the exact right term for it if you're not one of us?" His breath was hot on her face, but she refused to show how intimidating she found him on a physical level.

"Because of this." She pushed her hair aside and showed her NIEC. Perhaps it was a mistake, but someone had to start telling the truth, or they would never get anywhere—and she wanted to get back to her ship—to Holly.

"A neural interface expertise connector…" The fact that Neo'Toya took two steps back and stared at her as if she'd just grown fangs spoke volumes, but of what it was hard to say.

"Yes."

Looking undecided for the first time since she'd met him, Neo'Toya then tapped the side of his metal band at the level of his temple. "Find Elder Member Quantia. Have her meet us at the secondary site."

"But sir," a younger voice said, only to be slammed down.

"It's an order." Neo'Toya nudged Claire toward the edge of the railing. "Secondary site." Pushing at the railing, he opened a gate, and the twin cruiser moved closer.

Not about to look down, as they were at least twenty stories above ground, Claire gripped the gate and resisted. "Where are you taking me?"

"Get on the cruiser. Now." Neo'Toya's grabbed Claire's arm and practically lifted her onto the passenger seat. Immediately two straps wrapped around her thighs, keeping her in place. There was a short backrest, but little else to hold on to, and Claire closed her eyes to not reignite the vertigo.

Neo'Toya mounted the twin cruiser, and as soon as his hands were on the controls, it took off. Claire wished she had thought to put her helmet on, but she didn't dare let go of the backrest, even if she was strapped in. Neo'Toya weaved in and out of the air traffic between the buildings so fast, it became a blur. Though Claire was only two seconds away from a full panic attack, the NIEC kept the logical part of her brain occupied by absorbing details. Residential areas, financial blocks, and larger districts with lower structures containing factories and farms, as well as schools, libraries, and hospitals, flickered by. She saw recycling units so advanced her NIEC nearly gave up.

After a sharp turn to the left, Neo'Toya let the twin cruiser slow down and dip low until they were at ground level of a ten-story building. He drove the vehicle in through an opening that shut behind them. Claire drew a trembling breath. How would she be able to contact Holly from here? And how could she hope for her friends to ever find her?

"Come on. We're expected." Neo'Toya gestured toward a door, made of wood, for once, at the far end of what looked like a garage. Several vehicles were stored along the walls—twin cruisers, small shuttles, and something that looked like cars, but without wheels. Taking a closer look, Claire saw how they hovered a few inches above ground, even when parked. The car-like design made her think of her father, and the sharp pain that followed made her push those thoughts far back into her mind. She noticed that the belts around her thighs were no longer strapping her in, and she jumped off the twin cruiser.

"Can you at least tell me who we're meeting?" Claire asked as she walked next to Neo'Toya toward the door.

"Elder Quantia. Trust me, she's your best bet of one day getting out of here." Neo'Toya stopped at the door and pressed a sensor in the middle of an elaborate woodcarving. It looked like something between a dragon and a bird, and the sensor resembled a large, square emerald. The door swung open, and they stepped into a hallway adorned by beautiful tiles that resembled precious gemstones. Amethyst purple, emerald green, topaz yellow, and crisp, clear diamonds, as large as the average tiles on a kitchen backsplash, they lined the walls and floor in an intricate pattern. Four doors, two in front, and one on either side of them, made the space look like the set of a game show back home.

"What's behind door number one?" Claire murmured.

"What?" Neo'Toya barked.

"Nothing. And what did you mean by 'one day getting out of here'? I haven't done anything wrong. You have no right to keep me here against my will."

"Probably true, but I think you owe us an explanation," a sonorous female voice said from "door number four" to Claire's right.

Claire swiveled and blinked at the sight of the tall woman standing there. She was dressed in a green suit adorned with an embroidered pattern of flowers in every color around the edges. Her hair was the shade of rose gold, and she kept it in a large bun at the top of her head, which added to her considerable height. She was almost as tall as Neo'Toya.

"Elder Quantia." Neo'Toya bowed his head quickly. "As you can tell, this is the woman our sentries managed to prevent from leaving. There were three others, but they escaped in the transport system."

"And why didn't you alter said system's course?" Elder Quantia asked and waved for them to follow her. She walked through yet another hallway and opened another wooden door, which turned out to be an office. Large and breathing of luxury, it obviously was meant to show off this woman's power and wealth.

"I wanted to track where they were going. There are bound to be more, and we need to know how many and if this is a unit spearheading an invasion force—"

"Oh, for God's sake!" Claire had had enough. She took one step away from Neo'Toya, flinging her hands in the air. "We're not an invasion force. We have no hostile intent whatsoever—on the contrary." She glowered at the other two. "And yes, I know explanations are in order, but if this is how you treat visitors, it doesn't exactly make us feel welcome or that we can trust you."

Quantia looked taken aback for a fraction of a moment and then sat on a tall stool next to what appeared to be a glass table. When it buzzed to life in all kinds of colors, Claire surmised it was a computer console. Her NIEC was starting to catch up, which made it easier to make educated guesses.

"Sit down, please." Quantia motioned for another stool in front of her.

Claire climbed onto it but wasn't surprised when Neo'Toya preferred to stand. "Thank you."

"You are a visitor? I will need more than that reassurance if I'm going to keep you from being incarcerated. Not all elders are willing to listen and reach conclusions that force them to think independently. They prefer to travel in packs, and as we haven't had any 'visitors' for a very long time, your presence here will cause a stir and, no doubt, political upheaval, unless we present you and your people to them in an orderly fashion."

Claire studied the stark beauty of the woman before her. Her features were sharply chiseled, with high cheekbones and perfect lips. Her eyes glimmered an amber color that reminded her of Darian's.

"I know a woman with eyes like yours," she blurted out before thinking.

Quantia had opened her mouth to continue speaking, but now she closed it and tilted her head. "Really?"

"Yes. She's our chief of security." Feeling increasingly ridiculous, Claire decided this was still an opening. "Your technology is far more advanced than ours. Scan my DNA, and that will tell you the reason we're here."

Neo'Toya took a step forward. "What are you talking about?"

"Wait." Holding up a hand, Quantia stopped him. "An interesting approach, at least. Are you willing to separate with some of your blood as well as some strands of your hair?" She rose and opened a cabinet in the beautiful wooden shelf unit.

"No problem if it gets me closer to being reunited with my crew." Claire watched Quantia pull out a set of glass instruments. "Wait. You're going to do this yourself?"

"I was once a physician. This skill has often been quite useful. Right, Neo'Toya?"

To Claire's astonishment, the enormous man colored and muttered something inaudible, which made Quantia chuckle as she reached for Claire's hand. Taking it between hers, she studied it closely. "You're a young woman," she stated as she took a glass rod from her kit.

Claire had no idea how the people measured time here yet, only the basic knowledge of the planet's rotation compared to the twin suns. "Yes, I am," she said.

Quantia pressed the rod against Claire's wrist, and like magic, something resembling red sewing thread appeared at its center. Then Quantia yanked out a few strands of Claire's hair, making her jump.

"Let's see what you're so eager to share," Quantia murmured, moving over to the cabinet, where she pulled out a small, octagonal apparatus. She pushed the rod inside, and after pressing a glass clasp around the roots of Claire's strands, she inserted that as well. "We have less invasive methods to examine DNA, but this is a field unit for emergencies," Quantia said as she sat down at her computer again. Flicking her fingers over the controls, she then sat back, lacing her fingers. "It will be a few moments."

It seemed longer, and the silence in the room grew while they waited. Claire would have given everything to be able to pace back and forth to work off some of her nervous energy.

"Ah. There it is." Quantia leaned in closer to the screen, and Neo'Toya moved to stand behind her.

Claire could see exactly when Quantia found the marker. Her back went from perfectly poised to rigid, and she shifted her gaze to Claire and then to the screen again several times.

Neo'Toya gripped the low backrest of Quantia's stool, as if he suddenly needed support. "How can that be?" he whispered.

"It should be impossible, but there it is. Proof. If it were just the blood, I could have argued tampering, but the roots of her hair show the exact same thing." Quantia pushed back, covering her mouth with a hand that showed a faint tremor. "You have the genetic markers of our people," she said and then cleared her voice.

"I know." Claire remained still, knowing these two needed to process the news. "If you are willing to listen, I'll let you know how it happened—"

Neo-Toya's hands changed into impressive fists. "Yes, you will share all that, but more importantly, you will tell us how you can carry the DNA of our people—together with the DNA of our enemy."

Chapter Twenty-seven

Holly exited the elevator, growling at the raised weapons that met her. Pushing the muzzle of Brewer's rifle aside, she nearly ripped her speaker off the space suit when she paged the bridge. "Crowe to Walker, come in!"

"Walker here. What's going on, Captain?" Walker's voice, normally so calm and assertive, gave away his concern.

"We reached the inhabitants of this planet via the elevator. When they called for reinforcements, we tried to fall back, but—" Holly swallowed hard. "They have Claire."

A prolonged silence clawed at Holly's nerves.

"I see," Walker said, his voice back to normal, but it wasn't hard to imagine how deeply he had to dig within his many years in law enforcement to keep calm. "And the rest of your team?"

"All unharmed and accounted for." Holly breathed in deeply through her nose and expelled the air between tense lips. "I'm not sure how this is going to play out—if they'll use her as a hostage or a bargaining chip. We have to prepare for any conceivable scenario."

"We haven't seen any indications of them having ships or satellites in orbit, but that doesn't mean they don't. If we can cloak, they can too." It sounded as if Walker was pacing.

"I want you to take the *Velocity* into low orbit. We need her superior sensors to scan for other elevators. If we can tell where they might surface, we reduce their element of surprise."

"All right. I'm placing the ship in a lower orbit in the mesosphere. It's possible to go lower, but that's a good start." Walker gave the order. "As soon as we're in place, we'll engage all external sensors."

"Good. I will get us back to the speeders and brief the crew. When you're in a steady orbit, I'll send one speeder with the older scientists back, and consequently I want you to then fill it to the brim with crew and passengers in tactical gear and dispatch them here. Darian has provided you with a roster of the ones that have impressed her the most?"

"She has. And it sounds like you're preparing for war," Walker said.

"I am, but I'm hoping it won't come to that. We might be able to deliver proof to the people of this world that we're no different from them." Holly wasn't sure if she genuinely believed her own words. Her stomach felt like molten lead, and the rest of her was icy cold. "Brewer, I want you and Brandon to remain at this elevator. Stay out of sight of its opening in case someone is deployed this way before you get backup." Holly swiveled, meeting the eyes of the rest of the team. "We're returning to the speeders."

"Aye, Captain," Darian said and turned to Brewer and Brandon. "Don't take any risks. If you see movement that isn't one of us, I want to know about it asap."

"Understood." Brewer and Brandon moved around the corner of the partition wall, which would keep them out of immediate sight if the elevator opened.

Holly was already running back to the speeders. She heard the others behind her, but all she could think of right now, when she wasn't barking out orders and trying to figure out their next move, was Claire. Her own scream as she saw the hand yank Claire out of the elevator echoed in her mind, and she couldn't remember feeling such pain since Frances died. Back then, her grief had been mixed with relief that her wife was no longer suffering, and even if she had thought she'd never survive losing Frances, she had. Now, Claire was missing. Perhaps, best-case scenario, she was incarcerated and would be able to at one point to find someone who listened to her. Or she could be injured...killed.

Moaning, Holly forced the destructive thoughts from her mind. If she began to spiral into envisioning a hopeless scenario...She would work this problem together with her crew, assuming that Claire was alive and all right—and if that was the case, Claire would definitely be working the problem from her end.

When they reached the landing area, *Speeder Two* had already left with the older scientists. Carl and Nate, along with thirty tactical officers and ten of Darian's best trainees, waited next to *Speeder One.*

"Molly's at the helm. Rhian took the other speeder up to fetch reinforcements per your order, Captain," Carl said. He wasn't wearing his space helmet, but a smaller, tactical version. He handed over some headgear to Holly and the other four. "These are better now that we know the air is breathable."

"Agreed. Good job, Carl." Darian put her helmet on. "Whoa."

Holly had just snapped her chinstrap on and turned to ask Darian what was wrong, when she felt her add-on NIEC connect with the tactical helmet. The information flow was intense for a few seconds, and then she knew a lot more about the blocks around the square and how to access motion sensors, see all the specs about her rifle and sidearm, and communicate with every one of her crew hooked up to their helmets. Whoa, indeed.

"I don't want to wait until the other speeder arrives. It'll take them at least ten minutes, even with the *Velocity* in lower orbit." Using eye movements, Holly scrolled the menu of her helmet and found she would be able to access the sensors of her ship when it was low enough. "We'll know when that happens. In the meantime, let's use what we already have." She engaged her speaker. "Crowe to Molly. Take the speeder up to three hundred feet. Begin scanning for the same pattern of metallic framing that we found. There are bound to be more elevators."

"Aye, Captain." Molly already had the speeder on standby, and it began to rise immediately. "Scanning now."

"I can tell. Good job." Holly saw the scans as faint green lines mapping the surrounding part of the old, crumbled city around them. So far, the only metallic objects were the ones they had just left. She turned, meaning to issue orders for a ground search of the surrounding blocks, when a sharp tone pulsated five times in her ears.

"Proximity alarm," Darian said, pushing yet another visor down. "We have movement. Due north."

"How many? How far away?" Holly pressed down the secondary visor as well. She saw clear, white dots superimposed on the green-tinted map. "Ah. I see. Sixty-two contacts approaching. Not very fast, though. I'd say they're on foot."

"Two hundred yards, Captain," Nate said, "and closing."

"We're outnumbered, but reinforcement is coming." Darian pulled out her trackpad and worked it furiously. "These are the coordinates we need to reach. Three in each group. I'm sending them to your helmets now."

Darian was right. They had to take up a defensive position until *Speeder Two* returned. Even if Molly landed *Speeder One*, she could do little. The speeders possessed a powerful weapons array, but they would be clumsy to maneuver among the tall ruins. She tapped her speaker. "Crowe to Molly. Crowe to bridge. We're being approached by locals, their intent unknown. We're taking defensive positions. Keep sensors locked on us, and keep this channel open for quick hails." Walker and Molly confirmed, but Holly was already joining Nate and Carl. "We're going to the lower structure two streets northeast. That way we'll be able to track them and make sure we catch anyone breaking formation. I'm pretty sure they'll be able to scan our position as well."

Holly glanced at Samantha, who was joining two ensigns. She nodded toward Holly, giving her a thumbs-up with her right hand. In her left, she carried a large bag.

Darian was already running toward her assigned position, with two of her trainees right behind her. Holly hoped they would be all right and that whoever was approaching them wasn't hostile. Then again, she and her crew were trespassing, and those headed toward them had the right to defend their territory.

Holly took the lead until they reached a half-crumbled wall that overlooked a wide street that reminded her of parade streets on Earth. Trees still grew in the center of it, and even if half of them looked dead, some still had leaves. Nature was resilient and had reasserted itself to some degree after whatever had happened on Dwynna Major.

"Spread out, six feet apart along the wall," Holly said to Nate and Carl, pointing along the rock wall that described a quarter circle. It was just a little more than four feet tall and at a perfect height to rest her rifle's muzzle against. She scanned through the different visors of her tactical helmet. Most of her crewmembers were in place. When all of them were in position, they would have formed a shallow semicircle in front of the approaching contacts.

"Molly to Crowe. They're still moving at the same pace, but two parties have been deployed on the flanks. They might have noticed our presence on sensors."

Holly flipped back to the visors that showed the map of the streets and the contacts. Molly was right. Eight dots moved to the right and another eight to the left.

"Crowe to teams. Follow the contacts on your visors. We have a new pattern," Holly said over her speaker.

"Walker to Crowe. *Speeder Two* has launched back toward your position. Forty souls on board, including medical personnel."

Holly thought fast. "Understood." She browsed the map visor quickly. "Crowe to Rion." She waited impatiently for the pilot to acknowledge.

"Rion here. Go ahead, Captain."

"Set down on the square again and deploy the teams. I'm sending the coordinates. Keep the medics on board." Holly checked her visors again. The contacts were getting closer and seemed to move faster.

"Negative, Captain," another voice said. "Raoul instructed us to bring a medical habitat with us from the cargo bay. He wants us to find a sheltered place close to the square and deploy it there."

"This is the first I've heard of this procedure," Holly snarled. This was their first potential combat situation, but they had to maintain the chain of command. She wasn't even entirely sure what a medical habitat entailed. "Crowe to Raoul. You're about to risk your medical staff if they aren't kept on the speeder."

"Sorry about this, Captain, but I didn't have time to brief you." Raoul was breathing hard, as if he was running. "I'm on my way to a good spot for us to erect a medical habitat, which will be easy to defend and make it possible for us to actually save lives, should we need to. We won't do much good if we're up in the speeder while people are bleeding out planetside."

"Are you sure?" Holly asked pointedly.

"Absolutely."

"All right. I give you full autonomy for now. We're about to engage whoever's approaching. Crowe out."

Looking through the digital scope of her rifle, Holly kept the far end of the broad street in focus. The dots on the visor showed they would appear any moment. The crewmembers currently getting off *Speeder Two* would have to handle the dots on the flank. Holly could hear the familiar humming sound of the speeder setting down. What a relief to get more boots on the ground.

"Captain!" Carl whispered. "What the hell's that?"

Holly widened the view in her scope. In the distance, she could see the air billow just above the ground, reminding her of how hot asphalt heated the air above it on Earth. Behind the trembling air, she saw people walking, but also an enormous, dome-shaped contraption that she quickly measured to be twenty yards across.

"No idea. A vessel. Or a vehicle. Or both." Holly murmured. Or a weapon, she thought.

"It's like they're marching. If they hadn't deployed the people on the flanks, I'd have sworn they hadn't spotted us," Nate said.

"Holly to crew. Focus. I don't want anyone to shoot first just because you have an onset of nerves. This is not why we came here. We're here to reconnect. To learn."

"Walker to Crowe. New scans are in. Multiple sites for metallic bars like the ones you found earlier."

"Any close to my position?" Holly asked.

"Two hundred yards due west. Sending the results to you," Walker replied.

Holly cast a quick glance at the sensor readings and then placed them over the green-tinted map. Another elevator was within reach—if it worked. She watched the contacts come closer, and now they were near enough for her to see more details through the scope. They were clad in coverall-type uniforms, some deep red, some light yellow. Helmets, gloves, and boots. Some wore rectangular backpacks, others long, narrow objects that could be weapons.

The increased hum showed that Rion had taken off with her speeder.

"Holly to team leader *Speeder Two* crew. Deploy to your positions." She made sure she'd sent the positions she needed them to take.

"Affirmative, Captain. Already on our way. Medical habitat being deployed at this position as we speak."

A red dot appeared two blocks south of the square inside a ruin, on Holly's visor.

"Got it." Holly watched the people approaching and moved the scope along the first row of eight individuals. "Here they come."

One beat after she uttered the words, the contacts stopped, and the dome-like vessel rose off the ground. It began to spin, about one rotation every five seconds, creating a completely different, whirring sound than the speeders did. Sparks formed at the top of the dome, making Holly grip her rifle harder.

"What's that? A weapon?" Carl asked, and Holly saw he had his ops trackpad out, trying to scan.

"Not sure." Holly wanted to get closer. She wished she could see the faces of the individuals poised so still around the spinning dome. This was not a standoff by any means, but it was nerve-racking all the same.

Holly's speaker gave a low, whistling sound that she recognized as an alarm. "Walker to Crowe! We see movement in several places where we think there could be more elevators! You may be facing an attack from below as well!"

CHAPTER TWENTY-EIGHT

Delusional. That had to be it. A reaction to the crisis of being in the hands of strangers—aliens, even. Claire stared at Quantia and Neo'Toya. "What enemy?" That was all she could think of to say.

"You carry DNA markers—in fact, partial strands—of us and of Dwynnites." Neo'Toya towered over Claire. Strangely enough, his presence infused energy into her, and she placed her hands on her hips and returned his glare.

"Who the hell are the Dwynnites? And what are your people called?" She pushed her face up under his. For all she knew, he might knock her down, but after all she'd been through to get to this planet, she refused to be intimidated.

"We're Tantozians. Our nation is called Tantoz." Quantia spoke softly, while Neo'Toya merely huffed and turned away from Claire. Winning the stare-off was rewarding, to a degree. "You really don't know very much about us, do you?" Quantia said.

"We have traveled a long way to get here." Claire knew this was the best opening she was bound to get. Those other sentries, or soldiers, had seemed to just want to throw her into a dungeon and forget about her. These two were suspicious, but at least they were communicating. "We're descendants of people who left this planet a long, long time ago. We have all had this enormous *yearning* to reconnect. Before we found our spaceship, the *Velocity*, we couldn't even dream of anything like this…" Claire quieted when Quantia held up her hand, her expression unreadable and her eyes opaque. "What?"

"Exactly." Neo'Toya nodded as he sat down on the edge of her desk. "That's what she said earlier too. The *Velocity*."

"Yes. We're in orbit as we speak, and all we want is to find out about our ancestors. Where we originate. It was never an option for us not to come."

"She wears an old-fashioned NIEC," Neo'Toya said quietly. "That's why I brought her. It's not just an old artifact. She's using it."

"Are you sure?" Quantia placed a hand over his. Looking back at Claire, she raised her chin. "Show me?"

"All right." Claire turned around and lifted her braid. "There."

"No. Show me how you use it." Quantia stood and rounded the desk.

"I'm not taking it off," Claire said sharply and stepped back.

"I'm not asking you to. I want you to show me how you use this device." Quantia folded her arms over her chest. "Now."

Not sure what to do, Claire pulled out her engineering trackpad. She unfolded it and began running a diagnostic of her surroundings. The way her device began to ping, and the amount of data downloading via her wartime-expanded NIEC, nearly sent Claire to her knees. Her head ached, and the room twirled around her. Reaching out, she found Neo'Toya's steady arm and gripped it hard.

"She's not faking that." Quantia's voice sounded as if the woman were underwater—or Claire was. "She's using obsolete Dwynnite technology, and look at that…what is it? An old pad? It's upgrading."

"She said she's an engineer on the ship," Neo'Toya said. He pushed Claire down onto a stool. "Sit before you faint and fall down."

"Good idea," Claire said, managing to not topple over only by gripping the sleeve of his uniform jacket. "This…is a…lot."

"What do you mean?" Quantia said, taking Claire's left hand.

"All this data." Swallowing against new vertigo and nausea, Claire wanted to shake her head but didn't dare.

"She's downloading!" Neo'Toya yelled and began sliding his hand up the back of Claire's neck.

"Don't!" Claire cried out, pulling away from him. "If you yank it out now, I can sustain…brain damage. Just close my trackpad. Just— close it." She half-expected him to ignore her and tear the NIEC from her scalp. Wincing, she pushed at his strong hands.

And then the stream of data stopped. When Claire opened her eyes, she was still gripping Neo'Toya's sleeves, and Quantia was standing next to them, holding the closed trackpad.

"This downloaded and then transmitted to you?" Quantia asked.

"Yes. Thanks for shutting it off. If I'm to learn all that, I'll have to go by the rule of baby steps."

"Excuse me?" Quantia blinked. "Baby steps."

Claire sighed and offered a faint smile, mostly to appease the two before her. "It's an Earth way of saying 'doing it in increments.'"

"I see. Yes, that would be advisable since the *Velocity*, famously known as the last of the warships, disappeared more than thirteen generations ago. The long war was already on its third generation, and when the Dwynnites lost their flagship...it was the beginning of the end of life as our ancestors knew it. Both parties blamed each other, and the conflict has not been resolved to this day."

"And you thought, or still think, I'm a Dwynnite spy? Are you nuts? You have to have seen more in the DNA scan that corroborates my story. Yes, so what if I have a mix of DNA from you and your enemy. I must have even more of Earth human DNA."

After exchanging glances with Neo'Toya, Quantia nodded. "Yes." She ran her hand over her forehead. "How can you have strands of DNA from both peoples? It's impossible."

"No matter who took the flagship, both peoples must have been represented aboard the ship." Claire thought fast. "It isn't the first time that individuals have come together even if they're supposed to be enemies."

"Unlikely," Neo'Toya said, snorting. "I believe Dwynnites forced Tantozians to join them, perhaps even used them as labor on the ship, and then left."

"What for?" Claire had to relax her tense muscles and shook her hands at her side to help the blood flow better. The room wasn't cold, but the way her skin erupted in goose bumps every now and then suggested it was. "Tell me, if Dwynnites and Tantozians became friends, how would that have been looked upon back then?"

"Back then? To this day, that's considered treason," Quantia said. "Punishable by death, if severe, or many years of incarceration on the rainforest islands. The Dwynnites' punishments for the same offense are even more severe."

"Aha. So, it still happens." Claire slapped her knee in triumph. "It's not as unusual as you try to tell yourself, I'm sure. And I bet they're not all spies."

Groaning now, Quantia walked back to her desk. "We're going to have to find a way to get on board this ship and figure out the truth," she said, sounding tired. "We have a unit returning from the border shortly. I know they're bound to be exhausted, but they could—"

"Do what? Board a ship in orbit?" Incredulous, Claire got up and leaned over Quantia's desk, resting her hands on its glossy wooden surface. "One thing we didn't see from orbit when we scanned your planet was spaceships or satellites. Nothing. Not a bleep. With your technology, which must have developed tenfold, since the *Velocity* was on Earth for a long time before we found it, you should be able to fly rings around our ship by now. Still, nothing." It was a mystery and one they had touched on only briefly, which was, in retrospect, not smart. They'd all been so eager to go planetside, to set foot on the homeworld.

"That is a well-known part of the truce." Neo'Toya pushed at Claire to remove her from the desk. "After a long and bloody war, we needed a truce, and four generations ago, a disarmament of all above-ground ships was decided. Hovers, vehicles, floating structures are not part of the agreement, as they don't pose the threat of being able to deploy weapons of mass destruction. Your ship, though, can."

"And we're not part of your war, or your peace process, albeit commendable." Claire sat down on one of the stools. "Still, since you can't go into orbit, you can't board our ship. It's as easy as that."

"Not entirely true. You said it yourself." Neo'Toya smiled joylessly. "You're the chief of engineering, a vital member of the crew, no doubt. Important for the survival of the crew and the return to Earth."

Claire's heart grew icy, and her pulse appeared to slow down as she listened to his thinly veiled threat. "I'm good at my job, yes. I'm, however, not the only one who can repair the ship. I'm not sure if you are used to placing all your eggs in one basket, but that's not how we do it, trust me. We learn each other's duties, and as much as we are loyal, we all knew that for some it might become a one-way journey."

Frowning, Quantia leaned back in her desk chair. "Bold words."

"True words." Claire straightened her back. She returned to the other part of the information they'd just let slip. A unit was on its way back from the border, presumably against Dwynna. Was that part of this world more their home, their origin, than Tantoz? Did everyone who carried the specific alien DNA marker have a mixed heritage when it came to Dwynna and Tantoz? Why hadn't Raoul seen this pattern when scanning all their DNA strands?

Then her thoughts went to young Belle, who could read other alien signs that the NIECs couldn't interpret. She remembered how they'd talked about the possibility of other DNA, of more alien races, but it had been mere speculation. Raoul had, after getting everyone's permission, performed extended DNA scans, but he hadn't spoken about more alien DNA than what they had already theorized about, because of young Belle. Or, she realized, perhaps he had with the girl, and Belle's mother had asked him to not share this information. It was a sensitive situation, especially for a teenager, to be different.

Quantia's and Neo'Toya's heated but inaudible conversation brought Claire back to the present. She was getting very tired. "Listen," she said, not caring that she interrupted them. "There's an easy way to do this if you'd just slow down and listen."

"Excuse me?" Quantia pressed her lips together.

"By all means." Claire was losing her patience. She wanted to return to her crew—to Holly. "Let me contact my captain and open diplomatic channels. If you need to explore the ship and find out what happened all those, um, generations ago, I'm sure we can arrange for that to happen. And to not risk your truce with the Dwynnites, they need to be involved too." Claire hoped she wasn't stretching the truth too much. "Or, if that can't occur, and if your nations risk another conflict over this situation, we'll just leave." It would hurt like hell, Claire knew. To leave Dwynna Major before getting a real crack at exploring and learning the ways of these people would break everyone's heart. What it would do with their yearning was anybody's guess.

"We don't have diplomatic channels with Dwynnite." Neo'Toya looked as close to embarrassed as this man probably ever did.

"Well, that's just plain stupid." Claire sighed. "Do they too live underground, like you?"

"Yes, of course," Quantia said, looking surprised. "We've only been able to send out patrols for the last two generations. The planet's diseased as a result of—" She stopped talking and merely shrugged.

"As a result of weapons of mass destruction." Claire filled in the rest, and Quantia only nodded. Claire's stomach clenched at the thought of such massive violence. "The way I see it, you have nothing to lose. Sooner or later, the Dwynnites will know of the *Velocity*'s existence. If they find out you already knew and didn't inform them, even if you're not on speaking terms, I can see that going only one way."

Claire rose and approached Quantia's desk again. "I get the feeling you have a high position among the Tantozians. Neo'Toya wouldn't have brought me to you unless he knew you could actually do something, learn about me and put your knowledge to some use." Clenching her hands, Claire barely refrained from pounding the desktop. "I won't do much good for anyone in a Tantozian prison. Put me to use. Let me contact my people, and we'll initiate conversations with both your people and the Dwynnites. Remember we, or a lot of us, anyway, obviously stem from both nations. We can be neutral. We can use your help in deciphering some of the texts we've found that are hard for us to read, despite our NIECs. By doing that, we can figure out the truth—which I take it is the one thing you're interested in, right?"

Claire wasn't a fool. She wasn't certain the Tantozians were interested only in establishing diplomatic channels, if at all. They could be lying from beginning to end, but somehow, she found that too much to believe. Claire did know that nothing good would come if the wrong scenario played out with her as a prisoner and the *Velocity* and her crew caught in the middle.

"With the risk of sounding like a 1950s sci-fi movie," Claire said, knowing instinctively that she would, she stood at attention and spoke succinctly. "You better take me to your leaders."

CHAPTER TWENTY-NINE

Holly made sure her crew was spread out according to plan and that the medical habitat was nearly set up. She trusted Raoul to run that part and deliberately wiped it from her mind. Switching to a magnifying visor on her helmet, she scanned the still-immovable forms in the distance. Expanding the scan, she grew rigid.

"Damn it. Can you see the ones on the flanks?" she asked Nate and Carl.

"Negative," Carl said, and Nate echoed the word a second later.

"Holly to Walker. Scan for the ones on the flanks."

"Was just going to page you. They're gone. Both teams slipped into elevator shafts." Walker sounded frustrated. "They're fast when they get going."

"Then we can expect them to bring reinforcements." Holly tapped her speaker. "All teams, this is the captain. We have reason to believe that more contacts will approach from below. Stay vigilant, but do not—I repeat, do *not* fire first. Should the contacts commence a hostile conflict, you're authorized to engage in battle, but only then."

"I really hope we don't have to shoot at anyone," Carl murmured. "But I suppose they might see us as invaders. I mean, why wouldn't they?"

Carl was right. "That's why it's imperative that we don't initiate hostilities." Holly engaged her speaker again. "Crowe to *Speeder One*, *Speeder Two*. Cloak the ships."

The pilots confirmed.

"Good thinking, Captain," Nate said, shifting position and scanning along the perimeter through his scope. "Another perceived threat minimized."

"Unless they have superior technology that allows them to detect the speeders despite the cloaking feature." Holly switched to the map filter and studied the position of the strange, floating dome. Movement among the contacts gathered under and around it made her get up on one knee. "Look sharp now. They're shifting position."

Her speaker gave the alarm tone again. "Walker to Crowe. Activity around the dome."

"We see it." Holly didn't even dare blink.

"Not only that. Check your flanks, Captain. Something's happening in at least eight elevator sites."

"Damn." Holly scanned in a full circle around her, seeing the activity transmitted to her helmet both from the *Velocity*'s sensors and her own surveillance. "I can't penetrate the elevator cars to see how many are coming, but if it's eight elevators jam-packed with soldiers, we're completely outnumbered."

Carl moved closer to Holly. "Perhaps," he said, his voice filled with nervous energy, but he didn't look afraid. "Have you wondered why no spaceships are hurtling around here? No manned guns in the ruins? It's just that weird dome, which looks more like a high-tech umbrella than anything else. Nothing in orbit—not even satellites, unless they're cloaking them, and my gut says they're not."

Carl was right. "Good points, all of them," Holly said, "but even if we're just up against foot soldiers, there are still a lot more of them than of us."

"No, Captain, you don't understand. *We* have spaceships and a weapons array that can protect us if we're outnumbered." Carl's eyes grew darker. "That's a scarier prospect than anything so far. That we might have the upper hand."

Did they? Holly looked into the eyes of the normally idealistic and enthusiastic Carl, the nineteen-year-old high school senior whose aunt had joined him on this dangerous adventure. Now he resembled a seasoned explorer and someone who had perhaps been given too much responsibility, too soon. "I hear you, Carl. And yes, I understand what you mean."

"Walker to senior crew. Multiple contacts emerging from elevator sites at eight locations."

"Darian to senior crew. I have eyes on one of those sites less than ten yards from my position." Darian rattled off information. "Twelve individuals. Green and yellow uniforms, helmets, transparent facemasks, sidearms. Wait...They're just lining up outside the elevator shaft in two rows. They're not moving."

Holly tapped her speaker. "Crowe here. Hold your position. Don't approach." Everyone seemed to be holding their breath. They stood on a proverbial powder keg, and the smallest misjudgment, or any rash decision, could set it off, taking out them and the people coming up from their subterranean civilization.

"Look, Captain!" Nate whispered huskily just as Holly spotted movement to her left.

"Walker to Crowe. Captain—"

"I see them, Commander."

A group of people in green and yellow uniforms emerged from the closest elevator site. Among them, a man, taller than the rest, strode with lethal grace. A woman, not in uniform, but dressed in a long, billowing coat, walked by his side. Behind them...

Claire.

Holly heard her own gasp.

"It's Claire!" Carl said, moving as if to get on his feet. Holly and Nate pulled him back down.

"Don't move. We don't know what they want or what they've done to her." Holly's throat ached at the sight of Claire, and she adjusted her scope to zoom in as much as possible. Claire looked tense but unharmed. She carried her engineering trackpad in her hands, and the only things missing were her helmet and sidearm.

"That's one tall guy," Nate said quietly. "And look behind Claire."

"I see." Holly spoke through her teeth as she studied a group of eight other people, both men and women, out of uniform. They seemed oddly nervous, looking around and back at the uniformed people under and around the dome.

"Captain Crowe!" The tall man's voice boomed. "Show yourself!"

Blinking in surprise, Holly moved her scope to the man's face. He was definitely humanoid. Muscular, and with dark eyes in a broad, handsome face, he appeared entirely confident as he halted about twenty yards from her position.

"Don't take your eyes off him." Holly pushed her rifle onto her back.

"Captain! What are you doing?" Nate reached as if to tug at her, but she evaded his hand.

"The man wants to talk to me. They must've gotten my name from Claire. I'm going to walk over and have a chat. I trust you to cover me, Nate."

"Oh, I'll try my best, but if one of them is under orders to take you out instantly, I may not have time." He frowned.

"I don't think that'll happen." If her life had been in immediate jeopardy, Claire would have called out a warning, no matter the risk to herself. "Crowe to teams. I'm about to approach the locals. Hold your fire."

"Captain Crowe!" the man called out again.

Holly stood and, keeping her hands well away from her body, palms forward, she walked toward the people they had come to meet. She let her gaze travel between the man and Claire's face, and only when she saw Claire frown did she realize she wasn't easily identifiable when wearing her helmet with the visor down. She stopped ten yards from the man, who in turn stood a few steps in front of his people.

"I'm going to remove my helmet," Holly said calmly.

The man nodded, looking behind her. "Very well."

Holly slowly raised her hands and pushed the sensor for the visors. Unfastening the helmet, she pulled it off and felt the gentle breeze play with her hair. She heard whispers and a few gasps among the people before her.

"I'm Captain Holly Crowe. Is my engineer all right?"

"I'm fine, Holly." Claire answered before the man had a chance. "I've been interrogated, but nobody hurt me."

Holly knew Claire was telling the truth, since she was so in tune with every nuance of her voice. "Good."

"I'm Neo'Toya, Chief Sentry of the Capital of Tantoz. Your engineer insists she can prove she's telling the truth and that you will facilitate this claim."

"I see."

One of the women behind Neo'Toya stepped forward. She wore clothes as colorful as the others', but the way they parted for her to pass told of her high rank.

"This is Elder Member Quantia." Neo'Toya gestured toward the woman. "Your engineer managed the no small feat of persuading her—and me—to take her before the council." Neo'Toya didn't look amused. "Four of them are with us here," he motioned behind him, "with their cadets. I trust you can appreciate the risk they take to learn about the measure of truth in your subordinate's words."

"Risk. You have a lot of armed men and women around you and more where those came from. Not a lot of risk the way I see it."

"Captain. Please." Claire took a step forward, but a hand belonging to a uniformed sentry yanked her back.

"Don't do that again," Holly said, lowering her voice. "Is Claire your hostage?"

"No...for now, she's leverage." Neo'Toya didn't take his eyes off Holly. "We have scanned the area, and we know exactly how many of you are here, and where each one is positioned."

"Likewise," Holly said.

"Enough." The woman, Quantia, stepped closer until she stood shoulder to shoulder with Neo'Toya. "Enough rattling of pulsators. This is unproductive." She studied Holly without preamble. "Captain Crowe. Your chief engineer, Claire, has DNA that shows that at least part of your claim to be of Tantozian blood is true. You wear an old version of the leader crown, much like one that our city has on display in the Wartime Museum."

Holly hadn't expected this remark but nodded. "It's a captain's NIEC."

"It is. And one similar to it used to belong to the chosen ruler of Dwynna, long before the war." Quantia took one more step toward Holly. "It's been told through generations how it governed great vessels, but that was a long time ago."

"How long ago?" Holly asked.

"More than thirteen generations," Quantia said.

"Captain." Claire glared at the sentry who had yanked at her arm and then took a step forward, unhindered. "As far as I've managed to calculate, that's at least four hundred Earth years."

Holly quickly did the math. The *Velocity*'s crew had settled on Earth around 1776. That was almost two hundred and fifty years ago. Could this be correct? Had the *Velocity* been in space for that long? How was that possible?

"Most of our Elder Council believe this is all a ruse by the Dwynnites and a way to reignite the war." Quantia spoke faster now. "If we can't produce the proof Claire insists you can provide, we might face a bigger disaster than you and your crew arriving at Dwynna Major."

Holly began to see the truth behind Quantia's world. She opened her mouth to respond but was interrupted by Neo'Toya pulling at Quantia and shoving her behind him.

"What is that?" he said with a growl, pointing to the sky behind Holly.

She looked behind her and saw a hovering figure thirty feet up in the air. Samantha. "It's my chief pilot. She's in a hover suit. She poses no threat," Holly said. "Nobody among my crew will act with hostility unless I give the order—or if you shoot first. You have my word."

"A word in Tantoz is sacred. I do, however, not know if it's the same on Earth." Quantia rounded Neo'Toya, furtively rubbing her arm where he had grabbed her.

"My word is sacred as well, as I too carry the DNA of the ancestors that left this planet." Holly made a judgment call and took the last few steps, extending her hand to Quantia. "On Earth, we seal our word by shaking hands."

Looking back and forth between Holly's hand and her face, Quantia slowly took it. Holly gave the soft hand a gentle squeeze and then let go.

"Interesting," Quantia said and then looked over at Neo'Toya. "Come. Perform the handshake."

The burly man didn't look awkward, that was probably not in his nature, but he was clearly not thrilled about Quantia's order. The exchange confirmed that Quantia outranked him and thus the rest of the Tantozians.

Neo'Toya's version of a handshake was apparently to try to crush the bones in Holly's hand, but she made a point of not showing how painful his strong grip was. She flexed her fingers stealthily after he let go. "No need to overdo, Neo'Toya," she said, infusing amusement in her voice. "It's not a contest."

Quantia's chuckle made Neo'Toya scowl, but he didn't respond. She remained at arm's length, now looking up at the hovering Samantha. "I would feel a lot safer if your pilot did not hover directly above me. I'd like to meet her and the rest of your senior crew."

"Of course." Holly tapped her speaker. "Planetside senior crew, converge on my location, weapons holstered. Teams, hold your positions and maintain status quo."

Carl appeared from behind the crumbled wall, his rifle pushed onto his back. He strode up to stand a few feet behind Holly. Above them, Samantha lowered herself to the ground, and she was a sight in her red, luminous hover suit. She removed her helmet, and her long, blond hair broke free in the breeze, billowing behind her, as she strode up to stand next to Carl.

Darian approached, running at a steady pace. She too carried her rifle on her back as she studied Quantia and Neo'Toya, her brown eyes sharp. "Captain," she said as she flanked Samantha's other side.

Holly's speaker buzzed once. "Raoul to Crowe."

"Crowe here. Go ahead."

"I respectfully ask to be exempt from leaving the medical habitat. I have two wounded that I'm tending to." His voice didn't give anything away, but knowing him as well as she did, Holly knew something was up.

"Report," she ordered, keeping her gaze on Quantia. "Who's wounded?"

"Agent Brewer has sustained a dislocated shoulder and—a sentry has torn a ligament in her left knee. No, lie still, ma'am, or you'll do greater damage to your leg."

Neo'Toya stepped closer. "They have one of my sentries in custody?" He snarled the words out.

"No," Holly said, easily picturing what had happened at the elevator site where Brandon and Brewer had remained after Claire was taken. "My chief medical officer is *treating* an injury that your sentry sustained. She'll be free to go whenever he's done." She tapped her speaker. "Crowe to Raoul. How long before the sentry is able to return to her unit?"

"Oh, she's with them right now, as they're all here at the habitat, all twelve of them, crowding us. Brandon's fine."

"You are certain?" Holly asked.

"Absolutely. Raoul out."

Holly continued. "As I said, your sentry is in no danger, and her injury will be dealt with." She groaned inwardly. She would deal with Brewer later.

Shaking off her annoyance, she turned her focus to Quantia. "All my senior staff that are planetside are here now, barring the doctor and one crewmember, Brandon. Claire, of course, belongs in this category and should join us."

"Claire remains by our sentries," Quantia said. "She's our only reassurance."

Holly wanted to scream at them to release Claire, but if she didn't play the game right, they might take her back underground, where they definitely had the advantage. "Very well. For now." Holly saw how Claire merely nodded and gave her a subtle thumbs-up.

"About the proof," Quantia said casually. "I'd like to see that—now."

They were all at a crossroad. This was where their mission might become a success—or fail completely. Holly had one chance to get this right, and a multitude of ways of getting it wrong. She looked back at her senior crew behind her, who regarded her with overwhelming trust and confidence. She tapped her speaker, praying that her plan would not ignite catastrophe.

"Crowe to Walker."

"Walker here. What are your orders, Captain?" As arranged, the bridge had kept an open link to her speaker.

Holly drew in a deep breath and held it for a moment. After slowly expelling it, she said, "It's time to land the *Velocity* on the square."

CHAPTER THIRTY

Claire stood surrounded by sentries, and, right behind her, stood the constantly murmuring members of the elder council and their cadets. The latter buzzed around the elders, taking notes on their glowing pads, as if they were equally busy upstaging each other when it came to efficiency.

She focused, however, mainly on Holly. She looked every inch regal where she stood, wearing the crown-like NIEC and its add-on. Speaking in clear, measured ways, as she always did in an official setting, she obviously both impressed and frustrated Quantia and Neo'Toya.

Quantia had quickly taken Claire before a select few of the most powerful elders in a chamber higher up in the building Neo'Toya had escorted her to. Quantia's influence seemed enough for them to accept Claire's DNA test and to agree to listen to her story. That meeting had brought them this far—and it also brought reinforcements to the people Claire's crewmembers had already encountered.

Holly was paging Walker on the bridge now, and when Claire heard her say, "It's time to land the *Velocity* in the square," she clenched her hands as Walker merely answered, "Aye, Captain." What was Holly's plan? Did she honestly consider bringing a heavily armed spaceship into a potentially volatile situation was a good idea? The senior crew standing behind Holly didn't so much as blink. Perhaps they had agreed on this plan beforehand.

"Are you setting down a ship containing weapons of mass destruction?" The way Neo'Toya's voice lowered into a formidable growl made Claire wince. This was not going well.

"You wanted proof of our claims. I'm landing the ship so you can see for yourself." Holly placed her hands on her hips. "We can stand here and argue for days, but until you have solid proof, and we feel like you're not going to incarcerate the entire crew and their families—"

"Families?" Quantia raised her hand and interrupted Holly.

"Almost all the crewmembers have family members or friends with them on the ship. Children. The youngest can barely walk."

Claire saw Neo'Toya's shoulder go down. For a moment, she thought he might be going for Holly's jugular, but apparently, the fact that vulnerable people were on board the *Velocity* seemed to mean something.

"As we're being transparent now, I'd like to know what the dome-shaped thing behind you is, Neo'Toya." Holly motioned behind Claire.

"It isn't outfitted with any weapons. It's merely a shield for our border-patrol sentries." Neo'Toya appeared to have accepted that Quantia expected him to be more forthcoming. Claire thought that was only fair, since he was the one who broke protocol and took her to see Quantia in the first place.

"A shield. Why do you need a shield at the border, if there's a truce?" Holly asked.

"Not the world's greatest truce," Claire said, before Quantia or Neo'Toya came up with something more political than correct. "They still consider the Dwynnites their enemy." She shrugged at Neo'Toya's scowl. "I have ears."

"So, more a stalemate than détente." Holly nodded at Claire.

"I don't understand the reference," Quantia said.

"It means you are still wary of each other, but neither party is prepared to risk a wrong move." Claire took a couple of additional steps forward. Two sentries followed but didn't grab her. "And if the other side can't see you, they can't misconstrue that you need to keep an eye on the border. Quite sure the Dwynnites do the same."

"Makes sense," Darian said.

Holly used her speaker. "Crowe to Raoul. How are Brewer and the sentry doing?"

"Raoul here. Brewer is well enough to be furious. The sentry is undergoing non-invasive surgery. If the authorities are concerned, four other sentries here are keeping a watchful eye that we're treating her well."

"Good to know. Crowe out." Holly disengaged her speaker, only to have it beep again.

"Walker to Crowe. Setting down in three minutes."

"Understood." Holly turned back to Quantia. "That was my next in command. They're about to land. I suggest we move closer to the square, but at a safe distance, of course." She turned to Claire and extended her hand. "And you belong over here with us."

Claire didn't even look at the sentries but took the last steps toward Holly, and when she stood by her side, she finally began to breathe easier again, despite everything that still hung in the balance.

Samantha knew her duties were far from over. "Captain. I need to be up there to oversee the landing. The surrounding structures aren't safe. I suggest that you keep everyone on the northeast side of the square. That's also close to the medical habitat."

Holly nodded. "Good point. Go ahead."

Taking the time to kiss Darian, which she saw didn't escape Quantia's sharp eyes, Samantha put her helmet back on. The shiny red suit clung to her, and she rolled her shoulders underneath it as she engaged the flight function. It was more than a hover suit. She could go anywhere, at any height, even in space, for as long as it produced oxygen. Pressing the handles sticking out on the inside of her cuffs, she pushed off and pierced the air straight up. Despite the tense, crucial moments they were all facing, a part of her still felt the exhilaration of being able to fly.

Samantha twirled as she reached her intended height. From here, she could see the gathered Tantozian forces and their own crewmembers migrating to the northeast part of the square. The roar above her permeated her helmet, and she looked up just in time to see the first sign in the overcast clouds that the *Velocity* was breaking through. Moving well out of its way, Samantha used the magnifying visor and looked down to find the crowd she had just left.

Quantia stood next to Holly, and behind them, with his arms crossed over his chest, Neo'Toya had his face turned up to the sky.

Samantha didn't have to look at the ship to know when it broke through the clouds. The expressions of every Tantozian told her all she needed to know. They had never seen a spaceship of this magnitude. Fear, shock, and awe appeared on their faces, and many covered their mouths as they stared up at the majestic *Velocity*.

"Samantha to Walker. Let me help you. I'm in my suit, and you'll need me to guide you to set down safely among these buildings. They're not exactly stable."

"Walker here. We're grateful for your assistance."

"Hold your current hover level. Let me circle the ship." Samantha pressed her handles and began her sweep around the *Velocity*. "You're looking good both on port and starboard. As for your aft section, you're too close to the block where the medical habitat is set up. Move forward fifty yards, and then set down in a complete vertical trajectory. You have no margin for error." Samantha knew she had trained her pilots well, but both of her best were maneuvering cloaked speeders right now, and Walker had to oversee the ones manning the helm on their mothership.

Slowly, the ship deployed its struts. Once they locked into place, it began the last of its descent, slowly and regally. Only when it contacted the marble stones on the ground of the square did Samantha feel as if she finally remembered to exhale.

As the crew onboard went through the shut-down protocol, the ship made the ground shake and rattle so much that loose stones and debris began to fall from the surrounding buildings. Samantha was relieved she had thought to warn people away from the immediate area, and she moved out of the way as she saw how one of the buildings on the ship's port side began to tilt. Luck would have it that the top part swayed enough to finally fall into itself and not across the side of the ship.

Afraid that people would get too curious too fast, before the ship's propulsion system was completely shut off, Samantha placed herself twenty feet in the air between the densest part of the crowd and the *Velocity*. She barely had a chance to get into place before a few of the cadets rushed forward, holding what looked like some type of recorders up to their faces. A young woman was several steps in front of the others, clearly eager to move closer to the ship.

Samantha reacted instinctively and swooped down in front of the woman, holding her hands up before her. "Stop. It's not safe yet."

"I need to take pictures for my elder representative," the woman said, not even removing the device from her eyes, and kept walking forward.

"I think not." Samantha reached out, wrapped her arms around the young woman's waist, and lifted her nine feet off the ground, then returned her to the rest of the spectators.

The woman's shrill scream caught the attention of the rest of the cadets, who hurried back to their elders, looking startled.

Holly looked up, shaking her head. "Efficient, but still…" She shook her head. "We're trying to build a diplomatic rapport here, not scare the living daylights out of the junior officials."

"That, and we're also trying to keep them safe and alive, Captain," Samantha said calmly. "I'm sure Elder Quantia appreciates that."

"I do." Quantia looked, if not impressed, then at least interested in the maneuver. "Do you all have suits that allow you to fly on Earth?"

"Ah, no. This is technology from your area, actually," Samantha said. "Just like everything else aboard the *Velocity*."

Quantia blinked. "I thought you realized…This ship, the *Velocity*, was not built by Tantozians. We have never been a space-faring nation."

Samantha made sure that nobody else was trying the same stunt as the young cadets and then landed. "Excuse me? You didn't build it?" She looked over at Holly, who appeared stunned.

"That's why we need to see logs, and perhaps old personal archives," Quantia said. "We have to find out once and for all how your chief engineer can have both Tantozian and Dwynnite DNA, when traveling on an old Dwynnite warship."

Chapter Thirty-one

The elders, led by Quantia and Neo'Toya, stood in the center of the *Velocity*'s bridge, and even though Holly wouldn't suggest they looked relaxed, at least they seemed to have abandoned the idea that this was some elaborate Dwynnite ambush. From what Quantia had told Holly on their way through the ship's corridors, the Dwynnites no longer possessed any warships. The war that had torn the planet into shreds had focused on destroying their respective technology.

"We were forced underground many generations ago, and even if the planet is reestablishing its ecosystem, we are not ready to risk rebuilding a world neither of us has experienced," Quantia now said. "The Dwynnites are not as far underground as we are, as the topography of their nation consists mainly of mountains and oceans. They live inside the mountain bedrock and underwater."

"If you have no connection, how do you know this?" Holly asked.

"We have no contact via official channels, but both sides have spies, though I'd firmly deny admitting to that statement, officially." Quantia smiled.

"Sounds familiar." Holly thought of how the people of her own planet had conducted political business for hundreds of years. Nothing was ever straightforward.

"Captain? We're ready for you in the mess hall." Darian had showed up at Holly's side. "We have removed the partitions to fit everyone. Marjory Hopkins and several of the other passengers have prepared food for the crew and visitors."

Grateful, Holly placed a hand on Darian's shoulder. "And security outside? The medical habitat?"

"The habitat is treating minor scrapes and cuts, mainly among some of the Tantozian people that are coming up from underground in droves. Guess they're not used to crowd control, as they're so eager to see the ship, they're ready to walk right over each other. We have practically our entire medical staff down there."

"Good job. Keep assisting those who need it until they go back underground." Holly turned to Quantia, who looked quizzically at her and Darian.

"Are you saying that civilians are coming topside?" She frowned as she turned to Neo'Toya. "Why am I hearing about this only now?"

"*I'm* only hearing it now. It must've started after we came on board this ship," Neo'Toya said. "If you will excuse me, Quantia, I'll go sort this out. You have enough sentries present to guarantee your safety."

"This entire crew personally guarantees the safety of all your people." Holly narrowed her eyes, knowing full well how this remark signaled her authority.

"Of course. Be well." Neo'Toya bowed. Holly watched him pass Claire and Samantha, who stood by the door, watching the elders and their entourage. He nodded briskly at Claire, who, for some unfathomable reason, grinned broadly at the massive man. Holly wasn't sure she wanted to read Claire's report from her visit underground. Claire seemed unharmed and at ease, but it had to have been an ordeal, no matter how you looked at the outcome.

"Let's move into the mess hall," Holly said and motioned for the Tantozians to follow her.

Someone had given the placing of the chairs and tables a lot of thought. Instead of having to face each other over the expanse of a table, thus reinforcing everything that stood between the crew and Dwynna Major's inhabitants, they sat in chairs that faced each other in small half-circles, where small tables had been erected. Holly instinctively knew this was Marjory's doing. Carl's aunt was invaluable.

The elders moved as one person, and if Marjory hadn't showed up at that moment and interjected herself by showing them to seats in several different semicircles, Holly was sure they would have congregated in the same corner of the mess hall. Now they were evenly placed together with their sentries, cadets, and the *Velocity*'s senior staff and officers.

Marjory waved her staff over, and soon everyone had a serving of bread, fruit, and water. Not knowing what the Tantozians ate or were used to, Marjory had made a smart choice that would hopefully please most palates.

The door slid open, and two men—she recognized Crewman Schneider as one of them—came in with a hover cart holding a container. They pushed it up to Holly, glancing at the Tantozians with obvious interest. "Here are the scrolls you asked for, Captain."

"Thank you. Please. Available seats are in the back. If you want, you can stay for a while and have some fruit."

"Appreciated, Captain." The men lit up and hurried over to an empty table.

Holly sat down next to Quantia in the semicircle that faced the large screen on the bulkhead and waved Claire over. "Sit here, please, Claire." She patted the seat next to her, relieved when Claire sat without hesitation. She thought she saw a new look in Claire's eyes, something less opaque, and it was as if her features had relaxed, and she didn't seem to have a problem leaning into Holly as she reached for a plate of fruit. "Ah, time for the scrolls. I'll help you."

"Thank you." Holly felt Claire's touch acutely. The fact that she had Claire back safely on board the ship made her want to pull her into a tight embrace, which of course was impossible—especially right now.

"What do the scrolls contain?" Quantia asked and bit into a plum. As the juice from the ripe fruit dripped onto her chin, her eyes widened. She caught the drops with a finger and carefully took another bite, this time closing her eyes. "What is this?"

"It's a plum from Earth. We have a small tree in our hydroponic bay. We're fortunate to have had some truly skilled people join us on our adventure."

"It's...like nothing I've ever tasted. Amazing." After taking another bite, Quantia pointed to the thin scrolls. "The scrolls?"

"Ah, yes. These are personal logs from the crew that came to Earth. We have read some here and there, but our journey has been such a learning experience on so many levels—it hasn't been the priority it should've been."

"And now you think it's time." Quantia reached for another plum.

"I do. I believe the answers to some of your questions are in here, as well as in our medical records. We are willing to share our DNA scans with you, if that would help determine our sincerity and good intentions."

"It might."

Browsing through the scrolls, Holly chose one at random, as they might have to look through several before they reached the information she hoped was there. "Would you mount this on the reader, please?" She handed it to Claire.

"Absolutely." Claire moved over to the screen and inserted the scroll in the slot beneath it. She entered a few commands, which adjusted the resolution on the screen. The murmured conversation in the mess hall died down when Claire turned around. "Should I read from the scroll, Captain?"

"Yes, thank you. Go ahead." Holly took a piece of bread, but her stomach was suddenly in knots. What if the information wasn't there? What if they all found out something that made their situation worse, rather than improved it? And, considering the never-quite-resolved conflict with the Dwynnites...what if their presence on this planet reignited the war? Claire had been adamant earlier when trying to convey how important it was for the crew to not appear to take sides in a barely resolved conflict. She was right, of course. It wasn't ideal to let the Tantozians into the ship first—but this was the situation, and they had to make it work somehow.

Claire stood to the side of the screen. She reached for a glass of water and gulped down half of it. "All right. This is the personal log by Casta'Lloy. She was, um, thirty seasons old when she made her first entry in the time of the Silver-Saber." Claire paused and looked back at her audience. Her full lips stretched into a wry grin. "I would imagine that means more to the people of this planet than it does to me without sitting down and performing some serious calculations with the help of a star chart."

"From the name alone, we can be quite certain that she was Tantozian—not Dwynnite," Quantia said, her voice betraying her surprise.

"Ah. I see. Well, let's continue." Claire turned back to the screen.

Holly kept her focus on Claire, as always concerned for her wellbeing, Still, for Claire to carry herself so well after everything she'd been through was impressive.

"There is tension on the bridge," Claire read, her voice changing quality. Perhaps it was because she was such a voracious reader, but she was obviously a born narrator. Holly relaxed against the backrest of her chair and crossed her legs as Claire continued. "I think it's probably normal, as we have all left friends and family members behind. Our nations will brand us as thieves and traitors alike, and that means it will be impossible to return. No wonder everyone jumps at the slightest glitch. We're maneuvering the last of the great warships, the last vessel that can fly through interstellar space from our planet. And though we have several members that have done so before, without the NIECs, we would never have even gotten it off the ground.

"Deshim suggested early on that we need to form an elder council of our own, and though some are strongly against it, most seem comfortable with the idea. After all, even if our nations are at war with each other, they're governed by the same method, if not by the same political principles.

"My NIEC placed me at the helm. I went from being a librarian at the governmental building in the capital of Tantoz to being a pilot and navigator." Claire stopped for a moment and looked over at Samantha, but then she kept reading.

"We're using the extra wartime NIECs right now, not for any sinister purpose, of course, but to understand Tantozian text better. The Dwynnites constructed them for wartime, and for spying. Now we use them to be able to add the most advanced Tantozian technology to the ship, little by little. The most important part is the amazing sails that one of our Tantozian engineers has created. They once used them on their satellites, but he's brought enough material for us to create them large enough for the ship. Then we hope to be able to stow the wartime NIECS, once those of us from Dwynna better understand the Tantozian signs.

"I think Deshim had hoped to be a pilot as well, but he was selected to head up engineering. Gillmay, our captain, far too young, of course, but still exuding such authority and wisdom, sits behind me on the bridge. She notices everything, and I think the NIEC determined in one single moment that she was it. Now that we're shooting through space, all three hundred cramped souls aboard the *Velocity*, searching for somewhere we all can live together in peace, I'm praying that we did the right thing. Most of all, I hope my parents aren't persecuted further for my actions. But how could I possibly live without Deshim? Meeting in the tunnels and caves for several years, knowing that a Tantozian and Dwynnite would never be allowed to form a union, was unbearable. The war raged around us, killing our family and friends. It was clear that something had to be done, and so we used the contacts we had on the Dwynnite side to steal a ship."

Claire kept reading, snippets here and there, and they followed Casta'Lloy's life on board the ship. Through trial and error, dangers and calmer times, they surveilled a multitude of planets but didn't find any suitable ones during Casta'Lloy's lifetime.

"So Casta'Lloy entered a union with Deshim...a Tantozian and a Dwynnite. They had three children and lived their entire lives aboard the *Velocity*." Quantia seemed to speak to herself, but when she turned her head to face Holly, her eyes were wide and glossy. "Were they all leaving Dwynna Major because of love, or did others have different objectives? Political perhaps?"

"I don't know." Holly looked over at Claire and saw how she leaned against the closest table. She looked exhausted. "Thank you, Claire. Take a seat. Carl, please choose another scroll. Perhaps a newer entry?"

"Of course, Captain." Carl bounced up from his chair and picked another roll, entering it into the slot below the screen. "This one is the personal log of Riam'than. Wow. He was only six years old, if I calculate this right, when he started it."

"Six?" Quantia blinked and gripped the armrest of her chair.

"Go on, Carl," Holly said, grateful that Claire had chosen to sit down next to her. Not even considering that they were within sight of everyone in the mess hall, Holly gently patted Claire's knee. "You okay?" she whispered.

"Just a bit tired," Claire murmured. "Carl will make more sense than me—I think I was starting to slur my words."

"You did fine. Just relax." Only now realizing that she was still touching Claire's leg, Holly stroked it twice and then removed her hand.

"I don't like my teacher. He yells a lot, and I like it better when my mother teaches us math. She never yells, and she keeps telling me that we'll find a new home soon. I think the ship's our home, but mother says we will one day live on a planet and be free. I'm not sure what that means. I feel free now.

"We celebrated my mother becoming captain. She said it felt wrong to enjoy the festivities since old Captain Tere'cai passed away in his sleep. Mother, being the second in command, had to take over his duties, and I can tell she sees it as her duty rather than something she wants.

"Becoming an adult officially isn't at all what I anticipated. Only yesterday, I had free time to spend as I pleased with my friends. Now that I'm an adult and outfitted with a NIEC, I have a long, boring career in the infirmary to look forward to. The only good part about working as a medic is that Losanta is a physician. I'll make sure I work the same shifts as her."

Carl paused and scrolled even farther down. "Seems to be about him entering a union with an entirely different girl and having a son. Here. Oh, wow. Look, Darian. Your ancestor. Gai'usto."

Darian stood and pulled Camilla with her. Walking closer to the screen, they still held hands. "Anything about when they reached Earth?"

"Let me check." Scrolling farther down, Carl browsed the text. "Here. He enters a union with Bech'taia. See?" He pointed at the screen.

"These are individuals you know of?" Quantia asked.

"Yes. We found an old journal in our chief counselor's home on Earth, kept by Bech'taia after the *Velocity* set down on our planet." Holly motioned toward Camilla and Darian. "That's Camilla and her granddaughter, Darian." She hesitated. "Camilla is also my mother's sister."

"I see," Quantia said, but Holly wasn't sure that was true.

"Here." Carl stopped scrolling. "Want to read?" he asked Darian, but she shook her head.

"I do." Camilla wrapped her arm around Darian's waist, perhaps for comfort, perhaps for support. Probably both. "We have been in orbit around this blue-and-green planet for more than thirty rotations. Our scans show a rich wildlife, plentiful, uncontaminated soil, and nearing one billion humanoids spread out over the continents, some locales denser than others. Our elders have decided that we will settle here, since living on a generational ship isn't optimal in the long run. I'm the third generation aboard the *Velocity*, and since Bech'taia and I want to introduce children into our union, the idea of raising them under a blue sky is quite enticing. Bech'taia is less enthusiastic and concerned with what she sees as the volatile nature of many of the humanoids on the planet.

"Today, a small part of the crew will take a cloaked speeder down to the planet and scout for a remote area to settle down. We have decided on a less dense area in the northern hemisphere. Bech'taia and I are both going, which I hope will ease her mind about what our future will be like on this planet.

"We've been given the order to scuttle the ship, since the people on this planet are far behind us when it comes to technology and firepower. I know the elders also feel we have to eliminate any chance of going back to space or, worse, return to Dwynna Major. This decision has created factions among the crew and their families. Some of us carry an intense longing for our homeworld, which none of us has ever actually set foot on. Even the oldest among us are children or grandchildren of those who stole the *Velocity* and left. Personally, I am a third-generation refugee. My grandparents were very young when they fled in the ship that carried us here. My parents were both born in space, as was I. Bech'taia was born on a desert planet where the older generations tried to excavate and create a habitat underground there—and failed.

"We have emptied the ship of some of our technology, and for now the vessel is hidden in a remote area in the mountains until it is time to carry out our elders' orders. In the meantime, we're excavating a place to hide our speeders since our elders have agreed we need to keep them close as a precaution. We might at one point realize that this part of the planet isn't the best for our purpose of survival. It is vital that we work clandestinely. Our technology allows for excavating and building, using any natural material from bedrock to wood. I would imagine the indigenous people of this world would think it sorcery if they witnessed our sound-lenses cut through the bedrock and create space, building blocks, or fine dust.

"This will be my last entry in this scroll, as we are establishing ourselves as immigrants to this planet, this North American continent. Nothing can be used or displayed of our old technology or our former way of life. I'm sure it will be a challenge for us to learn the simple life of the inhabitants of this world, but I'm ready to face it.

"I have called a meeting tonight, as I am adamant about not scuttling the ship. I think we can persuade, even coerce, the elders to agree to hide it. If we have to rise against them, we will. Bech'taia feels the same way about the ship, but she insists that it can be done peacefully, though I'm doubtful. She is, however, the mathematician and has the best brain among all of us, Tantozians and Dwynnites alike. We will see tonight if our idea is valid.

"Bech'taia is calling me, and as always, her voice fills me with such joy. She would consider me a sentimental fool for writing like I've done in a scroll that will be sealed and stowed in oblivion forever, but perhaps someday someone will read this, and if so, I want them to know that this is my existence, my truth, and Bech'taia is my universe."

Camilla read the last sentence and then pressed her fingertips against her lips. "And that's where Gai'usto's scroll ends and Bech'taia's journal continues. Gai'usto ended up sharing her vision, and the refugees in Dennamore excavated the area under the lake where the ship slept all this time. That is, every year, something went on below the lake that made it, and Dennamore, rather famous. It created the most beautiful light show, and we have always theorized that it had to do with a function that kept the systems going over time. Our ancestors also constructed the opening mechanism that allowed our chief pilot to maneuver the ship and bring it out from under the lake for us to use to return to this planet. We're living proof of that fact by our mere presence here."

Darian hugged her grandmother and led her back to her table. Walker rose and took Camilla into his arms.

Holly stood and waited until the murmurs around her died down. "Respected Elders, Tantozians, you are welcome to examine the scrolls, DNA scans, and the ship's logs that describe our journey here. These will give you proof of our sincerity. In return, we request that you share it with the Dwynnites, using whatever means necessary to bring about a diplomatic exchange between the nations."

Quantia rose and walked with sure steps over to Holly. "You have given us a lot to think about. The return of the Dwynnite warship *Velocity* is controversial and miraculous. Part of the fragile treaty between the Dwynnites and the Tantozians states that neither of the Dwynna Major nations may possess long-distance space-faring technology.

"Under these remarkable circumstances, Captain Crowe, you and your crew have conducted yourselves honorably from the moment you made contact. We have no idea how the Dwynnites will react to the *Velocity*'s return, but if we can share this proof with them that the theft of the last warship was a joint venture centuries ago, an act of desperation, or perhaps even an act originating in a hope for a better future, when all our nations knew was perpetual war, they might listen." She bowed to Holly and then extended her hand. "Creating new diplomatic channels will be our responsibility, but we will need your assistance, Captain."

Holly squeezed Quantia's hand. "You'll have it. I know I speak for my crew and their families when I say that we'll do anything we can to help you in your efforts to reach the Dwynnites. From our Earth history, we're well aware how difficult and vulnerable the peace process between sovereign states can be."

"I want to invite you and the crew to visit our capital underground anytime you want. It is one of many similar cities, but it is the greatest. Perhaps we should wait a few rotations, as we are all overwhelmed and need to come to terms with this unexpected turn of events?" Quantia smiled.

"I know we're all curious and interested in learning more about our mutual history and how you manage to exist underground, but I also agree that we have to let the dust settle a bit first," Holly said.

"Exactly." Quantia motioned for a cadet to bring the long coat she had placed over the backrest of her seat.

"Bridge to Crowe." As if on cue, Holly's speaker interrupted them.

"Go ahead." Holly excused herself and walked back to Claire, who was still sitting on the chair next to Holly's.

"Our speeders have decloaked and landed on either side of the ship, which means we take up pretty much all of the old square," the lieutenant on the bridge informed them. "The medical habitat is still out there, and the doctor authorized four of the medics and four security officers to remain outside and keep assisting anyone who might need help. Approximately four thousand people are in the streets, and it's becoming dangerous, as they're not entirely aware of the risk that walking among the debris poses."

"I'll take that up with the Tantozians. Good idea about the habitat. Keep guards aboard the speeders and around the *Velocity*."

"Understood. Already in place, Captain."

"Excellent. Keep me posted. Crowe out." She turned to Claire. "I know this wasn't how you hoped our first diplomatic contact would occur. I agree that starting with the Tantozians might create difficulty with the Dwynnites."

"I do get the feeling that Quantia sees this as a true opening—a golden opportunity—to reach out to their neighbors. I wonder how many botched attempts they have made, diplomatically speaking, over the centuries." Claire shrugged and grimaced, as this reflection seemed to bring her pain.

Holly wanted to continue their conversation, but in private. "I'm going to see our guests off the ship and make sure they know how reckless some of their population is being around the ruins. Once that's done, we'll have something more substantial to eat and then rest. Would you like to join me in my quarters for a meal?" It was both natural and nerve-racking for her to ask.

Claire studied Holly for a good ten seconds. Her hazel eyes looked nearly transparent, luminescent, even. "All right." Her reply was noncommittal. "I'll just clean up first."

"Same here. It was dusty outside today." Holly tried to sound casual. "I think I could taste the grit when I tried some of the bread."

Claire smiled faintly. "Yeah." She stood, and her smile widened when Samantha and Darian came up to them, together with Walker and Camilla. "I'm going to my quarters. Anyone care to join me in the elevator? I'm afraid I'll fall asleep and keep riding it up and down until someone stops me," she said.

"Look no further," Walker said and placed his free arm around Claire's shoulders. "We'll make sure you get to your quarters."

Holly was relieved, as she still had to see Quantia and the elders off the ship and inform them about joint crowd control when it came to the Tantozians' understandable fascination with the ships. "See you later. I'll page you when the food's on the table." It didn't escape Holly's attention that the others exchanged knowing glances. She wanted to roll her eyes at them, but a persistent headache, no doubt because she was starving, made her stop herself.

Claire gently touched Holly's sleeve. "See you later."

Returning to Quantia and the elders that waited for her in the center of the mess hall, Holly still felt Claire's brief touch, and for a few seconds, it was all she could think of.

Chapter Thirty-two

The meal was hardly imaginative, but more geared toward nutrition with a hint of comfort food. Claire hesitantly took a seat across the small table from Holly, who had just placed two bowls of macaroni and cheese before them.

"Who did you bribe to give up their precious brought-from-home mac and cheese?" Claire pushed her fork into the steaming-hot, creamy goodness and blew on it.

"Actually, it's from my own stash." Holly smiled and sat down, then poured them both water. "One of my culinary weaknesses."

"One of them? Name a few others." The taste of the food brought memories of home, of sitting in the kitchen with her father, or even on the couch, watching TV.

"You know. The major food groups. Chocolate, ice cream, and homemade caramel." Holly took a bite. "Mm. Not bad for coming out of a box."

They ate in silence for a while, and Claire could see her own fatigue reflected on Holly's face. Where Holly's black eyes were normally scrutinizing and, the last few months, opaque and sharp, they now drooped a little at the outer corners. The dark circles underneath them were also the same as Claire's, though more noticeable against Holly's pale complexion.

"You're staring," Holly murmured and glanced up from her bowl.

"I know. I mean, I'm sorry." Claire winced. "You look like I feel."

"If by that you mean exhausted, trepidatious, and carefully optimistic, then that's correct." Humor was hiding in her words, but mainly fatigue. "I don't think I've ever had such a day. So many emotions—fear, anger, hope, surprise..." Holly sipped her water. "How was yours?"

"Ha. The same. Not so much fear for my own safety. I mean, I sort of felt that I wouldn't be physically harmed, though I did worry about being incarcerated, kept from you and the rest of the crew. And, oh God, I worried what might be going on with you topside."

"Topside. You already speak like them." Holly tilted her head, resting her chin against her palm.

"Hm. Yeah. I suppose. I can be somewhat of a mimic at times." Claire shrugged and took another bite.

"I know you've filed a short brief of your experience into the computer, but can you tell me some more?"

Claire nodded. "Sure. People or the city?"

"Start with the people. I'm curious about Neo'Toya, especially," Holly said. She pulled one foot up on the seat of her chair and wrapped one hand around it while she ate with her other. If it hadn't been for her exhaustion carving deep lines around her eyes, she would have looked like a teenager.

"Neo'Toya is rough in many ways. And by that, I mean, he seems harsh, but he was also the one who seemed to realize that I wasn't some damn spy or terrorist—and that my story has some truth to it. He sent his sentries away and took me to Quantia. I could have stabbed him in the back, literally and figuratively, for all he knew. As I didn't, I guess he's got some good instincts."

"If he hadn't been a man of honor, you should have." Holly's brow furrowed.

"Stab him? Attack him?" Claire snorted. "You did catch how big that guy is, right? He would've broken me like a twig."

"You're resourceful."

"True." Claire smiled wanly. "And to be truthful, I was more nervous about meeting the elders. I have only our elder-council chairman back home to compare him to, and Desmond Miller isn't very impressive. He's also a bit corrupt, if you ask me. For all I knew, these elders could have been cut from the same cloth."

"But?"

"They were suspicious, even disdainful. But Quantia seems to carry a lot of weight, and the elders seem to hold her in high esteem. Their actual chairman is apparently old and frail. I bet she'll be elected once he steps down or passes away. I'm not sure if they're a democracy the way we know it, but as I understand, they hold some sort of elections."

Holly nodded. "And the city?"

"Like nothing I could ever have imagined—and I have a lot of sci-fi imagination. The buildings are almost as tall as the ones out there," Claire said, pointing to the outer bulkhead. "If it started as a series of caves, I'm not sure, but obviously, the people on this planet are skilled at creating spaces underground. They have shuttles and hovercraft down there. Everything is bright, and the architecture is beautiful. The building materials are the same as the walls of the city—white, marble-like rock. And wood. I hope I get to go with you when you see it for the first time."

"I hope so too. I actually hate that you were there alone today. I feared the worst when they took you." Holly pressed her lips together. "When that sentry tore you from the elevator was one of my worst moments ever."

Holly's words were so unexpected and came out in such a raw tone, Claire lost her grip on her fork, which clattered back into the almost-empty bowl. The last few months had been all about keeping up with a barely functioning NIEC that caused her pain. That, combined with trying to maintain her distance, emotionally, from Holly, despite how much she loved her, had often made her life unbearable. And now, Holly said that the idea of losing Claire was one of her worst moments.

"Do you really mean that?" Claire pressed her palms against the table, trying to hide how badly they shook.

"Yes." Holly sounded almost angry, but Claire didn't think the emotion was directed at her. "I stood there, forced to ride the elevator back to where we entered it, and all I could think was...how I had wasted precious time. With you."

"We've both avoided each other. You, for not wanting to compromise the command structure, and I...because the command structure was more important to you than I was."

"I thought so. I honestly thought I had to separate myself from the crew, and you, especially, as the captain of this ship." Holly grimaced. "I suppose I've learned a lot about myself during our journey. More than I ever thought possible since I now know the truth about my birthmother." Shrugging, she looked at Claire with a hint of exasperation. I had envisioned my life—had painted a picture of her in my head—all wrong. She didn't abandon me. She died. The family didn't abandon me—but they did that to her. Camilla, Darian, and I are still trying to figure out our respective roles out, but I'm grateful to have them."

Growing silent, Holly wiped at her eyes. "Damn, I'm so tired." The tremor in her voice made Claire extend a hand across the table. At first, Holly didn't seem to notice it, but then she clutched it, and Holly's icy fingers didn't surprise Claire.

"I'm not sure why we're having this meal together now. Apart from ingesting nutrition, you must have had a reason to ask me to join you. Is that…" Claire gently cleared her throat. "Do you need me… my support, or whatever?" She wasn't sure where she found the guts to put her heart on the line again, but after this day, after all that had happened, it seemed the only way to go. Claire drew a slow, cleansing breath. "Holly? You do have me. I know I risk yet another rejection by saying that, but it's the truth, and—"

Squeezing Claire's hand firmly, Holly shook her head, making her hair dance around her face. "No. I mean, I don't intend to reject you ever again—in any way." Only a few moments later, Holly seemed to realize what she'd just said. Her cheeks flushed, and she let go of Claire and stood so quickly, her chair tipped over.

"Holly?" Claire got up when she lost her grip on Holly's hand but remained by the table.

"Have you ever felt as if your entire world has just snapped back onto its correct axis?" Holly pushed her hands into the deep pockets of her flowy, white cardigan.

"I think it did, just now."

"Now?"

"When I said that you have me." Claire had to avert her gaze for a few moments. The feelings between them seemed to swirl around them in the room and make the air too thick to breathe. "You do. If you want to."

Holly moved so fast, Claire wasn't prepared, despite her words. Strong arms wrapped around her as Holly pulled her into a fierce embrace. "I thought I'd lost you. That I'd traveled so long through space and fought so hard to keep everyone safe, only to lose *you*. All I could think, very selfishly, was that I might never get a chance to tell you how I feel, how much you mean to me, and that I hated that I pushed you away, even if I thought I did the right thing at the time. I fought for our crew out there, for maintaining a peaceful return to this world…but I stayed calm and focused only because your life was at risk, Claire."

Claire hid her face against Holly's neck, inhaling her clean, fresh scent. "And I thought I'd never get the chance to convince you that we could make it work. That we, together, are worth a try."

Holly gave a muted sob and then pressed her lips to Claire's hair. "I know I'm a stickler for protocol. I can be too rigid. Just ask my students back home. Frances used to call me a puzzle box, said that a person had to locate all the hidden doors and traps to find the real me. She did. And you're doing it. You have from the moment we met."

"W-what?" Claire tipped her head back, hoping she wasn't having auditory hallucinations.

"I do love you," Holly said. Tears clung to her lashes.

"I love you too. I have for a while," Claire whispered. "I told myself I could stop, since it hurt too much, but that was a big lie."

"Same here. I never thought I'd be able to let anyone close, but—here we are." Holly wobbled and took a step to the side.

"Hey. Let's sit." Pulling Holly over to the couch, Claire remembered when they kissed the first time—the same night Holly pulled back from her. This was going to be different. It had to.

Holly drew her legs up and leaned sideways against the backrest, looking at Claire through slitted eyes. "You feel it too, right?"

"Déjà vu?"

"Yes." Pushing her hair from her face, Holly sighed. "I can say a ton of things hoping you'll realize that I'm not in the same frame of mind now as I was then, but it all comes down to if we have any trust left—or not."

"I've always trusted you—as a person and as my captain. I think time will show us that things are different now. We both feared we'd never see each other again. We both dared to tell each other how we truly feel." Claire had to smile at Holly's confused expression. "We don't need to plot and plan everything tonight. We're too tired. Tomorrow, we have more information exchanges to deal with...not to mention potential war to avoid. We have to be aware of the risk that we won't have a lot of time for each other. I'll be busy in engineering and working with the Tantozians, and you'll be even busier dealing with all the diplomatic entanglements."

"Thanks for reminding me." Holly chuckled, her exhaustion obvious. "And you're right. Our personal feelings—or should I say *lives*—will have to take a backseat. But there's one thing we could do, if you agree."

Claire took Holly's hand. "Yes?"

"Every so often, and in my mind, it can't be often enough, we could set aside time for *us*. Even if it's just minutes. Your quarters or mine, I don't care, but—time. Just us?"

Claire threw herself forward and pulled Holly close, pressing her lips against hers. She tried to keep the caress soft and gentle, but Holly responded with the same passion, the same abandon. Parting her lips, Claire invited Holly's tongue, welcomed it, caressed it with hers. Intoxicated. That's how she felt when Holly pushed her fingers through her hair and held her even closer. Claire moaned into Holly's mouth, changed the angle to make the kiss more perfect. Her heart was racing so fast she was sure it was trying to leap forward to meet Holly's.

Claire had dreamed of this, never dared hope that Holly would change her mind, and now...here they were, so close she didn't know where she ended and Holly began. She wanted to mimic Holly and push her fingers through her hair, but she still wore the captain's NIEC, and Claire had to settle for cupping Holly's cheeks. That turned out to be even better, as Holly tipped her head back and offered her silky skin where her pulse was visible underneath. Claire didn't hesitate. She pressed her half-open lips to Holly's neck, kissing every inch of it, over and over. When that was no longer enough, she pushed the cardigan aside, just a little, and found the soft protrusion of Holly's collarbones. They looked so fragile, and Claire gently traced them with her tongue.

"Oh, God…Claire…" Holly arched and kept holding on to her. "Claire…"

"Mm." Claire found no words at all. Painting a trail with her tongue back and forth from one collarbone to the next, she conjured up images of devouring Holly's breasts, of how she one day would make love to this fantastic woman.

Slowly, the intensity of their caresses and their deep kisses stilled. Part of Claire wished she weren't so exhausted, but another part knew her fatigue kept them from going too fast, too soon. In the long run, this might be better. With a hint of regret and several deep, long kisses later, Claire pulled back, trying to remember what Holly had been saying when she interrupted her. Ah, yes. Making sure they set aside private time. "I'd be happy to have Walker put our private time on the duty roster," she said, winking at Holly.

"What? Oh. Oh!" Holly had gone rigid but now sank back into Claire's embrace. "Very funny." She smiled as she shook her head. "So, you agree?"

"I agree completely. Time for us. Done." Claire nuzzled Holly's temple, mindful of the protrusion of the NIEC.

They remained in each other's arms, settling into semi-reclined positions on the couch. Claire absentmindedly studied the viewscreen on the wall, displaying the outer sensor images, and tried to grasp that it wasn't showing distant stars, but the ruins outlining the square. She ran her hand up and down Holly's back, and every so often, she kissed the top of her head.

And in less than a few minutes, they slept.

Epilogue

Two months later

The oval table was set for ten. The plates shimmered a, by now, familiar silver-white, and the utensils were made from some matte black alloy. Beautiful, frosted glasses were filled with Tantozian wine, and the dark-red color reminded Darian of some grapes in California—which seemed like a lifetime ago.

"I'd like to propose a toast, and I promise to be brief," Walker said. He sat next to Gran, who glowed in the artificial sunset created by illuminated orange crystal ore in the cave ceiling above the city. Darian never tired of seeing her grandmother look so healthy and happy. "It took me a few days to realize that the yearning I've experienced all my life, whenever I left Dennamore for some reason, was gone. When we arrived, my duties and the constant adrenaline surges kept me occupied, but as soon as things started to calm down a bit, I knew. The pull that became even stronger on our journey here, sometimes painfully so, was no longer there, tugging at me. You know when you've had a persistent headache, and then you wake up one morning and it's not there anymore? It was like that for me. I knew something was different, but it took me a while to figure it out. When I did, as soon as I set foot on this planet, I knew it had vanished. Part of me is at home here." Walker gave a lopsided smile. "And another part is of me misses Dennamore. Not a very big part, as I have everyone I love here." Walker held his wineglass in one hand and Gran's hand in the other. "I want to toast to our entire journey.

For persevering. For reaching the home of our ancestors. For the crew becoming our family."

"Hear, hear," Gran said, raising her glass to Walker's.

"To the journey," the rest of them echoed and drank the wine that tasted sweet, spicy, and rich.

Darian looked around the table, knowing she would never forget this evening. This wasn't the first time she'd been to a restaurant in the capital of Tantoz, but they had never managed to gather all the senior staff at the same time. Seeing them together reminded Darian of how they had met at Gran's house in Dennamore, where they'd shared all their latest finds and theories and eaten Brandon's excellent food. Here they sat now, all nine of them, plus Carl's Aunt Marjory.

"During today's briefing that Walker and I had with Quantia and Neo'Toya, they shared that a Dwynnite delegation will arrive within days," Holly said, lowering her voice. "I'm supposed to attend, and I want a few more of my senior staff to accompany me. Apparently, they're immensely interested in the *Velocity*."

Samantha placed her left arm on Darian's backrest and frowned. "Immensely interested?"

"Not as in reclaiming it—or at least I hope not." Holly leaned closer. "But I imagine they'll also have enough questions to keep us busy for the foreseeable future."

"Quantia said the Dwynnites are mobilizing at the border," Walker said. "Neo'Toya in turn deployed more units of sentries. There's even talk about them building new border stations."

Philber huffed. "Of course, they will. The ancient conflict with Dwynna is so ingrained in the Tantozian minds, that's their knee-jerk reaction. I have a contact at the capital university, and she insists that new tunnels, similar to those used by our ancestors to move between the nations unhindered, are very much still in play."

"A contact." Holly had raised her glass to have another sip but now set it down again. She was out of uniform for once, as this dinner was their first private get-together since they arrived at Dwynna Major, but of course they still talked shop. "You mean you've established an unofficial contact among the Tantozians?"

Darian knew Holly was as by-the-book as they came, and, from the look on Philber's face, so did he.

"Don't worry," Philber said, playing with his utensils. "It's a civilian contact, and from what I understand, it's a somewhat official secret."

"Uh-huh." Holly raised her eyebrows. "I want a report of what your contact has shared with you—tomorrow. And no, I don't need to know who they are." Lifting her glass again, Holly sipped the wine.

"Geez. Don't give the old man a heart attack, okay?" Claire grinned at Philber, who nearly downed his entire glass of wine in one gulp.

Darian leaned into Samantha and placed a hand on her thigh. "They remind me of us."

"What? Who?" Samantha looked quizzically at Darian but then smiled. "Ah. Yes. I agree." She took Darian's hand under the table. "I doubt their love could possibly be stronger than ours, though." She winked, making Darian chuckle.

"As a matter of fact, there's a lot of love around this table. Romance. Friendship. Loyalty. Bravery." Darian looked at Marjory, who sat next to Carl, her nephew, and who beamed so proudly at the extraordinary young man. On Carl's other side sat Brandon, who, with Philber, had taken it upon himself to function as a father figure for Carl, whose parents left a lot to be desired when it came to appreciating their son. Raoul, the young doctor who lived and breathed his job, had kept saving them, one after another, throughout their journey.

The restaurant staff brought food, all vegetarian, as the Tantozians had huge gardens and fields underground but prohibited hunting No animal above ground was fit for human consumption, as radiation still remained too high.

"Holly," Samantha said quietly. "Are you nervous about meeting the Dwynnites when their delegation gets here?"

"Apprehensive, perhaps." Holly leaned closer. "We had planned to reach out to both nations at the same time, but that's not how things unfolded. It will be a major diplomatic feat to make the Dwynnites understand that we don't intend to take sides and, most of all, that we are not going to use our ship as a weapon against either nation—or give it back to them. I'm sure both nations will argue for the latter, but that won't happen. If we put a potential weapon of mass destruction into either of their hands, all we need is one hothead too many, or a corrupt megalomaniac, and we will have helped undo what the nations have struggled to overcome. We know our ancestors, Tantozians and Dwynnites alike, stole the *Velocity* to escape the planet—and to stop the war before the Dwynnites wiped out the entire Tantozian nation. That was, according to our calculations, around 1710, Earth time."

Darian nodded. "And they crisscrossed through space, desperately looking for a planet that could sustain life, trying several, for almost a century, until they found Earth. And after all this time, we inherited the ship, so to speak."

"And it will stay in our hands. That is why I keep emphasizing how important it is that we don't share technology. We can't afford to. If we give away enough for them to learn how to operate the ship, we could lose it, and if that happens, we can never go home." Holly shifted and looked at Claire, who placed a hand on top of hers. Darian had sensed how the ambiance between the two had changed after that first dramatic day when they set down on Dwynna Major. Claire had told her a few times about how she and Holly did their best to navigate between their duties and their feelings for each other. Darian could relate, even if she and Samantha were much more established and actually lived together.

"And if we can't return, we can never hope to establish diplomatic channels between this planet and Earth," Samantha said calmly, breaking Darian out of her reverie. "Returning is our ultimate goal, long-term, right?"

"It is." Holly nodded. "And now that we seem to have figured out what it takes to calm down the yearning, I guess, after a while, most of us will eventually feel rather homesick for Earth instead."

Holly had a point, but sitting here, with the amazing underground city carved out in white marble at their feet, Darian knew it would take her a while. As long as Samantha was by her side, and Gran, she wouldn't mind exploring the city or taking a speeder and mapping the planet for quite a long time to come.

Samantha nudged Darian's shoulder with her own. "Isn't it amazing, when you think about it? No matter if we're here, or back on Earth, we'll be home."

"Now there's a thought I can toast to," Claire said and raised her glass. Her eyes glittered as she looked at Holly. "What do you say, Captain? Here's to being home, wherever we are."

Ten glasses were raised and clinked against each other, and then ten voices blended. "To being home!"

❖

"Your Excellency, it's almost time."

Shadena looked up from her workstation. "Already?" She eyed the long caftan that Limmin, her long-time senior aide, held up on a rod to keep it from wrinkling. "Blue?" She frowned.

"It's the stateliest of colors, Your Excellency." Limmin didn't even blink as she regarded Shadena.

"Very well. It would be a sad state of affairs if I didn't look stately when I meet the elders of Tantoz." Shadena hadn't decided whether to see this summit as a challenge or a reconnoitering mission. Perhaps both.

She stood and allowed Limmin to dress her. Her thoughts drifted back to the early years of being elected Governor of Dwynna, how she had cringed at the old traditions like these. She snapped back to the present when Limmin took a step back after smoothing down the back of the caftan. Examining her reflection in the tall mirror on the wall opposite her desk, Shadena had to admit Limmin was right. The deep-blue caftan with its iridescent threads woven in accentuated her long, black hair piled on top of her head and the dark yellow of her eyes. It would do.

The armored aircraft that would take her to the capital of Tantoz sat in the courtyard, ready to go. Was she ready? She had no other choice—she had to be prepared to face the people with whom the Dwynnites had warred for many generations, until a truce had been negotiated after the last of Dwynna's spaceships disappeared.

And now it was back. Shadena's marshals had found images and schematics of the *Velocity*, which would make it easier to identify the ship. And if a positive identification could be performed, the next step would soon follow. By then it would be obvious to anyone adhering to any type of law that the ship should be delivered to its rightful owners.

If this indeed was the long-lost ship, the *Velocity*, it belonged to the people of Dwynna—and certainly not some aliens making claims that sounded more outrageous every time the head of the Dwynnite spy units briefed Shadena.

This fact had convinced her to make up her mind. The Tantozians expected a civil-servant delegation to arrive at their capital today. After giving the situation considerable thought, Shadena had decided to take a more direct approach. She would join the delegation and thus pull the proverbial rug from underneath the feet of both the elders and the newcomers. Before they could gather their wits, she would have sized them up and gained the advantage—the edge, as it were.

She pulled on stark-white gloves and turned to Limmin. "I am ready to depart. Have the crew start the aircraft."

"Already done, Your Excellency," Limmin said and bowed. "Safe journey."

"Thank you." Shadena briefly touched Limmin's shoulder before she exited her office.

It was time to set history right, once and for all.

About the Author

Gun Brooke, author of almost thirty novels, writes her stories, surrounded by a loving family and two affectionate dogs. When she isn't writing her novels, she works on her art, and crafts, whenever possible—certain that practice pays off. She loves being creative, whether using conventional materials or digital art software.

Web site: www.gbrooke-fiction.com

Books Available from Bold Strokes Books

A Champion for Tinker Creek by D.C. Robeline. Lyle James has rescued his dad's auto repair business, but when city hall condemns his neighborhood, Lyle learns only trusting will save his life and help him find love. (978-1-63679-213-2)

Closed-Door Policy by Erin Zak. Going back to college is never easy, but Caroline Stevens is prepared to work hard and change her life for the better. What she's not prepared for is Dr. Atlanta Morris, her gorgeous new professor. (978-1-63679-181-4)

Homeworld by Gun Brooke. Headed by Captain Holly Crowe, the spaceship Velocity's crew journeys toward their alien ancestors' homeworld, and what they find is completely unexpected—and they're not safe. (978-1-63679-177-7)

Outland by Kristin Keppler & Allisa Bahney. Danielle Clark and Katelyn Turner can't seem to stay away from one another even as the war for the wastelands tests their loyalty to each other and to their people. (978-1-63679-154-8)

Secret Sanctuary by Nance Sparks. US Deputy Marshal Alex Trenton specializes in protecting those awaiting trial, but when danger threatens the woman she's falling for, Alex is in for the fight of her life. (978-1-63679-148-7)

Stranded Hearts by Kris Bryant, Amanda Radley, Emily Smith. In these novellas from award-winning authors, fate intervenes on behalf of love when characters are unexpectedly stuck together. With too much time and an irresistible attraction, anything could happen. (978-1-63679-182-1)

The Last Lavender Sister by Melissa Brayden. Aster Lavender sells her gourmet doughnuts and keeps a low profile; she never plans on the town's temporary veterinarian swooping in and making her feel like anything but a wallflower. (978-1-63679-130-2)

The Probability of Love by Dena Blake. As Blair and Rachel keep ending up in the same place despite the odds, can a one-night stand turn into forever? Or will the bet Blair never intended to make ruin their happily ever after? (978-1-63679-188-3)

Worth a Fortune by Sam Ledel. After placing a want ad for a personal secretary, a New York heiress is surprised when the woman who got away is the one interested in the position. (978-1-63679-175-3)

A Fox in Shadow by Jane Fletcher. Cassie's mission is to add new territory to the Kavillian empire—murder, betrayal, war, and the clash of cultures ensue. (978-1-63679-142-5)

Embracing the Moon by Jeannie Levig. Just as Gwen and Taylor are exploring the new love they've found, the present and past collide, threatening the future they long to share. (978-1-63555-462-5)

Forever Comes in Threes by D. Jackson Leigh. Efficiency expert Perry Chandler's ordered life is upended when she inherits three busy terriers, and the woman she's referred to for help turns out to be her bitter podcast rival, the very sexy Dr. Ming Lee. (978-1-63679-169-2)

Heckin' Lewd: Trans and Nonbinary Erotica by Mx. Nillin Lore. If you want smutty, fearless, gender-diverse erotica written by affirming own-voices folks who get it, then this is the book you've been looking for! (978-1-63679-240-8)

Missed Conception by Joy Argento. Maggie Walsh wants a relationship with Cassidy, the daughter she's only just discovered she has due to an in vitro mix-up. Heat kindles between Maggie and Cassidy's mother in a way neither expects. (978-1-63679-146-3)

Private Equity by Elle Spencer. Cassidy Bennett spends an unexpected evening at a lesbian nightclub with her notoriously reserved and demanding boss, Julia. After seeing a different side of Julia, Cassidy can't seem to shake her desire to know more. (978-1-63679-180-7)

Racing the Dawn by Sandra Barrett. After narrowly escaping a house fire, vampire Jade Murphy is unexpectedly intrigued by gorgeous firefighter Beth Jenssen, and her undead existence might just be perking up a bit. (978-1-63679-271-2)

Reclaiming Love by Amanda Radley. Sarah's tiny white lie means somehow convincing Pippa to pretend to be her girlfriend. Only the more time they spend faking it, the more real it feels. (978-1-63679-144-9)

Sol Cycle by Kimberly Cooper Griffin. An encounter in a park brings Ang and Krista together, but when Ang's attempts to help Krista go spectacularly wrong, their passion for each other might not be enough. (978-1-63679-137-1)

Trial and Error by Carsen Taite. Attorney Franco Rossi and Judge Nina Aguilar's reunion is fraught with courtroom conflict, undeniable chemistry, and danger. (978-1-63555-863-0)

A Long Way to Fall by Elle Spencer. A ski lodge, two strong-willed women, and a family feud that brings them together, but will it also tear them apart? (978-1-63679-005-3)

Barnabas Bopwright Saves the City by J. Marshall Freeman. When he uncovers a terror plot to destroy the city he loves, 15-year-old Barnabas Bopwright realizes it's up to him to save his home and bring deadly secrets into the light before it's too late. (978-1-63679-152-4)

Forever by Kris Bryant. When Savannah Edwards is invited to be the next bachelorette on the dating show When Sparks Fly, she'll show the world that finding true love on television can happen. (978-1-63679-029-9)

Ice on Wheels by Aurora Rey. All's fair in love and roller derby. That's Riley Fauchet's motto, until a new job lands her at the same company—and on the same team—as her rival Brooke Landry, the frosty jammer for the Big Easy Bruisers. (978-1-63679-179-1)

Inherit the Lightning by Bud Gundy. Darcy O'Brien and his sisters learn they are about to inherit an immense fortune, but a family mystery about to unravel after seventy years threatens to destroy everything. (978-1-63679-199-9)

Perfect Rivalry by Radclyffe. Two women set out to win the same career-making goal, but it's love that may turn out to be the final prize. (978-1-63679-216-3)

Something to Talk About by Ronica Black. Can quiet ranch owner Corey Durand give up her peaceful life and allow her feisty new neighbor into her heart? Or will past loss, present suitors, and town gossip ruin a long-awaited chance at love? (978-1-63679-114-2)

With a Minor in Murder by Karis Walsh. In the world of academia, police officer Clare Sawyer and professor Libby Hart team up to solve a murder. (978-1-63679-186-9)

Writer's Block by Ali Vali. Wyatt and Hayley might be made for each other if only they can get through nosy neighbors, the historic society, at-odds future plans, and all the secrets hidden in Wyatt's walls. (978-1-63679-021-3)

Cold Blood by Genevieve McCluer. Maybe together, Kalila and Dorenia have a chance of taking down the vampires who have eluded them all these years. And maybe, in each other, they can find a love worth living for. (978-1-63679-195-1)

Greener Pastures by Aurora Rey. When city girl and CPA Audrey Adams finds herself tending her aunt's farm, will Rowan Marshall—the charming cider maker next door—turn out to be her saving grace or the bane of her existence? (978-1-63679-116-6)

Grounded by Amanda Radley. For a second chance, Olivia and Emily will need to accept their mistakes, learn to communicate properly, and with a little help from five-year-old Henry, fall madly in love all over again. Sequel to Flight SQA016. (978-1-63679-241-5)

Journey's End by Amanda Radley. In this heartwarming conclusion to the Flight series, Olivia and Emily must finally decide what they want, what they need, and how to follow the dreams of their hearts. (978-1-63679-233-0)

Pursued: Lillian's Story by Felice Picano. Fleeing a disastrous marriage to the Lord Exchequer of England, Lillian of Ravenglass reveals an incident-filled, often bizarre, tale of great wealth and power, perfidy, and betrayal. (978-1-63679-197-5)

Secret Agent by Michelle Larkin. CIA agent Peyton North embarks on a global chase to apprehend rogue agent Zoey Blackwood, but her commitment to the mission is tested as the sparks between them ignite and their sizzling attraction approaches a point of no return. (978-1-63555-753-4)

Something Between Us by Krystina Rivers. A decade after her heart was broken under Don't Ask, Don't Tell, Kirby runs into her first love and has to decide if what's still between them is enough to heal her broken heart. (978-1-63679-135-7)

Sugar Girl by Emma L McGeown. Having traded in traditional romance for the perks of Sugar Dating, Ciara Reilly not only enjoys the no-strings-attached arrangement, she's also a hit with her clients. That is until she meets the beautiful entrepreneur Charlie Keller who makes her want to go sugar-free. (978-1-63679-156-2)

The Business of Pleasure by Ronica Black. Editor in chief Valerie Raffield is quickly becoming smitten by Lennox, the graphic artist she's hired to work remotely. But when Lennox doesn't show for their first face-to-face meeting, Valerie's heart and her business may be in jeopardy. (978-1-63679-134-0)

The Hummingbird Sanctuary by Erin Zak. The Hummingbird Sanctuary, Colorado's hottest resort destination: Come for the mountains, stay for the charm, and enjoy the drama as Olive, Eleanor, and Harriet figure out the meaning of true friendship. (978-1-63679-163-0)

The Witch Queen's Mate by Jennifer Karter. Barra and Silvi must overcome their ingrained hatred and prejudice to use Barra's magic and save both their peoples, not just from slavery, but destruction. (978-1-63679-202-6)

With a Twist by Georgia Beers. Starting over isn't easy for Amelia Martini. When the irritatingly cheerful Kirby Dupress comes into her life will Amelia be brave enough to go after the love she really wants? (978-1-63555-987-3)

Business of the Heart by Claire Forsythe. When a hopeless romantic meets a tough-as-nails cynic, they'll need to overcome the wounds of the past to discover that their hearts are the most important business of all. (978-1-63679-167-8)

Dying for You by Jenny Frame. Can Victorija Dred keep an age-old vow and fight the need to take blood from Daisy Macdougall? (978-1-63679-073-2)

Exclusive by Melissa Brayden. Skylar Ruiz lands the TV reporting job of a lifetime, but is she willing to sacrifice it all for the love of her longtime crush, anchorwoman Carolyn McNamara? (978-1-63679-112-8)

Her Duchess to Desire by Jane Walsh. An up-and-coming interior designer seeks to create a happily ever after with an intriguing duchess, proving that love never goes out of fashion. (978-1-63679-065-7)

Murder on Monte Vista by David S. Pederson. Private Detective Mason Adler's angst at turning fifty is forgotten when his "birthday present," the handsome, young Henry Bowtrickle, turns up dead, and it's up to Mason to figure out who did it, and why. (978-1-63679-124-1)

Take Her Down by Lauren Emily Whalen. Stakes are cutthroat, scheming is creative, and loyalty is ever-changing in this queer, female-driven YA retelling of Shakespeare's Julius Caesar. (978-1-63679-089-3)

The Game by Jan Gayle. Ryan Gibbs is a talented golfer, but her guilt means she may never leave her small town, even if Katherine Reese tempts her with competition and passion. (978-1-63679-126-5)

Whereabouts Unknown by Meredith Doench. While homicide detective Theodora Madsen recovers from a potentially career-ending injury, she scrambles to solve the cases of two missing sixteen-year-old girls from Ohio. (978-1-63555-647-6)